ROUGH MUSIC

ROUGH MUSIC

PATRICK GALE

BALLANTINE BOOKS ▪ NEW YORK

A Ballantine Book

Published by The Ballantine Publishing Group

Copyright © 2000 Patrick Gale

Originally published in 2000 in Great Britain by HarperCollins publishers.

www.randomhouse.com/BB/

Library of Congress Cataloging-in-Publication Data

Gale, Patrick, 1962–

Rough music / Patrick Gale.—1st ed.

p.   cm.

ISBN 0-345-44236-9

1. England—Social life and customs—20th century—Fiction. I. Title.

PR6057.A382 R68 2001

823'.914—dc21   00-068012

Manufactured in the United States of America

First Edition: May 2001

10 9 8 7 6 5 4 3 2 1

FOR AIDAN HICKS

I turn away, yet should I turn back the arbour would be gone and on the frozen ground the birds lie dead.

(from *The Rake's Progress*,
W. H. AUDEN & CHESTER KALLMAN)

"I often dream about walking down a Cornish lane in the summertime with high hedges on either side full of butterflies."

(Ronnie Biggs, train robber,
The Daily Telegraph, July 23, 1999)

"Let us shut it out," coaxed Elizabeth-Jane, noting that the rigid wildness of Lucetta's features was growing yet more rigid and wild with the nearing of the noise and laughter. "Let us shut it out!"

(from *The Mayor of Casterbridge*,
THOMAS HARDY)

ROUGH MUSIC

She walked across the sand carrying a shoe in either hand, drawn forward as much by the great blue moon up ahead as by the sound of the breaking waves. The moon had a ring around it which promised or threatened something, she forgot what exactly.

The chill of the foam shocked her skin. She stood still and felt the delicious tug beneath her soles as the water sucked sand out from under them. The water was as cold as death.

If I stood here long enough, she thought, *just stood, the sea would draw out more and more sand from under me and bring more and more back in. Little by little I'd sink, ankles already, knees soon, then waist, then belly.*

She imagined standing up to her tingling breasts in sucking, salty sand. When the first, disarmingly little wave struck her in the face, would she panic? Would she, instead, laugh, as they said, *inappropriately?*

She dared herself not to move.

The moon was nearly full. She could see the headland on the far side of the estuary mouth and its stumpy, striped lighthouse. She could see the foam flung and drawn, flung and drawn about her. He was striding across the little beach behind her; she could tell without turning. Would his hands touch her first or would she merely feel the jacket he draped about her? Would he call out from yards away or would she hear his voice soft and sudden when his lips were only inches from her neck?

Her resolution not to turn stiffened her spine. Watching weeds and foam rush away from her for long enough made it feel as though the sea and beach were motionless and it was only she who was gliding back and forth on mysterious salty tracks.

I love you. She felt the words well up. *I love you more than words can say.* Which was true, of course, because when she felt his steadying hands about her shoulders at last and the brush of his lips on her neck, all that came from her mouth was, "I turn you. Turn my words away?"

BLUE HOUSE

"Actually I feel a bit of a fraud being here," Will told her. "I'm basically a happy man. No. There's no basically about it. I'm happy. I am a happy man."

"Good," she said, crossing her legs and caressing an ankle as if to smooth out a crease she found there. "What makes you say that?"

"That I'm happy?"

She nodded.

"Well." He uncrossed his legs, sat back in the sofa and peered out of her study window. He saw the waters of the Bross glittering at the edge of Boniface Gardens, two walkers pausing, briefly allied by the gamboling of their dogs. "I imagine you usually see people at their wit's end. People with depression or insoluble problems."

"Occasionally. Some people come to me merely because they've lost their way."

He detected a certain sacerdotal smugness in her tone and suspected he hated her. "Well I'm here because a friend bought me a handful of sessions for my birthday. She thinks I need them."

"Do you mind?"

He shrugged, laughed. "Makes a change from socks and book tokens."

"But you don't feel you need to be here."

"I . . . I know it sounds arrogant but no, I don't. Not especially. It's just that it would have been rude not to come, even though she'll be far too discreet to ask how I get on with you. If I didn't come, I'd be rejecting her present and I'd hate to do that. I love her."

"Her being?"

"Harriet. My best friend. She's like a second sister but I think of her as a friend first and family second."

"You have more loyalty to friends than family?"

"I didn't say that. But you know how it is; people move on from family and choose new allies. It's part of becoming an adult. I feel I'm moving on too. A little late in the day, I suppose."

"Your best friend's a woman."

"Is that unusual?" She said nothing, waiting for him to speak. "I suppose it is," he went on. "I'm just not a bloke's bloke. I never have been. I find women more congenial, more evolved. I mean I'm perfectly happy being a man, but I find I have more in common with women."

"Such as?"

He did hate her. He hated her royally. "The things we laugh at. The things we do with our free time. And, okay, I suppose you'll want to talk about this—"

"I don't want to talk about anything you don't want to talk about."

"Whatever. We also share sexual interests. I mean we like the same thing."

"You're homosexual?"

"I'm gay." He smiled, determined to charm her, but she was impervious and vouchsafed no more than a wintry smile. "I told you. I'm a happy man."

"Your sexuality isn't a problem for you."

"It never has been. It's a constant source of delight. Not a day goes by when I don't thank God. If anything I'm relieved. Especially now my friends are all having children."

"You never wanted children."

"Of course. Sometimes. Hats jokes that if she dies I can have hers. But no. The impulse came and went. There are more than enough children in the world and I'm not so obsessed with seeing myself reproduced. Besides, one of my nephews is the spitting image of me, which has taken care of that. I love my own company. I don't think I'm selfish exactly but I'm self-sufficient."

"What about settling down? You're, what, thirty-five?"

"Thank you for that. I turned forty earlier this year. I have settled down. I have a satisfying job, a nice flat. I just happen to have settled down alone."

"And watching all those girlfriends settled with their partners doesn't make you want a significant other."

"Oh. I have one of those. Sort of, I suppose. He's really why I'm here. I made a promise to him. It was a joke really, but I told Harriet and—"

"Tell me about him."

He paused. Glanced out at the view again. "Sorry," he said. "It's private."

"Whatever you tell me—"

"—is in strictest confidence. Yes. I know. But we've barely met, you're still a stranger to me and I'd rather not talk about him just now. It's not a painful situation. He's a lovely man. He makes me happy. But I didn't come here to talk about him."

A slight, attentive raising of her eyebrows asked, *So what did you come to talk about?*

"Shouldn't we start with my childhood?" he said. "Isn't that the usual thing?"

"If you like."

"I warn you. I wasn't abused. I wasn't neglected. I love my parents and I loved my childhood. It was very, very happy."

"Tell me about it."

BEACHCOMBER

"You can't possibly go to bed yet. It's only four," Ma sighed. She was packing food, most of it tinned, into a big box. He saw corned beef, grapefruit segments, fruit salad, rice pudding, baked beans, yellow pie filling, red pie filling and the detested steak-in-gravy. She had on his favorite of her summer dresses, very short and covered with enormous daisies, and the white Dr. Scholl sandals he liked to try to walk in sometimes. She looked up from her labors and saw his face. She smiled. "You're so excited you're not going to sleep for hours in any case. Have you finished packing?"

"Yes."

"Teddy packed?"

"Yes, and books and crayons and everything."

"Monopoly."

"And Totopoly and Scrabble. They're all in the hall where you told me. But Pa said there'll be games in the house."

"Well, you can never be sure. That dreadful place he rented in Northumberland only had Spin Quiz. Remember how boring that got? Oh, but you're too young to remember, I suppose. Now . . ." She sighed and carried on packing things from the larder. "Have an apple to clean your teeth."

"No, thank you."

"Well how about getting your bed all ready, then go and play in the garden for a bit so I can get finished in here?"

"All right."

Secretly delighted, he left the room slowly, pretending she had set him a chore. She called after him.

"How about Lady Percy?"

"She's already in."

As he ran up the huge spiral of stairs, the hall clock struck four. First he moved the lunar module model, finished that morning, off his bed to the relative obscurity of a bookshelf. It had bored him really. The kit was a present from the same godfather who religiously sent him baffling first-day covers for his nonexistent stamp collection. Julian had only made it up out of politeness and now it felt as out of place in his bedroom as a football or cap-gun would have done. He snatched the pillow off his bed and the sheets and blanket, then, doing his best not to trip, carried the boulder of bedding back downstairs, out of the open front door and across the drive to the car. He laid it carefully on the gravel, which was fairly dry, then opened the hatch at the back with a grunt of effort, standing on the bumper for a better reach. Whistling to himself, he began to make his bed for the journey on the short mattress that lined the shelf at the vehicle's rear.

Referred to by Mrs. Coley, the awestruck cleaning lady, as a *dormobile* it was, strictly speaking, a Volkswagen Devon Caravette. Julian always thought of it as the *Height of Extravagance*, however, because that was how his father referred to it whenever the subject arose. Ma had bought the gleaming red and white thing on impulse with some money a dead person left her. Ma's theory was that they could save money by going on camping holidays instead of renting or that they could, at least, spend the occasional night in it instead of stopping at a bed and breakfast. It was beautifully equipped. There was a little gas cooker that smelled funny and a fridge and even a sink with a dribble of running water, which all disappeared into cupboards when you didn't need them. There was a table with sofas on either side so Julian could do drawings and play games and face forward or backward as they drove and never commit that cardinal childish sin of getting bored. And at bedtime the table sort of dismantled and combined with the sofa cushions into a grown-up bed for Ma and Pa while Julian slept on the shelf behind them. This seemed incredibly intimate, as though they had stopped being people and had become furry nesting animals, like foxes or badgers. The pleasure it gave him was so intense that he could not understand why they did not sleep in it at least one night of every week. They had only once gone camping as a family, for a disastrously wet weekend on the Isle of Wight, when tempers had run high and Pa had said *Bloody Hell Frances* a lot and had insisted on frying breakfast on the little stove with the door shut against the wind and rain. When Julian pressed his nose to the curtains or itchy upholstery he could still detect traces of the smell of burning bacon.

Since then, the Height of Extravagance had rarely served her purpose, although she made Ma popular on the school run. On a few bewitching occasions, Ma had *kidnapped* Julian, as she put it, bundling him back in as soon as he was changed after school and running away with him for spontaneous nights in a field somewhere without Pa, on the educational pretext of showing him a castle or a battlefield. Otherwise she was merely a car, only bigger; a room on wheels. Her chief justification was on occasions like this one, where Julian could be put to bed in her in Wandsworth and wake up halfway across the country after Ma and Pa had taken turns driving through the night or dozing. He loved the idea that his holidays thus started several hours before theirs. Ma had rightly guessed that a destination was immaterial to him; he would be perfectly happy if they tucked him into bed then merely drove in a large, all-night circle. Woken at regular intervals through the night by the gunning of the throaty engine beneath him or by a food cupboard door which occasionally came loose and struck him on the head, he loved to lie watching the lights flash by overhead and hear his parents talking in low murmurs from the front. Even though the house was protected by dogs and guards and high barbed wire, he never felt so entirely secure in his bedroom as during these nights on the road.

Bed made after a fashion, Julian checked on Lady Percy, his Abyssinian guinea pig, whose hutch he had stowed beneath the table. He had actually wanted a dog called Shadow, a large black dog that frightened other people, but Pa had said he would have to wait until he was old enough to walk it himself, and how about a guinea pig? Lady Percy was a lush bronze color with exotic whirls in her fur, a pink nose and sharp, pink feet which tickled if you lay on your back, lifted your shirt and put her on your stomach. She would sit quite happily on your lap munching a carrot and did not mind being groomed with a powder-blue baby's hairbrush and Julian loved her language of squeaks which *Caring for your Cavy* said was called *pinking*. But she didn't do a great deal beyond run in a straight line when one set her on the lawn or run in manic circles when placed inside an old car tire. He had overheard Pa say that the whole point of small pets was to teach children about reproduction and death but Lady Percy remained in robust good health, a resolute spinster, so seemed as wayward of purpose as the Height of Extravagance.

"We're both going to Cornwall," Julian told her. "But you must be very patient. Here." And he jiggled an old piece of cabbage leaf under her nose. Lady Percy sniffed the offering disdainfully, pinked a few times then retreated into her bedding. Julian climbed into the big front seat which stretched the width of the vehicle, tried on Ma's driving gloves and driving shoes and helped himself to a sugar-dusted barley sugar from the tin she kept hidden there. Then he let himself out and obediently went to the garden to play.

An only child, he saw nothing strange in being told to play when there was no one to play with. In fact he much preferred playing alone to playing with other children since other children invariably imposed rules and systems and overruled his suggestions—mildly posed through lack of aggressive group practice—as to what they should make-believe.

The Governor's House had always seemed to him to be enormous and now that he was going to school and gathering points of comparison, he was coming to see that the home he had taken for granted was undeniably strange. Nobody else he knew—he knew at least four other people well enough to visit and he had been to eight birthday parties— lived in a place with so many rooms that several of them were left empty. Pa told him it only seemed big because he was small and Ma said he was never to forget that the place didn't belong to them but merely came with his father's job. Neither could deny, however, that with its blackened masonry and louring tower and numberless windows, the place was a far cry from the stylized two-up-two-down pictured on *Play School*. The house had a vast basement, reached by a rickety set of steps through a trap door in the wooden floor of his father's downstairs lavatory. In this sinister series of musty rooms, moldy wooden chairs were stacked and tattered posters about the Home Guard and First Aid Procedures curled away from yellowed walls. The Guides and Brownies used to meet down there but apparently they had stopped coming because they had found somewhere more congenial.

At the top of the house, sunnier and drier, but no less dusty, there was an answering sequence of attics where ancient leather trunks and broken furniture were stored. There were moldering dresses and hats to try on, even a long black veil which scared Julian so much he had only tried it on once, and a First World War gas mask like a skull with a metal box on a long caterpillarish tube. Julian knew that bats nested here, although no one would believe him. He had also found, in strictest secrecy, that he could climb through one of the attic windows and explore the valleys, chimney stacks and unexpected skylight views of the roof. (Another great advantage of being single, he had discovered, was that one could stray into the more dangerous side of play with no risk of talebearing betrayal to grown-ups.) From up on the tiles he could see all Wandsworth, from Trinity Road and the gloomy church to the Common, and the railway cutting spanned by multiple bridges. Closer to, he could see the extent of the prison walls, see the uniformed officers coming and going through the door where Pa went to work and even see down into the yard where the prisoners exercised.

Most secret of all, he could venture past the point where the internal dividing wall marked house from prison so that he was over the prison itself and could lie flat on the roof and peer gingerly down through one of the skylights that gave on to the nearest wing of cells. It was like a view into a strange kind of monkey house, where all the monkeys wore ties; a vista of cages and walkways full of harsh shouts and laughter and the clatter of heels on metal. He would watch for hours. It was as fascinating as watching an ants' nest or the glass-sided beehive in the Horniman Museum. He knew that the men in tight uniform with hats on and truncheons were officers, controlled by Pa—who, like the queen, was so powerful he was never seen—and that the men in baggy blue suits, without hats or ties, were prisoners controlled by the officers. He also knew that the prisoners were said to be doing *stir* or *porridge* and that they called the officers *screws* and that he was never to say this word in front of his parents.

The garden was bounded by high walls on three sides. Two, shaded by sticky-scented limes, had pavement and road beyond them. The third, unshaded for security reasons, divided Governor's House from prison territory and was overlooked, for most of its length, by the prison factory where the inmates worked up hessian sacks for use by the Royal Mail and potato farmers. The humming of sewing machines and shouts and chatter from the workers so struck Julian that the word *factory* would never acquire quite the grim connotation for him that it had for others. From the sounds, at least, it seemed to him a place of release and even joy.

"Men need to work," Pa explained when questioned on the matter. (He always called them *men*, never *prisoners* or *convicts*.) "Without work, they become demoralized, which can lead to all kinds of trouble. Never underrate the dignity of labor, Julian."

It was through one of the factory windows that Julian had his first encounter with one of the men, apparently. He was too young to remember it but it was a story his mother liked to repeat in his hearing so that it had become a memory of sorts.

"I opened the drawing-room window and I could hear him burbling away. Well naturally at first I assumed he was talking to himself, the way they do at that age. Then I realized there were gaps and I was hearing one half of a conversation. I looked out and there he was, all of four, chatting to one of the men through the factory window. Another man must have joined in as I looked out because I heard someone call out, 'Wotcha Ginger!' and this one got quite shirty and said, 'I'm not ginger, I'm a nice little boy!' I had no idea they could see out. I mean, I knew they could see the sky and the trees but nothing more. I put a blind in the downstairs loo the same week . . ."

There was no other story about such conversations, so Julian assumed it was either an isolated incident or that he had been discouraged in some way. He could not remember her ever trying to stop him talking to the men and, so far as the trusties were concerned, she *actively encouraged* him. He knew this from an argument he had overheard between her and Pa when they were all sitting out in deckchairs after Sunday lunch once.

"It's not right to use him like that," he had said. "You actively encourage him to talk to them."

"It does him no harm, John. He likes them," she replied. "They're harmless lifers rotting away in there. He's like a grandson to them."

"Two wife-killers and a robber who raped his hostage. Quite harmless. Frances—"

"They *love* him."

"Just be careful."

And she was.

"You would tell me, darling, wouldn't you, if any of the trusties—Bert, say, or Henry—ever said anything that was, well, not quite nice?"

"Of course," Julian assured her, very much the nice little boy. But his curiosity was piqued. Which were the wife-killers? How could one tell? How had they done it? And what was a rapist? Judging from the only picture he could find, *The Rape of the Sabine Women,* a rapist made ladies cross by picking them up in the air and tickling them with his beard when they had nothing on.

The trusties said plenty of things that were not quite nice. Trailing around after them as they painted rooms, pruned the roses, mowed the lawns or forked out horse poo donated by the rag and bone man and the coal merchant, he had compiled a rich vocabulary of forbidden words.

Unrepeatable and broadly incomprehensible, they were none the less precious for being useless.

Rounding the corner from the drive, he found the trusties at work. They were also known as red bands because of the armbands they wore that showed they could be trusted. Friday was their gardening day. Joe was riding the lawn mower up and down, creating stripes and obviously enjoying himself. (The trusties took it in turns to mow the lawn, officially because it was considered a *cushy number* but actually, Julian believed, because the old machine was fun to ride and, as with a prize toy, they each wanted a go.) George and Bert were weeding. Henry was working his way around the edges of the grass, chopping off the straggly bits the lawnmower only squashed, using a pair of long-handled edging shears. As always, the screw in charge was sitting on the steps of the Wendy House looking bored. Today it was Mr. Prescott, who always looked as though someone had stolen his Easter egg. Ma said everyone had to overlook this and be extra nice to him because his wife had died or left him or something, so Julian threw him a cheery, "Hello Mr. Prescott!" which met with the usual resentful stare.

Meanwhile Henry looked up from his trimming, said, "Afternoon young Ginger," and carried on. (He persisted in calling Julian Ginger despite the fact that his hair was brown and would only offer the maddening explanation—"You'll find out soon enough.") Judging by appearances, Mr. Prescott seemed a far more believable cutter-up-of-wives than the men he guarded and Julian was surprised this possibility had occurred to no one when Mrs. Prescott went missing. But then perhaps Henry was only a rapist and a bank robber. Bank robbers were often the heroes in cowboy films, unless they had Alan Ladd in them, who was always the sheriff. Perhaps you had to be a rapist too for it to count as a serious offense. It was all very confusing.

Julian walked along behind Henry, picking up handfuls of the turf he had been shaving off the lawn's edge and adding them to the heap in a wheelbarrow.

"That's very kind," Henry said. "See that funny car of yours is all packed up, then."

"We're going to Cornwall. All of us."

"Very nice. I was in Delabole during the war. Evacuee. Nothing sweeter than Cornish flowers. How long you going for?"

"Two weeks." Julian stared at the mermaid tattooed on Henry's forearm. Once, when he was a bit younger, Henry had let him touch it, running his fingers through the hair to trace the voluptuous design. He wanted to touch it again but it was difficult to know how to ask and he feared the request would be viewed as not quite nice. He had a brief vision of Henry on the beach with him, wearing trunks for once instead of his oddly respectable prison uniform. He imagined his father telling him to guard Henry closely the way Mr. Prescott had to, imagined Henry's grinning obedience as Julian buried his big legs in the sand for his own good.

"Dad going too?"

"Of course. He has to share the driving. Can I help you make a roll-up?"

"Best not. Him Indoors is watching."

Julian glanced back and turned on Mr. Prescott a smile of such cloying sweetness that the officer turned away. "Not anymore," he said.

Barely interrupting his work to do so, Henry tossed a matchbox on to the grass. Well trained, Julian snatched it up and sat with his back to the Wendy House. There were some matches inside, a tiny foil packet of tobacco and some Rizla papers. Julian sprinkled a very little tobacco on to the paper as he had been taught, licked one side and rolled it up neatly. Small fingers, Henry said, did this job so well that in some countries children rolled up cigarettes in a factory instead of going to school. Julian had a small puff of one once, behind the Wendy House, when Henry let him. It made him feel sick and the taste was bad. He liked the smell, however. It was part of the smell the men gave off even out here in the open, with all the roses scenting the air about them, a good, brown, male smell, like the man who came to mend a window once or the car when you opened the bonnet when the engine was still hot or Pa when he came back from playing rugger with the prison officers' club. It was a smell that once breathed in seemed to curl like a snake around Julian's stomach so that he felt excited and rather queasy at the same time. He had the same feeling when he got close to Tom Sherry at school when they played Lions during break, only Antonia Pauffley kept joining in and spoiling everything.

"So how do you get up on the roof, then?" Henry's question was casual enough but he saw Julian flinch. "It's all right. I won't tell. I don't want to spoil your fun. I know you're safe enough. Not like some nippers."

Julian glanced toward the house. Ma was wedging a box of groceries under the dormobile table. Turning, she waved to him and headed back inside.

"When did you see me?" he asked.

"Yesterday afternoon. Must have been around three 'cause I was coming off my shift. My cell's in that block. I just happened to glance up as we was coming up the stairs and I sees you peering down through the skylight like a bleeding pigeon. Pardon my French."

"That's all right."

"So how'd you get up there, then?"

"Easy. Through our attic. There's a window with a broken catch at the far end and you go through on to a sort of valley in the roof. Then there's a little wall at the far end, between the chimney stacks, and on the other side is the prison roof. I've been all over it. But . . ."

"What?"

"I've never told anyone."

"Don't worry. It's our secret. You don't tell anyone you told me and I won't tell anyone I asked. Deal?"

"Deal."

"So how do you get to your attic, then?"

"Up the stairs, silly."

"Course you do. Now listen. You know how to use the jelly bone, don't you?"

"Course."

"Do you want to make a call for me?" Henry quite often asked him to make calls, usually about things that meant so little they might as well have been in code. Henry said they were about bets and dogs but Julian had his doubts.

"Only if you tell me, you know. Another word."

Henry glanced over at his mates who were still working but out of earshot.

"You're on. When your mum's not looking, I want you to ask the operator for Plaistow 9595."

"Plar's Toe 9595."

"That's it, and a nice lady'll answer and you're to tell her, 'Henry says his mum's birthday's on Tuesday.' "

"Is it really, Henry?"

"Course."

"So what's my word?"

Henry looked about him, then whispered, "Beef curtains." Julian was thunderstruck and delighted. "Look, your mum's waving again. Reckon she wants you."

Julian scowled toward his mother, affecting manly reluctance. "Suppose so."

"Have a good holiday."

Julian got back on his feet, noting how the grass and daisies had left indentations all over his hot knees, and went to rejoin Ma. Soon she would let him call Pa on the internal telephone to ask how much longer he'd be, which is when he could make Henry's call to Plar's Toe. Then there'd be supper and a bath and then, still in broad summer light, he'd be allowed to cross the drive in his pajamas and dressing gown and go to bed in the car. He turned back to Henry, who looked up from the wheelbarrow and dismissed him with a wink of his startlingly blue eyes. The realization that Henry would never go on holiday, at least not until he was even older than he was now, however sad, somehow made the anticipation of pleasure all the sweeter.

When he asked for Plar's Toe 9595 a woman sounding like Mrs. Coley, only younger, answered. She was not very nice at all.

"Hello," Julian said politely. "Henry says to tell you his mother's birthday is on Tuesday."

"Right you are, love," she said. "And what's your name?" He told her. "And where do you live?" When he told her Governor's House, HM Prison, Wandsworth, London, she couldn't speak for a while because she was laughing so much.

Julian was rather cross. "Why are you laughing and why did you want my address?" he asked.

"Nothing, darling. He's got a nerve, that's all. Keep your mouth shut and a token of our esteem will be coming your way."

She hung up first.

Token of Esteem was almost as good as *Height of Extravagance* but both paled by comparison with the sinisterly suggestive *Beef Curtains*. Curled in the hall armchair, waiting for Pa to answer the internal telephone, he imagined the not quite nice woman in her palatial bedroom in Plar's Toe drawing magnificent drapes made of dripping steak.

BLUE HOUSE

In his more vulnerable hours, throwing a fortieth-birthday lunch-party for himself, however casually, even dismissively he did it, struck Will as akin to inviting people to a wedding with no spouse to parade. It was obscurely a failure, like buying your own scent or recognizing the family hand behind a Valentine's card.

A late starter in the relationships race, by virtue of virtue and confusion, he had not acquired a lover until he left home and went to university. Like many who choose to save themselves, he had perhaps dangerously high expectations: a great student love affair, too passionate not to go up in glorious, mildly tragic flames and then, later, a marriage of sorts, with dogs and artworks in lieu of children, in which the growing beauty of house and garden would lay out public evidence of a rarefield meeting of minds as of bodies.

His fantasies fueled by Waugh and Forster, he found university life overpoweringly heterosexual after ten years of protective schooling. At party after sordid party he found himself leaning against the fridge lugubriously watching the Noah's Ark proceedings with variations on the same waspish huddle of more-or-less gay onlookers. In so overlooked,

overcritical and confined an environment, the great love failed to materialize. There were, however, three encounters repeated often enough to
be hungrily counted as boyfriends. After two and two-thirds terms of reluctant chastity, he met a geologist from New Zealand, a comparative
ancient of twenty-one. Then there was a period of horny mourning followed by liaisons with an impossibly sensitive drama student from the
nearby polytechnic, so convinced everyone despised him that they came
to, and with a depressive fourth-year linguist with no friends.

Finn the geologist might have become the great love or even the ex-
emplary marriage, but he was a light-headed finalist when they met and
had no sooner turned Will's life and heart upside-down than he headed
back to Christchurch and a summer job on a sheep farm followed by a
lengthy seismology doctorate. In the years that followed he kept spo-
radically in touch, just enough to fuel the embers of a fantasy from
which Will would unwittingly forge a romantic template. Finn remained more or less single. He pursued his rugged research unencum-
bered by any company but a dog. And despite the fact that in their one
fortnight together they had never spoken of love, their involvement had
clearly meant something to him because he seemed keen to keep in
touch.

Will should, perhaps, have put his life on hold and saved for a ticket
to New Zealand when he graduated or even flown out earlier. Every
holiday seemed to be spent in grinding poverty, however, slaving to pay
off the debts run up the previous term and, once he graduated, times
were frighteningly hard so he felt compelled to accept a librarian post in
Barrowcester when it was offered him. Besides, much of Finn's attrac-
tion lay in his self-sufficiency and, in his early twenties at least, it was
hard for Will to see how he could fit in to a life as ingeniously self-
contained as its owner's camping equipment. In time Finn's letters had
petered out. He had either met someone, found Jesus or gone pot-
holing once too often.

The great marriage had failed to materialize for several reasons
but the chief of these was Barrowcester. A ravishingly pretty provincial cathedral town in the country's middle, it called itself a city but

offered none of the risky subcultures implicit in the title. Perhaps the fact that its name was not pronounced as it was spelled—the correct pronunciation rhyming with *rooster*—should have been chintzi-ness enough to warn him off. But he was lulled into passivity by the relative cheapness of the attractive housing, the security of his job—managing a well-financed children's department in the city library—and the fact of its being the nearest he had to a hometown in a rootless youth. His parents had moved on every five years because of his father's work as a prison governor but he had been a choirboy at the cathedral choir school, then a music scholar at Tatham's, the city's ancient college, and boarded throughout so that the place was full of youthful associations.

His parents had lived there when his father ran Barrowcester prison when Will was at choir school. Like him they retained happy memories of the place and, having scrupulously requested his permission to en-croach on what they saw as his town, chose to retire to a house on its rivery fringes. They made few demands, at least until recently, and scarcely intruded on his life but they could not fail to inhibit him. He was not in the closet exactly, but he had never discussed his sexuality with them because the idea was as embarrassing as discussing theirs. And it was a small community. And people talked. And perhaps it was just an excuse but, if pressed, they and their aging would have been the reason he gave for remaining a bachelor at forty. Will had invited them today but they had declined, with characteristic tact, saying his mother found it a trial to stand for long these days and disliked being parked in a stately chair where she was expected to hold forth to the *young things*. They would celebrate with him later, as the obituarists had it, quietly and at home.

The party had reached the point where it would bubble on under its own social momentum. Will had slaved to produce a two-course buffet for thirty from his galley kitchen. Coffee and birthday cake had been served and the few who were still drinking were happy to fend for them-selves. At last he could relax and possibly even begin to enjoy himself. He poured a glass of Chablis—having cooked all morning and much of the previous night, he had no appetite for food—and walked out on to the brightly painted fire escape which served as a terrace and led down to the garden.

Someone pressed a hand on his rear and planted a nuzzling kiss on the nape of his neck. Harriet.

"Hi, Hats."

"Precious," she said. "I couldn't resist. You look about eleven with that haircut."

"You don't like it."

"On the contrary, I like it too much."

"Oh. That old thing."

He drew her briefly to him and easily kissed the top of her head. Harriet had always refused to dance with him because, she said, the difference in their statures made them look like a pixie with a waltzing bear. Then they leaned on the railing and surveyed the guests.

"Oh God," she sighed. "Children everywhere."

"There are quite a lot," he said. "It's almost surreal."

"I'm sorry."

"It's not your fault. Only one of them's yours. Anyway, I love children. I've just become a godfather again. Della and Kieran."

"Which?"

"The solicitors from over the road. Little thing called Jemima."

"Isn't there some official limit?"

"Apparently not. But I'm calling a halt at six. Christmas is nightmarish enough as it is and children *cost*."

"Tell me about it. Corporate Raider Barbie didn't come cheap."

His garden had indeed turned from a city oasis into a sort of crèche. A paddling pool had materialized beneath his fig tree. Several toddlers were lolling in it while their mothers cooled their feet. Each child, however small, appeared to have brought at least two toys, all of them in primary-colored plastic, all of them noise-producing. Vera, Harriet's four-year-old, had acquired a scarlet plastic trumpet and was calmly circulating in the crowd parping it in the ear of any infant who came close.

"God, she's hell," Harriet said, doing nothing to stop her. "You know she's all yours if I die. It's in my will and everything."

"Try to stay with us just a little longer. Till she can cook, say, or plaster a wall."

Harriet laughed and kissed his shoulder. She was carrying a wine bottle in a spirit of survivalism. She topped up their glasses. "Happy birthday," she said.

"Thanks."

"Oh, sorry. That was white in there, wasn't it?"

"Doesn't matter. The claret's better."

"Soon be time for your presents."

"But I said no presents. I hate presents."

"You're so controlling. You hate the thought of being given something hideous and having to sound convincingly grateful."

"Well, don't you?"

"You can trust me." She grinned. "I always give you something that doesn't hang around. Like opera tickets. Or Calvados. And after that difficult waistcoat thing Poppy gave you last year we had words and she knows to do the same."

"God, you didn't tell her I didn't like it?"

"No, no. I just said you were going off material things in your old age and preferred presents that came and went."

"Oh. Thanks."

"I still haven't got you anything yet. Can't make up my mind. But her present's rather brilliant. For her."

"They haven't gone mad, have they?"

"Only a little. I'm planning on treating you to something spectacular."

"Hats," he groaned.

"Humor me. I earn more than you and I had another raise last month."

After years of high-stress, low-pay jobs as press officer for various publishers and publicist for an opera company, Harriet had quietly stepped into a high-stress, high-pay one containing press crises on behalf of the prison service. When there was a breakout at Camp Hill or a riot in Strangeways, she faced the cameras and fired off the press releases or spoon-fed them to the appropriate minister and pushed *them* into the firing line. Almost stealthily she had gone from being mad, sad Hats who drank too much at parties and could never hold down a man to being sane, wryly amused Hats who now had a nanny to pick up Vera from school but frequently canceled dates in favor of ministerial briefings.

"I suppose *someone* I know has to become a Dame," Will joked.

Short and vampy, still drawing heavily on *Cabaret* for her style references, she had gatecrashed his life when they were students. Enrolled in the year below him, she appeared during his period of mourning for Finn and sniffed out his insecurity amid the hall of residence hearties as a tidy match for her own. A notoriously easy lay with a notoriously acid morning-after tongue, she would drop in on his room to borrow his steam iron or his purple braces, to split a facepack or a bottle of wine and to ask his advice on how to keep a man. Advice she then pointedly ignored. Whenever he found a lover, she caustically disapproved. Whenever she found one, she became unavailable for the duration of the liaison. He forgave her, however, because she was the only person who knew when he was lying and because long after he had acquired a modicum of maturity and style, she continued to remember him living off cottage cheese and pining for a geologist with no dress sense which, however galling, made him feel young again.

They had always joked that they would marry if they reached forty and were still unclaimed. What had started out as an oft-repeated jest came increasingly to resemble a threat as they remained outwardly single and more and more of their contemporaries married. When Harriet elected, amid some mystery, to reproduce, even his mother had suggested it would be *tidier* if he made an honest woman of her. Harriet had no intention of marrying anyone, or so she maintained, least of all her oldest friend, but there were times when he wished she would at least set up home with someone, to give her somebody else to needle. He hoped she was going to have the sensitivity not to remind him of the pact today.

"So," she crowed. "The big four-ho-ho."

"Don't," he murmured.

"Oh spare me. You're aging better than I am. You defy gravity. You've got cheekbones."

"So've you."

"Make-up."

"Oh."

"So you're probably still not ready to steer me up the register office."

"I'm answered for."

"Master Mystery." Her eyes narrowed. "It's a bit convenient, saying you've got someone but not letting anyone meet him."

"I've told you before; he's married. He's not *sortable*."

"Is he going to leave her for you?"

"I sincerely hope not." Will did his best to look airily at no one in particular but she caught him.

"He's here!" she gasped.

"No he's not. What do you take me for?"

"A shameless home-wrecker. Which is it? The *love-rat bastard*!" She scanned the men below them. "Paddy? No. George? I've always had my suspicions . . ."

"Stop it."

"It is. It's George!"

"No, it's not. George has childbearing hips."

"Then it's one of these people I don't know. Who *are* they all?"

"People from the shop. Neighbors. Kieran and Della. Simon the nice vet."

"The Nice Vet. It's him!"

"He's straight," Will sighed. "Brought his girlfriend. See? In the blue with the hair."

"So?"

As Harriet continued to scrutinize the crowd, the erring husband in question, who *was* there of course, caught Will's eye over a child's shoulder, grinned and might have given the game away by waving had Vera not saved the day by causing a violent diversion, slamming another child over the head with her toy trumpet. The child screamed and Vera watched it with her customary analytical coolness and a ghost of a smile.

"Oh look," Harriet sighed before walking down to dispense a weary reprimand, "I made a psychopath."

Will's sister bore the wailing child, one of his nephews, up the fire escape and Will bribed him back to silence if not quite happiness with a home-made Tia Maria truffle.

"Sorry," he said, catching the soft reproof in Poppy's gaze. "It's what uncles are for."

"You know we don't give them sweets."

"Why do you think he likes me so much? It's not for my conversation. Little boys *need* sugar so they can stand up to Vera and her kind."

"Could I have another, do you think, please, Will?" Oscar the nephew asked with measured innocence.

"Not now, dumpling," Will told him. "Your mum and I want to talk. Have a strawberry. Look. Tasty? Go and ask Daddy for a piggyback ride. He needs the exercise."

Poppy caressed the boy's red hair as she set him down, gently pushing him back into the fray. "So hey," she said, once they were alone, and gently mimed punching Will's arm.

Always so free in her gestures of affection with others—husband, children, friends—she remained oddly shy toward him and the inhibition was catching. However pleased Will was to see her, they rarely advanced beyond the formal frigidity of a single cheek-kiss. They remained alike in many ways. They were both tall and each had failed to lose the stooping self-consciousness of the beanpole adolescent. Their voices and accents were similar too—an approximation of Will's mother's low, amused speech. These resemblances only served to highlight their dissimilarity however. With auburn hair, freckles and eyes so pale they seemed almost bleached of color, she could look more her husband Sandy's sister than dark-haired Will's. She was cheerfully dim, not a reader and gave every appearance of finding marriage and motherhood entirely fulfillling. If she entered his shop as a customer it was to buy books for the children or to ask his suggestions for presents to

friends. Though prepared to tolerate each other for Will's sake, she and
Harriet shared their narrow common ground with reliable frostiness.
She claimed to find Harriet "rather sad and brave" while Harriet maintained that, for all her amenability and affection, Poppy was a mistress
of passive aggression.

Will had given up defending Poppy long ago as it only encouraged
Harriet's spite. It was enough that he knew there was more to Poppy
than she betrayed. He knew the affection and amenability were genuine.
He knew that it was Poppy's conventional dress and manner, precisely
those qualities that irritated Harriet most, that were a mask. Only when
she was alone with him, as now, and sometimes when she was playing
with the boys, unaware that she was watched, did Poppy allow her
blunter, quirkier self to emerge.

"So. Many happies, big boy."

"Thanks. How's things?"

"Oh. Fine," she said, pushing her sunglasses up on her hair then
pulling them down again when her weak blue eyes could not face the
sun. "Sandy's working too hard as usual. Loads of late nights. The boys
have both had mumps, which was a relief to get out of the way. They
really suffered though. We all make light of the kids' illnesses; it's easy to
forget how scary it is at the time. Poor Oz actually thought he was dying
at one point."

"But how are *you*?"

"Oh. Fine. You know me. Terminally placid. No worries. No illnesses." She sounded like their mother. "Sandy says I should take a
lover to give my life some interesting tension." She laughed and they
both looked at Sandy, who now had a son on his back and was racing
two other fathers in a piggyback derby. "I think I might just take up
squash," she said.

"Great. I'll play with you if you like. I've always meant to learn."

"Don't be stupid. You can hardly catch. I'll join a club. Play with
whoever I can find there."

"Find yourself some fun among the coaches."

"Will!"

"Only kidding."

"As if I'd have time," she sighed. "How are the Aged Ps?"

"He's coping, I suppose." Will drank and grimly contemplated the image of their parents a moment.

The nice vet and the luscious proof of his straightness came to make their early farewells, oppressed in their nascent coupledom, perhaps, by so many children. Will marveled at the finesse with which Poppy admired the girl's pretty dress. She fooled everyone. She almost fooled him. He wondered if she had reached the point where it was no longer an effort. Of course she never took a job; being herself was employment with overtime.

"No problem with an empty retirement," he told her when the vet had left. "Mum's going to become Dad's work-substitute. It seems to come and go. The stroke didn't help. She's showing most of the early symptoms and it depresses her which makes her spiteful to him. But they won't talk about it. They're not ready to face the reality. Not really."

"Who can blame them? Jude Farson didn't offer any hope at all, and he's a specialist. Mind you, when I got her to fill out that questionnaire of Sandy's the results seemed fine. Well, fine-ish. Oh shit. It just makes me feel useless and I hate that. I should see more of them, shouldn't I?"

"Don't be daft. You've got your three to care for. At least I'm dependant-free. I go over there every Wednesday now to give him a day off and try to get her over one night at weekends too so he can escape. She still loves the cinema but videos are easier because she gets restless if she has to sit too long."

"Maybe you should spend more time with him rather than her?"

"I couldn't. We've got nothing to say to each other. We never did. I just take her off his hands and let him pretend it's because she and I have lots to talk about or that she can still play cards with me, which she can on her good days. He goes for walks and visits museums or sits in a pub nursing a half. I ought to break the habit of a lifetime and take the two of them on holiday somewhere."

Her face lit up. "Oh good!" She made an effort to backtrack. "I mean . . . really?"

"What?" He smiled.

Looking confused, she glanced around them and called out to Sandy but he was now embroiled in a conversation with the other fathers and already distracted by Oscar who was swinging irritably on his arm.

"Well I might as well tell you," she sighed. "It's our present to you. Not a holiday with the Aged Ps but a holiday, anyway."

"That's so sweet."

"We've rented you a cottage in Cornwall. Right on a little beach. First two weeks of August. We were meant to tell you together. I mean, you could take the Aged Ps if you like but I think the idea was to take, well, you know, someone *special*. If you had anyone in mind. Harriet seemed to think you might."

Will smiled and hugged her. "It's very, very kind," he said. She did not flinch exactly but she was stiff in his embrace, like a reluctant boy hugged by an unappealing relation and he found himself wondering, as he often did, what she was like in bed. "I'll take the Aged Ps," he told her. "They'll love it. Sandy?" he shouted. Sandy looked round at last. "Thank you!" Will called out. Harriet excused herself from an animated argument with the girls from the shop and ran up the fire escape to join them.

"You're not to take your parents," she said.

"It's too late," his sister sighed. "He's already decided."

"But that's so *sad*. It sounds incredibly romantic. It's bang on a little cove with a veranda and I want you curled up with Master Mystery watching sunsets and sipping Nuits-Saint-Georges, not playing whist and having early nights. You *can't* ask them."

"They might not want to come," he suggested.

"Of course they'll come," Poppy said lightly. "They haven't been to Cornwall for years. I found it through an advert in the paper and rang up and it sounded perfect so I booked it for you. But the photo only came yesterday. Look."

She was the kind of mother who was never without a capacious bag. At a moment's notice she could produce tissues for a child's tears, plasters for its wounded knee, Wet Wipes for its sticky fingers and a sugar-free pastille to reward its bravery. One sensed she could always find passport and driving license, always had pen and paper handy *before* picking up the telephone and maintained a small notebook of important birthdays and anniversaries as well as a tidy diary. Will knew all this was in reaction to their mother who had always found affectionate gestures easier to summon up than stamps or car keys. Now, in seconds, she produced a small color photograph of a bright-blue bungalow with a green picket fence and veranda. "Blue House," she said. "That's what it's called."

"It's amazing," Will said. It struck him as faintly familiar. "Haven't we been there before? When I was tiny?"

"You don't remember, do you?" She sounded disappointed. "Maybe it isn't the same place. You weren't *that* little."

He stared at the picture, searching for clues, but even as he stared any familiarity faded. "This is the place we went to? I don't remember it at all."

"Maybe they've changed the color," Harriet suggested. "And places you saw as a child you remember as twice the size."

Will continued to stare at the picture but it gave up no secrets and set off no more resonances in his memory. It might have been anywhere at all. "No," he said. "Sorry. I don't just remember it wrongly. I don't seem to remember it at all. Not just the house, the entire holiday. I remember bits I suppose; the drive down there mainly, and trying to surf and the smell of the place but, well . . ." He shrugged. "I must have blanked it out."

"Scary," said Harriet. "Christ knows what staying there is going to dredge up from your unconscious. Maybe you should book somewhere else?"

"Oh no," he insisted. "I want to go. I'm curious. And it'll be good for Mum. Old familiar places seem to stimulate her."

"But you *can't* take her," Harriet wailed.

"It's no good," Poppy told her. "His mind's made up. He's already planning which books to take and what goodies to pack for picnics."

Curious, some of the others had gathered. Freed at last from their sons, Sandy had slipped an arm around his wife's neck.

"Well if he's not taking a significant other after all," he said, "maybe some of us should invite ourselves."

"Taking the Aged Ps is bad enough," Poppy said firmly. "He doesn't want whole tribes tagging along."

"Oh, I dunno," Will told her. "It might be fun and whoever came could take the Aged Ps off my hands now and then."

There was a quick flurry of present opening, during which Will became mildly hysterical because three people had given him vases, then gradually the party dissolved. The girls from the shop and Harriet buried their differences by loading the dishwasher and the solicitors tidied away leftovers. The younger and poorer of Will's employees gleefully accepted his offer of doggy bags. Children were borne away, fractious from sunshine and social competition. Cheeks were kissed, promises made to stay more closely in touch. The groomless reception was done.

Left alone at last, Will noticed that he had been left with the paddling pool. Barefoot—he had kicked off his new shoes as soon as the last guest was gone—he trod down one side of it to let the water spill out and soak away into the grass. Then he folded the incongruous object away into a large carrier bag and left it by the front door to await collection. He did not have to wait long. He had barely had time to flop on to his bed and close his eyes when the doorbell rang.

"Hi," Sandy said, slipping in and kicking the door shut behind him. "Managed to forget the paddling pool. I've got half an hour," he added, taking Will in his arms and kissing him. "Happy birthday. I've been wanting to do this all afternoon."

"But . . ."

"Trust me. I'm a doctor."

Will had been his brother-in-law's lover since the week after Sandy and Poppy returned from their honeymoon. If heavy petting counted as commitment then the relationship actually predated the marriage. Will had suffered from a weakness for Scottish accents, red hair, muscular legs or any combination of the above since developing a doomed but loyal crush on an ex-policeman who gave gym classes at his school.

When Poppy announced she had fallen in love with a young general practitioner who mended her puncture on a cycling holiday in the Borders, he was as glad for her as he was jealous. When he was allowed to meet the happy couple, it became rapidly evident that Sandy was one of those men who had a problem with their girlfriend's gay playmates. In Will's company, he became surly, either unforthcoming or aggressively male.

"He thinks I'm hopelessly effete," Will told her. "But that's fine. He may be a jerk but he's a sexy one. You love him and I'm very happy for you. After all, you're the one that's got to sustain a relationship with the bastard."

"But I want you two to be friends."

"Poppy, let me break it to you gently: it's not going to happen."

"But I think I want to marry him."

"Oh. Well it's still not going to happen. No cozy drinks with the brother-in-law. Don't look like that. We'll survive!"

"I don't understand it. Normally he's so sensitive. Maybe it's because I told him you had a thing about Scotsmen . . ."

"Well reassure him, for God's sake! Tell him he's not my type. Tell him I only go for swarthy Celts."

The happy couple became engaged. Relations between Will and Sandy did not improve. Sorrowing, he resigned himself to seeing less of Poppy and more of Harriet, who did her best not to let her triumph show. Then came an invitation to the stag party. Appalled, Will trusted that Sandy was offering an olive branch, not planning to humiliate him. He accepted to avoid family ructions, also because his spiteful side sensed that Sandy had counted on a cowardly refusal.

"I could no more deal with a lap dancer than I could drink hog's blood," he told Poppy. "I hope you appreciate what I'm going through for you."

"It'll be fine," she insisted. "There aren't going to be strippers or anything stupid. I've made his best man promise. It's just going to be dinner and a load of booze in some dining club in Birmingham with a bunch of his medical school pals."

If that sounded bad, the reality was far worse. Will had spent a lousy morning protecting the library from an invasion of destructive school-children and a draining afternoon trying without success to plead with the finance committee to raise his budget to allow for visits by celebrity children's authors. He arrived in Birmingham late and fractious to find everyone drunk already so he spent the whole evening being always that crucial bit nearer sobriety than anyone else. The conversation consisted of medical school gossip, anecdotes that meant nothing to him and smutty jokes whose misogyny and racism made him blanch. The wait-resses were molested, the (admittedly filthy) food insulted, bread was thrown, napkins set on fire. At the far end of the table from Sandy, who appeared to be enjoying himself immensely, Will guessed he was seeing a side to his brother-in-law elect which his sister willfully ignored or in-nocently assumed to have been outgrown. There were no strippers or lap dancers. There was, however, pudding and no spoons. And pudding consisted of a young woman borne in on a large catering tray, naked except for a liberal coating of raspberries, whipped cream and little meringues.

"Tuck in, boys," she invited as the tray was set down amongst them. As luck would have it, Will found himself sitting by the pudding's head so, while the others ate with slavering gusto, he could at least make con-versation to take her mind off her ordeal. Did she do this on a nightly basis, he asked her. Was she trying to earn her Equity card? No? And she also danced with a python. Oh, how interesting.

As if this experience were not sufficiently excruciating, the manage-ment then asked them to leave when the partying grew too rowdy and, in the ensuing kerfuffle, the friends proved less than loyal, scampering off to some nightclub leaving the bridegroom behind in their drunken haste.

"It's OK," Sandy assured Will. "Didn't want to go there anyway. Look. Come back to my place for a nightcap."

All Will really wanted was an early night with a good book but he was fairly sober still and owed it to his sister to see her intended safely home. Sandy had lost his keys, however, and his wallet—or they had been snatched by one of his friends in lieu of chaining him naked to a lamp-post. With deep reluctance, sensing it would involve him in all manner of complications as the wedding day dawned with Sandy cashless, key-less, suitless and in the wrong place, Will helped Sandy fall into a taxi and gave the driver his own address in Barrowcester.

Sandy leaned heavily against him all the way home, sustaining a monologue along the lines of, "That was so disgusting I can't believe they sprang that on me that poor kid you won't tell her will you God that was so disgusting . . ." He continued to lean heavily on Will as they lurched up the stairs to his flat, a heavy arm clamped across his shoulder, only now the monologue changed into a less chest-beating, more hesitant mode, full of false starts and pauses which seemed to spell out volumes Will would much rather not read.

"It's not as if—" he now began. "I mean I don't even—I mean I *do* but, well, not always and not even then. Do you see what I'm saying? I didn't actually *enjoy* it back there any more than you. Not that I'm, well, you know."

"I know, Sandy," Will said briskly. "Believe me, I *know*." He un-locked the door, swung Sandy inside and lurched him in the general di-rection of the sofa. But Sandy became suddenly immobile and was holding him even more tightly.

"Could I just . . . ?" he began.

"What?"

"Could I just kiss you?"

"Sandy, you're drunk. Very, very drunk."

"So? I still want to kiss you."

"Is this some stag-night thing? Like paying a last visit to a tart or get-ting a tattoo somewhere silly because if so then—"

Sandy's embrace was a kind of ravenous assault, a feeding frenzy of boxed-up desire. He had the strength of drunken impulse as well as sur-prise on his side and several seconds passed before Will could fight him off and back away, eyeing him warily.

"You don't know what you're doing," he stammered.

"This is what I *want*," Sandy said, with sudden, horrified certainty. "It's what I've wanted all along if only I'd—"

"You're just saying that. You're scared. It's understandable. She's a strong character and tomorrow's a big day. A Huge Commitment. Think of Poppy. You *love* her."

"Yes. Oh God. Yes, I do. But I want you. Come here."

"No!"

"Come here. Please?"

Will was aghast. But he was also excited and, cheaply, flattered. He stepped over to where Sandy was slumped against the wall, took his trembling hands in his and kissed their palms then raised his head and kissed his frightened eyes closed then wrapped his arms about him and held him tight, so that they could talk without having to meet each other's eyes.

"Why did you have to leave it so late?" he asked.

"I suppose I was scared," Sandy said and Will felt him shudder at the admission.

"Has Poppy got any idea?"

"What do you think? She'd *die* if she knew!"

"It's not too late, you know. You can still back out."

"No!"

"You may think she'd die now but she'd die a whole lot more and a whole lot more expensively if you marry her, start a family and *then* let her find out. For all you know she'll still want to marry you. I mean, you do love her?"

"Yes. Oh yes."

"And you fancy her."

"Yes. Only . . ."

"Only not as much."

"Mmm."

"And you want to be a grown-up married person."

"Fuck off."

"Just checking. You know, I could stand up in church tomorrow and call the whole thing off, bring down the whole tidily bourgeois edifice? I mean I won't, but I'll still be tempted."

"For her sake?"

Will thought a moment. "No. Probably for mine. We've got to stop this now, Sandy. You're going to sleep on the sofa. I'm going to sleep in my room behind a locked door. We'll sort out your suit and things in the morning, you'll get happily married and none of this ever happened. OK?"

"OK."

They were kissing on a more equal footing now. They slid to the landing carpet and rolled around, bruising chins and hip bones. For a beginner, Sandy showed remarkably good instincts and for a man who had drunk such incapacitating quantities, he regained his vigor with impressive speed. One thing had led most of the way to the inexcusable other when Will remembered he was desperate to piss and stumbled off to the bathroom, where he caught his reflection's accusing eye and, unabashed, found a condom that was only slightly past its use-by date. Returning to the landing, he found Sandy deep in a sleep from which it would seem like rape to wake him. With the inward sigh of one saved from damnation at the eleventh hour and not entirely grateful for the favor, he refastened Sandy's shirt buttons and trouser fly, tucked a pillow under his head and furled him in a quilt. Then he took several deep breaths before ringing Poppy, who had not yet fallen asleep at their parents' house, to reassure her that her *caro sposo* was safe and virtuous but in need of her spare key.

The next morning it was impossible to judge whether Sandy's verbal paralysis was due to guilt, panic, alcohol poisoning or stiff bones. Dispatched by the bride, the best man fetched his wordless charge before Will had a chance to find out and the wedding passed off with no conscience-struck confessions or altar-side pleas for psychosexual understanding. Will was kept too busy by relatives and the need to stop Harriet (who was not yet in her capable, Dame-ward phase) cheapening herself too publicly, to lend the matter much thought. He fancied he detected an edge of desperation to Sandy's manly handshake and muttered thanks for *saving his bacon* but assumed that the laughing couple on a tandem they waved off to a honeymoon in the Western Isles would be sufficient unto themselves for at least a month or two.

A series of circumspect postcards arrived, some of them penned by groom alone, then Sandy appeared on Will's doorstep the day after their return to Barrowcester, expecting, no, demanding conclusion of the business deferred on his stag night. Will shut the door on him and ignored the telephone all evening. In the weeks that followed, during which Sandy repeatedly called up or round, he tried to be a responsible adult. He tried in all honesty to be a loyal brother and a trustworthy friend, but Sandy was not a man to be denied. He also had a Tweedside accent, cyclist's legs and red-gold hair in his favor. If only the sex had been perfunctory or Sandy's bedside manner odious or his nature as harsh and judgmental as Will had always assumed it to be, their crime against the family would have gone no further than this one outrage. The chemistry between them was all too effective, however.

As though viewing the experience through Sandy's eyes, Will found it was like making love for the first time. His experiences with the drama student, fourth-year linguist and, even, Finn paled by comparison. He was disturbed at the depth of reaction it drew from him and at the brutal demand that there be a second and a third time regardless of guilt and danger. Rattled too, lowering his defenses at last, Sandy revealed a vulnerable, even sweet side to his personality and was as tenderly solicitous after the act as he was impatient before it. He refused, often angrily, to lay plans or to analyze the situation into which they had stumbled. He was married to a woman he loved, but regularly bedded her brother, whom he loved no less but differently.

Thus two marriages grew where only one was visible. Confided in by the sister as regularly as he had knowledge of the husband, Will was made an intimate party to their relationship and tasted their joys and apprehension as keenly as if their various house moves, job changes and children had been his own. Poppy had demanded a lunch with him the morning after he and Sandy first slept together and Will attended dreadheavy, expecting guilt to garble his wit or cause him to blurt out a confession. Life would have proved simpler if it had. Instead he found he could greet her and receive her happy confidences as easily as if it were not a husband she spoke of but a mutual relative. Which, of course, Sandy had become.

The only active deceit Will had to practice was in making his revision of his judgment of Sandy's character seem more gradual than it was. He was aided in this by the fact that merely because he had started to sleep with the man and found he could not stop, he did not find his friends any more acceptable or sympathize with his love of football, find his politics any less reactionary or his jokes any funnier. Qualities that were galling in a brother-in-law, however, became piquant in a lover, a peppery substitute for a gender difference.

Will would have been checked only if the liaison had begun to steal obviously from the marriage, if Poppy had begun discreetly to complain of neglect. But on the contrary, Sandy seemed to thrive on having two outlets and Poppy actually glowed when she spoke of the attentions he paid her. Her eagerness that they should become close did not help either. As far as she could perceive, Will and Sandy had started to make an effort for her sake, and she was touched. The occasional brotherly drink together, the occasional manly bike ride . . . "What do you find to talk about?" she asked, fascinated, and Will would quite truthfully answer, "God knows. Not much. You mainly. And, well, you know, guy stuff."

Sandy taught him to drive and called around occasionally for long afternoons to help fix problems with the third-hand Mini Cooper he helped him choose. When Will took the plunge of leaving the children's library to buy a place with a shop on the ground floor so that he could open a bookshop and café, it was Sandy who donned overalls to help him decorate and rewire the place. With the arrival of the boys, Will proved a devoted uncle and babysitter. And if Sandy took time to stay for a quick drink when picking the babies up, that was only to be expected.

As a busy man, Sandy made full use of those adulterer's toys, the mobile telephone and the pager, although this meant that a quickie snatched with Will on the pretext of visiting a patient was made very quick indeed when a call came from a genuine patient whose need was more painful, if no more urgent, than his.

Habit, and the illusion of a balanced domestic arrangement between the three of them, dulled Will's guilt but it was inevitable that such constancy in betrayal should drive a wedge between the siblings. Poppy

wanted him to be happy and now that she was married could not imagine anyone being happily unattached. She became an inveterate match-
maker, often crudely assuming that any two single gay men had only
to be introduced for gratitude to blossom into love. Will would be invited to dinner parties where he was pointedly placed opposite her
latest find—Fergus, her sad pet decorator, was the example that sprang
most painfully to mind—while Sandy masked his jealous anxiety in a
show of blokish insensitivity, breaking into any conversation that might
well up between his lover and the latest candidate or even insisting on
swapping places with Will on the pretext that some female guest had an
urgent need to discuss something with him. Happily, the arrival of children and the consequent erosion of Poppy's energy and free time prevented her from wondering if there were any *other* reason for Will and
her spending less time together. When she complained of it, she did so
in a spirit of shoulder-shrugging apology rather than any tone more ac-
cusatory. If she felt sorrow at the distancing of a friend, he convinced
himself, it was swept aside by the compensations of motherhood and a
life apparently fulfilled.

"So were you serious about asking us to join you in Cornwall?"
Sandy called out from the shower.

Lolling across the rumpled quilt, Will thought a moment. "I never
asked you. You invited yourself," he pointed out.

"So?"

"What about Poppy?"

"She's been angling to sign up for some intensive squash course at the
sports center. If I took the boys, it would set her free to go." Sandy
emerged, toweling himself. He had perfected the art of showering without suspiciously wetting his hair.

"Well, sure," Will said. "Come. The Aged Ps would love having Oz
and Hugo around and I'm sure we could come to some arrangement as
to who gets which bed."

"Great." Dressed in practiced seconds, Sandy kissed him quickly on
the lips. "Got to go. I'll ring you."

Will heard the crinkling of wet plastic as the paddling pool was grabbed up, then the opening and closing of the door, hasty feet on the steps and the gunning of Sandy's car engine. He reached for another Tia Maria truffle and suffered a brief twinge of what Harriet called *Other Woman Syndrome*.

BEACHCOMBER

"Frances? Frances?"

Frances emerged from a deep sleep to find John crouching beside her in the dark. Reassembling her mental self, she became aware of the strangeness of their surroundings, the car around her, Julian's rasping, childish snores on his bed behind her head, the rodent scuttlings of the guinea pig, the stiffness of her legs where they had been scrunched up on the seat beside her.

"Where are we?"

"Somewhere between Stonehenge and Dorchester. Sorry darling, I hated waking you but I was nodding off at the wheel and I—"

"It's fine. You've done more than your share. Come on. Swap."

Alert to the thick country night beyond the open door and to the fact that he had woken her in the middle of one of what she privately classified as her *bad* dreams—bad as in wicked, not unpleasant—she slipped out from under the car blanket and offered it to her husband.

"Promise you'll wake me," he said urgently. "I only need two or three hours."

"You look shattered," she said. "We're mad. Go to sleep." She leaned past him to tuck Julian's leg back under his hopelessly disor-dered bedding. He had a tendency to windmill in his sleep.

"There's still coffee in the Thermos."

"Oh good. Sleep."

John first insisted on unscrewing the table to make up the bed properly then, satisfied, he lay back with a yawn, stretching long legs across hidden grocery boxes and on to the seat opposite. He pulled the rug up about him, relishing, perhaps, the residual warmth she had left in it. Looking down at them, man and boy, she had one of those unsettling moments in which she felt more the child's age than the parent's, or at best like an older sister to the one and a responsible daughter to the other. Shudder-ing, she slid the door closed on them as quietly as she could.

The road was deserted, the landscape almost featureless. With the small stretch of road and verge picked out and lent color by the lights around it, the dormobile might have been an island. She looked up. No wonder it was so cold. There were no clouds. Stars seemed flung like a falling hunter's net overhead, their blue-white brilliance only adding to the chill. Opening the driver's door, she reached across for her sheep-skin car-coat and pulled it on. Then she stepped out of her shoes and pulled on the old suede moccasins she retained for driving. The shoes with heels, the last vestige of her smarter London self, she tucked into a bag and slipped behind the seat. With luck, she would not need them again for a fortnight. The house gave directly on to a beach, if the letting agency was to be believed. She intended to go barefoot as much as pos-sible, although she suspected that John found this flower-child tendency in her distressing. His own feet were crumpled and gnarled by years of army boots and constricting brogues. She guarded Julian's feet like soft treasures, encouraging him to go barefoot or wear sandals whenever the weather was warm enough, so that his toes should grow as straight and long as a Botticelli angel's.

In an effort to rouse herself by rousing her stomach, she ate a corned beef and tomato sandwich and poured herself a plastic beaker of tepid coffee from the Thermos, making a mental note to replace the latter with one of the new models that fastened with a screw-on lid rather than a leaky cork. Then, munching an apple to clean her teeth, she slid up behind the steering wheel and drove off, adjusting the mirror angle as she went.

The dream John had interrupted was the same uneventful one she had been having for fifteen years or so, since she was thirteen. She was in the prison garden, wearing a sort of muslin shift so diaphanous she felt more exposed than if she had been stark naked. And she knew there were prisoners, hundreds of prisoners, watching her from behind hundreds of broken windows. John was at her side, talking and talking to her in a tone that was just beginning to shade into anger. He wore a dark suit and was tapping a stick against the side of his leg to emphasize the points he was driving home. Governors were moved on every five years to prevent compromising familiarity breaking out between governor and officers or indeed governor and prisoners. She had experienced the same dream against the background of Her Majesty's prisons at Liverpool and Durham and, before that, with her father replacing John in the lead role, at Portland and Camp Hill. She had told no one of the dream, still less of the guilty excitement it continued to cause her, but at Wandsworth fantasy threatened to become a reality when she realized, through Julian's idle chatter, that prisoners in the mail-bag factory were indeed watching her as she went about the garden or lay in her deckchair reading. Her first intervention into prison management had therefore been to ask John to have the lower panes of the factory windows whited out with greenhouse paint. She had worried that he might demur or even suggest that she venture into the garden less often if she did not like being watched, but he was courteous discretion itself and had the panes painted by a work party the next afternoon. His only concern was that she had not told him sooner.

The coffee and sandwich started to work and she found she was wide awake. She enjoyed driving. Taught by her father, it was one of the things she knew she did well—unlike cookery or dressmaking. She had even taken her advanced test but had long since abandoned her girlhood fantasies of becoming a racing driver or stuntwoman. Motherhood had made her sharply aware of risk. Where she would once have relished the thrill of speeding in her Triumph Vitesse with the roof down, she now appreciated this great bus of a vehicle, more house than car, for the unathletic virtues of security and bulk.

Her mother disliked her driving such a thing. She said it was unfeminine. But then her mother had long since despaired of Frances blossoming into the feminine paragon she felt she deserved in a daughter. The late, last child of a tribe of six, Frances had felt all the pressures of being an only and overdue daughter in a rowdy nursery. She had tried to answer the needs of either parent but found her father's easier to satisfy. At once their mascot and arch competitor, she aimed to outshine her brothers in his eyes. She could hit a tin can with the nursery air gun, drive his car, name the principal towns, rivers and mountains of the world and even set a school speed record in the swimming team.

Her only remotely feminine skill was playing the piano. She might have tried to become a professional, had she not come from such a stultifyingly correct background. As it was her gift soon became an awkward accomplishment, since she favored not the *nice* pieces her mother wanted, but dark, brooding Liszt, Brahms and Scriabin.

Fearless on a diving board or lacrosse pitch, she was ambushed by shyness when thrust into parties. She had no facility when clasped by a sweaty-palmed stranger on a dance floor and no small talk to hold his attention once off it. An older sister might have shown her how things were done. Older brothers merely daunted and oppressed her with their easy expectations. As the social torments of adolescence overcame her and she realized too late that paying more heed to her mother's lessons rather than her swimming practice might have prepared her better for coping with dances and her brothers' army of friends, the piano became her wordless escape route, a safety valve for her frustration with herself and her surroundings.

John came to her rescue. Her father's newly appointed deputy, he had two left feet and an endearing way of bypassing all small talk—of which he had even less than she—to plunge directly into conversations of high seriousness about subjects that mattered. She liked him because she perceived from the way her brothers and father teased him, that he was a fellow sufferer. He asked her out to a concert—a very bad and over-long *Messiah* given by an Isle of Wight choral society, offered her a maladroit embrace beneath an oak tree as they were walking home and asked her to marry him ten minutes later. She accepted with all the alacrity of relief but had the sense to make him promise to say nothing to her parents until he had taken her on three more evenings out.

A kind of triumph ensued, a vindication; she was a girl after all. Her mother was satisfied, her father pleased. Her mother made inquiries of *Burke's Landed Gentry*, her preferred afternoon reading, and it emerged that John came of a stable, old, West Country family, landless and relatively poor now but gratifying to her unquiet snobbery nonetheless. Frances declared herself in love because that was what she assumed herself to be. She was an old woman of eighteen. John was the first and only man to have kissed her. She assumed that he had enjoyed more experience because he was twelve years older and a man. She was mistaken. Theirs was not a whirlwind romance. As virginal as she was and even more inhibited, he labored under the illusion that she would know what to do because she was a girl and her mother would therefore have told her. On their brief honeymoon in Normandy, they kissed and talked of many serious things until their lips were pink and their voices hoarse but it was several weeks later, after a hot-cheeked perusal of a dog-eared book from the library called *Things a Man Should Know*, that their marriage was finally, clumsily consummated. The pain of losing her virginity was such that it was weeks more before a repeat attempt was made.

Months passed before Frances realized that John too had married to escape. His only family was Becky, an academic sister who had moved to California after receiving her literature doctorate up at Rexbridge. Their mother had died when he was a child and since their father's death in the war when an incendiary bomb caught their house, he had lived in a sequence of all-male environments; university, the army, the prison service. By the time he met her, his private life had dwindled to a wretched set of rented rooms where he read his way through the scant shelves of the local library when not being served prompt breakfasts and suppers by a lugubriously respectful landlady. From the eagerness with which he seized on the chance of marriage and the wider domestic scene and broader social acceptance entailed upon it, she guessed that he had given up hope and begun to fear that his future would consist only of more of the dutiful same. Sure enough, now that he was married, he seemed to win new respect in the eyes of the prison service. Just as priests and army officers required wives for promotion beyond a certain level, so there was an unwritten rule that prison governors, like house-masters, should be family men, as though convicts, like small boys at boarding school, would benefit from the overspill of mother love from a woman installed on the premises, however remotely.

After some months of living in cramped, married officer's quarters, John was promoted and the new couple moved to the gaunt, turreted Governor's House at Wandsworth. Frances was gleeful. She had es-caped her parents, escaped the provincial restraints of the Island. She had a big house to redecorate and furnish, a drawing room large enough for a grand piano which she could play as loud and as long and as un-girlishly as she pleased.

John encouraged her playing. He had high-minded ideals about the salvation and rehabilitation of the prisoners and had her play to a group of them occasionally on the battered Blüthner upright in the boomy acoustic of the prison chapel. He also began discreetly to make up the shortfalls in the education her mother had so studiously circumscribed. He put books her way and indicated newspaper articles for her to read.

Then their sporadic attempts at a love life paid off and she became pregnant, an event she fancied John welcomed with a certain relief, as though it represented a temporary suspension of duties. It was only once the pregnancy and the early years of motherhood curtailed her culture-hungry movement about London that she realized they had no friends. Forming lasting friendships had never been easy for her with her father's frequent changes of post but her parents maintained a social bustle of sorts and she had fondly assumed that marriage would do the same for her and John. John would bring in people, she thought. He had been in the army and up to Rexbridge; he would have friends and by now his friends would have wives. But John, it transpired, had been too conscientious a student and soldier to have much time left for socializing and had long since cultivated a monastic self-reliance. Happy enough to go out and meet people, he was just as happy to stay in with his wife, baby and a good book. Her parents came to stay from time to time—chiefly to shop—and just once the elusive Becky visited in a self-dramatizing flurry, but for day-to-day society she had to make do with the prison chaplain and his wife, the local rector and his wife, the headmaster of the local boys' school and his wife and a succession of stilted evenings with various senior prison officers and their families. They were none of them friends. It was all duty. For the first time in her life, Frances was lonely and mildly bored.

John worked long hours. He insisted on tasting every meal the prisoners ate, which meant being on the other side of the wall early as well as late. He held daily "surgeries" at which he would hear the prisoners' grievances or punish their misdemeanors. He was the perfect father to them, albeit along distinctly nineteenth-century lines, which meant being a less than present husband. By the time he passed back through the succession of gates between prison and Governor's House after he had returned to work following a brief supper with her, he was drained of energy and character. She learned to fight down her need to tax him for entertainment, seeing what it cost him to be lively.

When Julian was younger, the boy was her near-constant companion. She played with him, read to him, encouraged him to draw pictures and make things. As he grew older, she took him on excursions around London and further afield. They had recently discovered the delights of watching old films together in the afternoons or snatching guilty matinées in the cinema on Lavender Hill. He would sit miraculously quiet beside her, never fidgeting even though the larger part of the storylines must have been far beyond his comprehension. But once he was enrolled in primary school, term-times presented her with crises of empty days. When he began boarding at choir school that autumn, a prospect she could hardly bear to face still less discuss, she would find herself with empty evenings and weekends too. She threw herself back into practicing properly at her piano, for two hours a day. This, she began to perceive, was dangerous for as her old agility and speed returned so did the old fantasies of professional performance, fantasies that could only feed her restlessness.

This holiday had been her idea. Inspired by an advertisement in the Sunday newspaper, goaded by a particularly maddening combination of glorious weather and no social prospects, she made her demand over supper and was astonished to hear John accept with the sole proviso that they could not travel before the last days of August and she and Julian would have to cope on their own for the second week. She had spent the intervening weeks in a fever of anticipation. A whole fortnight in a house by the sea, a house without guards, prisoners, the unremitting male gaze! A whole fortnight away from Wandsworth's dull routine! But now that the adventure was upon her she found herself oddly shy at the thought of having John around her day after day, at the novelty of seeing him in something other than a suit. She knew Julian would let them have lie-ins. She hoped. She hoped for many things.

The value of marrying young—she could see this now—was that one had few if any points of comparison with which to gauge the success of one's marriage. But the problem with marrying young was the same. Married at eighteen, a mother at nineteen, Frances was beginning, at twenty-eight, to mistrust what she had taken for an approximation of perfect happiness. During the summer term just past, as well as taking up the piano with a vengeance, she had been filling her sonless hours by helping out at a church kindergarten three days a week for pin money. Her colleague there, and the first friend she had made in Wandsworth independently of John, was Beverly Thomas. Beverly affected astonishment that Frances had married so young. She was not sure, she claimed, that she wanted to marry at all. She was pretty and had boyfriends she liked to discuss in suggestive detail while supervising the paddling pool or sandpit but she claimed to relish her freedom too much to settle down just yet. She was eased in this by a trust fund as well as the Pill and John had suggested, rather cattily, that Beverly's boyfriends remained keen precisely because there was little threat of her demanding any formal proposals from them. Bravado or no, Beverly's accounts of her love life inevitably made Frances examine her own, as did the crude magazines she insisted on passing on to her like so many evangelical tracts for a brash new faith. *Things Every Man Should Know* notwithstanding, Frances had thought she and John were fairly normal. Now she began to realize that something must be wrong.

Lovemaking seemed to be painful, brief and even frightening. Naturally modest, she had never seen him naked or paraded herself naked before him. She was sure he would be deeply shocked if she once suggested he leave off his pajamas. John always turned the lights out first then stole upon her like a silent assassin. It happened about once a week, with no preamble and no discussion afterward. He usually muttered an apology when he was through, which was nice, and kissed her tenderly. Her mother had warned her that men were beasts and this painful sating of themselves, presumably, was what she had meant. It was not so bad once she got used to it, indeed she would probably have missed it if he stopped. Nonverbal communication was honest because beyond cleverness or guile and in nonverbal terms, he plainly needed her, as a hungry boy needed bread.

But now, through Beverly and her wretched magazines, Frances discovered that she was meant to be enjoying lovemaking as much as him. She did not betray her simplicity, for she felt far too stupid, as though she had been caught out in ignorance of the proper use of a knife and fork. She listened, however, imbibed, and did her best to practice what she learned. To no avail. She was coming to accept that she was what the magazines called frigid, one of those benighted females who could not enjoy sex. For the next week, however, she would persevere. At the risk of shocking him, she would encourage him to approach her night after night. For she wanted another child desperately, and not merely to please her mother. (Her brothers had sired a bounty of grandchildren.) Purely, selfishly, she wanted a daughter. In the kindergarten she had caught herself favoring the girls over the boys, caressing this one's ringlets as she beavered over a toy oven, encouraging that one to sit on her lap for a story. If her need could only be assuaged by answering his, then so be it.

The long journey to Cornwall was mapped out in old market towns. Dorchester, Ilminster, Exeter, Okehampton. Ever cautious and mistrustful of her (actually splendid) map-reading prowess, John always used the AA's route-charting service. A small sheet of paper duly sent by the organization was now clamped in the ashtray lid. Frances ticked off the still sleeping towns with a pencil as they passed through each. She drove fast, far faster and more surely than John, who had learned to drive on a tank and taken no lessons since. Childishly, she wanted to surprise him with how far they had traveled while he slept. But it was Julian who woke first, mumbling soon after dawn that he needed to spend a penny. Shushing him, she pulled into a field entrance and walked round to release him from the back. As he stood, shivering in his pajamas, to water some cow parsley, at once hunched and self-important, his father's soft-eyed miniature, she felt her eyes grow heavy. She tucked Julian back into bed, stilling the excitement that threatened to bubble up, so that he might sleep again, then slipped the side door open. John was still sound asleep.

"Darling?" She caressed his hair and he frowned in his slumber. Watching, Julian giggled. "Ssh!" she told him. "It's hours before we get anywhere."

"Where's Lady Percy?"

"Fast asleep. Now ssh. Darling?" John woke with a start then relaxed, seeing her, and she wondered whether, like her, he suffered dreams too disturbing to avow. She smiled down at him, unable as ever to resist the temptation to reach out and smooth away with her thumb the anxious crease between his eyes. "Your turn," she murmured.

BLUE HOUSE

Will's mother was playing patience in the conservatory, dimly aware of her husband tidying away lawn clippings beyond the open door. The air was thick with the unsummery richness of roasting beef and potatoes. She dealt card upon card for several minutes before realizing that the reason it was not coming out was that she had only four aces. Then she remembered that there *was* no ace of squares and saw that she was having one of what she and John had taken to quaintly calling her *bad days*. She shuffled the cards back together. She knew there were only four suits. Of course she did. Wherever had the idea of a fifth one come from? It was characteristic that rather than despair or seek to tidy the problem away, she confronted it head-on and asked questions of it. As she had done with dreams since reading the Jung book Will had given her for her fiftieth, she looked for significance in her misreadings and spontaneous fabrications.

"Square," she asked aloud. "Why on earth square?"

"What?" John had come in and was obediently wiping his shoes on the mat. The tang of mown grass he brought with him cut through the smell of roasting meat.

"Cards," Frances told him, adding, "nothing," when she saw his worried face. She could never look at him without thinking how unfair it was that he, twelve years her senior, should be aging so well when she was aging so disastrously.

"You're having a bad day, aren't you," he said. "Cup of tea?"

"Why not? I'll get it."

"No no. Stay put. I'm there." He paused on his way to the kitchen to ask, "Is supper *meant* to be cooking now?"

"Yes."

"But it's barely five."

"Oh hell!"

"Could you turn it off and start it again later?"

"I suppose so. Not really. Oh hell." She heard him proceed to the kitchen, open and close the oven, then turn it off.

"I'm sure it'll be fine," he called back. "Don't worry. You can finish it off when Will gets here." He filled the kettle, humming to himself, and stayed in the kitchen. He would be leaning against the sink, washing his hands in that slow, methodical way he had. When she next saw him, his fingers would be as clean as a surgeon's.

She saw tears splash on to the card table and wiped crossly at her cheeks with her blouse. "Don't worry," she repeated.

"What?" he called back, hearing as sharp as ever.

"Nothing." She was hot. She needed air. She thrust herself upright, ignoring the twinge in her dodgy knee. "I must go swimming tomorrow. It helps my knee. Nothing hurts when I'm swimming."

"What?"

"Nothing." She strode into the garden and down to the Bross so she could stand in her favorite place, out on the landing stage, and fume.

How could he say not to worry? She was like a woman fallen in quicksand and people kept telling her not to worry. Never mind, they said. It doesn't matter really. She called them by the wrong name or turned up to lunch a day early and they said honestly it couldn't matter less. As though she might be anxious that she had given offense or caused inconvenience, when all that was on her mind was that her brain was sliding into terminal, premature decline.

Some memory loss she could cope with. She had long ago accepted that memory was like a pair of hands and could only carry so much at a time; you forgot something but that left space for you to pick up and remember something else. Besides, Sandy had taught her that, like an obsolete computer, she retained a stolid but still functioning search mechanism. "When you can't remember a name," he said, "pretend your brain is a librarian and send it off in search of it then get on with something else and don't fret. It may take a while but then suddenly it'll come up with what you were searching for."

What she could not bear was the deterioration in her powers of reasoning.

She had suffered the stroke out of the blue, while buying shoes. She was trying on a pair which pinched slightly. She bent over to see if she could loosen them at all then suddenly felt dreadfully sick and faint and keeled over, toppling a whole rack of the things she had clutched at for support on her way down. She lay on the floor, convinced she was about to be sick, feeling as though she were the center around which the shop was slowly spinning. There was a terrible fuss. Sales assistants trying to make her sit up and put her head between her legs. Customers offering advice. When she found she could not speak and that her right side refused to move, she gave up, assuming she was about to die and distantly amused because she happened to be wearing brand-new Marks and Sparks underwear Poppy had helped her choose.

Death apparently had other treats in store for her however, for she came round in a hospital room with her family all about her, wearing a strange nightdress and with the tight shoes she had been trying on and had not paid for tucked under a chair. The paralysis passed and her speech returned in hours. Everyone assured her she looked just the same but she was convinced one side of her face had slackened. "What would you know?" she told Poppy. "You just see an old woman. But when it's your own face you can tell. I look drunk, I tell you."

It was more depressing than frightening. Overnight, although she was only sixty, she became someone people worried about. Her independence felt curtailed by the concern of others. In the past, "Do you think you should?" had always goaded her on to do the inadvisable. Now the question planted a small, prickling doubt. Little by little, blunder by blunder, it became apparent that the stroke had hastened into motion a process she did not care to name, even when she could remember its medical title. Some days she was fine but on others it was as though she had been force-fed cooking sherry in her sleep and woken sozzled. She would call her husband Mervyn or call Will Mary. Her body clock would go briefly haywire so that she found herself preparing for bed when they had just finished lunch. Worst of all were the panic attacks, as unexpected as they were vindictive. She would become quite dissociated from herself.

"Who's that woman in the bed with us?" she had once asked John in a tone of quiet concern.

Poppy became indignant when she voiced her fears. "You're *far* too young yet. Dad's much older than you and he's fine."

"But all the women in our family go doolally. Granny did."

"That was drink."

"It wasn't. Then her mother went when she was only sixty-five. They shut her away in that place in Esher."

"Listen. I'll get you a test you can do. I saw it in Sandy's waiting room. If you're so worried."

Poppy reappeared days later with a small booklet entitled *Senility, Memory Loss and Alzheimer's* and made her complete the questionnaire at the back. Ever cautious, she did not hand over the whole booklet, which might have proved alarming, she merely tore out the questionnaire. Striving to be as honest as she could, Frances pored over such questions as "How often do you forget close relatives' names? Often. Sometimes. Never." and "Do you find it hard to concentrate throughout a television program? Often. Sometimes. Never." Promising to look up and grade the answers when she had time, Poppy had taken the questionnaire away. The result could not have been to her liking because she had yet to make a report. Or perhaps she had forgotten? As she never tired of saying, brains began to die off at seventeen and everyone suffered memory loss with time. This was unconvincing in the mouth of someone who not only remembered everybody's birthdays and their children's names but even what she gave them to eat when they last came to dinner and who they sat by. Poppy kept lists in a small leather book in her desk.

"Here." John held out a tray.

"Thanks." She helped herself. He set the tray on the nearby bench and came to stand beside her, munching. Two rowing eights sped by toward Barrowcester, barked at through a megaphone by a cyclist on the farther towpath. A red dog was with the cyclist. It stopped to sniff something and lift its leg, then raced to catch up. A barge piled with compacted rubbish glided past the other way. The tide was high. Brown water swirled around the posts of the landing stage making small sucking noises. "Would you be all right on your own?" she asked.

"What? Don't be silly."

"No, but would you? Well of course you would."

"There's no need—"

"Don't pretend there's nothing wrong."

"I won't."

"I can't bear it."

"I said I won't. Drink your tea."

She sipped. His voice was always so equable now, never seemed to lose its equilibrium. When did he get to be so calm? Had he always been like this? Suddenly her biscuit seemed huge and impossibly dry. She tossed it to some ducks who fell on it with such savagery it barely had time to get wet. "Promise me something," she said, staring at the thumping wings and lashing bills.

"What?"

"You won't try to be noble when it gets bad."

"It's not going to."

"Now you're being silly. Promise you'll put me in a home when I get really doolally."

"If you're truly doolally you won't know if I have or not."

"So promise."

"You won't know if I've kept my word." He was actually smiling. A dry smile over the last of his tea.

"Don't tease me," she snapped.

He stopped smiling. "I promise."

"Thank you. It's just that—"

"Please don't let's talk about it anymore," he said, turning to dead-head a late rose. "I find it quite extraordinarily depressing."

"Sorry."

"Will should be here soon. What are you giving him to eat?"

"The house is already full of it."

"Of course. I forgot. All right, all right. So I'm not the only one." He smiled again, more warmly this time.

"You don't have to go out, you know," she said.

They turned as one away from the river and started to walk back up the garden's shallow slope.

"I know. But aren't you going to play gin rummy?"

"I doubt it. Aren't those lovely this year! Such a success."

"Schizophrenics."

"Even I know they're not called that. They're Schizostylis. Schizo-stylis Jennifer. Lovely." She smiled with private triumph. "I thought that pink would be too hot but I only seem to notice it at this time of day, when they're in the shade."

"I'll still go," he said, ignoring her feat of memory. "It's nice for you to have him to yourself."

"And it's nice for you to get out. You didn't say it. Didn't need to. I know."

He refused to rise to this. "I'll probably go for a walk along the tow-path to Arkfield and back then have a quick drink."

"You needn't make it quick. Enjoy yourself."

There was a "hallo" from inside the house and Will appeared bearing a bottle of wine and a large pot of basil he had promised her from the pannier market. It struck her afresh how the young man she had always thought looked so like her was maturing into the very image of his fa-ther. *Look!* she wanted to say. *Can't you see?*

But John was not the sort of man to notice a thing like a family resem-blance. Having thanked them again for the birthday present, which she had again forgotten giving him, Will poured himself a cup of tea and walked around the garden with them both, stopping regularly to admire

or be introduced to this plant or that and asking for a cutting of an interesting curvy-leafed sage they had found in an open day somewhere
recently. John then muttered about getting off for his walk before the
best of the light had gone.

"Before you go," Will said. "What would you think of a holiday in
Cornwall?"

"Lovely, but we've paid to have the house repainted so we couldn't
really think of—"

"No, no. It would be my treat. Well, Sandy's treat really. Didn't they
tell you?" John looked at her. She shook her head. Will went on. "They
booked me a seaside cottage for a whole fortnight. But it's really soon.
Week after next. We'd just have to drop everything and go. Please say
yes. I'll drive and cook. Ma can just put her feet up and go for swims
and Dad can walk himself silly on the coast path. It's literally right on
the beach so we can hear the sea from our beds. And Sandy says he'll
come and bring the boys during the second week to give Poppy time off
to go and learn squash. Look. I've got a picture somewhere." He bur-
rowed in his rucksack and proudly produced a photograph. "They
found it in the *Observer* apparently."

He held the picture out. She looked. It was delightful. A bright blue
wooden bungalow, like a proper Indian one so it was probably quite
old, with a green veranda and deep purply-red geraniums in pots and
what looked like lavender hedges, or was it just tamarisk, behind a green
picket fence.

"Lovely," she said. It made her think of bucket-and-spade afternoons
on the Island when she was a girl. But John was grimacing, a rare look of
real thunder on his face.

"Poppy thinks we've been there before," Will went on, not noticing.
"But I don't remember. She didn't realize until they sent her the picture
and by then it was a firm booking. I mean, of course I remember that
holiday. Well. Bits of it. But not the house. Dad? What's up?"

"It's only that—" John began, staring at Frances in a way that un-
nerved her. "You don't remember it either, do you?" She shook her
head obediently and saw he was reassured. "Well, in that case I don't
see why it should matter." She saw the effort it cost him to lighten his

expression. Extraordinary man. "But are you sure there's no one else you'd rather . . . ?"

"No one. Honestly." Will grinned. "I just thought it would be fun."

"Well in that case . . . Darling?"

"I can't wait," she said.

"That's settled then. Thank you, Will. That's very kind. I'll see you both later."

"Have a good walk."

"Bye Dad."

"Bye."

And he was gone. They heard him lock the front door behind him out of force of habit then unlock it again, realizing he was shutting them in.

"Doesn't want us to escape," Will joked. "Shall I get us a drink?"

"Why not?" She sat back in her customary chair in the conservatory—it seemed she had sat nowhere else for months—and shuffled the cards out of habit.

"Do you mind if we eat early?" he called out from the kitchen. "I'm starving."

She smiled at his customary tact, knowing he must be aware from the fumes that their dinner was already on its way to spoiling. She would make an effort to play cards with him after all. She hated to see him worry.

BEACHCOMBER

They stopped in Exeter to stretch their legs in the cathedral and ate an indifferent lunch in a restaurant on the edge of the Close, then stopped again in Okehampton for an ill-advised but celebratory clotted-cream tea and a walk around the castle. So, by the time they had crossed both Dartmoor and Bodmin Moor and cut up through Wadebridge to the north coast, the sun was low in the sky and Julian had passed from boredom to a premature fever pitch of anticipation and back to slack-jawed dissatisfaction. One of the many disadvantages of the dormobile was that Julian ended up seated so far away that he had every excuse to shout over the thunder of the engine.

"I think Lady Percy's dead."

"She can't be," John sighed. "She'll just be asleep."

"She never sleeps. She's far too quiet. I'm going to let her out."

"No," Frances stated. Spoil him as she might, Frances never shied away, as John did, from the full force of a blunt prohibition. "We're nearly there. Ten more minutes. Look. There's the sea!" She unfurled the smartly-headed letter from the house's owners, which could now safely take over from the AA's instructions fluttering on the dashboard. "So," she read, "*Follow road out of Wadebridge (do not cross bridge!)*

then left at top of hill, following signs to Rock then signs to Polcamel." She wound down her window and the car filled with hot sea scents—pine needles, seaweed, salt. Ten minutes later, when they had passed a sequence of perfect beaches grouped at an estuary mouth, she read on, *"Leave Polcamel, take second turning on left, skirt car park in a clockwise direction*—I say, aren't they bossy!—*and take the gated track now directly ahead of you.* Julian! Gate to open!"

Excited again, Julian unfastened the gate, then they followed a track so steep it must have become unusable in icy conditions. At some stage gravel had been spread, but heavy rains and traffic had carried most of it downhill. But they must have taken a wrong turning because they found themselves carried away from the promised sea, along a gorse-lined valley to a rugged manorial farmhouse John judged as Jacobean with the inevitable Victorian extensions.

"Well this isn't it," he said, preparing to turn round.

"I know, but isn't it *lovely*," said Frances, who had proved herself utterly fearless in the past of exploring the drives of grand country houses out of curiosity. "We can always say we're lost."

"Because we *are!*" shouted Julian. "There's a lady coming and she looks cross."

A middle-aged woman in summer tweeds had emerged from a walled garden. There were dachshunds yapping at her heels. She eyed the dormobile without amusement. John leaned out of his window.

"I'm so sorry," he said. "We were looking for the holiday cottage."

"Beachcomber. It's called Beachcomber," Frances hissed.

"I guessed," said the woman, still not cracking a smile and raising her voice above the yapping of the dogs. "I'm your landlady and it's back the way you came and first on the right before the lane starts to climb. My fault really. The tamarisk needs pruning. If you need anything, don't just turn up. There's a telephone in the car park." She turned on her heel but John saw her in the side mirror, standing in the garden door to watch them leave. He hoped she did not hear Julian's flawless imitation of her accent as they pulled away.

Like most of the houses they had passed to this side of the small resort, Beachcomber dated from the early twenties. Nestling in a patch of reclaimed sand dune, it was a dark-stained clapboard bungalow effectively doubled in size by the addition of a deep wooden veranda on its three seaward sides. In contrast to most such places in the area, which were white and blue or white and black, its bargeboarding, window frames and veranda railings were a startling canary yellow.

Only one other house was visible from down here, a sprawling place on the headland. Their landlady's lair was tucked into a fold in the valley and quite invisible. The view behind the bungalow was across steeply climbing fields of sheep—hers presumably. Ahead lay uninterrupted sand and sea. The bungalow nestled at the top of a cove at the less populous end of the broad expanse of Polcamel Strand. When, as now, the tide was high, it effectively boasted a private beach.

"I wonder if she used to entertain her lovers down here, like Rebecca," said Frances.

"She probably still does."

"Who does?" Julian asked. "Are we there?"

"Heaven. It's heaven," Frances exclaimed and impulsively kissed John's cheek. Julian had already jumped down from the dormobile, taking his cue from the silenced engine, and run up on to the veranda. "Let's explore before we unpack. Her letter says the cleaner will have been and left the key under the mat. Do you suppose she's always so unwelcoming?"

"Oh, I don't know. Isn't it more fun this way? Like breaking in? God I'm tired." He rubbed his eyes.

"Me too," she said. "There was a fish and chips in Polcamel and that pub up the road would probably let you get beer by the jug."

"Mind reader."

Exhausted, they sat on, watching Julian scamper around the veranda, peering in at each window in turn. Frances sighed. "Look at him. Do you think he's happy?"

"Of course. Why ever shouldn't he be? A whole fortnight by the sea. I'm quite envious. All we got at that age was my purse-lipped aunt in Lowestoft."

"Being on his own, I mean."

"You think we should have asked one of his little pals from school?"

"No. I meant generally."

Before John could answer, however, Julian came racing back and tugged open his door. "Come and see. It's lovely!" he exclaimed. "I've already chosen my room. It's the little one on the end with windows on both sides like a sort of lookout tower. You wouldn't want it anyway 'cause it's got a single bed. Oh do come *on*!"

John slid down from behind the wheel into the relative cool of outside. Touched that Julian had appealed to him for once rather than his mother, he let the boy tug him by the hand across the springy, sandy turf to the bungalow.

"Steady on," he said. "The key's under the mat. You can let us in."

"OK." Julian ran ahead. Watching him scrabble for the key and fit it into the lock, he marveled at the boy's stout self-sufficiency, the speed with which he was becoming less child than person. He was glad they had resisted asking some sort-of friend from Julian's school. He remembered from his own boyhood how such arrangements had a way of turning sourly awry in the course of a long holiday. Besides, with no other company the boy would spend time with his father. John saw him so little in the course of a working week that this, he considered, was half the value of the seven days he had agreed to spend with them. Then, just as she came in behind him, he saw what Frances had actually been driving at. She wanted, or felt she should have, another child.

As she busied herself opening windows to dilute the paraffin smell of furniture polish, he hid his confusion as best he might. Unable to answer in even her elliptical terms, he tried to express his agreement in a show of pleasure at the truly very charming house her skill had tracked down for them. There were two good-sized bedrooms with bay windows, smaller ones to either end, a large central sitting-cum-dining room with views in two directions which had a door on to the veranda.

"Darling, it's great. How did you tell it was this good from just a little advertisement?"

"I didn't," she said, evidently pleased all the same. "I got her to talk me through it room by room. Isn't it sweet? I'll get the bags."

"This is my room," Julian announced proudly, bouncing on a bed. "But if I don't like it, can I try one of the others?"

"I don't see why not," John told him. "Come and help your mother. That Shakespearean guinea pig of yours is probably dying of heat."

"Really?" The child was alarmed and John cursed his failure to gauge childish conversation properly.

"Figure of speech."

"Oh. Well can I let her run about?"

"Don't for God's sake lose her."

"I won't." Julian ran out to the car. John turned to watch him go and found Frances standing in the sitting room with a small case in either hand. She was grinning.

"Which shall we have?" she said. "He's still left us with a choice." He followed her into the nearest of the two double bedrooms. As she slung a case down on the candlewick coverlet, the bed springs twanged alarmingly. She chuckled then blushed.

"Maybe not," he said and carried the cases across to the parallel room to their right, which had an identical view but a newer, more discreet mattress.

"Maybe that's why she didn't advertise it as having two doubles," she said, shaking the folds from a dress as she hung it in the wardrobe.

I agree. I so agree, he wanted to tell her. *I want another child too.* But all he could muster was, "I'll get those boxes of food in."

She had become pregnant with Julian so swiftly that in the first months of their marriage he had worried, ironically enough, at how he was going to support the tribe he thought would inevitably follow. When no further children made their presence felt, John had guessed that, since she had managed to conceive, any problem probably lay with him.

He secretly took pills bought by mail order and read cloudily-printed pamphlets found through small announcements in the back of the Sunday papers. He tried everything from red meat and teetotalism to limiting lovemaking to a fortnightly outlet. Unable as he found himself to tell her his worries or explain any of these activities, he became stern and even withdrawn from Frances as the time for lovemaking approached. His fear that she would discover the truth and find him wanting as a husband appalled him and left him the more inhibited. He almost

laughed aloud in desperation when one pamphlet suggested he persuade his wife to sit astride him, the better to spare his energies for the
exertion of an efficient ejaculation. The idea of being able to hold a conversation with someone as pure as Frances about sex, still less to ask her
to adopt a position anything but submissive and long-suffering, was
alien to the point of the ludicrous. Now that she finally had raised the
subject, however indirectly, he dared not reveal what he had known for
six years lest she feel he had practiced a deceit on her, like a seller of
shoddy goods.

After unpacking the dormobile, they celebrated their arrival with a
swim so icy John was sure it would undo any potency the last week's
painful abstinence had stored up. Then, in the fading light, Julian yawning fiercely between them but insisting he would be up for hours yet,
they walked around the headland to fetch fish and chips, a jug of powerful local ale and a bottle of lemonade. Ever the romantic, Frances found
and lit hurricane lamps and they dined on the veranda, greasily fragrant
newspaper spread across their laps. Shandy-drugged, Julian fell asleep
on his rocking chair and barely murmured as John carried him to his
elected bed and tucked him in.

In films couples always began the amorous part of the evening with
prolonged and increasingly passionate kissing and John could quite see
how this could stoke a woman's amatory fire. But what had been possible, just, when they were still courting and thus barely known to one another, became less and less so as marriage deepened familiarity. Under
cover of darkness and bedding, he could be a creature of urgent need
and rough-mannered desires but so long as Frances could meet his eye
in the seconds before his approach, he felt too much himself, too much
the stiffly polite ex-army governor of HM Prison Wandsworth to do
more than peck her cheek. The evening, the lit part of the evening that
was, thus ended with the two of them queuing to use the bathroom and
change in it—there were no dressing rooms as at home—before climbing into the unfamiliar bed, each with the sure armor of a book.

For several minutes she read her Georgette Heyer Regency romance,
probably full of tight-trousered heroes behaving precisely as he could
not, he the latest, rather unpromising novel from C. P. Snow. She made

attempts at conversation but when steeling himself he found light conversation as impossible as heavy petting.

"We should have brought our own bedding," she began. "These are the sort of sheets that catch on your toenails. I can tell. Who'd have thought she'd be such a cheapskate!"

"Hmm," he said and there was a pause while they both read.

"Isn't it heavenly to be able to lie here and listen to the sea!"

"Hmm," he said. "Yes." And there was a longer pause.

"Are you sleepy, darling? Shall I put the light out?"

"All right," he said and found himself yawning in earnest. She turned out the light. "Sea air," he added, by way of explanation. "And a jug of Doom Bar."

"Night darling," she said.

"Night."

And she leaned over to kiss him, once, lightly, on the lips. As ever, he found the scent of the cream she rubbed in at bedtime powerfully erotic. "Listen to the sea," she murmured. "Isn't it wonderful! It sounds so close. Listen!"

For what felt like five minutes but was probably only seconds, he lay there dutifully listening to the sea but really only aware of her regular shallow breaths against his neck, where she lay curled against him. Then he could bear it no longer and he reached out to feel her thigh through her nightdress, then ran his hand up to cup one of her breasts through the lacy material that hid it. Then he rolled over and began to kiss her in earnest.

By his standards, he considered his lovemaking was remarkably expert for once. He did not drag it out for too long—it was over in five minutes (he glanced at the alarm clock)—and she didn't cry out or anything so presumably he had managed not to hurt her. Afterward, as they lay side by side, hot beneath the prickly nylon sheets, he dared to mutter, "It *would* be good to have another. I mean, if we could," and she reached for his hand and squeezed it and said:

"Darling." Then suddenly she was startled awake by something. "Oh my God! I completely forgot!"

"What?"

She turned the light on. "Post. You got an exciting-looking letter from abroad this morning and I packed it so I'd remember to give it to you and—"

"Well, can't it wait?"

"Hang on." She slipped across the room to where the empty suitcases were stacked beside the wardrobe. She opened the larger one, hers, and took out an envelope from the frilled pocket that lined its lid. "Here," she said and glanced at its stamp. "From America."

He saw no reason why he should read it now but she seemed excited so he glanced at the unfamiliar handwriting then tore the thing open. *"Dear John,"* he began and glanced over at the signature. "It's from Bill Palmer," he said, surprised.

"Becky's Bill?"

"Who else?"

"But he *never* writes."

"I know. *Dear John,"* he read again aloud. *"Haven't heard from you since Christmas but I hope all is well. Our little lives are in upheaval—or are about to be—since I've accepted a teaching post at your new university in Norwich. I was getting very aware that Skip was growing up a little too all-American and I'd always promised Becky I'd stop that happening. So when I failed to get tenure here and the offer came up, I jumped at it. So much to pack and ship over, even after we've given half away and sold the bulky furniture we can replace. Don't worry, John. No heirlooms! Anyway, as it's Skip's first time out of the States, I'm taking her on a whirlwind tour of various friends in Europe before we turn up in England and I wondered if we could come visit during the summer holidays given that she's never met her young cousin and London is such a key historic center etc., etc. But also, of course, because I would like to meet the three of you properly. Don't worry if you consider this would be an imposition or inconvenient. I'm sure we can arrange something else in the course of the year. But I suggest you leave a message care of my secretary at VEA who I'll be phoning at regular intervals. All good wishes. Bill.* Good Lord, I suppose I'd better ring the woman and suggest they join us down here."

"But it's the other end of the country!"

"Well I can't very well entertain them in Wandsworth without you."

"I don't see why not. You're the relation."

"Julian too. Anyway, I'm curious. And I feel a certain responsibility toward Skip."

"That's not really her name?"

"Course not. She was christened Petra Louise or something but they never used it. Well, they never actually christened her. And if she's going to be living in England now . . . She is my niece after all . . ." His words petered out, then Frances seemed to realize she was scowling.

"You're quite right. It was only that, well, I'd so looked forward to having you all to myself. Just you and Julian."

"Funny."

"What?"

"Nothing," he sighed but it had occurred to him that she was looking on the holiday as a time for spending more time with her husband so as to get pregnant and he was looking on it as a time for getting to know his son better and his son was looking forward to a fortnight of blissfully Oedipal access to his swimsuited mother. The three of them were locked in a circle of unrequited need and probably required some healthy interruption from outside. "I'll go up to that telephone box in the car park on the cliff and call his secretary tomorrow," he said. "Suggest they might like to join us before I have to go back to work. They probably won't be able to make it—we don't know for sure when they get here from Europe anyway—but at least we'll have done our bit. Happy?"

"Of course," she said and turned the light out again.

But then she had to get up to pee and, as always, the sound of distant flushing got him going so he had to pee too. By the time he slipped back into bed, Frances was fast asleep and he was wide awake. He lay there listening to the sea and her touchingly adenoidal breathing which was never quite a snore, more a series of clicks and halting sighs. And he thought about Becky.

His elder sister by four years, Becky was cleverer, funnier, prettier than he was. Trailing, unwanted, in her wake, he had idolized and tried in vain to despise her. Once she deemed him old enough to notice, she judged him stuffy and conventional. Their mother died when he was nine and Becky had fought against the obligation to mother him and his father in turn. She escaped at the first opportunity to Rexbridge, then on to Berkeley where, in one of her rare, maddeningly sketchy letters, she informed him that she had fallen in love and married. The husband was studying for an English doctorate, like her. She expressed no qualms about turning her back on England. She wrote to John to announce the birth of his niece. The alienation between brother and sister reached rapid completion. He had no interest in visiting America and, after her one visit to Wandsworth to meet his young wife, found he could not miss a woman who had made herself so unlike the golden girl he remembered. This made the reality of her sudden death all the harder to accept.

The husband, Bill, by then a writer who did some teaching or a teacher who wrote on the side—the emphasis varied from year to year— sent two newspaper clippings in an envelope. To be accurate, one was from a newspaper and reported how Dr. Palmer died when she danced out of a tenth story window during a faculty party. It went on to state that she left behind husband, daughter and an unfinished book on Blake. She died instantly and her blood was found to contain high levels of alcohol and a homemade hallucinogen derived from a certain cactus. Her husband was being questioned in relation to the drug but was distraught and no foul play was suspected, since Dr. Palmer had been a known experimenter in mind-altering substances privately, justifying it as part of her research into Blake's visions. The second clipping was from some counterculture journal, apparently printed on home-made paper which caused the ink to spread as on a blotter. By way of an obituary it said that Becky had a big soul and had expressed her wish to be reincarnated as a seagull. Bill attached a note, scribbled on the back of a crude drawing of a frowning flower—presumably by poor Skip. *So sorry, John,* it read. *I know you'll miss her as much as we do. Bill.*

There was no funeral, just a party. John felt no compulsion to attend, especially when he learned that there would be no grave to visit. Becky was swiftly cremated and her ashes taken to India for scattering on the Ganges by some devoted pupils.

It was only in the weeks that followed, during which the numbness of shock gave way to the relentless workings of memory, that it struck him that his sister had affected his choice of wife. In many ways, Frances resembled the pre-American Becky; restless, rebellious even but still rooted. He wondered now whether his brother-in-law would notice or whether, like Becky in her catty letter of "congratulation" after her visit, he would merely see her as a wife in John's own image; inhibited, conventional and quiet.

BLUE HOUSE

John strolled by the Bross then went to his usual pub—not quite his local. A residual Puritanism made him slightly ashamed of drinking in public and he fancied that a greater distance from home lent him a measure of anonymity. However, contrary to what he had told Frances, the walk was short and the drink was anything but quick.

Sylvia was at their usual corner table. She had none of his wife's inhibitions about entering a pub on her own. She gave him a little wave as he entered. He smiled at her on his way to the bar and pointed at her gin glass but she covered it with a small hand to show that she was all right for the moment. Joining her, he marveled afresh at how very neat she was. White hair, discreetly assisted so that one could tell she had once been a blonde, curled neatly about small ears. Her pink blouse was creaseless. Her thin legs were tucked neatly away into the recess beneath her settle. The only untidy touch was her jewelry, of which she wore a profusion, but even then she favored gold over gems; the glitter combined with the sharply pressed outlines of her clothes to lend her appearance a hint of the military. They did not kiss.

"How are you doing?" he began instead, their customary greeting.

Sylvia spoke lightly, raising her glass. "If Teresa hadn't arrived when she did, I think I'd have pushed him under a bus."

"Not good then."

She drank then laughed bitterly. "Funny, isn't it? Good used to mean a sunny holiday, a comfortable retirement or, what was it you called it that time? *The tenuous possibility of very cautious sex.* Now it's what? A smile that might be meant for you or might just be wind. A morning when he hasn't pulled his nappy off in the night. A day when he's calm, even nice. I tell you, I used to want him to be aware so badly. I wanted him to recognize who he was. Now I want his brain to hurry up and fry itself. When that look comes into his eyes and I know he's aware and he's like 'what's happening to me?' I can't stand it." She drank again, lit a cigarette, hand shaking slightly with need as she inhaled. "Listen to me," she said and restored neatness with a smile. "I'm fine, John. *I'm* fine. How are you?"

"Fine," he said, smiling. "I'm fine and Frances is fine too. I mean, relatively. A bit forgetful. A bit . . . But compared to what Steve's going through . . ."

"I know," she said quietly, adding words that were both reassurance and threat. "Early days yet, John. Early days."

Given the way they had found each other and the clandestine manner of their meetings, they ought to be having an affair. In a woman's sense, he supposed, in an emotional sense, they already were. Certainly Frances would be as wounded and jealous if she knew of the depth of their shared confidences as if he had set Sylvia up in a love-nest. Generous colleagues had bought him a personal computer as a retirement present over ten years ago. He had found little serious use for it at first, merely using it to play chess, to keep the household accounts and to write the occasional formal letter. When Will bought him a modem and organized Internet access, he had made an effort to use the thing, out of politeness at first, but had swiftly become hooked. A lifetime's user of any local reference library, a lover of facts and arcane information, he now found that the Internet was like having the great libraries of the world and an unlimited newsagent accessible, Narnia-fashion, from one small corner of his study. Now if he had any query, about the safety of a rose spray or the timetable for trains to Haverfordwest, he switched on his computer. Not only were there documents out there, but people, helpful if opinionated people. An intensely private man, moved on repeatedly through most of his working life, John had never been a great one for chatting over the garden fence but the Internet was like having neighbors one could switch off.

The family nettle-grasper, Poppy, had taken action after her shock at bringing the grandsons to a long-arranged birthday lunch only to find that Frances had laid in preposterous quantities of knock-down Rioja and nothing else.

"I'm bringing Jude Farson round to look at her. We'll keep it very casual. He's a friend, after all, as well as a specialist. So you can just pretend we were passing and dropped in."

Jude and she came and went, then Jude rang up a discreet hour or two later and said that he feared it looked like early-onset Alzheimer's. He had called on one of Frances's bad days.

"What can we do?" John asked.

"Not a great deal. I mean we can run some tests, even book her in for a scan to check there's no other cause, but . . ." The doctor was not hopeful.

Frances was watching television very loudly. John retreated to his study, turned on his computer, logged on to the Internet and ran a search on *early-onset Alzheimer's*. He found a welter of references to Alzheimer's, many of them humorous, and a surprisingly high number of articles on potato cultivation, then a direct hit. *Early-Onset Alzheimer's—A Wife's Story*. In three bleak pages, someone described how her husband had become more than usually absentminded soon after his fiftieth birthday. Forgetfulness progressed to the point where he would make a telephone call then forget who he was calling or even who he was. He also suffered terrible depressions, in which he became wordless and withdrawn and which he described, in a lucid moment, as *entering a black pit with no certainty of return*. He became doubly confused when losing his job forced the pair to move to a cheaper neighborhood and wandering was added to his list of problems.

The prognosis is never good, the writer finished. *Depending on how*

early the diagnosis was made, the patient (not the sufferer—you are both
going to suffer here) will have ten to fifteen years. Decline will be steady
and, this being a disorder of the central nervous system, double inconti-
nence is a treat in store, along with irrational terrors, violent mood
swings, and the knowledge that your loved one is going somewhere you
cannot follow. Or at least you can and may follow, God help you, but it
will be as a fellow patient, not as a traveling companion. But to be reading
this you are probably still young and feel cheated of the retirement you ex-
pected. You are not alone. To prove it, you can e-mail me and I promise to
get back to you or to have a colleague do so. Just click here.

John e-mailed her, outlining his situation. She e-mailed him swiftly
back, giving the telephone number of the Alzheimer's Society and at-
taching her standard help pack of advice. E-mailing her to thank her, he
felt he must relieve the one-track nature of their doomy correspondence
so added some personal details, mentioning his wife's name, his son's
bookshop and that he lived just outside Barrowcester and was a keen
yachtsman on the river. This in turn inspired a more chatty reply from
her and soon they were corresponding every few days, always with their
partners' conditions as a pretext or opening gambit. Once she admitted
that she lived in nearby Arkfield it was merely a matter of days before he
found the courage to suggest they meet.

She was about Frances's age, perhaps a little younger, and had retired
as a personnel manager in local government so as to care for her husband. She had the flat vowels and nasal twang of the local accent, which
had always conveyed for him—quite irrationally, of course—an air of
easy moral slovenliness. Tonight was not exceptional in that he had no
sooner sat beside her than he felt a dispassionate desire to kiss her, if
only because he felt he could, because he sensed she would not make a
scene about it but would, at best, encourage him, at worst, laugh.

"Will's with her tonight," he said.

"Playing cards?"

"Not tonight. Bad day. Crisp?"

"No thanks. They catch in my plate. There's romance." She laughed.

"He's asked us on a holiday. To Cornwall."

"That's nice."

"But it's a place we went to before. Years ago."

"But that'll do her good. Familiar places can be far more stimulating than new ones. It'll stoke up her memories without unsettling her."

"I'm not sure these are memories we want stoked up."

"Did you argue there, or what?"

"I've never told anyone."

"Tell me."

"I . . ." He looked at her tidy, expectant, careworn face then imagined it registering her shock if he did as she asked. "I don't think I can," he said. "And I'm not sure I should."

"I can respect that," she said, lighting another cigarette. She always mutely offered him one, although she must have known by now that he would refuse. He liked it. One day he might surprise her. "There are things I'd never tell a soul about Steve and me. Not even my sister, and I tell her everything. That's a lie for a start. I haven't told her everything since we were about twenty and I fancied her boyfriend. In a funny way I've got closer to him since he got ill than I ever was before. We never used to share a bathroom. I didn't even see him shave. He was so sensitive of my ladylike sensibilities, he even used to wait till he'd got to the office before he'd have a crap."

"What did he do at weekends?"

"Public library lavvy on Saturdays, pub one on Sundays. He'd *die* if he knew I knew. And now, well, there's not a thing about him I don't know. Not that it's much compensation for what we lost. I've got the answers to the little things I'd always wondered—his savings accounts, his wine cellar, his toenail clippings. I've even got rid of the hairs in his ears and nose that always used to drive me crazy. But it's a bit like, what's it called? What's-her-face's box."

"Pandora."

"That's the one. I've opened the box. I know everything. But now it's just me and the box and the box is empty and not half as exciting as when it was locked."

"Pandora's box wasn't empty."

"Yeah. I know. It was full of nasties like war and famine and plague that the silly moo let out."

"Yes, but she slammed the lid shut just in time and kept back one feeble, fluttering little thing."

"Euthanasia?"

John smiled. "Hope."

"Spare me."

A young couple came to sit at the table opposite. The girl smiled briefly across at them and he wondered how she saw them. Husband and wife? Father and daughter? Viagra-fueled illicit fling? Anything but the truth.

"My box is still so much fuller than yours," he said. "We still talk. She's still . . . She hasn't stopped feeling like herself. The odd thing is that I suppose, if I'm honest, I've never really understood women. Women's things. Maybe if my mother and sister had lived longer. Women have always been alien to me. I've always lived in male worlds."

"Do we scare you?"

"A bit. Yes. In that I don't understand you. You'll laugh, but in a way, living with Frances has made me a bit of a fetishist."

"You old devil."

"I said you'd laugh."

"No. Sorry. Honestly. Go on."

"I just . . . well . . . I suppose I've always focused on the surfaces. Her shoes. Her slips. Her hats. Her soap. Her lipstick. I've identified the outside with the flesh beneath for so long that on one level that's something that won't change much. The surfaces, I mean. I suppose I find them easier to love because they're so comprehensible. In a way, as she becomes more helpless, the little things I associate with her will come more and more into my grasp. Sorry. I've lost you."

"No you haven't."

"I don't know why I find you so easy to talk to. All this *stuff* I come out with . . ."

"Me being a woman, you mean? It's because I'm common."

"No you're not," he said automatically.

"I certainly am compared with you. Don't worry. I'm not offended. Common's only a perspective, not an insult, like me finding you a bit posh. I can't see it from here. It's the same as you wanting to kiss me."

"I never said that."

"You didn't need to."

"Well."

"Just to see. Because you could. That's because I'm common too. I don't remind you of your mother. Frances probably does."

"Now I've made you cross."

"I'm not cross, I'm thirsty."

"Sorry. I'll get you another."

After their second drink, he saw her to her car then walked home. The sun had not quite set as he entered their quiet, leafy street but lights were coming on. He saw through windows to where families stared at televisions. A man dandled a baby. A bunch of young people stood around self-consciously clutching wine glasses. He froze below a bedroom window where a neighbor he knew faintly, a man around sixty, was unzipping his wife's dress, then hurried on as the woman turned to draw their curtains. Had they seen him staring, they would have assumed he was an old man hankering after a tantalizing glimpse of bra or breast. Nobody could guess it was not flesh he lusted after but the ordinary, practiced intimacy of the moment.

The last tableau was displayed in his own conservatory, which branched out to one side of the house and was clearly visible from one point on the pavement. Frances was sitting with Will and playing cards after all. He saw her laugh at something Will had said and flap her cards as though to swat the witticism out of the air like a passing fly.

Deep in her second gin, Sylvia had raised the old theory, much discussed in Alzheimer's chat rooms and fund-raisers, that early onset of the disease was particularly common in people whose lives had been basically unhappy, even traumatic; the bereaved, mothers of murdered children, survivors of persecution. Publicly he scorned the theory, finding it as crudely metaphorical as the insulting myth that sad, repressed personalities were more prone to cancer than sunnily open ones, so that child-blessed wives were favored over unloved virgins. In private, however, he had lately found the theory like a mental burr that stuck and chafed however hard he tried to dislodge it with reason.

He had always thought of Frances as someone who had led a happy life. All or most of his images of her were happy. The image he had carried in his mental wallet all these years was of her grinning, in a swimsuit, on a sandy beach. But perhaps he was confusing her feelings with the ones she evoked in him? She always spoke of herself as happy, basically happy, fortunate too. Could it be that she was trying to convince herself? Repeat the statement often enough and it became true? Had she been protecting him or had he been fooling himself? Certainly they had undergone their trials—what long-married couple had not?—but theirs was a sound marriage and, he had just learned from Sylvia, to be counted a successful one. "You're still together forty-one years on? It's a successful marriage."

Frances looked up and, seeing him loitering on the pavement, waved.

BEACHCOMBER

Julian would have been perfectly happy to be left alone. He was happy with his room with its lookout window and its sounds and smells of the sea. He was happy with the beach, especially when the tide cut it off from the bigger one around the corner and it became *Our Beach*. He was happy sitting among the rocks reading *The Story of Troy*, making sand castles, fishing in rock pools, buying cornets from the ice-cream van that drove around the bay twice a day. In the evenings he could barely keep his eyes open long enough to eat and in the mornings made himself a picnic breakfast rather than wait for his parents to appear. The grown-ups, however, seemed to feel that his happiness could not be complete unless it directly involved them and kept pestering him to swim, to go for a walk to visit some old church or another beach not nearly as nice as the perfect one on their doorstep. He knew his parents liked peace and quiet—"Ah! Peace and quiet!" was a typical exclamation of theirs on returning from some excursion—and by the same token that they enjoyed doing nothing at all because leaving their deck chairs or beach towels was always accompanied by such protestations of effort and a sort of nasty-medicine insistence upon doing what they believed to be the right thing. They baffled him.

When it was announced that his uncle and cousin were coming to join them for a few days, Julian had been excited. The mystery cousin was especially intriguing. He had become accustomed to obedient signings of Christmas and birthday cards to the enigmatic Skip and sensed, from people's reactions, that it was unusual and therefore faintly glamorous to be able to talk of *my cousin in California*, but she remained unreal to him, less real even than a character in a book because she entered his life supplied with fewer telling details. He sensed from the way his parents dismissed certain television programs and their thinly-veiled disgust when a well-meaning but distant relative gave him some Charlie Brown books for his last birthday that there was something *not quite right* about American culture. Judged against the things they did value—Bach, Rievaulx Abbey, Shakespeare—it must have seemed too new, too brightly colored. The romantic matinées he watched with his mother were usually American (at least the best ones were) but it was understood they were an indulgence not to be discussed in his father's hearing, like the chocolate bars they sometimes wolfed between meals, *all the better for being secret.*

Julian could tell his parents were unhappy about the unexpected visit from the over-bright way, all smiles, in which his mother announced it to him. "And you'll be able to play with Skip! Won't that be fun!"

He had probed their unease with questions. How long were they staying? Where would they sleep? What did Americans eat? Until something in his father's vexatious, "You'll find out soon enough," told him they knew little more than he and were afraid of what lay beyond their ken.

Until now he had always been glad his cousin was a girl. She would prove a more interesting playmate, should they ever meet. This was his first thought when he heard she was coming. A girl would enjoy his quiet sandy pastimes, making seaweed gardens, collecting shells, exploring rock pools for shrimp and baby crab, poking sea anemones with shells to make them close. A girl would prove no threat and would not expose his male deficiencies the way another boy might. Then a chance remark of his mother's—"I suppose the poor thing will be glad of some female company for a change"—undermined this fragile certainty. He pictured the doll-like perfection of the creature bearing down on them—even her name suggested Shirley Temple bounce—her poise, her wit, her feminine guile, and he saw how, by polarizing their little household with her mere presence, she would expose his corresponding lack of brutish capability.

"You must be especially kind to Skip when she comes because she doesn't have a mummy."

"But she's older than me."

"You must still be kind to her. She's only got her father and this'll be her first time in a foreign country."

"We're not foreign. We're Great Britain."

"You know what I mean. Foreign to her. Apart from your Uncle Bill, we're all the family she's got."

"Doesn't he have any relatives, then?"

He saw that this thought had not occurred to her but that she masked her ignorance with her usual retort when he had her cornered. "You're so sharp you'll cut yourself."

He resolved that his only recourse would be extreme politeness. It was plainly impossible to be *kind* to someone you didn't know but he could be polite, studiously polite, so as to highlight her American not-quite-rightness even as she exposed him. Meanwhile he resolved to preempt the effects of her arrival by striving to be all his parents could wish for in a son. He embarked on the expected holiday diary without prompting, sticking in postcards of the churches and villages they visited along with pieces of dried seaweed, lolly sticks and museum tickets and writing a drowsily dutiful report at each day's end. He swam when his mother told him to swim, although the brine stung his eyes and made him retch when he swallowed it, although he stubbed his toes on unexpected pebbles and had a horror of Moray eels. This morning he had agreed to play cricket with his father for the same reason.

Last year, one of their overnight camping trips had unluckily coincided with his short-lived devotion to the novels of William Mayne and he had expressed a wish to remain in the Height of Extravagance reading the last chapters of *A Swarm in May* rather than walk through the drizzle-sodden field where they had spent the night to peer down some ancient well.

"God, you're so *boring*," his mother had shouted.

She had probably forgotten saying this—it had goaded him into action and so served a temporary purpose—but it wounded him deeply. Wounded and warned him. For it made him aware of the terrible possibility that her love and loyalty were not automatic, that she or his father might look at him with coldly assessing eyes and find him not the boy for whom they had hoped. They might reject him as they threw out cakes that were stale or returned clothes that had revealed signs of shoddy tailoring. He knew they could not send him back to some factory or abandon him in a wood, like the parents in a fairy tale. Or rather, they could—he knew about child-killers, Henry had told him—but he knew this was not their style. He knew they could not put him into Borstal or approved school unless he broke the law, but he knew they could send him away. Boys were sent away all the time, sometimes to the other side of the world, so far that they could only go home in the longest holidays and sad, unsatisfactory arrangements had to be made for the shorter ones. He had read of such things in several books.

They did not truly play cricket, of course, because there were only two of them, but his father produced bat, ball and a set of stumps. Pa had played cricket up at Rexbridge, played in the university team at Lord's, and Julian sensed without anyone saying as much, that it would please him immoderately if Julian turned out to excel at the game too. He had tried. Elements of cricket appealed—like its relative stillness, the bulky pads, the linseed oil, the arcane method of writing down scores, the words *silly mid-off*—but he had an unshakable horror of the rock-hard ball and the damage it could do. He had been shown a horrible photograph of a bird killed by a flying ball at Lord's and subsequently stuffed. He fumbled even the easiest catches because at the last minute his concentration was thrown by the memory of the bird or an image of broken fingers or pulped brain. Why should the ball be stained bloodred if not, like the floors of the *Victory*, to disguise the marks of carnage?

They tried bowling and catching practice first. The idea was for him to attempt to bowl his father out. Failing that, Pa would endeavor to hit the ball so as to grant him an easy catch. Occasionally he would grow impatient and whack the ball far over toward the cliffs so that Julian had to run for it. His mother clapped when this happened and called out *bravo* from behind her novel in a voice not her own.

Julian had always bowled daisy-cutters, not daring to attempt an overarm bowl lest it betray his lack of coordination and send the ball off at a dangerous or merely ludicrous angle.

"At least have a go," Pa insisted. So he did and the ball flew wildly off course. "If you learn one thing this week," Pa said, "it'll be this."

"It's a holiday, darling," his mother murmured. "Not a boot camp."

"Well we wouldn't expect you to understand," Pa said. And he winked at Julian.

He had never winked before. It was extraordinary; like hearing him swear. And his use of *we*, admitting Julian to the select circle from which as a mere girl his mother was excluded, was briefly thrilling. In fiction and the playground, Julian much preferred the company of girls since most traditionally male interests bored him and girls were better at make-believe, relying less slavishly than boys on the previous after-noon's television. Now, however, he wondered if his boredom were not a worldly mask for fear of failure. If he could kick a football without people laughing or bowl a respectable overarm that even stood a fight-ing chance of dislodging the bails it might change his whole view of things.

"Never mind the run-up for now," Pa said. "Just whirl the ball round and round." Julian did as he was told. How could this ever feel natural? It seemed as effortful as doing the crawl. "Now let go." Julian let go and watched the ball fly high in the air and land uselessly between them. "Don't worry. At least it was in the right direction. Now. Try again." Amazing himself with his own eagerness, Julian ran for the ball and tried again. He began to whirl it over and over. "Just let go," Pa said, an edge of impatience entering his voice.

"What if I hit you?" Julian asked, chastened.

"No chance."

Julian let fly the ball, causing his father to lunge aside in a way that made his mother laugh.

"See?" he said, laughing too, but Pa was unswervable.

"Well try it again but without me there. See if you can just hit the wicket without me getting in the way and worrying you."

Julian tried it again, with a run-up this time, and somehow sent the ball yards wide of the mark. His father caught it and shouted *Owzat*. It must have stung his palms, Julian knew it must, but he caught it without a flicker of pain. Manhood was astonishing. Maybe he enjoyed the pain? Maybe that was what men did? Like pulling off sticking plasters without crying and shaving and boxing and putting wounded rabbits out of their misery with walking sticks.

"I'll never get it," he said, taking refuge in a risky show of sulkiness.

"Of course you will."

"Show me."

"All right. Good move." Pa seemed pleased. "Your turn to bat."

"Not too fast, darling," his mother murmured and turned a page.

"I won't," Pa said and, catching Julian's eye, winked again.

He must have misjudged the distance or had the sun in his eyes. Julian had expected it to bounce a yard or two in front of him. Instead it seemed to come so fast that he lost sight of it entirely. Then something struck him so hard in the face it seemed best to fall down. He was briefly aware of the sudden chill of damp sand on his cheek, then everything went blank.

He heard crying in the distance, recognized his own voice and fled back into the darkness to hide. When he came to his senses, he was lying on his bed under a quilt and a strange boy was staring at him from near his feet, frowning. He had short reddish hair, freckles, a stripy T-shirt and he was chewing gum.

"Did they rub it with steak?" he asked. His voice was gruff and he talked American. Like Samantha in *Bewitched* only not so sweetly.

"I beg your pardon?" Julian asked back.

"They should've held a piece of steak to it, right after it happened, all raw and bloody. It stops it going black. You're going to have a real shiner if they didn't. You'll look stupid."

"Who are you, please?" Julian demanded.

The boy gave no reply but merely hollered over his shoulder through the half-open door, "He's awake!" As adult voices drew nearer, he turned to go, pausing only to say, "Don't let it get to you. Cricket's only for sissies anyway. Tomorrow I can teach you baseball."

"Is the ball soft?" Julian asked.

The boy gave a sullen grin that made him look much nicer but also rather frightening. "Not when I hit it."

He was replaced by Ma, who kissed him and rubbed his head, and by a doctor, who examined his swelling eye with fingers that smelled of fish, asked him a few silly questions, like who he was and where did he live and how many fish-smelly fingers was he holding up before making up a cool, witchhazelly wad of cotton wool for Julian to press on his bad eye and declaring him as right as rain.

The doctor left but the voices continued, those of his parents and somebody else. There was laughter—the kind Pa only produced when he was with other men—and the unmistakable sound of ice in glasses. The strange boy was talking too, though not much. Julian began to feel slightly silly. The doctor had said he was as right as rain but Ma had not said he could get up. He did not feel ill and there were few things Pa despised more than malingerers, so he sat up. The soggy bandage slipped. Julian retrieved it and held it back against his eye, although it no longer felt so deliciously cool. He walked to the looking glass and peered at the damage. Reassured that he was indeed wounded, and quite dramatically, he padded out toward the voices.

His parents were in chairs on the veranda with a man in a black leather jacket and jeans. Not like Darrin in *Bewitched*, more like someone in *The Virginian* only less reassuring; a cattle rustler, maybe. A bad man. He had very thick black hair, much thicker and longer than Pa's, and a mustache like Lord Kitchener's on the England Needs YOU poster Ma had stuck up in the upstairs lavatory as a joke. Incongruously, the boy was sitting on his lap, swinging his legs. The grown-ups were all drinking. The boy appeared to have a whole bowl of Cheese Footballs to himself. The man looked up expectantly and said, "Hi there," in a voice that was nicer than he looked.

The boy just stared.

"Oh darling. You're up," said Ma. "I didn't think we should bother you till you felt ready. This is your Uncle William. Bill. Sorry. And this is Skip, your cousin. And guess what? They came all the way from Sussex on a motorbike like Steve McQueen's."

Julian remembered his resolution to be polite. "How do you do?" he said.

As he extended his palm to shake hands, the unsupported bandage fell from his eye and plopped wetly to the floorboards. Everybody laughed so he did too. He pretended he had done it on purpose and did it again. But nobody laughed the second time and he could tell from the way Skip looked at him that she was not deceived.

BLUE HOUSE

Taking time off did not come easily. Will was not one of nature's travelers and was never happier than when doing what he usually did, holding the fort for others. He had been to Paris and Florence as a hostelling student and been inspired by Finn's example to go backpacking across England in a last mad bid for freedom before sitting his Finals but in the twenty years since had only traveled alone once. After his first year in the children's library, he took a cheap flight to Naples, spent a week in the second-best hotel he could find, sight-saw until his feet bled and was so wretchedly homesick and unhappy with no one to talk to that he finally swallowed his pride and came home a day early. Holidays might not have been the preserve of the married but they were, he decided, group activities. Since then he had confined himself to spending weekends away, visiting friends, sometimes even visiting friends in the middle of their holidays abroad. He always took a make-me-welcome present, entertained difficult children and aunts, left while he was still wanted, wrote a witty thank-you letter and was inordinately pleased to return home.

Kristin, who helped him in the bookshop, was quite capable of running it on her own for a fortnight. Gaia, to whom he sublet the café, ran it as an independent business with her retinue of underwaged devotees, and expected little of him anyway. Nothing in his life had been a great success up to now and he could not quite believe what his accountant and cash register had begun to tell him. He was convinced the delicate balancing act, the small economic miracle, would all slip sideways into chaos if he turned his back on it.

When one of the big chain bookstores opened a branch in town, he had been prepared to see his custom decimated. It had wavered, certainly, dipped, but he had weathered the storm and his loyal customers soon returned. He could not carry a huge range, but he gave a personal service. He knew what his regulars liked and so could recommend new titles to them when they came in. He also ran a popular mailing service, sending out small parcels of novels or biographies to customers isolated or expatriate, on the understanding that they would return anything they did not want. And returns were remarkably few. Like the chain stores, he invited famous and not so famous authors to give readings, but his Saturday meet-the-author lunches remained popular because lunch was free to anyone who bought a hardback first—regardless of who wrote it. And his lazy Sunday morning book-brunches had become a cult ever since a national radio program suggested they provided an excellent opportunity to pick up love or consolation. Kristin said the popularity was down to Will's policy of letting customers browse on sofas or the little café terrace before they bought, resulting in an irritating stream of books which had to be reduced because of food smears. Gaia attributed sales to the excellence of her brownies and biscotti. Whatever the reason, it was a business that Will had conceived, set up, decorated and often run on his own—give or take some advice from Sandy—and he was loath to entrust it to others, however capable, for even a fortnight. Kristin said that if he telephoned her more than once in his absence, she would walk out on him.

Everyone he told was appalled that he was taking his parents on holiday. Holidays, apparently, were all about sex or adventure and the presence of elderly parents was assumed to stifle either. He could hardly explain that on the contrary they were, in this case, to provide the perfect mask for both. Sandy astonished him by accepting as his due that his wife should be offering him illicit romance on a plate. Not for the first time, Will felt a pang of envious irritation at the confidence with which he seemed to accept the gifts of fortune as being his by right.

Deep down he was appalled too. At first. He had not spent so much time with his parents since leaving home. Christmas rarely lasted longer than a long weekend and by the end of that he was usually climbing the wall with vexation and a desire for less innocent conversation. Even with a sunny beach attached—and this was Cornwall, not Tenerife, so the sun was not guaranteed—and the promise of a visit from Sandy, the arrangement loomed with every passing day ever more like a sentence in an open prison to which he had needlessly committed himself. However, the more he was called upon to defend his decision, the more convinced he became that doing the right thing might turn out to be enjoyable for once. He amassed a heap of novels to read, optimistically bought new sunglasses and the best suntan lotion he could find. At least until Sandy and the boys arrived, he would see that the experience was quite unlike a traditional family holiday. They would dine on crab and lobster, drink good wine, maybe even go out to one of the Cornish restaurants one read so much about these days. No one would be forced to do anything so there would be no silly arguments. Even if the weather turned nasty—which it showed no sign of doing yet—they could enjoy the independent pursuit of adult pleasures. They might even have grown-up excursions to St. Ives or the Scillies. Now that he was taking a holiday at last, he began to feel the need to indulge himself in compensation for all the summers he had stayed put.

The drive from Barrowcester to Cornwall lay entirely on motorways and dual carriageways. Will was determined they should go to their destination by the most direct route possible with none of the cultural stoppings-off at castles, cathedrals and burial mounds that had made the long drives of his youth so interminable. He feared some opposition on this. His mother found it extremely hard to sit still for long and his father regarded motorways as an immoral waste of countryside. However, after talking incessantly through various domestic worries—Had they watered the flowerbeds enough? Was the garden door locked when they left? Was the milk bill paid? Had they packed Pevsner as well as Ronnie Barclay? Was Will truly insured to drive their car because honestly they wouldn't mind squeezing into the back of his?—they both fell into deep and apparently relieved slumber within minutes of joining the southbound M5. He was able to listen to a taped reading of *The Woman in White* in peace as far as Somerset, where he left the motorway to stop off for lunch in a village pub that was not as excellent as he remembered but was at least less soul-destroying than a service area. They woke as he drove into the village, sensing the slackening of speed perhaps, and both apologized as though sleeping were bad form in a passenger rather than an ideal.

Dad insisted on paying which made asking for anything more than a half and a Stilton ploughman's awkward. In the sly hope of fueling further sleep so that he could hear the rest of the Wilkie Collins uninterrupted, Will bought everyone another half and a helping of treacle tart richly crested with clotted cream.

"The holiday starts here," he said when Ma made her customary protest about the state of her still excellent waistline. He allowed half an hour for pottering in the village's overpriced antique shops and over-restored church and felt a treacherous glow as first one then the other let the motorway's monotony lull them back into a doze. Dad stayed awake just long enough to observe, "Your ma's not used to beer really," in a touching we're-all-men-together tone.

Will woke them as the A30 crossed the Cornish border, releasing a trickle of confused reminiscence. They showed no great excitement until the first glimpse of the sea, which Mum claimed proudly as though demanding a boiled sweet by way of a prize. As the car rounded the curve in the estuary road and the view of the open sea and the Camel opened before them, she let out a gasp.

"You do remember it, then?" Dad said, for she had been protesting since Bodmin that nothing looked even faintly familiar.

"It's all changed so," Mum said, then turned, uncertain. "It has, hasn't it? I don't really remember but . . ."

"It's more built-up," Dad confirmed. "None of those bungalows were there. Or the camp sites. And *Surf Shack Pizzas*," he pronounced the name with an audible curl to his lip, "certainly wasn't."

"It's rather fun, though," she added mischievously, as a tanned youth with a pierced navel and wetsuit unpeeled to his thighs somehow contrived to cross the road looking like a sexy panther rather than a person ridiculously skirted in wet rubber. "All these young things with nothing on. I like it. *Much* more fun."

Unlike most villages in North Cornwall, with roots in fish, mines or cattle, Polcamel had no history beyond the dawn of bucket-and-spade tourism. A vast sandy beach, the Strand, just far enough past the point where estuary met open sea to allay one's darker fears of sewage, panoramic cliff-top walks without the punishing valley climbs for which most of that stretch of coastline was notorious, and an easy supply of cheap seafood attracted the first holidaymakers in the nineteen-hundreds. The resulting straggle of villas and nostalgic ex-Raj bungalows only became a fully-fledged resort complete with post office, butcher and general stores, in the thirties, when a young Rexbridge poet laureate-to-be, Ronald Barclay, inherited a house there, invited his friends and made it fashionable among the intelligentsia too impoverished and/or child-laden to afford places in the South of France. It had grown steadily until the fifties, when its floating population reached critical mass.

It was never, strictly speaking, a community. There was a post office, certainly, and one could buy basic food and a newspaper, the newest paperbacks and suntan oil, but there was no school, no medical center, no policeman or midwife. Off-season the population shrank and aged dramatically, since the year-round residents were chiefly people who had chosen to retire to holiday houses their youthful selves had merely visited. In the eighties, an unscrupulous district council had conspired with desperate farmers to encourage development around the village's outskirts. On what had been a majestic green headland sporting three or four spacious thirties houses, mean pebble-dash homes now huddled around a campsite that was gaudy with caravans in summer and a sea of scarred mud in winter. The Strand remained, huge and fairly golden and, thanks to the arrival of a self-consciously macho surfing culture, wetsuit hirer, surfboard shop and chippy were kept open all year long.

The greatest change, however, was not immediately discernible. It lay in the curious process by which Polcamel had evolved from being the half-humorous playground of Ronnie Barclay, Jacoby Tate, founder of the nearby music festival at Trenellion, and their circle of artistic Fabians and pacifists, into the jealously guarded territory of their golf-playing, cheerfully philistine successors. In high season one could close one's eyes in the post office queue and, but for the powerful scents of Ambre Solaire and Cornish pasties, think oneself in Fulham.

Will soon gathered that the house was not, after all, the one where Mum and Dad had brought them as children. At least Mum was confused and Dad was uncertain. It was blue—a deep, electric blue the color of Greek fishing boats—with blue-green shutters and veranda. Pa recalled the other place had a more fanciful name than Blue House, like Spindrift or Bladderwrack. The other place had belonged to a land-owning family who lived in an altogether grander place at the far end of the same drive whereas Blue House's steep drive led nowhere else. A high hedge of sea buckthorn now displayed its silver leaves and orange berries. Like the earlier cottage, it was set in sand dunes in a little bay but this had a fenced off garden where the other had only veranda blurring into drifting sands. Within a picket fence, the owner had persuaded hedges of lavender, tamarisk and rosemary to grow as well as sea buckthorn and to the rear of the house, where two stunted Monterey pines afforded shelter from the salt-laden winds, planting was lush, even subtropical, with yuccas and cabbage palms, their huge summer flowerheads still on show as they dried out, two great agaves and a multi-colored raft of phormiums. They grew in raised beds formed from railway sleepers and attractively bleached driftwood, discreetly watered by a pipe from the bungalow's gutter and fertilized by a colorful and rather smelly mulch of seaweed.

The only blot on the horizon, apart from the people on the little beach, lay to the rear. The unnatural green of a golf course had taken over from farmland and in a scrubby field between that and the beach lay some sort of New Age encampment. There was an L-shaped tent, an ancient caravan, a great heap of what looked like wooden salvage from ruined houses and was probably fuel, a couple of hens scratching about and a pitiful dog tethered in the shade of a gorse bush. Two dustbins, a cascade of vivid plastic rubbish and a laden washing line completed the scruffy picture.

"Never mind," Mum sniffed. "At least there aren't dozens of caravans. It might have backed on to that pass we placed earlier. I mean—"

"Judging from the deeply trendy crowd hanging around as we drove through," Will said, "we'll probably be subjected to a rave before the fortnight's out."

"What *fun*!"

"She has no idea," Dad sighed, sniffing his hand after rubbing it on the lavender. "There'd be used syringes in the sand and coupling couples in the garden. Where are the keys?"

"Hang on." Will dug in his back pocket to retrieve the directions. They were creased with sweat from the long drive. He reread the last paragraph. "It says under the Welcome mat."

"Huh," Dad snorted, stooping to retrieve them. "Very trusting."

Mum was dreamily absorbed in the view of the sea. Suddenly she roused herself. "God I need to pee. Urgent woman coming through!" She hurried inside in Dad's wake.

Will's hopes of being spared the worst of a family seaside holiday showed every sign of being met. Modishly furnished, decorated in bold, fresh colors with sanded floors, a well-equipped kitchen and some abstracts and sculpture to which he would happily have given house-room, the cottage's interior was almost unnervingly fashionable, only a few years old.

"Are you sure this is the right place?" he asked, fingering a smooth, spotty pebble on a windowsill.

"It was blue and the key was under the mat," Mum said. "Can we have this room, please?"

"Have whichever room you like. Oh." Will tried to open a small room on the end which he had guessed would have views in two directions from its turret-shaped bay window, but found it locked. He rattled the knob then gave up. Presumably it was where the owners kept their private possessions. It was surprising, all the same, to find anything locked away in a holiday house so unlike the meanly-furnished norm. He chose instead the other double room, intending to make the most of it before the arrival of Sandy and the children forced him to give it up.

Not bothering to unpack yet, he eased up the window, whose sashes were sticky with salt, then flopped on to the bed where he shut his eyes with a contented sigh and listened to the sounds of sea and swimmers, relishing complete inactivity after hours of driving. For a few minutes he drifted pleasantly on the edge of a doze then became aware of the sound of his parents murmuring and walking about but doing so with exaggerated attempts at restraint. They should have been exhausted. They were the old ones, after all. They were the ones who would have been up since six A.M. fretting about preparations and the survival of tomato plants. Then he remembered that they had slept for most of the journey and forced himself to get up to join them.

Mum appeared to have brought most of the contents of her larder, which she was stashing away in the kitchen cupboards. She had on a toweling robe, through which he glimpsed her swimming costume. "You should be lying down," she said. "Don't mind us. You must be shattered from the drive."

"I don't need to sleep," Will said, the truth of it dawning on him. "I'm on holiday." Some of the herbs she was unloading looked older than he felt. In particular there was a pot of gray, dried tarragon that was on its way to becoming something else entirely. "Are you both going swimming?" Through their half-open bedroom door, he had caught an off-white glimpse of Dad in the throes of changing.

"It'll probably be freezing but I was feeling all hot and sticky anyway," Mum said. "Come too."

"Of course. I'll just change. I thought we'd agreed on no cooking."

"Oh well. You know how it is." She shrugged and continued stacking jars.

Pa stopped changing and seized the opportunity, declaring a wish to walk while there was still light along to the spectacularly bumpy headland he remembered known as the Rumps. The implication was that Mum was not safe to swim alone but now that Will had volunteered to mind her, he was free to play.

The tide had risen so far since their arrival that the small bay the house overlooked was now cut off from the main beach. Most swimmers and surfers had retreated toward Polcamel so as to be spared the arduous walk up the cliff and over the headland to their cars. Mum and Will thus had most of the remaining expanse of scuffed-up, sun-warmed sand to themselves. He felt self-conscious, nevertheless, because his skin was so pale and the new trunks, bought in a sale on a burst of short-lived fitness enthusiasm, had more orange stripes than he remembered. So, gasping against the Atlantic cold, he ran through the surf and dived into a wave. He swam a few strokes in an effort to acclimatize his body then turned to look for Mum.

She had always been a strong swimmer and continued to swim regularly in the city baths. It was highly unlikely she would get into trouble. Will was by far the likelier candidate for drowning. His body, it seemed to him, had always been too bony to be usefully buoyant. Where more rounded boys floated naturally and so could use all their strength for flying through the school pool, he had to use all his churning efforts just to stay above water. He had developed an inefficient, overly splashy technique at an early age and never managed to unlearn it. Although he lived as far from the sea as one could in England, a miraculous improvement in his crawl and backstroke remained his impulsive desire whenever birthday cake candles, Christmas puddings or roast chickens granted him a wish.

Mum was still standing on the line where surf melted into sand, apparently hypnotized by the bubbles breaking over her feet. When he called out to her, she looked up and took a moment or two to find his face before she could focus a smile on him. "Well come on, then," he urged. "It's fine." Which it was, in a bracing fashion.

She slipped off her toweling robe, tossed it on to the sand behind her and he was startled at how good her body still was, a testament to a life-time of weekly swims. She had the broken veins and ravaged skin of her generation, but her figure was not the kind that ballooned with age and her long legs and broad shoulders gave her an advantage. She was un-doubtedly flattered by the dazzle of low sun on water and by a struc-tured black swimming costume but as she strode toward him through the surf and expertly dived to avoid a buffeting, he imagined a glimpse of her younger, unconfused self.

She laughed, "Fuck, it's cold!" then laughed again, seeing the sur-prise on his face. She dived again and emerged a few yards away on her back, toes pointing to the cloudless blue, silver hair fanning out around her face. "Do I look hideously witchy?" she asked. "Should I wear a rubber cap with flowers on?"

"You look like a mermaid," he told her.

"Mermaid's mother, maybe. Aging thingy. Tritoness. Look. There's your daddy." She waved to a tiny figure on the cliff path to their left, who might have been anybody, and called out, "Hello, darling!" far too loudly. The figure waved back and walked on. "This is wonderful. No water! I mean, no stuff."

"Chlorine."

"Yes. Let's swim round to Polcamel."

"You're joking of course. Those rocks look lethal."

"Well I'll race you to that Lilo someone's lost out there."

"But—"

"See it? OK. Go!"

"I'm not sure," he began but she had already launched off in a decep-tively languid backstroke.

Swearing under his breath, conjuring up mental images of vodka and tonic, pistachio nuts and a grilled chicken salad, Will did his splashy best to follow in her wake. The waves were high. Even diving through them as she had taught him, he emerged to find himself drawn too fast for comfort into the trough before the next one. He was buffeted twice in a row, coughing on swallowed brine, then realized he was drifting dangerously close to the rip tide that was hauling out from the bay's edges. Abandoning the race—he could see neither Lilo nor mother now for waves and, whatever the state of her spoken English, had no fear for her ability to find her way back to shore unassisted. Instead, he struggled away from the rocks, parallel to the shore, until he judged himself far enough from the tide to be able to strike out for the sand without the humiliation of being reduced to swimming on the spot.

Breathless, and bruised where his foot had struck unexpected stone, cursing at once his lack of assertiveness and ineffectual parenting of his parent, he staggered back on to the still dwindling beach just in time to rescue Mum's robe from the greedy surf. Somehow the thing's wet edges sapped his confidence in her.

"I won't panic," he thought, "because there's nothing to panic about. I'm a weak swimmer, that's all. She's fine. She's having a ball and she's absolutely fine." Wincing from the mussel shells under foot, he clambered on to a great rock so as to be able to see beyond the roiling waves and keep a protective, albeit impotent, eye on her. The sun was beginning a garish setting and was fast losing its warmth. Shivering, he absently pulled on the toweling robe and screwed up his eyes.

The Lilo was now much further out. Presumably the rip tide had caught it and the owner was resigned to its loss. It was one of the odd facts of beachcombing that one never came across the remains of Lilos lost at sea. Did they sink on bursting? Did wily fishermen pick them up to sell afresh or did they merely sail farther and farther out to sea to become floating nesting pads for seabirds? There was no sign of her. Will glanced over to the Strand and saw that the lifesavers' flags planted there earlier had disappeared. Then he saw some late walkers on the cliff path pointing down to an inlet just out of his view. Then he made out Mum.

She was battling with the current, he assumed at first, then he saw a second head. It was another woman. Then he saw arm muscles and a flash of chest hair and realized she was struggling with a long-haired man. He appeared to be coughing and flailing and shouting all at once. Then, extraordinarily, she performed some maneuver whereby she seized him from behind, around his chin, and like an illustration on a lifesaving instruction notice, began towing him to shore. Will glanced desperately about him but the beach was now deserted except for children still absorbed in a huge sand castle they were defending against the encroaching tide. The cliff walkers had gone. From the houses on the Polcamel headland came the shouts and laughter of families uncorking wine and lighting barbecues. In the New Age encampment, the tethered dog set up a wretched howl.

Will leaped to the sand, ripping off the robe, and ran back into the sea, which now felt less cold. He had barely got in past his waist when she hove into view, still swimming strongly but with breath coming in great gasps. The man, who Will now saw was about his own age and had hair that hung in tight dreadlocks to his shoulders, was no longer shouting or flailing but floating quite limp in the water.

"If we can just . . ." Mum panted. "Get him on to the beach, he'll be fine."

"Here. I'll take his feet." Will took the man by the ankles, whereupon the man lashed out, kicking him in the chest and winding him before fighting clear of Mum's grasp.

"Of course I'll be fine. I was fucking fine to start with," he said.

"You were drowning," she said flatly.

"You brainless woman," he muttered and made *woman* sound like an insult.

"Don't you dare to talk to my mother like that," Will began. "She was only—"

But his words died as the man whirled around, eyes full of red sun, and glared at him so close to that Will could smell the wine on his breath. His face was blank for a moment or two as he seemed to read Will like a poorly-worded notice, then he assumed an expression that mixed contempt with a wintry bitterness and walked away up the beach as though nothing had happened.

Will stared for a second, then was freshly aware of Mum's heaving lungs. "Here," he said and threw the robe about her, rubbing her shoulders. "Hot bath for you the moment we get in, my girl. You're freezing."

"He was drowning," she said as they walked up the beach arm in arm. "I was heading for the whatsit. The Lulu."

"Lilo."

"Yes. And I suddenly saw him." Her teeth chattered. "He was already about two feet under. I saw his hair fanning out in the water."

"You saved the rude bastard's life."

"Judging from his reaction, I'm not so sure. Oh dear. Poor man. How ghastly. He'd probably waited all day for the beach to empty."

Her teeth were chattering so hard now she could barely form sentences. Shock was setting in. When they were back in Blue House and her bath was running, he poured them each a medicinal brandy from the selection of drinks Dad had thoughtfully packed along with the contents of her herb rack. He found that his teeth were chattering too and clunked against the rim of his glass. He pulled on a thick cotton jersey and took his drink out to the veranda while the place filled with the urbane fumes of her bath essence.

The few playground fights he had ever got into as a boy were set off by someone insulting her and this persisted into adulthood. By some piece of old-fashioned chivalric programming, he only lost his temper in the defense of women. Had the man not strode away as he did, Will might have hit him. He re-ran the odd scene in his head, adding in a Galahadish punch and confecting the exchange of manly indignation which followed, but the projector in his head kept jamming at the point where his knuckles brushed the man's lips.

The hazy sunset filled all the bay's small slice of horizon. Will heard whistling and looked up to see Dad descending the footpath from the cliffs. They would turn the evening's near-crisis into an amusing anecdote for him. He could already hear how it would be done, with exaggeration of his own feeble swimming, of Mum's derring-do, of her refusal to let a handsome suicide drown on a perfectly nice evening. He thanked God Poppy was not there to spoil the fun with her dogged insistence on the truth and responsible behavior. By now she'd have called in some defenseless local GP to check Mum over and contacted social services and the Samaritans about the presence of a man in need of psychiatric help. Handsome or no.

Will raised his drink in greeting. With his walking stick, Dad pointed at the stumpy, red-striped lighthouse on the far side of the bay and shouted something like "Fog!"

Will smiled in reply, uncomprehending but eager. "The very image of our relationship," he thought.

BEACHCOMBER

Everything about them was too loud—clothes, voices, manners, tans. And that motorbike was the last thing one expected which was, of course, precisely why he liked it. Frances could see at once that he was one of those people who would sooner die young and unappreciated than be found predictable. Something about his mustache confirmed this for her. What such people never seemed to realize was that in their pains to evade the norm, they became as fixed, as much creatures of habit, as the most staid conservative. The new university was the perfect nemesis for him. He would take drugs, sleep with his students, take sides with youth against age then wake up one day to find himself fossilized into a harmless campus *character*, no more scandalous than Gilbert and Sullivan.

The strength of her reaction startled her. She was not a snob and would always spring to check snobbery in Julian, but these self-invited guests made her feel like a curtain-twitcher of the worst kind and she resented them for it. When they arrived she was talking to the doctor who had been called in to deal with the pocket drama of Julian's being knocked out. The child had not been out cold for long. He came round as poor John was carrying him into the bungalow. He wept briefly with the pain then slid into a deep sleep. Worried about the wisdom of allowing this in case he had concussion, uncertain if she could safely give him painkillers, she had tracked down Dr. Hengist, interrupting his late lunch. The intrusive din of the motorbike angered her. Knowing it could have nothing to do with their landlords, she assumed it was some lout come to fool around on the sand. When John ran out and she heard him laughing and saw Bill and Skip coming in with him, she found the anger she had prepared for unruly strangers transferred to them. She smiled, laughed as she explained the drama, shook Bill's hand, but she felt the anger hot behind her brow and in the hours that followed it had not lifted. She was sure it was illegal for a mere child, even this self-assured eleven-year-old, to ride pillion like that even for short distances, and they had come miles. Bill assured her they had spent a night in Salisbury to allow for an excursion to Stonehenge as though he thought that made such irresponsibility forgivable.

At first she assumed that Skip dressed like a boy because it was safer on a motorbike and made it easier to disguise her age. Then it became clear from her manners, lack of them rather, that she felt more comfortable that way. She was a tomboy; scowling, monosyllabic, freckle-faced. Her actual, feminine name sat awkwardly on her slouching persona so it came as small surprise that her nickname had supplanted it entirely. Junior, Chuck or Beaver would have suited her equally. Frances did her best to draw her out, asking her about her trip and school and California but it proved such an uphill struggle she decided the girl was shy and that it would be kinder to leave her to scowl in peace.

Meanwhile something odd was happening to John. Talking to Bill, he was putting on a joshing, even loud, manner. He talked about distances and miles per gallon, things in which he never showed the least interest, became suddenly keen that everyone drink as much as possible and, she noticed, persisted in standing when the rest of them were sitting down, as though he needed to assert himself. What surprised her most, however, was the knowledge he revealed about all things California, not just history and geography but recent politics, student movements and what he called *counter-culture*. He had been researching. Not for this visit, naturally, which had taken him by surprise, but for the vaguer purpose of keeping abreast since Becky's death so that when fate brought him together with his niece he should not be found wanting.

Bill was handsome. Why should she deny it? He looked less like an academic than a farmer or cowhand, which would surely have pleased him greatly. He was shorter than John but thicker set, stronger-looking. He was the younger by several years but so tanned and weather-beaten that his face had more lines. Somehow the creases around his eyes and mouth and the lines etched in his brow contrived to look like signs of health whereas John's furrows spoke only of anxiety. But even as she compared them, perched on a creaking bench beside the sullen child and looking discreetly from one to the other, she despised herself for even seeking comparisons. Bill was handsome, certainly, but his awareness of the fact undercut its impact, on second and third examination. As did the arrogant fullness of his voice, his assurance of attention. He had brown eyes, good white teeth, a firm jaw and, if his daughter's bragging about his surfing prowess were to be believed, would have muscles to match. John was the better bred, however. She abhorred such terminology but there was no more effective way of distinguishing him. In purely veterinary terms, John plainly came of closer-matched bloodstock. His nose was longer, his cheekbones were more pronounced, his hands not flattened and spread as if by generations of labor. John was a gazelle hound to his brother-in-law's mastiff.

Supper was not a great success. On a whim, partly because it was a favorite of John's, she bought some local sausages and made toad-in-the-hole. But the oven was not hot enough so the batter failed to rise properly and remained unappetizingly flabby in the middle. Although it doubtless confirmed all the worst things Becky had told him about British cooking, Bill at least ate the sausages. Skip, whose eyes had already widened with disgust at the dish's name, announced that she was vegetarian and not hungry in any case. Although she was actually angry that no one had thought to warn her of this, Frances tried to cajole her into eating some vegetables instead but Skip only stared at her as if she had taken leave of her senses. Julian took this as his cue to show off and try to eat more sausage than was good for him, whereupon John ticked him off rather sharply and a mildly drunken gloom descended, unrelieved by Frances's production—what had possessed her?—of an unseasonably hot rice pudding. The business of sending the children to bathe and settling them into bed provided a much-needed diversion.

Frances returned from tucking Julian in—Skip, quite properly, had refused any such childish intimacy—to find the men smoking duty-free cigarettes and tucking into a second bottle of Wine Society claret. Succumbing to the urge to retire early with a novel, she bade them both good night. She felt Bill's eyes on her as she crossed the room to take refuge in a bath and knew she was being chilly and rude but she was too tired to care. In any case, to announce that she had changed her mind and was going to sit up with them and prove the life and soul after all would have appeared odd even had she possessed the confidence required to reverse her decision.

Had John not been drunk when he eventually came to bed, he would have been angry with her. As it was he merely expressed concern that she had *not been very nice* to Skip.

"But I've tried," she protested. "I talked to her. I helped her get ready for bed. I tried to make her eat."

"I think she's terribly unhappy," he said. "He can't see it, of course, and she makes a big effort to hide it from him. She doesn't want him to think it's his fault. And it isn't. I mean he didn't *kill* Becky. But she's just terribly unhappy."

She was astonished to hear him talk this way. She had no idea he thought in even this depth about any of them and actually felt a small pang of jealousy that he should wax sentimental about an ill-mannered brat he had barely met, even as she agreed and promised to make a special effort tomorrow. But then, even less characteristically, he started to make love to her without even waiting for her to turn off her reading lamp.

"Ssh," she managed. "He'll hear!"

He stifled her, however, with a not unpleasant, winey kiss, put out the light himself, knocking it over noisily in the process, and made love to her. It hurt, probably because she was so tense at the thought of a strange man and child lying and listening on the other side of the thin bedroom wall, and took longer than usual because of the alcohol.

As though she were drunk too, however, she drifted off in the middle of it, away from the discomfort of mind and body, to a small, imaginary room where her new daughter was waiting for her, a perfect, pretty, entirely loving, meat-eating little girl. She barely noticed when he was through with thudding into her and was subsiding without his customary apologies into leaden slumbers, rapt as she was with every perfect detail of the baby and the extraordinarily acute sensation of her milky-breathing presence.

When she returned, as it were, to the room and pulled her sweat-soaked nightdress back around her legs and prepared to sleep, she found herself breathing in time with the sea and feeling the house gathered about her as a creaking wooden shell, aware of husband, son and other sleepers as so many small animal presences she could bear effortlessly along on its frame.

The following morning, because the sea was uncomfortably rough for swimming, she had hoped to organize a trip inland to a church with famously beautiful pew ends. However, Bill returned with Skip from a reckless pre-breakfast dip wildly excited. Nobody had told him there was surfing in Cornwall and he wanted to go in search of surfboards immediately. Something about him, his unbounded enthusiasm perhaps, had reduced John to a state of clannish adolescence. He tossed aside his C. P. Snow, declaring this a marvelous idea, and claiming he had always wanted to learn, which was news to her. Skip insisted that even though Julian wasn't a strong swimmer he could still enjoy body surfing or they could find him something cheap and polystyrene. Julian, Frances could see, was torn between mistrust of this bolshy girl and puppyish awe of her father. At last he checked an impulse to linger mousily and tailed along.

"You don't want to come, do you?" John asked her in a fleeting way that made her feel he would have been disappointed had she surprised him and come too, so she smiled and shook her head, remembering last night.

"I'm exhausted," she said. "Just promise me a go on your board if you find one."

Left alone, she washed up breakfast, irritated afresh that her radio picked up nothing but pop music down here. She sat on the veranda with more coffee, anointed herself liberally with sun cream, and finished rereading *The Grand Sophy* in an unsatisfactory rush. Then, bored and feeling greasy, she went inside again to tidy up. She made her bed, scooped dirty clothes into a bag, did the same in Julian's little room then paused on the threshold of the room Skip had insisted on sharing with her father. It was odd how twenty-four hours could turn a neutral space, a spare room, into somewhere so intensely private. They had only swimming things and the clothes they traveled in. In an arrangement that had already struck her as both spendthrift and characteristically selfish, the belongings they could not fit on the motorbike were coming separately by train so would have to be collected. Despite this, father and daughter had managed to create a mess in the room. The bedding was all over the floor, an ashtray was overflowing on the chest of drawers and their wet swimming things were staining the bedside rug. The room had already acquired an alien scent; not just cigarettes, but something sweet and nutty she could not place.

She hesitated a moment, familiar with the bossy disapproval that could be implicit in a room tidied in one's absence. Then a breeze from the open window caught the cigarette ash and she felt compelled into action. She swept the ashtray off to the kitchen, wrung the bathing costumes out of the window before slinging them up on the washing line then made the bed. She realized, as she plumped up the pillows, that they must have slept in their underwear. Far from thinking the image sordid, she found it to be oddly touching.

The girl had no bedside reading, which was surely a shameful lack in a writer's daughter. He had brought a new copy of a novel, *Couples,* by someone called John Updike, and a dog-eared hardback of metaphysical poetry. She began reading the Updike where she stood then, turning a page, sank to the newly made bed. She was still reading, despite a certain impatience with the tone, when she heard the Volkswagen changing gear as it came down the track. She left the book as she had found it, open face-down on a folded-over page, tidied the bed again and hurried out. She was overcome by a surge of silly, hot-cheeked guilt, became panicked that she could not immediately settle convincingly to some other activity than snooping, so was discovered wandering the corridor like an inexperienced shade.

John was still in the throes of incongruously boyish excitement and announced, in tones that implied he would brook no alternative, that they had bought the entire small stock of basic but serviceable surfboards in a sports shop in Wadebridge and were going to try them out immediately.

"I hung your swimming things out to dry," she told Bill.

"You didn't have to," he said, "but thanks," and went to retrieve them. Julian insisted on showing her his bladeless, polystyrene board. He seemed unconvinced. She knew he would rather the money had been spent on a book.

"Very grown-up," she told him. "I'm glad they didn't make you get one with those nasty fins."

"Got us crab for lunch," John said, crossing to the kitchen with a large cardboard box, and he actually kissed her in passing.

"They're called Malibu boards," Julian told her precisely. "Bill knows how to use one. He said he'll show me how to do it standing up. But I'm not worried."

"Good," she said and ruffled his hair so that he looked less neat and vulnerable.

Skip stamped through in her swimsuit and grabbed him quite roughly by the arm. "Come on," she said. "That's only a baby's board but you can still go fast on it."

John ran after them without a backward glance.

"You coming?"

She turned and found Bill standing in his bedroom doorway, wearing the mustard-yellow shorts. They were still damp, she saw. They clung. "I'd better get lunch ready," she told him. "The sea'll make you all ravenous. I'll have a go later."

"OK."

"I started reading your book," she said. "Sorry."

"That's OK."

"The Updike one I mean. Not one by you. I'd finished mine and . . ."

"It's OK," he said again, grinning, and she saw she was being odd. As he pushed open the door to the veranda, she saw there was a still-livid scar across one of his shoulder blades.

They had bought live crabs. Expecting neat parcels of cooked flesh redistributed into cleaned-up shells, she opened the cardboard box and gasped absurdly to find rubber-banded claws and four pairs of stalky eyes. She slammed the lid back down in a kind of rage. She had never cooked crab before. John *knew* this. How dare he assume she could? It was so typical, so maddeningly typical that in his sweet, unworldly way he assumed it to be yet another standard part of feminine capability. And to think her capable of such cruelty. She had a good mind to carry them down to the shoreline and toss them one by one over the heads of the startled swimmers.

She had bought cheap Cyprus sherry to make a syllabub for supper one night. Seething, she sloshed some into a mug and sat heavily on a kitchen chair. She drank and felt better but she sat on, listening to the sounds of distant pleasure from the beach and the closer, secretive stirrings of the crabs in the box.

A pair of brown, sandy feet stomped into her field of vision.

"I'm hungry," Skip said flatly. "What are you doing?"

"Drinking cooking sherry and failing to make lunch. Oh hell. You don't eat meat."

There was a pause.

"Fish doesn't count. The water has to be at a rolling boil," Skip said. There was a clatter as she opened and slammed a series of cupboard doors and found a high-sided pan, filled it at the sink and slapped it on to a gas ring. "There isn't a lid but I guess we could use this baking tray thing."

Frances sat up and in her surprise drained the last of the sherry, which really was not at all bad. "I thought you were surfing."

"Yeah, well . . ." Skip began and she sat at the other chair and peered into the box at the crabs. "Julian needs to learn." Frances heard the echo of a jeer in the way she said her son's name.

"All boys together, then?" she asked. Skip merely nodded, stroking a crab's impotent claw with a finger. "They'll be tired after lunch," Frances told her, "and we can make the fathers even sleepier with beer. Then you can teach me. How's that?"

"OK," Skip said. She still did not smile but the atmosphere between them discernibly lightened.

"Tell me about your mother. I only met her once."

"She died. She fell out of a window."

"I know but . . . before that."

Skip met her gaze a moment then shrugged. "I was small," she said. "I don't remember much. If you're scared of dropping the crabs in when it boils, I could do that for you and you can butter some bread. Do we have mayo?"

"Mayonnaise? Er. No. There's salad cream. Would that do? It's Heinz." Frances stood. "And there are tomatoes and lettuce and, let's see . . ." She opened the cupboard where she had unloaded cans and jars. ". . . and there's a big can of Russian salad."

BLUE HOUSE

As a child, she recalled quite clearly, there had been few things so stressful as being expected to enjoy oneself. Birthdays, theater trips, even food could be ruined by the oppressive weight of others' hopes, by raised faces around a room requiring joy. There was something of that now. She felt them looking to her to enjoy herself, watching her for reactions. Men were like that, always needing to know they had pleased one. It made them so much easier to offend than women. She *was* enjoying herself. It was a lovely cottage, a beautiful beach, but she would soon stop enjoying it if they did not stop watching her.

"You don't have to watch me," she told John. "I won't fall to pieces just because you go off and enjoy a walk on your own."

"Sorry," he said. "Was I staring?"

"Sorry," she echoed. "That was rude of me."

And they both smiled and he took a Thermos and went for one of his long walks, with a little book on bird identification she had given him apparently.

It was the house. The same house. Beneath the tarted-up paintwork and pretty fabrics lurked the grim, brown bungalow scorched so deeply on her memory by events that no disease could quite obliterate. She recognized it at once, from the car, and foolishly began to say so. Realizing then that neither John nor, thank God, Will had recognized it too, she fogged her recollection in a nice show of elderly confusion. Still, she was watching them now. Not as the men watched her, for gratifying signs of pleasure, but for tokens that they were remembering and pretending as well.

She swam before the beach filled up, which was delightful. The water's iodine iciness smacking over her seemed to return her to herself so that she knew entirely who she was and felt everything about her, toes, fingers, scalp, as if it were brand-new, not old and wrinkly. The public pool never did this; warmth and chlorine and the faint suggestion of amniotic fluid prompted by the urinous presence of so many small children, some of them not even walking yet, dulled one's bravest efforts to strike out alone and one emerged without renewal or refreshment.

After that it was good to sit on the veranda. She was not supposed to sunbathe any more, since an outcrop of bad moles they cut off her a few years ago, and since her mid-fifties and the onset of what Poppy coyly called The Change, had found she overheated easily. It was as though menstruation had been a discharge of heat as well as blood and now the slightest thing, a polo neck, sunshine through double glazing, a department store scent section, could leave her feeling steam was about to burst through her eyes.

"My thermostat's gone," she would joke as she tugged off a layer of clothes or fought to open a window, and people would look the other way because aging woman and hot flesh in the same thought process was not quite nice. So; no more sunbathing. But she could toast her legs a little while the rest of her sat in shadow. That felt good. And Will erected a sunshade beside the veranda so it was shadier still. But once the car park at the top of the drive began to fill and the sands became congested, even sitting on the veranda was oppressive. It was not just the noise. People stared with envious curiosity because they wanted a house in such a place and wondered how such a woman, an overheating old woman, came to be there on her own. Even with the sunshade in place, Frances felt too much on display. She retreated to the patch of garden at the rear with its spiky plants, glimpses of gaudy golfers and view of the curious encampment.

She made an effort to read one of the novels John had borrowed from the library for her.

"Found you a new one by her. You said you liked her."

She had resisted asking do I because yes, it was by a novelist she enjoyed. She knew that as she knew her own name and that these were her pearls. But he need not have troubled to find her a new one because any of the old ones would have done. Their plots all seemed unfamiliar now and would probably have been jumbled in any case.

It was amusing enough, a waspish tale of a young urban widow forced to move to an insufferably cozy village she would doubtless come to love, but Frances soon tossed it aside, impatient at her inability to concentrate even long enough to remember the heroine's name. She made herself a cup of coffee and settled instead with one of the magazines Will had brought from the selection he sold at the shop. It was largely pictures. Pretty girls and pretty men, clothes nobody wore and houses where nobody normal could live. She flicked and stared, flicked and stared and found a kind of consolation in the thought that even to her son, who had all his faculties intact, the world these pages presented must seem like science fiction.

Will came around the side of the house. He had been swimming and had a towel slung over one shoulder. "There you are," he said.

"Here I am."

"Are you OK here? It's not very sunny."

"I don't really do sun anymore."

"Oh yes. But you're OK?"

"I'm fine."

"We can go out in a bit. If you like."

"I'm fine here. Honestly," she said and wished he did not look so disappointed. Like his father, he wanted her happy and amused. If only Poppy were here. Poppy could always be relied upon to make a woman feel useful. There would be little faces to wipe, little drinks to be made and messes to tidy away. "Crab," she added. "Crab and chips. Do you think we could find it anywhere?"

"I'm sure we could. Dad walking already?"

"Yes. He said he was doing a circular walk to Pentire Head and back. He said he'd be back in time for lunch but not to wait for him if it would cramp our style." She remembered this intelligence with a small sense of triumph, which in turn depressed her. "You've got a hairy chest," she said.

Will looked down and rubbed the mat of hair, abashed. "Yes," he said, as a complimented woman might say *this old thing*.

"You never used to have," she said, puzzled.

"I was probably younger then," he said, smiling. "You never used to read glossy magazines in Italian."

She looked down at the magazine. "Just one of my new talents," she said.

"I'll go and get dressed," he told her, patting her shoulder as he went in. "Then perhaps we can have an excursion. Go round a garden or something. Do you want an iced coffee?" he called from the kitchen. "I put a jug in to chill last night."

"Where did you learn to do that?"

He laughed. "I've always done it. Every summer. I think you taught me."

"Oh."

She flopped the magazine on to the gravel because it was making her hands sticky, then looked out at the scrubby field. The dog in the encampment there was tethered again, probably on account of the sheep beyond the golf course, but she had seen it playing in the waves this morning so there was no need to feel sorry for it. The young man with the suicidal urges emerged from his caravan, fed the chickens, stroked the dog then began to pick through the heap of driftwood and rubbish there. Finding what he needed, he went back inside. Above the noise from the beach, which she realized now was like the buzz from a huge party only with waves and seagulls among the guests, she heard the brief whirring of an electric drill.

"Talk to me while I shave," Will called from the open bathroom window.

"Shaving too, now," she murmured, joking. "Whatever next?" Then she added aloud, "I saw him when I was swimming. Our sad young man from the sea."

"Who?"

"Our sad young man."

"He wasn't so young. He was my age."

"You'll see. It's young. He was swimming too, with his dog, and he washed his hair then he shaved in a rock pool. Like a nymph."

"Nymphs don't shave."

"You know what I mean. Merman. Selkie."

"Did you talk?"

"No. I was swimming. Anyway I think he's decided it's politest to ignore us. Since we're so on top of each other."

"How do you mean?"

"He lives in the caravan over there. Hence the lovely long hair. He's a piecrust." There was a pause and she realized this was the wrong word.

"You mean crusty. A traveler."

"That's it. And the dog and everything. I talked to the woman in the stores yesterday and apparently there are lots down here. They don't really travel any more because the police were so beastly when they did and they like it here. They like the stone circles on the moor and hold ceremonies. Naked, she said. Bollock-naked ceremonies. She looked envious, if you ask me, silly cow. And she said the hospital down here is the first in the country to provide a white witch as one of its, you know, ministering people. Because of the heathens."

"Pagans."

"Yes. Look, there he is again." The young man re-emerged, wearing a shirt now and with something under his arm, a big wooden object. He untethered the dog, which jumped up to paw him in its excitement, then led it off along the track up the valley beside the golf course. The encampment looked vulnerable now that he had gone. He had not locked the caravan, if one could lock caravans, and anyone could have gone inside and helped themselves to whatever was there. She wondered what she would do if she saw an intruder go in. With sudden clarity, she remembered James Stewart desperate to warn Grace Kelly of the killer's return and powerless. She remembered the hot, unshifting feel of the film. The comic couple sleeping on their fire escape. The astonishing sexiness of Grace Kelly, provoking her crippled lover in a series of beautiful gowns. People always spoke of it as a murder film but it had always seemed to her that the murder was a red herring and it was all—murder and all—about relationships and commitment and the terror of getting involved with another life.

"What do you do for a love life?" she asked aloud. She should not have asked. He'd be cross. And she realized she had emphasized the you as though saying *as opposed to Grace Kelly*. But the shower was going so perhaps he had not heard. She wanted to know. She worried. It was not like men uselessly wanting women to be happy. Mothers were allowed to worry about sons. She knew it was forbidden territory however, because she had quizzed his sister about it often enough and been warned off.

"It's not our business," Poppy had said last time. "He'll tell us when he's ready. When he meets someone he'd like us to meet."

"But he's nearly forty. He might be lonely. I don't want him to be lonely."

"Well neither do I but asking him if he's got a boyfriend or a girlfriend or whatever is hardly going to make him happy if he hasn't, now, is it? And if he has, well then he has and presumably they make him happy enough. He doesn't ever *seem* lonely."

No. Will never seemed lonely, any more than he ever seemed unhappy. There were always friends and his friends seemed to overlap nicely with his job. But John had always been so controlled and aloof, at least until he retired, and she had always thought herself so restless and prickly and difficult. It never ceased to surprise her that such a pair should have raised such a son. Blithe, as the birthday rhyme had it. *Bonny and blithe and good and* the other thing. Poppy was much more the child they deserved. No, that was harsh and she did not intend that. Poppy was more the child that truly reflected them, bound their oddly allied natures in herself and reflected them back at themselves. Respectable *and* restless. Fixed, settled so *young*, and yet always obscurely riled. Whereas Will was so easily sunny.

So of course she worried about him. She worried he was lonely, but she worried too that he was pretending. His schooling, the harsh schooling she had acquiesced in but which she now bitterly regretted, had taught him perhaps to dissemble content in the name of good behavior and to choke back pain because that was the proper, manly way. Perhaps he placed advertisements and met people that way, which she gathered no longer bore the stigma it once had. Or perhaps he used the computer, an idea she did not understand but was afraid to have explained to her. She thought of the pain of girlhood Christmas lists, of laboring as hard over a letter to Father Christmas as one did over prayers, struggling for the just balance between tactful self-denial and naked greed, weighing up the image of one deeply desired thing against another, couching the whole, as her mother insisted, in a letter that had charm as well as a shopping list, gave news of home and family, asked kindly after the elves; only to thrust this labor of hours into the fireplace for a few seconds' brilliance. She remembered the panic if some fragment of charring paper failed to catch the updraft and fly up the chimney, the awful sense of failed ritual. Were these modern ways of finding love like that? Wish lists entrusted to the ether? She had no idea what Will wished for. Women tended to marry men who sooner or later revealed elements of their fathers and vice versa, but what of men who sought other men? Would Will end by pairing off with an approximation of her or of his father?

"Let's not wait for Dad," he said when he'd emerged, showered and dressed. "I want you to myself for a bit."

She knew this might be true but that it was also a kinder way of suggesting John might profit by a break from her.

The most likely pub to satisfy her yen for crab and chips was barely twenty minutes' drive in the direction John had set out to walk, overlooking the harbor at Saint Jacobs, a few bays around to the north from Polcamel. As with so many of the places they visited, Frances experienced an initial sense of having seen it before which was gradually muffled by a snowfall of unfamiliar details. She had a recollection of a rough-hewn fishing village winding steeply up two narrow lanes from a natural harbor formed by a dramatic fissure in the line of granite cliffs. She remembered, or thought she did, a working village with real fishermen mending nets and lobster pots while their wives sold the morning's catch or boxed it up for sending to London by train. Now there were more dinghies and yachts in the harbor than fishing boats. The uncompromisingly ugly ice works and pilchard cannery at the harbor's edge had become a gallery and a seafood restaurant respectively. The dirty beach where nets had once been hauled up for mending was now a low-tide car park where the vehicles were surely too new and German to come from so poor an area. Less Cornwall than Cornwall World.

The whole place was still pretty, prettier indeed than she remembered, for in making the painful transition from working community to holiday resort, it had taken on the look town-dwellers thought a fishing village should sport. Walls were newly whitewashed, their slates rehung. Window frames and doors were picked out in the Mediterranean blues and greens so common now as to have lost all boldness. Pelargoniums glowed on every narrow windowsill and the cats that still sunned themselves on the low, higgledy-piggledy roofs and garden walls were too sleek to be scraping a living off nothing but fish heads and discarded dogfish.

The pub had no music, at least, but was noisy with the booming bonhomie of visitors. By some miracle, Will found a freshly abandoned table on the harborside balcony and left her there while he fetched drinks. For a few minutes she nibbled at a packet of balsamic vinegar crisps and sipped her half-pint of local bitter, which smelled deliciously of elderflowers, and feigned contentment so he would not be disappointed. She pored with him over the menu which, far from the longed-for, unadorned crab and chips, offered only a lobster bisque, which she saw from a neighbor's bowlful was unpromisingly watery, and something rather complicated called a Medley de Mer. Will raised his eyebrows pointedly as the woman on the other side of Frances was joined by a family in identical fisherman's smocks.

"We're tourists too," she reminded him gently.

"Could we try to remember that we're hardly commercial tourists," he said, imitating a cruel old woman's voice. "It's bad enough to have to associate with tourists on board . . ."

She laughed, remembering another film she loved. *"In This Our Life!"* she exclaimed.

"Now Voyager," he corrected her.

"Bet you can't remember her name, though," she said.

"What, Bette Davis?"

"No. Gladys Cooper. She played the mother."

"Where did you dredge that up?" he asked, astonished.

"God knows."

The sailor-smocked children all clamored their lunch orders at once.

"This is hell," he said.

"It is, rather."

"Shall we have something in our fingers on the harbor wall instead?"

"Yes, please."

He fulfillled her yen to the letter, with a bag of vinegary chips from the fish and chip shop—a relic of the village she thought she remembered—and a couple of dressed crabs, which they picked from the shells with little wooden forks while sitting on the harbor wall.

"This is such fun," she said, meaning it. "You never tell me about your love life," she added because she was happy so did not care what prohibitions she flouted. "How do you manage?"

"Oh. I get by." He looked away, eating a chip. When he looked back and smiled his face had shaken off the look of pain she had surprised there.

"Don't you want a family?"

"Not really, Ma," he said. He mustered no smile for that.

"Are we so very off-putting an example?" she asked.

"Not at all." But his tone was too roundly affirmative to convince her. "Anyway," he added, deflecting her inquiry, "if there's any justice in heaven, I should probably end up with a gang of little thugs who preferred football to books and war games to either."

"Yes, but they'd be happy. You'd be a good father. When are the babies coming?"

"Tomorrow. And they're not babies anymore. Hugo's eight and Oz is reading already. They'd be livid to be thought of as babies. Hugo's start-ing to look so like me at that age it's unnerving."

"At that age you were good enough to eat."

"Was I?"

"You know you were." She smiled, remembering, then said, "Do you think Sandy's a good father?"

"Excellent, I suppose. Now how about an ice cream? We could drive home via the dairy at Trenellion. Buy some concert tickets while we're at it."

On their way back to the car she was drawn to the Ice Works Gallery. There was a gust of clattering sounds from inside the wide-open glass doors as of countless tiny hammers tapping.

"That noise," she said. "I'm sure that's the noise I've been hearing in the night." Other noises were added, cow bells, a football rattle, some-thing like handclaps, then they all stopped. "Shall we go in?" she said.

It was a sculpture show. *Roly Maguire: Pieces for Wind* a colorful poster announced. A big-boned, mannish woman was reading a news-paper behind a slate-topped table, a cigarette on her lips despite the "No Smoking" sign. Frances judged her to be seventy at least, or older. Her white hair, cropped in the French manner, was offset by a volumi-nous blouse in tangerine silk. She grunted hello without the cigarette leaving her lips. Everything about her said *I am a member of the local artistic community and I only work here as a favor.*

"You just missed them," she said shortly. "No wind in here obviously, so they're on a motor. Comes on every five minutes. Drove me mad at first but now I don't notice. Ha!" Her nervous laugh was like a bark. "Stay to look. It's worth the wait."

The sculptures were made from a variety of objects the artist seemed to have found. Driftwood predominated, much of it very rough still and unplaned by the tides, but there were also pebbles, fishermen's orange floats, green net, blue nylon rope and the strange, melancholy detritus left behind at the end of the beach season; dolls' limbs, a bereaved plas-tic sandal, a dog's studded collar, bouncy balls, water wings. Each piece was mounted on a pole or plank and formed an apparently accidental cluster of stuff. There were pleasing textures, the occasional splash of sun-bleached color, but no particular beauty and no meaning that Frances could discern. Then the woman turned a page in her paper and murmured, "Here goes," and one by one each sculpture was flung into motion by an electric motor. Some whirled like mad things, others turned slow circles like drunken beetles and some merely flapped back and forth like machines deprived of purpose. The common element was noise. Pebble clacked on pebble. A child's scarlet bucket jiggled up and down rattling a fistful of shells within. A sandal smacked repeatedly on the broken-off nose of a surfboard. Frances laughed. It was like being in a toyshop and having the displays about you spring to life. And some of the sculptures were surely intended to be funny. Then it all struck her as infinitely sad and she stopped laughing.

"It's wasted time, do you think?" she asked Will. "People thrashing away and getting nowhere for all their effort. Why not stand still?"

As if in answer to her question the power clicked off, and with one last click or whirr each sculpture flopped back into stillness. The mannish woman sighed in relief as she solved another crossword clue.

"Wonderful," Frances said.

"Good," said the woman.

"I mean I'll buy one."

"Mum, are you sure?"

"Of course. I want that one." She pointed at one in which a broken paddle was dragged over a series of pebbles set into a length of driftwood. "No. I'll have that. The one with the child's shoe. So funny! Don't fuss, Will. I've got some money put by. It can be a late childbirth present to myself," she told the woman, beginning to write a check. "It'll fit in the back of the car perfectly well."

"Ah, now you can't take these specific models," the woman said. "The motors are only for demonstration. He has to fit them out with the wind vane for you. Allow him a couple of days. I'll need your address for delivery."

"We're at Polcamel for another week," Frances told her. "It's called Blue House."

"I know the one. Very handy. He can drop it off in person and show you how to put it up."

Impulse purchases needed to be carried home at once, while the madness was on one. Already the sculpture was threatening to lose its fragile charm. Frances wanted to cancel the sale now, tear up her check, but felt borne along by the older woman's imperiousness, which was winning the day over Will's ineffectual caution.

"Of course, some of us preferred his earlier work," she was saying now. "He used to work in stone and proper wood. But it costs so much and then his other half died and he moved back here and started doing these. We all thought it would be a phase but he hasn't stopped yet."

The sculpture was growing in significance as she spoke.

"Well I love it," Frances said protectively. "There's a windy bit of our garden, on the river. It can go there and startle birds off the seedlings."

As planned, they stopped off at Trenellion on their way home to treat themselves to ice cream at the dairy and bought concert tickets as well as cornets. Frances wanted to see inside the former church but a rehearsal was in progress and a notice on the door barred their entry. As they drove back to Blue House the sun was on her face and she slipped in and out of an old-lady doze, starting awake when Will braked at junctions, mumbling an apology, then sliding helplessly back to sleep moments later. When they arrived, she felt sick and disorientated and went to her room to lie down in earnest, leaving Will to write postcards in peace. But she was no sooner on her back, shoes and skirt off and a nicely cool sheet pulled up to her shoulders than all sleepiness left her and her mind began to race in a kind of panic.

She had forgotten something dreadfully important—keys, a birthday, an appointment, a gas burner—and her thoughts were like a pair of hands feverishly opening a series of locker doors, opening and slamming each in mounting frustration as they found nothing within. And the longer their search was fruitless, the more she found she dreaded them finding something.

BEACHCOMBER

"Are you kidding?" Bill grinned across at John, who saw himself doubly reflected in his sunglasses. "After all that beer? I'm not even sure you should go in yet."

"It's been half an hour," Skip said. "I won't get cramp. I never get cramp."

"I'll take her," said Frances, folding down a page in the new novel she had started. "Julian?" But Julian was quite happy making a garden on the roof of his sand castle, a sun hat pulled down rakishly over his black eye. "Darling?" Frances turned to John but he raised hands in surrender.

"Too much crab," he said. "But it was delicious. You go. I'll guard your things."

She narrowed her eyes in what might have been irritation or an expression of complicity, picked up one of the new surfboards and followed Skip across the tide-ridged sand to the surf. John reached for the beer jug but found it empty. His tongue felt salty and he longed for water but could not muster the energy to go to the house. A variety of insects had emerged from the clumps of dried seaweed to feast on the fragments of crab and bread and butter that remained. He reached for his novel. He had abandoned the unsatisfactory C. P. Snow to reread *War and Peace*.

"You don't mind just being here?" he asked Bill. "I feel we should be showing you sights."

"After that ride yesterday I'd happily stay put for weeks," Bill said.

His torso was firm and tanned and covered in short black hair. Beside him John felt like a pale, newly-evolved creature lamenting its loss of coat and shell. His skin prickled in the sun. He knew he would regret not retreating to the shade of the veranda—he lacked Frances' enviable ability to turn brown without an intervening phase of lobster pink—but he was enjoying too much this unusual sense of having a proper family about him. "Three is such a vulnerable number," he said, surprising himself.

Bill started. He must have nodded off. "Pardon me?"

"You were dozing. I'm sorry."

"No, no. You were saying?"

"Three. It's a vulnerable number. I mean, it's good to have you with us."

"Oh. Good. Well it's good to be here, John."

They turned simultaneously as Skip and Frances shouted from the cold as a wave smacked their shoulders.

"She's so like Becky," John said. "It was quite startling when you arrived."

"Well, Becks was a tad more feminine."

"You didn't know her at this age."

"She was a tomboy?"

"Never that exactly," John conceded. "But she was formidable."

"You weren't close, though?"

"Not by the time you met her. She'd left me behind long before."

"And at this age?" Bill gestured to where Skip was falling off her surfboard in a valley of foam.

"I worshiped her. I'd have done whatever she told me." Saying this, John received a pin-sharp recollection of the taste of tears and the brutal finality of his sister's locked door. He snorted. "An abject slave."

"You going to have more?" Bill indicated Julian. John was taken aback at the baldness of the question.

"Possibly," he said, opting for bravado. Then heard himself add, "It's not easy."

Aware, perhaps, that the boy was listening, Bill rose and hunkered down beside Julian's castle. "How's it coming, buddy?"

"All right," Julian said, mortified at an adult entering into so childish a pastime.

"Maybe you can come for a ride on the bike later on."

"Yes please!" Instant enthusiasm. John thought of cricket and felt a twinge of envy.

"Well, I'm not sure . . ." he began.

"Aw, come on," Bill overrode him. "We wouldn't go far. It'd be fun for him. Eh, Julie? You ready for water in that moat yet?"

"It won't stay in. The sand's too fine," Julian said and continued arranging a neat border of mussel shells. Bill stood.

"Well try lining it with seaweed. I'll go fill the jug." He snatched the beer jug and headed over to the water's edge.

Watching him go, watching him pause to call out to the girls in the surf, John felt angry phrases surge up in his throat like bile. But there was nothing he could say without appearing a middle-aged killjoy. He pictured skidding tires, childish flesh flayed by hot tarmac. As if illustrating his thoughts, a motorbike engine gunned somewhere in the car park above.

"Julian?" Julian looked up. "How's the eye?"

"Bit sore. It's OK, though. I quite like it. I'm going to use crayons to sketch the colors in my diary as the bruise comes out. Do you think I could bring Lady Percy on to the beach and put her in the sand castle garden?"

"What if she got lost?"

"But she wouldn't."

"But she digs, doesn't she? Imagine if she dug herself down in the sand and you couldn't find her. She could suffocate."

Why do we do this? he wondered. *Why are we so ready to fill their heads with fears?*

"Gerbils dig, not guinea pigs," Julian said. "Not much, I don't think."

"All the same."

Bill was returning, the cut glass jug slopping seawater. Behind him, Frances thrashed out through the waves, surfboard under arm, tugging off her bathing cap as she came.

"There's another motorbike," Julian said. "Coming down to Beachcomber."

John turned and saw a post office bike gingerly maneuvering a passage down the stony slope to the bungalow. "Hell's teeth!" he said.

He intercepted the telegram boy, who was indeed looking for him, and identified himself. It was from his deputy, Mervyn McMaster, demanding he call the office p.d.q. He tipped the boy, fetched change from his trousers and climbed the drive. The call box in the car park was stiflingly hot. Where city ones invariably stank of a mixture of urine and ear wax, this smelled of sugar and seaweed. Every surface felt sticky, from ice-creamy fingers, perhaps, or dried brine. Mervyn told him nothing at first.

"Give me your number and I'll call you back," he said.

Sweat beaded on John's lip and ran down his temples as he waited for the telephone to ring. A couple came to wait outside. They stared and he felt absurd for calling one of Her Majesty's prisons in swimming trunks and faintly criminal for using a call box for a long-distance call without spending cash. At the muffled ring, he answered with something like relief and turned his back on the couple. Mervyn wasted no time on courtesies.

"Farmer's gone," he said. "It was an outside job during exercise this morning. They used a ladder from a lorry. Dobey was overpowered with a garden spade. All over in minutes. Then all hell broke loose. I mean, Farmer, for God's sake! He didn't have long to go anyway. Sorry, John. You'd better come back. It'll be in the evening editions and the men knowing you're not here doesn't help much."

John was changing when Frances found him. There was no point packing. He had only holiday clothes here and a weekend suit. Nothing he would need. "But why?" she asked. "What can you do? The police will catch him."

"I have to be there. The men are upset. There's been trouble. Not a riot exactly but . . . I have to be there. Sorry. Can you drive me to Bodmin Road?"

"Of course. We can pick up their luggage while we're there. Oh, darling. We'd been looking forward to this for such ages. Can you come back?"

"Maybe. We'll see."

"Come on, then. We'd better hurry."

She was still in her bathing costume.

"You're not driving like that?" he asked, only he was telling her.

Impatiently she pulled a blouse and skirt on top and stepped into her white, wooden-soled sandals. While John was turning the Volkswagen around, she hurried on to the beach to explain to Bill what was going on and to ask him to mind Julian for her. Only she came back with all three of them.

John checked his impatience as people raced around locking doors and stacking away lunch things. After all, he might have hours to wait for a train. He had forgotten his Tolstoy. He wondered for a moment whether he could risk losing face and further time fetching it then decided he should read some newspapers instead, to help him wind back up from this lazy, holiday mode. Then everyone piled in at last and they were off. John drove. Frances was faster, he knew, but he needed to exert a measure of control. Bill apologized for holding things up but implied there might be money to pay for his luggage. Skip sulked. She had not wanted to leave the beach.

The road between Polcamel and Bodmin might have been hosting a rally for slow-moving caravans and tractors towing trailers of straw. Frances suggested a shortcut, which led to roadworks and a further delay.

"Why did Henry escape?" Julian asked as they waited for an impassive workman to show a *Go* sign.

John glanced at Frances.

"He'd have found out sooner or later," she explained, adding less forcefully, "it just came out."

"He won't be on the run for long," John told Julian. "They never are."

"Will he be punished?"

"Of course. His sentence will be extended. There may be a charge brought against him for assaulting an officer, though I don't know the details of that yet. He certainly won't be working in the rose beds for a while." He rarely discussed the prison with his son. It felt strange.

Frances waxed conversational, perhaps out of nerves. "The escapee was a pal of Julian's," she explained to Bill. "*Such* an old character. Raped a postmistress."

"He wasn't a pal," Julian exclaimed hotly. "I hardly know him. And he smells funny. They all do. They stink."

"Don't show off," Frances told him mildly. "It's all right to have been his friend. Pa's explained to you before about debts to society. But he's done wrong again and he'll have to be punished. You can make friends with someone else. Maybe you can write him a note when he gets back."

"He most certainly can't!" John snapped. "Now could we please change the subject? I'm going to be hearing about nothing else for the next week."

"Yeah. You poor bastard," Bill said. "Oh. Sorry."

"Bill said a rude word," Julian crowed.

"It's a character in *King John*," Bill told him. "By Shakespeare. Gets all the best speeches."

"Look, children," Frances called out. "There's Bodmin jail!"

"Why can't you live here?" Skip asked. "Then you'd be near the beach."

"Closed down long ago," John told her. "More's the pity. Something tells me we're going to need more prisons, not fewer."

The children were left firmly in the car while Bill went in search of his luggage, which apparently included his precious typewriter so he was planning on working. John bought his ticket and newspapers and snatched the quiet moment with Frances they had been deprived of by acquiring passengers. "I'm so sorry," he said. "Leaving you so soon. And with all this."

"I'm sorry I snapped," she said, and fastened a button on his shirt which had worked loose. "It's not your fault after all. Bloody bastard Farmer."

"Frances!"

"Well he is. Spoiling our holiday. Most inconsiderate."

"While Bill's here, you won't . . ." he began.

"What?"

"You won't let him take Julian on his motorbike, will you? He's got some damned fool idea of a jaunt and even if they stay off the road, that track's lethal. It's illegal anyway. I'm sure it is."

"Of course I won't."

"Promise?"

She frowned. He too was unsure why this was suddenly so important to him. Perhaps he was still a little drunk from lunch. He wanted to kiss her. Properly. With hands. Right here.

"I promise," she said. "And I'll make sure he writes his diary and does one culturally enriching activity per day. At least. There's that music festival. Maybe we can all go to a concert."

"You think that's Bill's thing?"

"Probably not. But he's a guest so he'll do as he's told. Is this your train?"

It was only a clumsy, fumbled, off-to-work sort of kiss. He remembered too late that he had forgotten to say goodbye to Julian or the others. As the train snaked out along the wooded valley, he tugged down the window and leaned out. He saw the Volkswagen pulling out of the car park and waved furiously in case the children were looking but its steeply angled windows were catching the afternoon sun so he could not see if they were waving back or had failed to notice him.

He found an empty compartment, began to read a paper and fell heavily asleep as the lunchtime beer triumphed at last. He woke briefly at Liskeard and Plymouth then woke in earnest at Newton Abbot where the rails followed a long stretch beside the sea and dived in and out of crimson South Devon cliffs. Reading his clutch of newspapers from cover to cover, downing a pork pie, a Bar Six and a cup of stewed tea from the buffet car, he felt a lessening of pressure. Whatever the trials of his working life, there remained a masculine predictability to it, a quality of the known beside which family life was fraught with ambiguities and scrambled attempts at communication.

BLUE HOUSE

On one level John judged the holiday a success. The weather was glorious and the house charming. Frances was swimming every day and resting and enjoying having twenty-four-hour access to Will again. When they first came down the drive, despite the new tarmac and the drastic metamorphosis of the grand landlady's manor to a golf club, he had recognized the house and setting with a horrible shock, bad memories reaching out at him like so many pungent smells. But Frances appeared to remember little, certainly none of the bad things, and the house had been so altered as to conspire in her merciful amnesia.

If the holiday was a disappointment for him, it was so only because he had unwittingly subscribed to the false hope that the sunny break would beget change and renewal. Instead, naturally, it shed bolder light on unchanging problems. She was as ill here as she was at home, just as his joints ached as much, he still had to pee twice a night and he slept every bit as fitfully. Frances slept like a baby, curled rather heavily against him and not even waking when cramp forced him to kick a leg out from under the covers or to jump from the bed to pace about.

When the second day began with him taking a second long walk alone, he realized he had been cherishing naïve dreams of her reaching out to him in daylight as she did in sleep. But they were a long-retired pair, not some hardworking young couple eager to rediscover each other. In retirement, he perceived, they had carefully carved out a simulacrum of the parallel lives their marriage had presented during his life as a governor. They did not, like vivacious grayheads in advertisements, celebrate joint old age with cruises and birdwatching and shared hobbies, but continued to respect one another's privacy to the point of leading nearly separate lives under one roof. Only the garden united them, and grandchildren.

He longed for Sandy's arrival with the boys. Their way of eliding *grannyandgrandpa* gently pressed a coupledom on to him and Frances he had scarcely felt since the first years of marriage. Hugo and Oscar reminded them to be husband and wife rather than mere considerate companions, or to play, at least, the sentimental, Ribena-mixing, toffee-offering roles expected of them.

Meanwhile it was not entirely without relief that he accepted the opportunities Will created for him with such clamorous tact to go off and explore on his own. It was not, as Will thought, to escape Frances, however, and the constant, depressing responsibility she presented, but to escape from Will. He found himself unexpectedly shy of his son. The formalized stages of a birthday supper or Sunday lunch—arrival, drinks, meal, exchange of news, walk around garden, small piece of symbolic home improvement involving one of Will's power tools, departure—could hardly be practiced over a fortnight's holiday. Had his son been married or had a boyfriend or whatever, the problem would not have arisen since there would have been other people filling the conversational void and the well-established pavane for cohabiting couples to be paced through. As it was, the desire to ask unaskable questions was almost intolerable. The sense of what they were not discussing, of who Will might otherwise have asked on holiday, was a constant irritant beneath the idle chit-chat and self-indulgent small excursions to galleries, gardens and restaurants. Time was, John thought, when someone could be introduced as a maiden lady or confirmed bachelor and the mind accepted it without this restless searching after other, juicier explanations. It was not that earlier times were more innocent, but that they were more respectful of privacy, even to the restraining of thoughts. Now where lenses and biographers pried, one's curiosity felt compelled to follow.

Will was being scrupulous in observing their timetables. He ate when they normally ate, left time for little lie-downs and postprandial dozes. There was a weighty sense of a son doing his duty. John tried to imagine himself at that age, however, and found another early-middle-aged man wed as much to duty and job as to his family. The only real difference was children. He had never appreciated until now how much emotional clamor, interference almost, the presence of children set up, saving a relationship from listening to itself. One often heard comments made in envy of childless couples, of the money they saved, the selfish freedoms they retained, knew indeed this lay behind much of the mistrust that greeted couples of the same sex, but in truth the ability of such couples to endure the total, unimpaired scrutiny they could train on their relationship year in year out, meant they were owed more awe than envy. He wrote this in a long letter he composed in his head, a letter to Sylvia, then remembered how many same-sex couples were famous for their surrogate families of dogs and cats.

Dear Sylvia, he wrote instead on a postcard of the mouth of the Camel estuary, *we can see this view from our veranda, when the beach isn't packed. V. hot but doing a lot of walking. Stay sane.* He made to cross out the last comment then realized that would lend a sinister weight to it so let it stand. *All good wishes, John.* He addressed it, stamped it and added it to the combined heap he and Will were building on the veranda table. A walk to the village letter box would fill nicely the interval between tea and the evening's first, welcome drink.

Will was being extremely efficient. He had a list of names and addresses he had run off from his computer's database and was striking them out as he wrote to them. Their eyes met briefly as Will tossed a card on to the heap.

"Ridiculous exercise really," Will said. "Like Christmas cards."

"Only less depressing."

"How so?"

"You aren't crossing off the ones who've died since last year. And you can still remember who they all are."

Frances emerged in her toweling robe, refreshed from her sleep and keen for a swim now that the crowds were draining away. John would have liked to go with her for once but Will was up and offering before he could say anything. If all three of them had gone it would have entailed a tedious delay while the house was locked up. So he pretended to be tired and contented himself with watching their tall figures cast even taller shadows as, changed, Will ran out to join her crossing the sands. He was touched at the way she took Will's arm as they went and felt a sweet, familiar ripple of jealousy at her ease of confidence in the boy. Since Will was five or six, it seemed, John had been coming into rooms or round corners and surprising them deep in conversation. It amazed him that they had spent most of the day together yet could still find things to discuss. Challenged once, she had said, "Oh, you know. We talk about people."

It would have aroused his jealousy less had she said they discussed the deepest secrets of her heart. He knew *people* to be her favorite subject, the life-as-novel at which she excelled, a topic at which John, being too scrupulous for idle supposition, remained a pious dunce.

They began to swim and were lost to sight. He stopped watching and began another postcard. It was the same view as Sylvia would get. He had bought the same view fifteen times. Frances had teased him for showing so little imagination. His correspondents could hardly be expected to compare cards and what if they did? It was a good view, the view from the veranda, photographed with some accuracy.

It was odd writing to Poppy knowing that Sandy and the children would be at his side by the time she read it, as it meant he could write to her as his daughter, as a beloved child even, rather than address her as a careworn wife and mother. *Poppy darling. We can see this view from the veranda,* he wrote. *When the beach isn't too packed . . .*

Then a telephone started to ring and broke his concentration. It took him a while to realize it was Will's mobile and he hesitated before answering. Only the awful thought that Sandy and the children might be about to cancel made him snatch it up. "Hello?"

"Darling," a woman said. "How's the Sunset Home for the Young at Heart?"

"Er. Hello?" he said again. "Will Pagett's telephone?"

"Oh. Oh God. Sorry. Is that John?"

"Yes."

"Just the man I was after, actually." She coughed nervously, plainly mortified. John thought it was rather funny and admired her for not simply hanging up.

"That's Harriet, isn't it?" he said.

"Yes. And how *is* the bloody Sunset Home?"

"It's fine. Young at heart. We've got a wonderful view. Beach on the doorstep. Literally. You should come down."

"I wish."

He liked Harriet best of all Will's women friends. She was sexy and he liked the way she swung nervously between flirtation and trying to talk like a man. She had always shown him a refreshing lack of respect, which was flattering to his age and amusing, given that she had ended up working for the prison service too. Frances had nursed fond hopes of Will marrying her one day. John had been treacherously gleeful when the idea was categorically rejected. "Will's swimming," he told her. "Shall I get him to call you back?"

"No. Well, if you like. But listen, John, I was serious. It *was* you I wanted to speak to."

"You don't have to be polite, Harriet." He paced the room as he talked and caught sight of himself; sun-tanned old man with incongruously young communication device pressed to his ear.

"I know. I'm calling unofficially, John, but I'm calling from work on work business."

"Yes?"

"It's our mutual friend in Rio. I thought it only fair to warn you."

"Oh God," he sighed. "Another bloody color supplement feature! It's such an old story. You'd have thought that by now—"

"No, John. Listen, will you. They're going to extradite him. At long last."

"But he's an old man. Well. Not *so* old. My age. He must be, what, seventy-five?"

"And obscenely rich and on his third marriage. But not beyond the reach of the law, apparently. Not anymore. It's not definite yet but he's even been teasing us, talking about making his peace with the old country and coming back to face the music."

"Secure in the knowledge that he's become such a media favorite most juries would be rejected by the prosecution or would acquit him. Why?" John sat on the sofa. He felt faint.

"Once he realized extradition might finally be going to push through, despite his lawyers' best defense, he probably thought he should save face. After all, if he comes back voluntarily, even after all this time, it goes in his favor. John?"

"Yes. I'm still here."

"I just thought I should tell you. If it does happen, the press'll have a feeding frenzy, it being the silly season. They'll rake everything up. I thought you should be ready. But it's not official yet and it may not even happen. If it does though, we can't protect you like in the old days. The press isn't what it was. They know everything now and what they don't know, they'll ring you up for. Or they'll make something up. OK?"

"OK. Thanks, Harriet."

"Not at all. Give my love to that handsome orderly."

"I will."

Another telephone rang in the background. She swore like a navvy as she hung up.

John went directly to the kitchen, poured himself a splash of Scotch and downed it in one needy swig. Then he poured himself a second, longer one, with some ice, and took it back to the sofa. All at once that other house, that other time, were here about him. For all the girl's touching concern, this business scarcely stirred him now beyond a vague desire to grind his teeth when he saw their *mutual friend*'s bronzed, smug old face pressed up against some nymphet's in a magazine. It stirred up much, however, that he would rather have left untroubled and unremembered. Ugly revelations. Unholiday violence. Bad words whose damage had never been healed but merely scabbed over. What misguided nostalgia had possessed Poppy to send them back here?

Hearing a motorbike engine nearby, he ran out, still clutching his drink, heart in his mouth. But it was nothing, of course, or not what he had irrationally feared, merely a groundsman speeding a quad bike about the golf course.

"John?"

He spun round at the veranda's end to see Frances and Will returning through the gate from the beach. He waved, smiled, said he would fix them both drinks as well, but for a moment she had seen his face. For a moment, too, he had seen her younger self, ebullient on a young man's arm, blithely unaware of the effect she was having.

While they warmed up in the shower and dressed, he snatched the pile of postcards, although both he and Will had several more to write, and took it up the track to the letter box. He hoped to still his thoughts with walking but the flood of poisoned memories was such that he had posted the cards in a clumsy fistful before he remembered that Poppy's was still only half written. He imagined her concern as she turned it over in her hand, heard her sad assumption that such forgetfulness spelled the beginning of a senility so stoutly held off until now. He wondered again at her motives in booking this house and recognized the open-handed innocence of the gesture. He felt a glow of consolatory pride that there, at least, was someone they had always succeeded in protecting, someone undamaged, in her youth at least, by too much of the wrong sort of truth.

BEACHCOMBER

A gust of wind blew rain against the windows so abruptly that they both looked up. There was another gust and the door came open. Bill stopped typing and went to close it. Julian rearranged himself in the armchair, trying to be as much like a cat as possible while still reading *The Happy Prince and Other Stories*. He wanted Bill to notice but Bill merely strode back to the dining table and continued typing the moment he sat down, as though he had been mid-sentence when he broke off.

His words were an unstoppable flow apparently. Julian knew all about writers and painters having Muses—had recently learned all the Muses' names and disciplines by heart to impress his father, who had not been impressed at all but had merely corrected his Greek pronunciation. He had always pictured a Muse as a lovely blonde lady in a white pleated dress and gold sandals who would sort of kiss the writer on the back of the neck and murmur ideas in their ear so they believed they were having the thoughts themselves. But now that he was seeing writing in progress, he realized that someone like the lady behind the library counter was more appropriate, someone with huge bosoms but no children and with two sets of spectacles, who knew where every book was shelved and could even summon up its Dewey decimal number, even though it was obvious she thought nine-tenths of the books published not worth reading.

The words came and came and if they stopped for a minute or two, Bill frowned and kept his hands ready at the keyboard. It reminded Julian of Ma's relentless piano exercises and did not seem fun in the least. Julian had tried reading just one word to each click of the typewriter keyboard but it began to make him feel sick. He revised his ambition to become a writer and reinstated an earlier one of being merely very rich.

Overnight the weather had changed. Something called a *cyclonic gloom* had arrived bringing a thick lid of gray cloud and intermittent, stinging showers that soon emptied the beach. It was, Julian decided, rather pleasant. For once breakfast had brought no insistence on bracing outdoor activity or cultural expedition and, finding him guiltily curled up in an armchair with a book, Ma had merely stroked his hair and said what a relief it was that he knew how to entertain himself. A particular stress in her comment plainly indicated Skip, who had already complained loudly about the weather and how there was *nothing to do* and had twice been reprimanded for swearing. Ma was currently pacifying her with a shopping trip to Bodmin.

The prose drew him in again and he forgot to be a cat, forgot all about Bill in fact. It was a book he had read several times before and found himself rereading at least once a year. He felt compelled to do so only partly by the content of the stories, all of them sad and most of them unsettling. They were a little like Hans Christian Andersen's tales of cold Kay with the shard of looking-glass in his heart and the mermaid prepared for love to feel as though she walked on knife blades. Wilde's cruel Infanta and amoral Star-Child affected him in a similar way. He sensed there were darker truths, adult truths, behind the self-consciously fairy-tale tone. These were stories adults never offered to read at bedtime. There was something fascinatingly sickly about them too, like the fluttering of wounded birds or the terrible wincing of salt-sprinkled slugs. *Life is savage,* the stories said. *People are vicious. But there is love and there is a chill, unloving beauty in stars and flowers, and both can be admired.*

Julian was also compelled in his reading of them by an interesting fog of disapproval that seemed to hang about adults when they spoke of the book and its author. Ma implied that the stories were *not quite nice*, as though Mr. Wilde had gone too far, as though making stories so desperately sad were a kind of showing off. He sensed that what she was actually saying was no more about the stories than the stories were about what they said they were about. There was a darker truth at work. She disapproved of the author, or was frightened of him, but something stopped her saying this aloud so she voiced vague unease about the stories instead.

The Puffin edition said little about him other than that he had written the stories for his two little boys. However, Julian found *The Birthday of the Infanta* in a cherished Puffin anthology of his, *A Book of Princesses,* where a more detailed author biography said that Wilde's middle names included the wonderful Fingal O'Flahertie and that he had been sent to prison for two years and had subsequently died in France. He had gone to prison, it said, because he was convicted of libel in 1895. He had been criticized, it said, for his *eccentricity and morals*. Asking, with no specific reference, what libel was, he was surprised to find it was merely speaking ill of another, surely not a crime worthy of prison, not like abducting children or killing your wife.

Exploring his parents' big bookcases one day he found *The Complete Works of Oscar Wilde*. Like a bible it was bound in dark blue leather and stored in a special box. Only it was more frightening than a bible and he soon saw that the box was to restrain not to protect it. It had an unread smell and the paper was so thin you could see through it.

Julian hid behind the biggest sofa and turned the pages one by one, stopping to read now and then but too nervous not to keep moving on. The book clearly had a power, like a book of spells, and might do things to him that were not necessarily pleasant if he read too much at a go. There were pictures—surely a rarity in grown-up books—and they were strange, even nasty: Salome kissing John the Baptist's head on a dish, a portrait of a monstrously ugly man being stabbed by a terrified young one who looked like an angel and there, near the back, a dim photograph of a prison, Reading Prison, only the book rather quaintly called it Reading Gaol.

At first he had been amazed and thought it was a prison specifically for writers, where perhaps they were forbidden to read or made only to read the books the governor chose for them, like special Sunday books only all week. Then he had said the name aloud, in the car one day, when he saw it on a signpost, and Ma had laughed at him and said,

"Redding, silly. It's pronounced *redding*," adding, with sinister carelessness that sounded like a covert warning, "there's a prison there. You can see it from the train."

Daunted by his parents, he had resorted to asking Henry. A man jailed (as Will then suspected but now knew for certain) for raping a postmistress in the course of a robbery could hardly disapprove of a man who had been imprisoned merely for saying something bad about someone else.

"Henry, why don't people like Oscar Wilde?" he asked.

The answer was straightforward but sadly had met a mystery with a riddle. "'Cause he was a shirt-lifter," Henry said. "A chutney ferret. No one likes one of those and you shouldn't either. You ever find yourself with an arse-bandit like that you get your back to the wall and if he gives you any trouble you break his nose."

Henry was rarely so vehement. Something in his face frightened Julian and he hurriedly changed the subject by asking to roll cigarettes rather than demand a translation. He added the words to his forbidden list however. *Arse-bandit. Shirt-lifter. Chutney ferret.* Knowing they were bad, while having absolutely no idea of their meaning, anatomical or otherwise, only added to their potency.

The statue of the Happy Prince, stripped of its gold and no longer admired, was taken down and melted. Julian paused. He did not turn greedily to the next story as he sometimes did, but relished instead the odd ache the sad tale induced in him, a sort of hopeless, deep-down wish to turn back time and change things. It was almost remorse, as though by reading the story he had made the sad things happen for the selfish pleasure of feeling—what? This curiously pleasurable hurt somewhere in his chest? Then he realized the typing had stopped.

He looked up and found Bill watching him. He had amazing eyes. Dark as a dog's, they looked too close and saw too much. He was like a man off a big poster who had come to life but had not learned to tone himself down and look like everyone else. Ma often said of people that they were *too much*. Bill was too much. Julian looked down, turned a page and started to read again but he was only pretending and the words danced. He looked up again and found Bill still watching. Bill smiled.

"You're really into that, aren't you, Julie?" he asked.

"Er, what do you mean?"

"I mean you really like reading, don't you?"

"Sometimes I like it best of all," Julian admitted. "Better than real life. Once I pretended to be ill so I could stay in bed and finish *The Weirdstone of Brisingamen*. It was too scary to read at night but I had to know what happened."

"I wish Skip read like that. I mean, she reads when she has to, when she has a comprehension to write or a history chapter to do but . . . books have never grabbed her."

Julian remembered his parents' instructions that he was to be especially nice to Skip because she had a dead mother. "She likes other things," he suggested. "She runs very fast and she's a good swimmer. If we fell off a boat, I'd drown and she'd survive."

"She'd save your life," Bill said. "Got her gold lifesaver medal last fall." He stood and stretched so vigorously that his shirt came untucked and Julian saw his belly button. "You wanna come out on the bike?"

Julian glanced out. The rain had stopped and sunshine was breaking through the clouds at last. Nothing would frighten him more and yet he wanted it more than anything. "Why?" he asked, playing for time. "Have you finished your book?"

"No way near." Bill laughed and tugged a sheet of half-typed paper from the machine. "But I could use the air."

"The ground'll be wet. We might slip."

"We might but we won't. Come on. It'll be fun. Put some color in those bookish cheeks."

Julian felt himself blush. He hated blushing even more than being told not to show off or to grow up. "Pa said I wasn't to," he admitted scrupulously. "Ma told me."

"Well he's not here to see. Don't you want to? I mean, I don't mind. I just need some air. I'm meant to be keeping an eye on you and if you come too I can do both at the same time."

The way he said this made it seem as though Julian would be impolite *not* to accept. Besides, Bill spoke walking to his room, as though the answer were not something that mattered greatly.

"Yes please, then," Julian said.

Bill made him wear his huge leather jacket. "Makes you look bigger and it'll protect you if you fall off. Not that you're gonna."

He straddled the bike and Julian climbed on the back. He made sure Julian's sandals rested in the right place because there was a pipe that got really hot, and he told Julian to hold on to him tightly. Then he started the engine and they were off.

He must have sensed Julian was nervous and did not want a policeman to find them breaking the law so he stayed off the road. First they went up the drive to the car park and down again, which was frightening because the gravel slipped underneath them and the motorbike kept going sideways. Then Bill drove them out on to the beach. The tide had not long gone out so the sand was still damp and firm. They made big circles. They flew along on the water's edge raising a salt spray that splashed their legs. They described a figure of eight over and over until Julian was laughing so much he was afraid he might wet himself. Only he didn't care. Bill felt totally safe, the way a big brother was supposed to. He didn't bother wearing a jacket in case they fell off so Julian could feel the heat of him through his shirt and smell him. Close to he smelled different from Pa, who smelled of Old Spice and ironing. Maybe because Bill did not wear proper shirts like Pa's, you could smell him instead of starched cotton.

The speed took his breath away. Once Bill knew he was holding on tight and would not fall off, he caused the bike to fly along in great surges that made Julian feel he had left half himself behind and it needed to catch up. Because he was so much shorter than Bill, he could not rest his chin on his shoulder and he was a bit nervous of them stopping suddenly and him hitting his nose and making it bleed, so he pressed his cheek against Bill's back and watched the blurring sea sideways on.

When they stopped because Bill wanted to type more of his book, Julian had to fight the temptation to be babyish and demand they carry on. As it was, he was clinging on so tightly that Bill had to prize his hands off and laughed, saying how sweaty Julian had made his back. This made Julian feel awkward so he got off and quickly took off the huge jacket, even though it gave off a good smell, like horses and Henry's tobacco.

"I won't tell your mum if you don't," Bill said.

When they came back indoors, Julian needed to pee. But he also felt a strange need to be alone to adjust. It was as though all the flying up and down and around on the motorbike had blown his face into strange distortions, like astronauts in training, and he needed to sit calmly to let it settle. So he sat on the lavatory a little longer than was necessary. Washing his hands, he paused to examine himself because he still felt peculiar. The black eye was a shock, of course, now that it was turning a rich purple with greenish edges, but it was a surprise to find no other change visible for his lips felt hot and swollen and his eyes felt twice their usual size, like Johnny Morris's lemur's on *Animal Magic*.

While Bill continued to type, only pausing to light another cigarette or take hurried gulps at a mug of iced coffee, Julian found he could not concentrate on his book anymore. It was too familiar suddenly and the chair fabric felt too prickly on his bare legs and the urge to talk and be silly was almost overwhelming. Instead he went into the back garden to give Lady Percy a carrot. While she munched in frantic little rushes, nose quivering, wary of the shadows of circling gulls, he pressed his nose into her fur and hummed *Gentle Jesus Meek and Mild*.

When she came back with Ma, Skip knew immediately what they had been up to. "You rode on the bike," she said.

"You didn't!" Ma exclaimed. "Julian!"

Julian just stared, waiting for a cue from Bill, not wanting to get him into trouble. "What makes you think that?" he asked at last.

"What kind of babysitter do you take me for?" Bill asked. "I rode. Julie just made me coffee and watched, didn't you, Julie?"

Julian looked at him and nodded and Ma set him and Skip to clearing the table for lunch.

But after lunch, when the grown-ups were dozing on their towels by the rocks, Skip made Julian come surfing with her. She was determined he should learn how to learn to use his board. And he wanted to because when she did it, it looked like fun.

"When Bill taught me," she said, "I was only four and we didn't use a board. We just used him."

"How do you mean?"

"How do you meeen?" She imitated his voice. Sometimes he hated her but he felt he had to follow her around and do whatever she said so in some way he must have liked her too. She was a bit like a big dog that could be fierce on your behalf if only you could work out how to train her and win her respect. *"I meeen,"* she said, "we used him as a board. He'd float and get me to lie on his back and hold on tight then he'd swim out and line himself up and catch a wave coming in and he'd bodysurf and I'd just cling on for dear fucking life."

"You swore!"

"So?"

"I know some bad words too. Really bad ones. I learned them from the prisoners."

"The convicts?"

"Of course." He had never told *anyone* this before. It was a huge risk. He realized how desperately he must want to be her friend.

Skip narrowed her eyes, standing firm against the surf churning around her. "Bet you don't know what they mean," she said.

"I do," Julian lied. "But it's just silly."

"So did you enjoy the bike?" she asked suddenly.

Her question was like a little knife pushed up under his armor and he had to answer truthfully only it came out all wrong and gushing and babyish.

"Oh, it was marvelous!" he said and she mocked his accent and his enthusiasm. "I don't make fun of *you*," he said at last.

"What's to make fun of?" she asked, maddeningly confident.

"Your ugly accent. Your manners."

"What about them? I'm American. So fucking what?"

"You're common," he said. "Only I'm not allowed to say that because your mother was killed."

"She wasn't killed, doll-brain," she said. "She fell out of a window. You don't know anything."

Curiously this cross exchange did not lead to a furious argument but seemed to make Skip relax with him. She was patient, even kind, as she showed him how to use the polystyrene board. When he finally succeeded in catching a wave and was dragged all the way to the shore, triumphant despite the pain of scraping his belly on sand and pebbles, she seemed genuinely pleased with him. Later, however, her mood turned sour again, as though she had suddenly remembered their earlier hostility. He was showing her a deep rock pool where he was sure a vicious Moray eel must lurk beneath the weeds when she suddenly said, "God, Julie, you're such a *girl*!"

"I'm not."

"How can you stand to let Bill call you Julie, then. It's a girl's name."

"It's short for Julian."

"Jules is short for Julian. Julie is strictly for girls. You're weird. You're a weird girly-boy."

"I'm not."

"Prove it."

Desperate, he pulled down his shorts so she could see. She narrowed her eyes for a moment or two and really looked, he saw her looking, but then she merely sneered as though she'd asked for a lobster and he'd offered her a prawn.

"*That*'s no good," she said. "Put it away. You're still girly."

"I'm not," he said, hoping he wasn't about to prove her right by crying, for his eyes were prickling.

"So?" she asked. "Prove it."

He did something braver than anything he had done before, braver than climbing over the prison roof, braver than going into the cellar with no lights on. He thrust his forefinger deep into the waving tentacles of a sea anemone. It closed its scarlet fronds about him and the stinging was so sharp and hot and worse than a nettle that it was all he could do not to cry out. Skip just watched his face, watching for tears. When he could bear it no more and tugged his finger out, she looked briefly at the fingertip, which rather disappointingly was not blackened or dripping blood. Then she made a slight sucking noise between her teeth and stood.

"You're still girly," she said. "But I won't tell."

Julian watched her return to the waves, lugging Bill's full-size surfboard. He sucked his finger furiously. *Beef curtains,* he thought at her, making his thoughts an all-destroying laser beam. *Chutney ferret.*

Then he remembered Ma saying that Henry had broken out of the prison. At first he had been sad about this, disappointed that Henry had not said good-bye or thought at least to wait until his return. Now his thoughts on the matter turned fearful. Henry in the prison garden, under guard, where he was a trusty and had to be nice because Julian was the governor's son was one thing. Henry in the wide world where he was anyone and Julian was nothing, where Henry was a rapist, was something else. Julian glanced up at the cliffs, imagining that Henry was watching from the tamarisk bushes and tree mallows, was despising him for letting a mere girl tell him what to do, Henry who would not stop at raping her, who would think nothing of slitting her from gizzard to belly button with a penknife. He comforted himself with the thought that now that Henry could roll his own cigarettes or buy as many as he liked with the postmistress's money, which he had probably buried in a well like the one in *Moonfleet*, a mere boy was nothing to him, even a girly one, and would be the last thing preying on his mind.

BLUE HOUSE

Will sat on the veranda swathed in a jersey, reading but not reading a new biography of Poulenc and trying to convince himself the cold, penetrating drizzle was no more than a sort of sea mist that would soon be burned off by the sun. He was alone, blissfully alone, Mum and Dad having clearly plotted together to give him a day of rest before Sandy and the boys arrived. They were shivering dutifully around some gardens on the Lizard, consoling themselves that at least he would be enjoying his day of solitude, but here he sat unable to enjoy himself or settle to anything.

Long before Mum gleefully reported back her findings he had already seen *that sad young man*, as she had dubbed their neighbor, shave in a rock pool. Every day he watched him walk the dog up on the cliffs, gather driftwood for his fire, go for the early morning swim during which he washed. At the risk of behaving like a stalker, he had twice now plucked up the courage to swim at the same time but swimming was not a conversational activity, at least not between strangers, and he was cowed by the stupidity of their first meeting and the pompous way he had spoken. He was fascinated in the way only possible with people about whom one knew almost nothing.

Once he had gone through the *no-no-I-insist* motions of offering to be Mum and Dad's driver for the day, he was impatient for them to be gone. Only as Dad drove them off did he realize this sense of urgency came from the fact that Sandy was arriving the next day, which left him less than twenty-four hours to do—what? They were complete strangers. In all probability they were not even on the same team. What had begun as a holiday hobby, fit to be polished up into an anecdote for Harriet, was assuming an emotional importance out of all proportion to its scant raw material.

This situation had never arisen before. In all the time he had been involved with Sandy, or been Sandy's arrangement or however one could best put it, Sandy had effectively annexed the square yards of emotional territory not devoted to work, friends or family. There had been the occasional adventure or mild flirtation, usually involving someone's friend from abroad or a temporary worker at the shop, but nothing major and certainly nothing that made him feel, as he so absurdly felt now, like a spouse tempted toward adultery.

What he had with Sandy was entirely sexual; inevitably, since Sandy already had a wife and family, more than enough to furnish an emotional life. For Will, however, this must have left a void. This scowling man, who appeared to save all his affection for his dog, aroused his desire, certainly, but desire was a commonplace. What consumed Will, what made mere interest feel like infidelity, was the hunger to know. What was the sad young man doing here? How did he make ends meet? Did he have no friends? What were his secrets? What or who did he think about as he lay in bed? All this, Will recognized, was the essence of romance; the tantalizing stranger, the inconsolable, brooding male. It was not the banal exchange of sex, different with every partner but ultimately, deadeningly, always the same. It was instead the holding out of a possibility; the invitation, threat rather, to discover and be known.

Curtains of drizzle blew across the beach. Mum always claimed that swimming in the rain made the sea feel warmer. Will had put her theory to the test earlier, hurrying across the deserted beach for a dip in the hope that he and the man might coincide. He swam alone, however, and soon returned, shivering, to the bungalow, having ascertained that the sea was as cold as ever but merely less of a contrast to rainy air than dry. Perhaps the young man had felt there was less urgent need of an early swim with the beach kept clear by foul weather. Perhaps he was ill.

This was preposterous.

Feeling in urgent need of a dose of sane cynicism, Will slouched indoors, grabbed his telephone and rang Harriet's direct line. She was always busy but he caught her in a lull between meetings and she was so startled at his speedily confiding in her about affairs of the heart for once rather than being chattily enigmatic, that she blocked incoming calls and made time for him.

"So you've spoken?"

"Yes. But I don't know his name or what he does."

"So you haven't spoken really?"

"No. But I know that he lives in one of those shiny American caravan things."

"They're called Jetstream trailers."

"Really? Thanks. And he has a dog and he's about my age but with long hair, dark-blond, and these freezing blue eyes and he scowls all the time. I'm being absurd, aren't I? Tell me I'm being absurd."

There was a pause.

"Finn," she said at last.

"What?"

"You've found Finn again."

"Who said I was looking for another Finn?"

"Will, please. It's me you're talking to. A nun with no English could tell Finn is your yardstick. So what if you were only eighteen and it was only two weeks? So what if this was a man who preferred rocks to people? You've measured everyone since against him and no one's come close."

"But I haven't . . ." Will sat, perplexed. "Have I?"

"We all have yardsticks."

"Who was yours?"

She thought a moment. "Sister Damien, which explains a lot."

"But I don't even know this man."

"And you knew Finn? You sound less stable than you have in years. If he has that effect without even knowing you exist, doesn't that make him an improvement on Master Mystery?"

"You're not helping. You're meant to dissuade me." He paced to the French windows.

There was a bark and the subject of their conversation walked into view at last, dog at his side, jogged across to the sea, tossed a wash bag on the ground and dived into the surf. The dog sat immediately, watching for his reappearance, heedless of the rain.

"You asked for my honest opinion," Harriet said. "Which is, of course, immaterial until you get to know him. If nothing else, he might get Finn out of your system and set you free to compromise like everyone else."

"He's out there now, swimming. I'm too old to feel like this."

"From what my mother told me, the grim truth is that one's never too old to feel like that. Hang up and get out there too. Empty beach. The two of you in the rain. What could be more romantic?"

"A warm log cabin. He probably isn't gay, Hats."

"That was never a problem before."

"Harriet? Not helpful."

"OK. Listen. Time's running out so we'll do the Life Choice Test. Shut your eyes, think of Master Mystery and tell me the first three words that come into your head. Quickly! Stop thinking!"

Even with his eyes still open, watching the man come out of the surf, reach for a bar of soap and start washing his hair, Will had no difficulty.

"Guilt," he said. "Timetable. Family."

"Now open your eyes and tell me the first three words about Finn Revisited."

To be fair to Sandy, Will shut his eyes.

"Salt," he said. "Privacy. Compulsion."

"No contest, I'd say."

"He's coming."

"The man? Now?"

"His dog. Thanks, Hats. I have to go."

"All major credit cards accepted . . ."

As the man stooped to rinse his hair, his dog had broken out of its sitting posture and bounded up to him, long tail floating. The man had looked up briefly, directly toward the bungalow where Will, too slow to hide, was standing in the French windows on the telephone, and said something to it.

Immediately the dog had turned and raced across the beach, jumped the picket fence, pushed through the tamarisk and arrived on the veranda too fast to brake without comically skittering on the varnished wood. As Will turned from tossing the telephone on to the sofa, the dog nosed open the windows and bounded across the room, showering neat surfaces with sand and water, to greet him like a long-lost friend.

Nervous of dogs as a child, perhaps because he was never allowed one as a pet, Will had not acquired the art of dealing with them as an adult. This one was skinny and midnight black, with a tail like a whip and a long, snouty mouth like Red Riding Hood's wolf and teeth to match. It seemed to be everywhere at once.

"Oh God," he said. "Down. No! Off the sofa. Off! Get out. Shoo!"

It seemed to think he was greeting it for it bounced up, pressing its paws into his kidneys and bounded once around the place, as if to show it could, then obeyed him to the extent of flying out on to the veranda. But there it lay down, nose on paws, as promptly as if someone had cut its strings, and showed no desire to move further.

"Go home," he told it. "Home!" But it only watched him, showing the plaintive whites of its eyes.

The man was running up the beach shouting "Hey! Hey!" furiously.

"Perfect," Will thought. "Our second conversation and it's going to be another ugly scene."

But the man was only shouting the dog's name. "Fay! Get out of there."

Fay stayed put. Will sensed she was enjoying herself. Her tail was discreetly thumping the boards.

"I'm sorry," he called out. "I shouldn't have let her in but she sort of helped herself."

"Wretched mutt. Fay!" Fay wagged and stayed put. The man came in to fetch her and Will saw a justification for dogs which had eluded him until now. "She hasn't done this before," the man said. "Maybe it's the drizzle. Her coat's so short she can be a bit of a wimp." There were still flecks of soap on one of his collarbones. "I told her to go home and she came straight here. Fay! Come on. *Other* home."

Fay looked at him beseechingly as the drizzle turned to a downpour.

"She's being sensible and so should you," Will said, raising his voice above the clatter on the veranda roof. "Drink to warm you up?"

"Erm." The man stepped on to the veranda as he hesitated. "I don't."

"Oh. I meant coffee," said Will, thinking something stronger an excellent idea now it had been mentioned. Then he remembered the wine on his breath when they first met and Mum saying *I saw his hair fanning out in the water.*

The man smiled and immediately stifled his smile, as though he had forgotten himself. "OK," he said. "Black. No sugar."

As Will went in, he left the French windows ajar, assuming he would be followed, and made the coffee self-consciously, assuming he was being watched. He struggled for something to say to break the awkward silence. But he turned from the kettle to find himself alone and the man still waiting politely on the veranda, checking one of the dog's paws. Perhaps he was shy of bringing sand indoors. As an afterthought Will took him out a towel.

"Here," he said.

"Thanks." He used the towel on the dog then, standing again, saw Will's face. "Oh. Sorry," he said and used it on his own hair too before leaving it draped over the veranda rail.

"Is something wrong with her foot?" Will asked.

"No. She picks up thorns from the gorse when she's after rabbits. They don't seem to bother her but they can work their way right under her skin and could cause an infection." He had the faintest trace of a Scottish accent. Care seemed etched on his brow and around his eyes and was further suggested by the traces of gray at his temples Will had not seen before. Grief, depression; some trauma had marked him as surely as a knife.

"You said her *other* home just now," Will said.

"Her main home's here."

"Of course," Will said, baffled. "Oh I see," he added as the penny dropped. "How crass of me."

"We live out there in the holiday season while I let this to pay the bills for the year."

"It's beautiful. It . . . It doesn't feel like a house a dog lives in."

"It does once you take the covers off the sofas."

Will pictured the place with rougher edges, threadbare cushions, without all the bright colors and surface styling so carefully calculated to appeal to townies, and thought how much better it must look.

"Is everything OK, though? You've got all you need?"

"It's fine. Better than fine."

"I'd normally have called round on your first day but I felt a bit stupid after that business with your mother . . ."

"Christ, I'm so sorry. She's . . . She's not very well."

"Oh. Forgive me. She seemed incredibly fit," he added with feeling.

"In her head, I mean. She's got Alzheimer's."

"She's not that old, is she?"

"It's the early onset kind. She's fine most of the time but . . . Well . . ." Will felt a shiver of sorrow pass through him, so intense he had to make a conscious effort to pull the corners of his mouth out of a droop.

"How do you *do* that?" the man asked.

"Do what?"

"You were getting depressed and—"

"I wasn't."

"You were. I saw. You were on the point of crying and you sort of snapped out of it. I saw you. It was like a gear change inside your face!"

"Really? Sorry."

"No, I'm sorry. Forget it. I shouldn't have . . ." He seemed touchingly worried by the curiosity he had shown. He tapped the dog lightly with a bare foot and she jumped up. "Come on, you. No more rain." He drained the coffee cup at one go and handed it back. "Tell that mother of yours, when she gets back, that I can deliver her sculpture whenever she wants it."

"You're the sculptor?"

"I'm full of surprises today." He turned to go, Fay launching herself off ahead of him, clearing the fence again rather than wait for the gate to open.

"Well, I could come and get it now. Couldn't I?" Will asked, head reeling.

"You could." He walked on as if it were all one to him whether Will came or no.

Having locked the house behind him, Will had to run to catch up. "I'm Will, by the way," he said. "Will Pagett."

"I know."

"And you must be Roly Maguire."

"Yup."

They followed the dog along the top of the beach and under some barbed wire into the field behind the house.

"Your Jetstream's brilliant. So much better than those fat beige things you see holding the traffic up."

"Want to buy it? It's a nightmare. Leaks when it rains. Roasts when it's hot."

"Oh."

"Days like this, a *fat beige thing* would be a godsend." Fay waited hopefully by the trailer door but Roly took her by the collar and tied her outside under a canvas awning, where she had a bed and a water bowl. "She's not really a pet," he said defensively. "She earns her keep catching us rabbits."

"Us?"

"She gets all the bits I don't eat."

The sight of the dog tied up, curling herself into the bed in a sad, reproachful circle, reminded Will of what the woman in the gallery had said about a dead wife. How could he have forgotten something so crucial, so instantly disabling to his trite romantic projections? The entire adventure, the whole day home and parentless was fatuous. His ruder impulse was to save himself mortification, grab the stupid sculpture, which would no doubt fall apart after one winter and prove a useless waste of money, and go. He had no sooner entertained such low thoughts, however, than he felt the need to be sociable to compensate for them.

"Pretty idyllic," he said, taking in the scene around him. Closer to, the encampment was far less slipshod than it appeared from a distance. Three brown bantams scratched for grubs inside a wooden run, tomato and courgette plants were thriving in a grow-bag and strawberry plants cascaded from a filled-in car tire. Driftwood was stacked in one pile, pebbles and shells in another and what had appeared from the house as a mound of litter was revealed as a heaped hoard of beachcombed miscellanea awaiting recycling into sculpture. Because of the intervening gorse and sand dune, the site enjoyed a view of the sea without sight of the beach. During a crowded summer, the views from here would be better than those from the house. "So how long have you lived here?" he asked but Roly had already gone inside.

The sun was coming out at last and making the long silver trailer dazzle. Will wondered whether seabirds high overhead ever mistook it for water and dived to sudden deaths. A thick crusting of guano gave evidence of their visits. He came inside just as Roly was pulling a paint-spattered rugger shirt over his head, and glimpsed the discreet zip mark of an appendectomy scar before looking modestly away.

"Sorry," Roly said, "it isn't designed for visitors and I live like a pig."

True, there was clutter everywhere, discarded clothes, paint, glue, woodshavings, an unmade bed spilling on to the floor. Smells of man and cooked breakfasts mingled with heady scents of adhesive and acetone. Mum's sculpture stood in pride of place. He must have been working on it this morning or late last night. Where the drive of a small electric motor once turned its mechanism, a belt now hung loose for connection to a small wind vane made of beautifully planed and sanded wood, a work of art itself. "I tried it out earlier to test the balance but

I can show you again, if you like," Roly said, picking the two components up.

"No, that's fine. I'm sure it's all perfect. Just show me how it joins up."

Roly pointed with a much-scarred finger and Will smelled that his breath was sour from coffee and lack of recent toothpaste. "That belt stretches over that drive bar and you leave the nut on the end of the bar to stop the belt working itself off."

"And she can put it outside all right?"

"Of course. That's what it's for. It's all treated with ten-year preservative. Just give the moving parts a squirt of oil now and then but use a light one. I guarantee it for five years, too, because I can never be sure of the materials seeing as it's all recycled stuff."

"Right." Will took the sculpture and wind vane from him. "Thanks. And, er," he paused, "does it have a name? In case she asks. Rook-Scarer 56 or whatever," he added.

Roly scratched his head and frowned, staring at the mechanism. "Not really," he said. "I just make them. I used to give things names when I was younger and ambitious. Galleries expected it. Now I mainly sell through Bronwen and, well, I just make them and she sells them. But no. Not a rook-scarer. I call them Skimmington pieces."

"As in *The Mayor of Casterbridge*?" Will could see this had pleased him; nobody normally got this allusion. No doubt he rarely dared make it. Roly smiled fleetingly.

"That's right. You read."

"I run a bookshop. I do little else. Tell me more."

"Country people used to put on protests outside the houses of people whose sex lives displeased them. Not just adulterers and seducers but dirty old men who'd taken girl brides or men who beat their wives. Gay people too, probably, though the books are too coy to say. Sometimes they'd make puppets of the people, like they do in Hardy for the Skimmington ride, but they always made a big noise, not just with instruments but pots and pans, stones, spades, buckets of horseshoes. The noisier the better. The weird thing is it's a phenomenon you find all over Europe and America, only with different names. Charivari. Rough music. Loo-belling. Riding the Stang. Sorry." He scowled again, looked down at his hands. "You're getting me all enthusiastic. I don't talk about it much. Art critics don't exactly fight for Bronwen's invitations. And now you *are* surprised."

"How so?"

"Not only is the drop-out your landlord and a sculptor manqué but he's pretentious with it."

"Well don't take it out on me. You do *cultivate* that look."

"Only because it's cheaper this way," Roly said, pushing dreadlocks out of his face.

"Don't you get into trouble? Putting shampoo in the sea, I mean."

"It's eco soap." Roly grinned. "They make it with seaweed and sea salt. It stinks but it works and one bar lasts all summer. Razor blades are my only real expense."

"You could grow a beard."

"I could wear sandals with camel-colored socks . . ." Again that tic of wiping away his smile as soon as it surfaced. But they seemed to have passed some barrier because he was loosening up, becoming nervous if anything, restless where he had been stiffly aloof. "Look. Do you want a drink? Not a drink drink but I've got milk and mint tea and elderflower cordial."

"That sounds great." Will was about to avoid sitting on the unmade bed then remembered this man was straight so it didn't matter. Then he sat and heard Harriet saying *that was never a problem before.* But by then it was too late. He carefully put the sculpture on the sandy floor. "So these are people-scarers," he said.

"I think of them as early warning devices. To stop you getting complacent. To remember how illiberal people are. I mean not . . . It's just a joke, really." He sounded deadly serious. "Most people will use them as bird-scarers," he mumbled, in verbal retreat.

Will watched him splashing cloudy liquid into two glasses from an old milk container then topping them up from a water drum that took up half the fridge. Roly passed a glass over and flopped on the chair opposite that was actually just a half-inflated beach Lilo bent in two. Will sipped dubiously; there were actually some old, discolored elderflower petals floating in it. But it was delicious, like tasting a summer evening, heady and sweet. "Mmm," he said. "Good. What are the stars in aid of?"

There were small, yellow, star-shaped stickers dotted around the narrow space. He had not seen them at first but once he spotted one, on the kettle, he began to see them all over the place. By the light switch. On the tabletop. On the grimy windowpane above the bed. Even stenciled on the battered surfboard.

"You ask a lot of questions for a stranger."

"Sorry. Don't answer. But actually it's easier asking questions with strangers. Haven't you noticed that? When you get to know someone better you suddenly go beyond a question-asking stage. They tell you things or you tell them stuff but you stop, you know, *digging* because if you know them well then you're meant to know all about them and understand them already." He ran out of words.

Roly had fixed him with eyes all the icier for his face being so weathered. "But that's crap," he said gently.

"Is it? Maybe."

"You've never been married, have you? I mean, never lived with someone, even?"

"Is it that obvious?"

"Apart from the fact that you come on holiday with your mother at, what, thirty-five?"

"Thereabouts." How had they got this earnest this quickly? Which of them had performed the necessary sleight of hand?

"Yes," Roly said with another fleeting smile. "It is obvious. But in a nice way."

"Oh. Well. Sorry. It's all crap then, what I said. And I ask too many questions. But tell me anyway."

"I did a course. On happiness. I went through a bad patch. I was drinking, I wasn't getting any work done, I was obsessed with money worries." He paused. "I had depression, I suppose. I still do. It's like being alcoholic. Once you've been there, felt it in you, it's never safe to turn your back." He stopped again.

Will thought of the evening they had pulled him from the sea and the unmistakable smell, then, of wine about him.

"The lady in the gallery told me about your wife dying," Will said, thinking this might make it easier for him to talk.

Roly laughed grimly. "Was that how she put it?"

"Well, she called her your *other half*."

"My *other half*. How quaint. I like that." He stared down at his untouched glass of cordial then put it on the floor as if suddenly thinking better of drinking it.

"Look, you don't have to talk about this, you know," Will began nervously.

"I know," Roly said, "But I want to tell you." And he pinned him in place with those eyes again.

Oh Christ, Will thought. *Now I'm stuck in a lonely caravan with a psycho.*

"So I went on this course someone in my therapy group had talked about. She was sneering at it but I thought it sounded interesting so I went. And it was very simple. This man believes that happiness and unhappiness are only superficially to do with outside phenomena. Obviously you get cancer or your child dies, you're sad, you win the lottery, you're happy. But on a day-to-day level he believes that people who are basically happy have simply learned to think in a different way from people who are basically depressed. And he aims to undo the damaging way of thinking. It takes months, sometimes years, but the basic system is so simple that it's easy to keep up. You make a list of the things that make you happy. Sunlight. The smell of jasmine. Your father's smile. The thumping of your lover's heart."

Against all logic, Will felt his own heart knock against his ribs.

"Then you go over that list, refining it, questioning everything on it until you're absolutely sure of the things and can remember each of them. Really remember them, though, recall the smell or sight and that sensation of happiness that goes with it, not just remember the words describing it. And then the stars. Well, they don't have to be stars. That's just me. You put them on things you see or use every day, in your house and wherever you work, in your car. Then whenever your eyes catch sight of one you have to pause and summon up one of the things on your list. And that's it."

"And it works? It sounds a bit like counting your blessings."

Roly shrugged and looked away at where sunlight was now falling in an intense band through the open door. "It helps. I think about good things more often than I did. And I left London—which took courage—and made the move back down here."

"I thought you came from Scotland. Your accent—"

"I did. Originally. My other half had inherited a place here and left it to me. I sold it to my sister-in-law. I couldn't stand living there with all those useless memories but I loved the area and the sea and I was known here by a few people so that made it easier. And it's cheap. Very, very cheap. Which helps."

"The lady in the gallery—Bronwen—said you'd changed your working methods too."

"Yes, well, Bronwen's spiteful and disappointed and she says a lot, most of it opinionated, ignorant and harmful." His tone changed so abruptly it pulled Will up short. The temperature was rising fast. In so confined a space, humid after rain, his aggression was a bulky third presence.

Will stood. "I should go."

Roly did not move or look up. "Maybe you should."

Will gathered up the two parts of the sculpture. "This is great. She'll be so pleased. There's nothing more to pay you, is there?"

"No," Roly said, suddenly weary. "Nothing more to pay."

Will could not fit the two pieces through the door at once so he carried the main part down the rickety steps first, then turned to reach in for the wind vane. But suddenly Roly was there, on his feet, holding on to it. "Look," he said. "What exactly do you want?"

"I'm sorry," Will said.

"You've been hanging around like a puppy."

"You asked me to stay."

"I mean generally. You've been watching me. I've seen you watching me, hanging around, pretending to swim."

"I *was* swimming!"

Roly jumped out of the caravan so fast that Will flinched, thinking he was going to hit him, but Roly just stood there, so close Will could feel his angry breath on his face. The dog barked, sensing excitement.

"What?" Will said.

Sandy would arrive tomorrow and they would have to find ways of dodging both parents and children. The last thing he needed was a further complication. And he was too old for this. He might be sleeping with a married man on a regular basis but forty was too old to go fluffing up straight men's egos. Roly was standing so close their knees were brushing, however, close enough for Will to see the few tips of stubble his razor had missed. Some were pure white. There was a trace of a smirk on his lips.

"This is such a tired routine," Will said. "Making the fairy do all the work so you have someone to blame afterward. I have my pride. And incidentally I think this apology for a sculpture is a piece of tourist-rip-off tat."

Or he would have said it had he not been kissing so hard that Roly stumbled back against the steps. His body was not as godlike as novelty and mystery had at first made it seem. For all his swimming and nouveau-feral lifestyle, there was a slight thickness about his waist and softness to his ass that was both reassuring and exciting. But he was unyielding in Will's embrace. "You're not kissing back," Will muttered, sniffing the bonfire odors of his hair and neck.

"Sorry," Roly said. "I'm not very ... Maybe if we went back inside?"

This really was an old routine. Harriet was mistaken in her too-pat analysis. This was not like Finn at all. Instead, it was taking Will straight back to the frantic, joyless encounters between boys at school. Roly would put on a coy, undone footman act, the better to distance his manly pride afterward from what had passed between them. Will would have to make all the moves. It would all be over in a clumsy rush, leaving unspeakable awkwardness in its wake and they would have to spend the next week avoiding one another on the beach. And Sandy was coming tomorrow. Will could save this pressure-cooked horniness for the devil he knew.

"Look, I don't want you to do anything you might regret," he said. "We could just pretend this never happened."

Two hours later, the trailer had not exactly rocked but one of the piles of *Art Forum International* supporting the bed had given way, and he was sitting up in a sea of none-too-clean bedding feeling stretched and nicely bruised and tasted all over. He knew his hair was standing on end and he didn't care. Still naked, a smear of butter on his upper thigh, Roly handed him a plate of marigold-yellow, scrambled bantam eggs with a piece of sliced buttered bread and a fork. He fetched his share then clambered in at the opposite end of the lopsided bed so that his legs slid up on either side of Will's.

He grinned, immediately wiped the grin off his face and fell to eating but Will scratched at him with a big toe. "You're good at that," he said. "Considering."

"The plumbing's the same," Roly said with his mouth full, then swallowed. "It's just pointing in different directions most of the time. You want more pepper?"

"No, no. This is great."

They ate on in ravenous silence, communicating only through occasional movements of their feet. Then Roly slung his plate on the draining board behind him and the movements of his feet became more specifically intimate. "I have to go to Saint Just in half an hour," he said.

"Where's that?"

"Other end of the county, near Land's End. I've got to deliver some pieces to a gallery there. There's an opening tonight. Drinks and stuff. You could come too. It might be fun."

Will gave it serious thought. Possibly Harriet's analysis had not been mistaken. Now that the mystery was dispelled, however, and the stranger known, Roly was nothing like Finn. The similarities had been superficial and this coming together was all too reminiscent of the numerous, depressing, pointless encounters that had spotted his years since Finn left. Will imagined the teasing hours of wanting to get each other's clothes off again without being able to, the clumsy, standardized, this-isn't-really-my-thing brush-off at the evening's end. "My parents get back in a bit. I ought to be here for them. And my brother-in-law and his kids arrive tomorrow. We have to get beds made and so on. Sorry."

Roly had the good grace to make a convincing display of disappointment but there was a give-away air of relief about the way he jumped up and started to dress that made Will wish he had agreed after all, with galling eagerness, and played a lovesick dead-weight for the rest of the day for the simple pleasure of punishing him.

"So do you *live* with your parents still?"

"Certainly not! A fortnight's holiday is quite long enough. No. They live on the other side of town. We're from Barrowcester."

"Ah."

"What do you mean, *Ah*?"

Roly shrugged. "Nothing. It's pretty there, isn't it?"

"So? It's pretty here."

"Not in the winter. In the winter it's stunning. You should see it."

"I'd love to."

"Come and stay."

"Yeah, yeah," said Will, charmed enough but not believing him for a moment.

"Shutters bolted against the howling wind. Fire roaring in the stove. The house feels like a log cabin. It's great."

"I'm tied to the bookshop." Will explained about his business, the café, the readings and, modestly, the building success of the thing. He assumed he had sounded enthusiastic but when he was through Roly startled him by saying it sounded like a kind of imprisonment.

"You should be careful," he said. "If your mum's as sick as you think, you'll get trapped."

"But I like it there. It's home."

"Oh, well, in that case ..." Roly shrugged again, finished tying his shoes. "Better head off," he said. "Help yourself to whatever. The door doesn't lock. Just slam it when you go." And he ruffled Will's hair and left.

With him no longer charging it with his presence, his trailer's interior became a filthy, inhospitable mess once more. The bed was itchy. Lousy too, perhaps. The air was stale and unpleasantly musky. Will waited until he heard the dog jump into the van with her master and the van's engine gun uncertainly then he hurried to dress again and be off. He slammed the door as instructed, picked up the two parts of the sculpture and helped himself to two lengths of blue nylon rope from the salvage pile.

Two hours of sunshine had been enough to draw out the holidaymakers who had been hiding from the rain and the beach had filled already. The tide was rising so he had to pick his way through family encampments as he crossed the dune to the house and imagined inquisitive stares upon him. As soon as he was back on the veranda, he secured the wind vane to a wooden upright and twisted it until it caught the breeze, then he used the other length of rope to fix up the sculpture beside it. He stretched the drive belt into place and waited.

Nothing happened at first and he realized the belt was so tight as to be acting as a brake. He fiddled with the knots and moved sculpture slightly nearer to power source. Still no movement. He nudged a blade on the wind vane. It began to move slowly then caught the breeze and threw the sculpture into clunking, slapping motion.

"Thwack," went the sandal on the driftwood. "Thwack! Beware! They don't like your sort. Move on. Thwack! Beware! Thwack!"

He grinned to himself as a child stopped her game to stare and heads turned among the nearer sunbathers. He went to his room, threw off his clothes and tugged on his trunks, not caring now if they were too tight or too orange. As he walked down the beach to the encroaching surf, he could hear the sculpture still laboring on behind him. Almost drowned out by the hubbub of ball games, barking dogs and shrieking children, it was unmistakable once your ear focused on it; a slow but insistent tattoo, stopping altogether when the breeze dropped then picking up again.

He walked out until he was waist-deep then plunged himself under and came up rubbing his face and shaking the water from his hair. He caught the eye of a woman dandling a solemn, water-winged baby in the brine.

"Sorry," he told her and threw himself into a backstroke, recklessly splashing all around him.

BEACHCOMBER

"Is it much further?" Skip whined.

"Miles," said Frances. "Your feet will be bleeding by the time we get there."

It worked. Skip pulled a face, laughed and ran ahead to join Julian, who was petting some bullocks who were leaning over a hedge to inspect him. Frances had been thinking how much he had grown recently but now he looked tiny with the older girl beside him.

"I had a small breakthrough this morning," she told Bill.

"You bought her a dress," he said. "I'm not sure I approve of you corrupting her. I let her wear what she wants."

"But she wears jeans like a kind of armor."

"Are you saying you think she's afraid?"

"No, no. Of course not." His tone had warned her off. "She's been through a lot. If she's happy in school here I think the change might do her good. No one knows her here. She can reinvent herself."

"She won't wear it, you know. The dress."

"Don't be so sure. She chose it. Not me. She has very good taste."

Bill snorted, picked a fistful of flowers in passing. The rabbit-eared tower of Trenellion appeared above a curve of field before them. "John said she reminds him of Becky when she was that age."

Frances was uncertain what to say. She had not liked Becky, had been relieved, after meeting her, that she lived in California. "Really?" she said.

"You didn't like her much, did you?" he said.

"What gives you that idea? Did she say something?"

"She didn't need to. You didn't come to the funeral."

Frances stopped short at this, shocked. "John said there wasn't one!"

"There was a funeral," he said, walking past her. "Not what *he'd* call a funeral perhaps, but we praised and burned her. I think that counts."

"I'm so sorry." She hurried to catch him up. "As John didn't come though, I could hardly have . . . I hardly knew her."

"That's all right." He smiled, hearing how worried he had made her and she felt he had somehow scored a point. "What's this flower?" He held up the bunch of pink blossoms. She stared a moment, racking her brains.

"Campion? Bladder campion? Ragwort? I really have no idea."

He tossed the flowers aside. "I thought all Englishwomen love flowers."

"And ride horses and make jam and breed dogs and stitch their own wounds without wincing. Did Becky tell you that?"

"No. I think it was in some book. Lawrence probably."

"Isn't it stunning!" She meant the church. He looked up at it as blankly as she had looked at the flowers. "I was reading about it this morning," she went on. "Julian, you see this tower? It was made in Heaven."

"There's no such place," Skip said, at which Julian looked gratifyingly shocked.

"It's a granite quarry on Lundy, a tiny island out there. They shipped the stone over and dragged it up the cliffs. Odd really because there's masses of perfectly good granite all around here."

"They wanted to give you guides a good story," Bill said. "Can we go in?"

"Of course. But I think you'd better . . ."

He was already stubbing out his cigarette on the sole of his boot, however. He looked at her wryly, reading her mind. It made her want to tug his stupid mustache till he yelped. Instead she carried on playing guide because the role came more easily than honest irritation. "It's used by a local music festival," she said. "Rather a good one apparently. Has been for some time now. It fell into disuse and was deconsecrated a while back. At least they stopped holding services here."

"Good," Skip said and pushed open the door.

"Look," said Bill, stopping in the porch to point up at a carved face on the wooden beams. The children had already gone inside. Frances looked where he was pointing. "Jack-in-the-Green," he said. The face leered from a wrapping of leaves. It had leaves for hair and a ruff of leaves about its throat. It was disquieting. "Pure paganism. And see this one?" He pointed to another face, which was tugging its mouth wide with bony fingers. "The mouth represents female privates. They thought they would scare the devil away. In some churches the carvers didn't even bother with symbolism; they carved the real thing. Lips, hair and all."

"Goodness." Frances felt herself redden. She passed swiftly on into the church, or ex-church, whatever one called it.

The central roof was held up by ancient carved angels, most of them crumbling into dust, some so severely that they had been swathed in sacking. But their vigorous beauty shone through, more than answer to whatever question his smutty faces posed. Light flooded the place—untouched by meddling Revivalists, the glass was nearly all clear—and caught on rhythmic lines of arches and stout white pillars. Every capital was carved with writhing berries and vines. It was far larger than it seemed from outside, with north and south aisles as generous as its nave, and a broad, flagstoned space where the altar once stood. One could see why it had appealed to musicians.

A noticeboard gave details of the coming fortnight of concerts. She went to see if there was anything that tempted her but would not bore the children. Vivaldi, perhaps, or a mixed evening of songs and poetry.

Julian and Skip had found the piano, a concert grand, and were lifting up its padded cover for a better look. Skip began to play *Chopsticks*. Frances frowned. It was something she never let Julian do; a musical equivalent of swearing. She shushed but the sound would not carry. There had been signs of life in the old vicarage—voices in the garden, sheets drying on the line. The owner of the piano, a festival administrator presumably, would be angry if they heard. She waited for Bill to complain but he said nothing. The wretched girl thumped out the crude tune again and again, faster and faster, complete with a teeth-filing figure played with rocking fists on the black notes. Frances glanced round, angry now, unable to concentrate on the poster details, and saw him blithely reading the inscription on a wall tablet. Her patience snapped. "Stop that!" she shouted. Skip continued thumping. "Skip!"

Julian stepped away from the piano, dissociating himself from the crime. As Frances walked over, Skip finally stopped, turned and stared.

"What's the big deal?" Bill asked. "She was only playing."

"It's bad for the felts," Frances said with authority. She knew that any number of Brahms or Rachmaninov pieces would place far more wear on a piano's workings but saying it was bad for her nerves would hardly have sufficed. "And it's a horrible noise," she added lamely.

"So why don't you play?" Skip asked. "Julie says you're really good."

"Well hardly. And it's not our piano."

"They won't mind," Julian said. "Not with you playing it. Oh, go on."

He looked so pleading that it dawned on her there was a contest of sorts in progress and the home team was falling behind on points. She tossed back the front of the cover, raised the lid, adjusted the stool and thought a moment. There were not many pieces she had reliably memorized. She flexed her fingers and launched into a Scarlatti sonata. This was a cheat, really, since the piece was all show and dynamism and sounded far harder than it was. The piano was a Steinway and far too good to be left unlocked in an unlocked church, but perhaps most visitors would lack the nerve to sit down and start letting rip like this. She rocked as she played, unable to help herself, letting each phrase scour her out. It was a good sonata, one of the angry, arrogant ones, imperious as a long car or an asymmetrical hat. She let it express her several angers, at John for leaving and spoiling the holiday, at this vulgar American brat for calling her son by a girl's name, at this man for inviting himself and making her feel insular and fixed.

It was over too soon. Rather than wait for a response, she threw off something contrasting, a Debussy prelude, *Danseurs de Delphe,* all subtly melting rhythms and smoky chords, a tango almost had the title not denied it. The chordal writing suited the piano and acoustic better than the Scarlatti had; it made the space feel small and the piano vast where the other had seemed to shrink the piano. The sonata had drawn Julian and Skip to stand where they could watch her fingers let loose on the keyboard. Now she noticed they shifted and Skip in particular was watching her face instead, so that Frances became self-conscious and it was a struggle to keep her expression the elegant blank she would have liked.

She stood as soon as the second piece was over, closing the lid and feeling a need to break whatever spell she might have cast. "There's a dairy next door that makes ice cream," she said. "Any takers?"

The children were easily diverted by the prospect but Bill could not be bought. As they returned, feasting, along the footpath down to the sea, she caught him staring at her, refusing to be swayed by her nervous talk of how good real ice cream was and how hard it was to find. He was going to compliment her playing. She knew the signs of old.

"That was really good," he said.

"Oh, I should practice much, much more," she said. "But you know how it is. Marriage. Children. The Enemies of Promise. It's hard to keep up."

"But you should. I mean, I know nothing about classical music but I could tell you're good."

She made a noise of dismissal. "Maybe once, I might have been. But the world is full of wives who play the piano fairly well, who like to imply they could have gone professional if they hadn't, you know . . . ."

"I know." She suspected he was mocking her. His eyes wrinkled. The mustache made it hard to tell. They walked on in silence, then he added, "To be frank, I'd never have guessed you had all that inside you."

"All what?"

"That passion."

"I don't. It's just notes. I just follow a series of musical instructions."

"You don't fool me," he said. "That was memorized so there were no notes to follow. That was *you* back there. Hey, Junior?" Skip turned. Frances saw the game she played, her eagerness to be all her father wanted. It was heartbreaking. "Race you to the stile!"

He ran after the laughing children, leaving Frances to finish her cornet feeling wide and womanly and cross. She was getting a sunburned neck. She missed John keenly, not just his physical presence but—there was no other word for it—his courtesy. She often thought honesty about emotional states was overrated. All it did was stir one up to no purpose, creating directionless discomfort. All too often, it seemed to her, it was mere bad-mannered intrusiveness dressing itself up as some brave new virtue.

On the first night without John she had been able to use the children as chaperons, effortlessly persuading them that it was a treat to stay up later than usual, then using their presence as an excuse for playing one of Julian's supremely tedious and time-consuming board games, one about horse racing and stud management. Totopoly was a particularly cruel game, since just when one believed it to be over at last, the board was flipped to reveal a whole new system of dice, cards and arbitrary misfortune to be labored through. By the time Skip was deemed the Pyrrhic victor, gray-faced adults were quite prepared to retire to bed leaving children to play something else. Tonight she had no such luck. Bill had been giving Julian surfing lessons and by sundown the child was too tired even to eat. Even Skip waited no more than the quarter-hour pride required before she followed him to bed.

Frances could not pretend to be tired too. She had slept on the beach while he entertained the children. As they took their coffee to opposing armchairs, it felt like the resumption of business deferred. Dreading fresh, unwelcome analysis of her supposedly repressed character, she went on the offensive, asking questions of him. She imagined all novelists were flattered by discussion of their work so asked him what he had been typing all morning.

"You really want to know?"

"Of course."

"Because I never can tell with you when it's just politeness or when you mean it."

She smiled despite herself. "Isn't that what politeness is for? No. I mean it. Tell me. Is it a new novel? I'm afraid I still haven't read your earlier ones."

"Why should you? They're not even published over here and they probably never will be. Sure. It's another novel." He grinned down at his empty coffee mug. "I'm writing about Becky's death and my reaction to it."

"That must be hard."

"Not really. It's a shameless attempt to make some money finally. It's a big love story."

"About you and Becky?"

"Not really. More about the girl the boy meets afterward, the girl who helps him love again. It's all very simple, very heart on sleeve, exaggerated almost. I'm doing Becky as an out-and-out bitch so that when she dies—sleeping tablets, nothing messy—he and his little daughter feel this tremendous guilt at their sense of relief."

"But you—you didn't feel that about Becky, did you?" She smiled again. "I'm sorry. I just realized how little I know you."

But he had turned serious, wrapped in his memories. He had shifted on his chair to stare out to where the house lights spilled across the sand. "No. She wasn't a bitch," he said, shaking his head sadly. "But she was impossible. An impossible woman. It's hard to believe John's her brother. He's so reliable and *grounded*. Becky was a fantasist. Always living in the next day, the next week, spending money before she had it, running up credit on the slightest prospect of income. And so insecure you would not believe. She had enemies everywhere. Not real enemies, not really, just people she'd fallen out with, people she believed had slighted her or stood in her way. There were streets she wouldn't even *drive* down in case we ran into one of these people. Then there were forbidden subjects. Her eating habits. Motherhood. Her failure to gain tenure yet. *Not* to be discussed on pain of a week-long sulk. Her work."

"Her work?"

"We couldn't discuss it without her losing her temper. Either I didn't understand it or I was patronizing her, apparently. So I learned to stay clear. And ex-girlfriends. Another no-no. Even if they'd gotten married or fat. Not to be mentioned." He laughed, lit a cigarette, offered her one. For the umpteenth time that day she shook her head. "Becky was the first person I knew who could create a thundercloud on a phone line. You'd be chatting away with her from a call box or wherever, then fleetingly mention one of the forbidden subjects and it was incredible! You'd feel this thick black thundercloud of disapproval filling the ether between you. She'd carry on talking but something in her manner would go dead."

"But you loved her."

"I loved her." He seemed to try the words on for size. "Yes. I loved her," he agreed. "Because when she approved, when she loved back, it was like someone just turned the sun back on. Tina, this really smart friend of hers, anthropologist, totally hippie . . . When I broke the news to Tina, rang her from the hospital, she just laughed and said, 'But of course!' She'd never been able to picture Becky grown-up, Becky old, Becky a middle-aged mom. Hearing about her dying, in such a crazy, *stupid* way, in the middle of a drunken argument too, naturally, which she was losing big-time, was like finding the last piece of the jigsaw. Of *course* a woman like that would have to go that way. She cried afterward, actually. Tina. Cried and wouldn't stop. So I had to hang up on her. But when I first told her she laughed."

He broke off, stood to walk over and top up Frances's wine glass without asking then topped up his own and slumped back into his chair so heavily its springs squeaked. Frances did not know what to say. The house suddenly felt very small around them, the night very black and the idea of his dead wife very large and threatening. Less thundercloud, though, than the charged minutes before thunder.

He's telling the truth, she told herself, *so I might as well too.*

"I didn't like her," she said. "You were right. I only met her that once, when we'd just got married and moved to Wandsworth and she came to stay. I was very young and silly. Not that I'm sensible now, but you know what I mean. A newlywed. And she went out of her way to make me feel uncomfortable, as though I'd failed some test. She talked incessantly to John of people I didn't know, cutting me out of the conversation entirely, and when John had to go in to work, she made me feel as though I was a visitor in her house, not the other way around."

"You probably mentioned motherhood."

"Oh, I don't know. I probably gave her homemade jam or let her see me stitching lavender bags for the linen chest. Whatever it was, she struck me as unpleasant and rude and yes, quite unlike John, and I was very glad when she went back to America and left us alone." She laughed, amazed at herself. "And I've never told that to anyone and now I'm telling you. Of all people. I'm so sorry."

He was just smiling at her. From under that mustache. She leaned to scoop up her wine glass. She had intended to drink no more but it was there and she was thirsty and he'd laugh at her if she went to the kitchen for a glass of water. "Was she not a good mother?" she asked. "Why was she so sensitive about it?"

"I dunno." He shrugged and watched a moth that was crashing around the lampshade. "She was probably hopeless. It was probably amazing she was ever focused for long enough to give birth. She did a lot of acid, you know."

Frances had no idea what he meant by this but suspected it had to do with drugs and merely nodded in what she hoped was an understanding manner.

"She'd forget to buy food or forget to change Skip's diaper. Babies bored her. Once or twice she even left her behind in shops. But she was great once Skip started to talk. They'd play weird games. She could enter into a fantasy so completely it was almost creepy to watch, but the kid loved it. They'd have been fighting constantly by now. Skip has twice the stubbornness."

"And double the dangerous charm." They laughed then stopped laughing and for a few terrifying moments they just sat there and stared at each other. Frances felt a kind of space yawn open between them, a cool clarity in which it would be permissible to say anything. Here was a man without rules. Nothing seemed to bother him. She understood how this could have goaded such a wife.

There was a low mumble from Julian's room. She turned, listening. "It's a dream," she said softly. "He'll probably roll over and stop soon but sometimes they're really bad and he ..." She stopped to listen again. Julian's mumble quite suddenly became a muffled shout swiftly replaced by a thin, hoarse cry. She jumped up and hurried over. She knew not to turn on the light. Sudden light could make it worse, like waking a sleepwalker. "I'm here," she murmured. "Was it a bad dream? It's all right. I'm here." She crouched beside the bed and laid an arm across him as if to shield him. He sprang up and clutched her. He had taken too much sun on the beach; his body was fiery, his little pajamas damp with sweat. "Oof!" she sighed. "You're burning up. Tell me about it? Was it so bad?"

"I can't," he cried. "I don't know. I can't."

"Monsters?"

"No," he said, sounding almost cross. "Just people. Lots of people."

"Well I'm here now. It was only a dream." She rocked him gently. "Here. Magic pearls." It was a babyhood habit; he had always clutched at her pearls as she nursed him and they had come to acquire a potent ability to calm him; a sort of luxury comfort blanket. He clutched at them now, though in a spirit of humoring her rather than out of any real belief. "Try to sleep, hmm? Try to sleep. Listen to the sea. I'll open your window. No wonder you're so hot."

"The moths were getting in."

"They won't if you keep the light off. And they can't hurt you. They're just butterflies that prefer the moon. Here." She opened the window then returned to the bed to stroke his hair off his forehead and kiss his brow. It tasted of salt, of boy-bacon. "Hear it?" He nodded. "Count the waves on the sand in your head," she told him. "Bet you can't get to a hundred."

"One," he said sleepily. "Two."

"Night," she whispered. She kissed him again and rose to go.

"Ma?"

"What?"

"Leave the door open this time."

The open door was oddly sobering, like having a dressing-gowned child bearing mutely indignant witness from the room's corner. She did not sit down properly again but merely sank on the armchair's arm.

"Does he dream often?" Bill asked.

She nodded. "But he doesn't always have the words to describe them. Once you get the words you can control the dreams. He reads so much and he's so imaginative that he often doesn't seem to see the boundaries between dreaming and waking or films and real life. I *am* Lana Turner. John *is* Captain Hook. As often as not, it isn't a nightmare so much as a dream about things he doesn't understand. How about Skip?"

"After Becky died it was bad for a while. Now, not really. Or if she does, she doesn't tell me. Funny that. I almost resent it now that her dreams are getting private."

"Oh, I think they always were," she said, standing. "They tell us things to keep us quiet, like we tell them fairy tales. They learn the dreams we'll accept and pretend to have those ones. I'm quite sure they dream monstrous things we'll never get to hear about until they grow up to write novels and spill it all out. Now I *must* call John! It's late. Open another bottle if you want to."

"I'm fine," he said.

As she passed his chair on the way to the veranda he briefly caught at her hand with his. He did not clasp it so much as brush it, letting her fingers trail through his. It was so fleeting a gesture she was past him and outside before it had fully registered. And even then she wondered if they had merely touched by accident and she had misinterpreted it.

It was cold out now. She snatched a cardigan of John's she had left on the veranda railing and shivered as she pulled it about her. She was glad of the hard climb to the car park. It would sober her up even further than Julian had done. *John,* she thought. *John, John, John.* But John was now pictured in her head with his hard-faced sister, lost in cruel chatter with her, and only turned to his wife with a look of mild resentment, as to a meddlesome child. *No more wine tomorrow,* she decided.

The telephone kiosk's yellowish light loomed up ahead. She clicked open her purse and felt for change.

BLUE HOUSE

"Oh, now I feel awful about this," Frances said, seeing Will cross from one bedroom to another with his bedding in a great bundle.

"So don't," he told her.

She took the pillows off the heap he was carrying only her hands were having a bad day and she dropped them. "Sorry."

"Leave them," he said with quiet impatience. "I'll get them in a bit."

"But that room's so tiny," she said, following him.

"It's fine. It's got the same view. Look. Better. Windows in two directions."

"And those tiny twin beds. Let's put the boys in here."

"Mum, it would feel funny sharing a double with Sandy. I wouldn't sleep a wink and I'm sure he wouldn't either. Honestly. We'll be fine in here. And the boys are always sharing so they won't mind and they're nearer to the door in the bigger room so they can stomp outside in the morning without waking us all."

"Well at least let me help you make that bed up."

"Mum? It's fine." He threw the bedding down carelessly and took her hands, leading her out of the room again. "You've been fidgeting all day."

"Have I?"

"You know you have. You should get some rest before they get here. And don't let the boys run you ragged the way you usually do."

"Yes, sit down and be peaceful, for pity's sake," John muttered from inside a newspaper.

"All right," she said, with an abrupt understanding that she had been irritating them all day, and she forced herself to sit on the sofa and keep still, despite a kind of burning in her hands to be active. Her back ached and the backs of her legs, which she knew was a bad sign although she forgot now who had told her so or what it betokened.

Although there was little to be done, just two new beds to make up, she had woken up on a small rush of excitement and been able to think about little else all day. She had found a broom and swept the floors clear of sand. She had dragged poor John to a supermarket in Wade-bridge and half-filled a trolley before forgetting what it was Will had suggested they buy or what she had planned to cook. She had found some children's books in a secondhand shop in case the weather turned bad again and the boys brought nothing to read. She had even baked a cake; a Victoria sponge, which was to form a party pudding for supper tonight, sandwiched with fresh raspberries and brown-flecked vanilla ice cream from Trenellion dairy.

"We're only guests, remember," John told her quietly now. "Will's the host," and she felt sulkily checked, like an unruly child, and cross too that she should be treated like one. It was one of the things she had come to resent most about aging; not the physical aspect, the drying out and stiffening up, but the social one, of being hectored to do less, move less, live less effectively. It was as though the only acceptable way to face old age was in a spirit of glassy contemplation and composure, to become a fund of quaint old stories (so long as one did not repeat them too often), a calm old lap on which babies might be placed and an unde-manding extra presence at a dining table.

Grandmotherhood had taken her by stealth. It was assumed, because she was not an easy woman, that she would respond badly, resent being made to feel old and insist on the children calling her Frances, as though they were cosmopolitan intimates and not relatives at all. A year or two before she too might have predicted such a reaction. Nothing had prepared her for the sensation of near-idolatry each child inspired in her. It was like motherhood, only refined, all the worries and guilts burned off, so that all that remained was a slightly indecent hunger to feel their flesh and give them pleasure. Cake, ice cream, excursions, all the indulgences she had felt she must limit with her own children, she lavished on her daughter's, as though to buy them for herself.

Similarly her relations with her son-in-law lacked the difficulties others had led her to expect. It was like having a son only without the worry that she could have raised him better. It helped, of course, that Sandy had chosen to live so far from his own parents for the sake of marriage and work, and had thus chosen Frances and John much as he had chosen their daughter. He confided in her, but not too much. He advised her, but not unduly. He even flirted with her on occasion. The only complication in all this was the guilt she felt when she sometimes wished Will had turned out more like Sandy, less secretive, more—dirty word but no other would do—normal. She suspected that she appreciated Sandy more than her daughter did, who had a way of saying *The Boys* to indicate husband as well as sons, lumping them all in to the same parcel of weary, womanly caretaking.

Aware of John's keeping an eye on her, she behaved impeccably, occupying her restless hands by stabbing away at her tapestry while Will made the rooms ready. He moved his clothes into the smaller room. He laid the table, found extra chairs, conjured up a small vase of wild flowers from the hedge at the garden's rear and all the while she stitched and kept up equable chat. Tapestry was a habit she had acquired in the middle years of her marriage, pressed by a vicar's wife into making kneelers. She had long since given up pictorial designs, since her eyesight was too poor to count stitches in the patterns. She contented herself with geometric patterns in the Florentine style, and even after the onset of her trouble found they took less concentration than books and could be pursued quite successfully while her mind skittered elsewhere. Seeing her at such a placid, Victorian pastime had always seemed to please John, which amused her. She supposed the male equivalent would be for him to sit across from her while she stitched, reading aloud from some inspiring text.

At last she heard a car coming down the drive and a horn toot-tooting.

"Ah," said John, who had dozed off.

"They're here, they're here!" she cried and lurched to her feet, dropping the tapestry in her hurry and not bothering to pick it up. "Darling?"

"Coming."

But before she could reach the French windows, Hugo, the eldest, came racing along the veranda shouting. "It's brilliant. Granny!" he yelled, finding them. He threw his arms round her waist, hugging her tight and said something that was muffled by her shirt.

"What darling?"

He pulled back. "I'm so happy," he said.

"Well we're happy too," she said and laughed.

"Grandpa!" He threw himself at John in much the same way, then grabbed his hands and stood on his shoes. "Walk me," he said. He was too old for the game but it was a ritual between them and John took a few obliging steps. "Now show me where we're sleeping."

"You and Oscar are in here," John said. "In a big bed." Hugo kept hold of his hand as they went to inspect the room. Perhaps because Sandy was so easily physical with them the grandchildren were uninhibited with John as the children had never been.

She hurried out toward the car and found Sandy coming toward her with Oscar in his arms, still drowsy so looking about half his age.

"Frances," he said and kissed her. "Sorry we're late. Hideous motorway trouble after Bristol."

"You're not late. Cold supper anyway."

"Oz? Look who it is! Very tired small person, I'm afraid."

Oscar rubbed his eyes and peered at Frances, too sleepy to speak. She stroked his hair, which was still baby-soft.

"Shall I run a bath?" she asked.

"Straight to bed I think," he said and took in the bungalow. "What an amazing place! Boy heaven. These two'll run mad."

"Good. It isn't a proper holiday without children. It feels all sad and grown up and pointless." Will passed at that moment, carrying luggage, and she felt disloyal in case he had heard, so created a diversion. "And look what I bought!" she said and gave the wind vane a spin so that the sculpture sprang into motion. The sandal whacked on the wood and startled Oscar who jerked awake properly and started to cry. "Oh fuck," she said. "Sorry." While Oscar was borne off to bed, she fetched more things from the car.

John emerged with Hugo and led him down to the sea. Stooping to catch what the boy was saying, he looked suddenly the part of old man. A dog must have visited the garden. Frances walked on some shit on her way back in. Encumbered with bags, she scraped her shoe as clean as she could on a patch of rough grass then kicked both shoes off below the veranda meaning to clean them later. She had forgotten about Will's change of rooms. Thinking to look in on little Oscar before he fell asleep, she dumped the bags with the others on the sofa and walked to the small room on the house's near corner. And saw something she should not have seen.

Will was reaching up to slide a suitcase on top of the wardrobe and Sandy, sitting on one of the beds, placed his hands on Will's backside. The gesture was unmistakable; he did it with the same slow, tender absorption with which a man would cup a woman's breasts in his palms. She froze, staring, unseen.

"Oi!" Will said and shook him off, laughing, whereupon Sandy whacked his bottom instead. So it was only a joke.

Sandy saw her and grinned. "You have no idea, Frances, how long I have waited to share a room with your son."

"Oh, behave," Will told him, turning.

Frances did her best to laugh but this was not her kind of humor. Sandy was a rugger player, she reminded herself. He had a weakness for horseplay and the company of men. It was embarrassing but harmless. She went to soothe her startled nerves and indulge herself by tucking Oscar into bed.

He was already tucked in, tiny in the double bed, but the strange, new room had woken him up enough for a bedtime story. It was not really a little boy's tale but she sat on the bed beside him and told him "Goldilocks and the Three Bears" because it seemed suitable for an encounter with an unfamiliar bedroom.

They ate early, almost immediately, so that Hugo would not feel left out but could be hustled off to bed too. Her cake was a success, especially with Sandy who flattered her by having three helpings. She liked a man who was unashamed to eat. Will was a good cook, of course, but both he and John had always had a way of eating so little or so slowly that they made a hungry woman feel she must be greedy. Sandy made her feel, as John and Will had not, that she was a lone woman in an all-male household. It felt good, rejuvenating.

Hugo ate his pudding sitting on her lap because he was at once determined to eat it now and heavy with a long day's excitement. Despite being so exhausted, he continued to ask questions. Was that last piece for Oscar? When would Oscar eat it? How soon could they swim? Was it true that there were basking sharks here? If Oscar didn't know the pudding existed, would he miss his helping if someone else ate it? Will parried each question with all seriousness, as though the child were a fellow adult, and she felt afresh her sorrow that he had no children of his own yet. Yet? Dared she still use that little word even to herself? Miracles happened. "Bedtime," she murmured, kissing Hugo's hair.

"But it's still light," he said and wriggled around on her lap to play with her pearls the way her own children had, clutching them in a small fist and counting them between his fingers like a rosary.

"Those come from deep in the sea," she told him.

"I know," he said. "In shellfish. Does it hurt when they take them out?"

"I don't know," she said in all honesty. "I hope not. I think it's probably like having your wallet stolen; it doesn't hurt, it just makes you cross until you get another one." She looked up and saw Will watching them and smiling sadly.

"He must be the age I was when you sent me to boarding school."

"Surely not," John said. "Far too young."

She had a bad feeling, the kind she got when her words were not going to come out right.

"Nine next birthday," Sandy said.

"Exactly the same age, then," Will said with a kind of triumph. "Just imagine."

"It's different," she said, meaning now. "It's all different. Come on. Bedtime for Julian."

"I'm not called Julian."

In her confusion she stood, easing Hugo off her lap too abruptly. Whining, fighting dismissal, he had not let go of her pearls. The rope snapped and suddenly they were everywhere. "Shit," she shouted. "Shit!"

Hugo screamed with laughter. "Granny swore!" he gasped, but all the men were diving around, scrabbling after dancing pearls.

She had caught a fistful of them, still on their string, but watching the men on all fours, like pigs, was so odd that she let these fall as well so that John shouted "Careful" at her. "Bedtime," she said again. "Jiggedy jig." And she steered Hugo, who was already in pajamas, into the bathroom to brush his teeth.

"I'm sorry I broke your pearls," he said, as she saw him into his side of the double bed.

"Ssh," she whispered. "You'll wake Oscar. Don't worry. It happens all the time, Granny losing her marbles. Happens all the time. Kiss." He kissed her and she kissed him back. "Now. Say prayers. *Gentle Jesus—*"

"We don't do prayers. God's a myth."

"Oh yes." She stood with a grunt. "Sorry. Sleep tight."

When she returned, John was back at the dining table, trying to thread pearls on a length of cotton from a small mending kit retained from some hotel visit. Will and Sandy were still on the floor, looking under furniture.

"How many should there be?" John asked. "Any idea?"

"Forty?" she suggested. "Fifty? I've never counted them."

"The insurance probably says," Will told them, standing up. "Now. Who wants a coffee and who wants mint tea? I'm sure this is the lot."

"Tea, please," she said and sat on the sofa thinking, *Magic pearls. My magic pearls. No more magic.*

Sandy was still on the floor, only now he had moved on to the door of the fourth bedroom, the locked one. "There are several more under here," he said, maneuvering for a better view like a terrier at a rabbit hole. "If I could just see better . . ." He grabbed a table lamp, causing the room's calm lighting to sway wildly askew, and pointed it under the door.

"Fifty-three," John said. "That does sound like a curious number. Were there sixty, perhaps? Or seventy, even? How many times did they go round your neck?"

"Well if you can't remember!" she snapped.

"Twice," Will called out from the kitchen. "They went round twice but they didn't hang lower than her second button and there wasn't a clasp."

Sandy tugged a sheet of paper from the children's coloring pad. He slid it slowly under the door. "I think I can catch them," he said. "Shit!" He jumped up. "Isn't there a key for this?" He rattled the door.

"No," John said.

"What's in there anyway?"

"Bluebeard's wives," Frances murmured.

"All the landlord's stuff presumably. Private things."

Sandy rattled the door again and bumped the lock. "It would give easily," he said. "It's not bolted."

"Do you think we should?" John asked. "How could we lock it again?"

"We shouldn't," Will said, rather vehemently, coming back. "We can get the landlord to open it for us."

"But we don't know who they are," Frances said. "Didn't it come through an agency, Sandy?"

"No. Yes."

Will came to stand protectively beside the locked door. "That's right. But we can ring the agents in the morning and get it fixed. Much the simplest way."

"I haven't been without them longer than a night since I had them re-strung in 1970," Frances said, remembering. "They get so personal. Maybe because they absorb your skin oils. Apparently they never look their best until they've been polished with weaning. I mean—"

"Tribal, really," John said, not waiting for her correction. "Like decking your weddable daughters out in animal tusks to increase their value on the marriage market. Shame you've no granddaughter to leave them to. But the way society's changing, it'll probably be perfectly acceptable for Oscar to wear them by the time he's twenty-one."

"Why Oscar?" Will asked. "Why not Hugo?"

"He gets my gold cufflinks and signet ring, of course."

"Far too much bother," Sandy muttered, apparently uncomfortable with such chat, and he thudded harder on the door. With a slight complaint of splintering wood it flew open and the fourth bedroom was laid bare like a darkened stage set. Everyone fell silent and looked in.

The remaining pearls were on the floorboards where they had rolled up against the edge of a rug. Will crouched and quickly gathered them up. He made to shut the door again but Sandy stopped him. "Hang on," he said. "We might as well have a look while it's open." He strode in and tugged back the shutters, letting in the garish light of the setting sun.

"Don't," Will said. "Someone might see."

"Not at this hour," Sandy said. "And they're hardly likely to be passing anyway."

"I like that." Frances admired a pale stone sculpture. It appeared to be of a face pressing through a veil. "And those. Look!" There were other sculptures, huddling together on a table in the shadows. There were books, stacked two deep on the shelves, and a colorful, Hockney-ish painting of two young men on a sofa, one dark, one fair, the dark one holding a chisel and hammer, the fair one a violin. There were framed photographs propped here and there on the shelves. Two of them showed the same dark-haired young man. In one he was still a teenager, posed and composed. In the other he was older, laughing, at a wedding apparently, with another slightly older man who looked familiar. "I know him," she said, pointing at the familiar one.

"How could you possibly?" John said. "Don't touch anything, for God's sake."

While Sandy looked at the book titles and Will looked at the photographs, she sat on the bed and chuckled. "Sandy could sleep in here," she said. "Now that we've got the door open. They'd never know."

"Oh no. I don't think that's a good idea," Sandy said quickly.

"Why not?" she asked. "You're the one that broke in."

"It's private," he said. "This is obviously a very private room. All his life is tucked away in here. It wouldn't feel right."

"My God!" Will exclaimed so suddenly that she was startled. "This was my room!"

"What?" Sandy asked.

"It was, wasn't it?" He turned to Frances, turned *on* her rather. "This *is* the house we came to before and this was my room. I didn't get it in the other room because the windows are the wrong way round and it confused me. But here, with the one window out to sea and one looking up at the cliff path . . . I remember sleeping in here." Uncertainty clouded his expression. "I'm sure I do."

"It could have been any number of houses," John said quietly. "The whole bay was practically built in this period and in this style."

"No, but on the beach like this!" Will laughed. "My God. This was it!"

Frances stood and left the room. "You can't possibly remember," she said. "You were much too little. Sandy's right. It's private. We should shut it up again. And where's my tea?"

She felt better once the shutters were drawn again and the door closed, but Will's sudden enthusiasm had started a process in her memory she could not interrupt. This had been the house. She knew he was right. The changed name, the tarmac on the drive, the golf course, the new colors and garden, the French windows where there used to be a door, the shutters where curtains had hung, together had composed smokescreen enough for her to ignore what she knew. But Will's insistence and awful enthusiasm were a merciless current clearing the air. The events were still not there, not entirely, but every room in the building, and the view from every window, now glittered with an unwelcome familiarity and she was living in a near-constant state of déjà vu that was almost nauseating in its refusal to resolve into clear understanding and unbroken recollection.

John sensed her discomfort as they were going to bed. He thought it was about the pearls, of course, and she played up to that to reassure him, fretting about the cost of having them restrung and her stupidity in allowing the boy to break them. He held her in the crook of his arm, like a child, and ran his fingers in slow repeated strokes through her hair, which he knew always soothed her. He fell asleep first. He had walked miles that morning, apparently, and been on the edge of a nap all afternoon. Before he slept, however, he mumbled, "It's not the house. He's quite wrong."

She could not sleep, and his body gave off the heat it had absorbed all day and became uncomfortable to lie against. She extricated herself as gently as stiffness would allow and went to the kitchen for a glass of milk. She knew the way well enough now to get there without lights and once there the fridge gave illumination enough. She could see light coming from under the fourth bedroom's door. She poured her milk, shut the fridge and stood there sipping, feeling the cool air about her hot legs. In a while Will emerged. She opened the fridge again to let him see she was there and he came across.

"I'd left something in there," he said guiltily. He had shorts on and nothing else. "Can't you sleep either?"

"No," she said. "Have milk. It helps."

He pulled a funny face. "I'm going out for some air," he said. "Maybe Sandy will have stopped snoring when I get back. Night."

"Night."

He kissed her cheek sweetly enough but there was a tension between them that smelled sourly of deceit. She waited until his bare feet had padded the length of the veranda. She heard the click of the latch as he passed through the gate to the beach then she went forward to watch through the French windows, keeping back so the moonlight would not catch on her nightdress to betray her.

There he was, quite clearly, walking along the top of the beach, oddly purposeful for a man wearing nothing but shorts. Then she saw to her astonishment that he was making toward the encampment and the home of the sad young man. There were no lights on there. It was far too late. The dog barked once, startled awake perhaps, and he froze like a burglar. It barked again and he turned and was walking, running almost, back to the beach. He did not see a light come on in the trailer.

Frances hurried back to her room. John was still sound asleep. She sat in the armchair, watching him. Sometimes now sleep came more easily when she was not lying flat on her back. She heard Will come in, heard him pad across to the bathroom and then back to his bed. She heard, quite distinctly, a burst of Sandy's snoring as their bedroom door opened and closed. She sat on, and felt haunted by truths whose significance danced beyond her grasp.

BEACHCOMBER

John was not good at running the house on his own. Not that it took much running, and a cleaner came twice a week. The plumbing and heating system was shared with the prison, so was maintained by prison work parties, and he ate all his meals with the men, supper included, if there was no family at home to dine with him. Frances teased him that he had always been looked after by institutions and could not fend for himself. This was not strictly true. Had he remained a bachelor, he would have spent the money he saved thereby on laundry bills and membership of a club.

The things he was hopeless at were the small touches that made this barracks of a house feel intimate. Frances effected them without thinking, much as she ate or breathed, drawing curtains, turning on table lamps, bringing in flowers from the garden, playing soft music. He had watched her often enough, these were all things he could do, but it took a certain confidence to do them on one's own. Besides, it would have felt self-indulgent and he had far more important business on his mind. As a result, he would suddenly become aware that he was sitting at night with the windows still naked, in a room rendered flat and harsh by a single overhead light source. Or rather he would notice the phenomena

and be dimly aware of the cause but preferred to view the physical discomfort as a symptom of Frances's absence rather than as a sign of any
dereliction on his part.

When she said how smelly and cold the telephone box was, he could
truthfully say, "It's pretty wretched here, too," and felt closer to her. In
much the same way, when she asked how things were at his end, he
slightly exaggerated their badness. He did not mention that it had been
gloriously sunny or that one of the officers' wives had brought him
round a remarkably good Lancashire hotpot which he had heated up
with some beans from the garden that he had gathered himself. Instead,
he spoke of how the search for Farmer was now concentrated on the
seaports and airports and was drawing humiliating blanks. He spoke
of the restlessness of the prisoners, made worse by the heat and their being confined as punishment for the disturbance on the night Farmer
broke out.

"Well come back," she said. "You're still on holiday. What more can
you do there?"

"I have to be here until they catch him," he sighed, trying to be patient. "Or at least draw some concrete leads as to his whereabouts."

"He's hardly dangerous."

"He robbed a post office, darling, and raped the postmistress."

"She was probably some puritanical busybody."

"Frances!"

"I was joking. But it doesn't mean he'll do it again."

"Since when were you a criminologist?"

"The pips . . ."

"Give me the number."

"Penfasser 452."

He started to call her back then froze, finger on the dial. There had
been a noise on the stairs.

It was an old house, hatchet-faced mid-Victorian with fanciful castel-
lations, and was full of old timbers so that it creaked like a ship. In the
summer however, with no heating on, the noises were rarer and more
particular. There was one board on the curving staircase that squawked
like a hen when trodden on. It was unmistakable.

He went to his study door. Night had fallen since he came in and the rest of the house was in darkness. To reach the staircase light switch he had to leave the carpet of light spilling out from the study and grope by memory across three yards of pitch black. He thought of Julian and his way of diving on to his mattress from several feet away so as to avoid the grasp of the blue-handed troll who lurked under the bed.

"Hello?" he said foolishly as he went. It was always a mistake to talk aloud in an empty house; the silence that followed invariably had the effect of making the emptiness close in around one. He flicked all the switches on the panel for good measure, causing the familiar hall and stairs to spring back into place. There was nobody, of course. Perhaps it was the heat after all, but the heat of the day rather than the heat of the water pipes. As if to prove this, a staircase floorboard squawked again, with no one on it. He turned back to the study, thinking again of Julian and of how he relished the sinister little poem about reluctantly climbing the stair to meet a man who wasn't there. He hastily rang Frances back.

He fibbed to her, explaining the delay as being caused by a routine call on the internal telephone. It would not do for her to think he suffered night fears as much as their child. "Tell me about you," he pleaded. "Take my mind off all this."

But she was on holiday so had nothing much to tell; an old church, more surfing, fish and chips again. "And how about our visitors? Have you warmed to them?"

"They're fine," she said, then talked for five minutes about Skip, how funny she was once you dug through her defenses, not bright but funny and original, and how she was teasing Julian a little, which was probably good for him, and how good it was for both of them not to be only children for a change.

"And Bill?" he asked.

"Oh," she said. "He's all right. He's working on his novel so we haven't talked much."

The front door closed. He had not heard it open.

"Who was that?" she asked.

"Bartlett, probably. Coming in to check on me."

"Why didn't he ring the bell?"

"Oh. They're all jumpy as hell after all this excitement," John said, relieved now that he was telling her. "Me too, for that matter. I'd better go and see what he wanted."

"I'd better go too," she said. "It's rude to stay away like this too long and Julian will worry if he wakes up again and I'm not there. He had another of those wretched dreams tonight."

He told her they would speak tomorrow or the next day and not to worry about ringing to check up on him. He would be fine.

"Bye, darling," she said.

No sooner had Frances hung up than he used the internal line to ring the gatehouse where Bartlett should have been on night duty. There was no reply so he let himself out and walked down the drive and around to the gatehouse where he met Bartlett returning from replacing a broken light bulb.

"Something wrong, Bartlett? You might have rung the bell first. That was a private call I was taking."

"I don't understand, sir," Bartlett said, visibly shocked. "I haven't been near the house. I saw you go out five minutes ago."

"How could you have?" John snapped. "I've been in the study on the phone to my wife."

"Well obviously I only *thought* I did. A cab arrived, which we reckoned a bit odd at this hour but, well, you know . . . Then you came out of the house, well the person I thought was you. You had your hat and coat on. But you said good evening and not to wait up and you got into the cab and—"

"Quickly man! Which cab? Which firm?"

"A Luxicab, sir. Black one."

"Did you hear where he asked to go?"

"No, sir. He didn't say, sir. But he had a big briefcase under his arm."

"Very well. Thank you, Bartlett. I'll deal with this now. Not a word to anyone else just yet. Stay where you are for now but the police will want a statement from you later."

Bartlett paused in the gatehouse doorway, dull face bright with expectation. "Was it Farmer, sir?"

"Of course not, Bartlett. If he's got any sense he'll be on a banana boat by now."

"Yes sir. Night sir."

John alerted Scotland Yard, because of the remote possibility that Bartlett was right and it had been Farmer. Then he discovered how much the intruder had taken and had to call in the local police, as the victim of what looked like a routine burglary. Not only had the intruder helped himself to an overcoat and hat but to John's second-best tweed suit, shirts, socks, underwear and razor. He had also snatched John's wallet, which had still contained a wad of cash taken out for holiday expenses which he had meant to leave for Frances and had forgotten, some silver, a painting and, to stuff in what he could not wear, a briefcase consigned to Frances's jumble sale heap on account of a broken handle. The silver was nothing special. Neither was the painting hugely valuable—the old gilt frame was worth more than the picture—but it was a cherished one. A study of a sow and piglets, school of Morland, in need of a good clean. His father had given it to him to take to university. It had gone on to travel with him in the war and therefore been one of his few remaining links with his dead family to have escaped the incendiary bomb that destroyed the other heirlooms.

"Could have been worse," the police constable said who took his statement. "He could have done for you, sir, on the phone like that with your back turned."

"Oh no, I don't think so," John said but he thought about the possibility when they finally left him in the small hours and he promised never to leave the downstairs lavatory window open again.

The birds were already beginning to sing. He drew the bedroom curtains to block out the dawn but could not sleep. He lay on the bed, favoring Frances's side as he always did when she was away, breathing the ghost of her scent from the pillows. He thanked God she and the boy were so far away and safe from harm and as he did so was unable to prevent terrible scenarios playing out in his mind. Their rape and torture, with him a powerless gagged witness, were all the more hideous for being enacted among familiar furnishings.

"Just give me the sow and piglets," their American tormentor kept asking in reasonable tones, "and I'll stop."

BLUE HOUSE

John was not a concert-going animal. He liked music well enough, although a teacher in his nursery school had told him to mime rather than attempt to sing because he *had no ear* and he had taken her word for it. He preferred music with English words attached, like hymns, *Dream of Gerontius* or *Judas Maccabeus*; music with a story to give him something to follow and some idea of how near a piece was to finishing. He could not abide opera in any form, finding it dramatically inefficient. Ideally music should be domestic, as when Frances played the piano after dinner or found something on the radio. Then he could read a book or beaver at a crossword and be occasionally surprised and distracted by some passing beauty in what he was hearing. The enforced listening provided in concert halls could be like drip-fed torture.

Frances had chosen a *lieder* concert because she knew he preferred words, but the program was of Schubert and Wolf with only a thin, unpromising English-language filling of Britten folksong settings. The sketchy program, all too swiftly read, gave no translations. One had to rely on explanations from the girl at the piano, who was pretty but largely inaudible.

Will had been going to come—he was as passionate about music as his mother—but he dropped out unexpectedly, insisting on staying at home to babysit so Sandy could spend time alone with his in-laws. John could never think of much to say to Sandy once the initial family questioning was out of the way. The man was amiable enough but almost proud of his complete lack of culture; the most worrying kind of scientist, in John's opinion. And Frances was having one of her bad days, after a sleepless night, so they were not a merry party and John keenly envied Will who was probably playing Cheat with the boys or enjoying a good book, having put them both to bed.

It was a long-standing music festival, performed and attended largely by outsiders who owned or rented holiday houses in the area. Despite the high reputation and ticket prices, a self-consciously informal air prevailed. Seats were unnumbered so had to be reserved with cushions beforehand, a process involving a heartily Dunkirk spirit in the queue outside and Byzantine ruthlessness in the barely restrained rush once the queue was admitted to the church. The idea, part of the fun apparently, was to fill the interval between pew-claiming and concert with a picnic. Will had thrown together delicious sandwiches, fruit salad and cake for them but they had forgotten in their rush to bring a rug so ate in the car, all facing the same way. With Frances in so flat a mood, one realized how great a contribution her chatter normally made. The atmosphere was strained, and made less comfortable still by thick, prickly weather heralding thunder. They talked exclusively of absent family.

John had queued alone for their seats, leaving the others to talk. As they filed inside for the concert, spirits improved by a bottle of buttery Chablis, Frances remarked on the changes to the building. She had been here before, apparently, before the bold decision was made to replace much of the old slate roof with glass. A tall, masculine creature in a peacock-blue tent dress that looked as old as herself, was handing out programs as they came in. She knew Frances, it seemed.

"Happy with your clacker, then?" she asked.

"Oh yes," Frances said. "Although I'm a bit embarrassed to leave it going all the time as it's been so noisy."

"Look up when you get inside and take a look at what he *used* to do. Coffee in the rehearsal hall during the interval. You'll see more art there."

They dutifully looked up as they took their seats. The new glass roof was supported by a phalanx of carved wooden angels, replacements perhaps for old ones decayed past repair. Reminiscent of something by Epstein or Eric Gill, they were more muscular than spiritual and would not have looked out of place on some Olympic stadium of the thirties. Their faces were expressionless, their long hair streamed back and their robes were swept tight against their bodies to suggest a mighty wind bearing them up. They were not beautiful and John questioned their suitability for such a fine old building, albeit one already deconsecrated and buggered about, but there was no mistaking the skill and confidence in their execution.

"Bit of a comedown from those to rook-scarers," he said.

"His wife died," Frances told him. "He's still a broken man, apparently."

Sandy said nothing, his attention absorbed by the other concertgoers. He had that in his favor; when he had nothing to say, he kept his mouth shut. He was also, John supposed, a good husband and father in that he provided well for his family and they all appeared to love him. John was shocked however at how even the oldest child, who should at least be reading easy classics by now, spent all his free time playing games and surfing the Internet on Sandy's laptop computer. It was a lapse emphasized by the child's startling similarity to Will, who rarely had his nose out of a book at that age. When taken on walks or trips, neither boy asked questions unless they related to food or other things they wanted that would cost money. Flowers, birds, scenery, buildings—nothing seemed to stimulate their curiosity and he could tell from their reactions to things he said, about the Saxons or the tides or the lives of fishermen, that they knew nothing. Poppy and Sandy were raising two cultural blanks. Attractive, healthy, very good-natured and probably quite clever, but blank. John looked around the church at the other young couples and imagined them all producing similar offspring, then stopped because the idea frightened him. He did not like to be made to feel reactionary, even though he knew that within the family he was regarded as a social dinosaur; a man who still had a use for shoe trees, weekend ties and a Church of England prayer book.

There were three singers taking it in turns to rise from their chairs beside the piano; a woman and two men. The Schubert sequence was interminable, the smiley, inaudible explanations often lasting nearly as long as the brief songs that followed them. When the thunder finally sounded, one of the men threw off an impromptu performance of *Der Erlkönig*. When a burst of rain followed it, clattering on the glass overhead, the other man swelled a long program further with *Die Forelle*. John noticed Sandy stir impatiently at the sycophantic, cultured titters that followed the announcement of each addition and warmed to him with fellow-feeling.

Much as he could still recall reams of poetry learned by rote at school, he found himself remembering a trite, gallumphingly-accented English version of the song from the same hazy period in his life.

We see the merry TROUT as he swims alo-ong hi-is WAY.
We see his fishy TAIL and we wi-ish him good DAY!

Almost guiltily he craned his neck for a better view and began to enjoy himself, tapping a foot to the infectious rhythm.

Britten, in his experience, normally signified music to be borne with fortitude. It was either simply tuneless or tunefully creepy. In the course of Will's time as a chorister, John had endured both the *War Requiem* and *The Little Sweep*. Will had landed the title role in the latter, leaving his father with chilling memories of his son being stripped half-naked in public in the cause of a thigh-slappingly grisly number called *Sammy's Bath*.

There was some shifting around before the Britten sequence began and when one of their neighbors needed to leave to help the volunteer coffee-makers, John was tempted to escape with her, pleading that old man's silencing standby, a troubled bladder. Frances patted his knee, however, and murmured, "Isn't this a treat!" in a way that compelled him to stay and suffer.

The first item, *The Little Ploughboy,* confirmed his worst fears, managing to be not only tuneful and creepy but to induce little patronizing snorts of pleasure in the audience. Then came *Salley Gardens,* a tune John had always loved and which Britten had left well alone. It was with the unpromisingly titled *O Waly Waly,* however, sung by the bass, that he found himself transported. He realized he knew it, or a version of it, from a Kathleen Ferrier record he played sometimes when Frances was out. (The scratches on the record irritated her, she claimed, but he had reason to suspect she was jealous of his perceived attachment to the dead singer.) It contained the combination of despairing love and inexorability folksongs carried off so effectively and Britten had set it with admirable simplicity. The piano played nothing but chords in a rocking rhythm John could not have described technically but which put him in mind of water lapping round the landing stage at the end of the garden. For a young man, the bass had an amazingly mature voice, so that it was almost as though another, older man sang through a younger mouth. Where the words were saddest, he held back rather than letting rip, covering the brass in his tone as one might shade a candle.

"A ship there is, and she sails the sea," he sang. "She's loaded deep as deep can be, but not so deep as the love I'm in; I know not if I sink or swim." And thinking suddenly not merely of Kathleen Ferrier but of the sitting-room at Wandsworth where he first heard the record and the old Governor's House at Camp Hill and Frances young and careless in the garden, John was moved and it was his turn to reach out and touch her.

She sniffed and he saw she was crying. She had always been charmingly sentimental, crying easily at carols or songs that evoked a happy time. *How sweet,* he thought, squeezing her hand. *She's thinking about us.* Then he realized the words sang of betrayal and of love as a long, hard slog of a journey. He glanced over again and saw to his dismay that she was crying in earnest, not just misty-eyed but with proper tears streaming down her face. He squeezed her hand again, uselessly, hoping she would manage to rein herself in, but she could not apparently and began to cry more openly until she was actually sobbing and having trouble breathing. A couple in front turned, first the husband then the wife, their faces angry until the sight of her tears turned them hastily back, alarm in their eyes. Other people were turning. Someone even shushed her.

"Ssh," John murmured too. "It'll soon be over," which earned him a shush as well.

Frances struggled to her feet. She was like a woman gasping for air. "I'm sorry," she said and spoke aloud.

John jumped up and helped her out, past the eyes boring into them. The song finished as they were leaving and he fancied the applause was the warmer to show disapproval of the rude interruption. Under cover of a change in singer, Sandy hurried up behind them, carrying the cushions. John guessed he had been suffering and was happy with an excuse to escape.

When they reached the graveyard Frances began to wail. John held her tight and she clung to him like a frightened child. "What?" he said. "What is it?"

Behind her Sandy signaled that he would go to the field across the way to fetch the car.

At first she could only mumble incoherently as John continued at once to hug her and steer her away from the church porch so she would disturb the music less.

Then she said what sounded like, "Chopsticks."

"What?" he asked.

"It was a vision," she said. "I had a vision." And she gulped deeply, then bent over and was violently sick into the long grass beside the lych-gate.

John handed her his handkerchief and glanced behind them but the interval had not started yet. A handful of people who had not managed to capture seats were watching them from the porch with unfeigned curiosity.

Nobody spoke on the short drive home. John thought of many things to say but judged it better to remain silent. The boys were asleep. Will was sitting up reading. He was surprised to see them back so soon. Frances confirmed that something was wrong by saying, rather briskly, that bed was the best place for her and took herself off without greeting Will or looking in on the children. Will took the used picnic things off Sandy and, mind-reading, returned from the kitchen with the Scotch bottle and three glasses.

"I had no idea she had got so bad," Sandy told Will as they sat on the veranda. "Poppy's been making out she's just a bit confused."

"Poppy is in denial."

"But she's not so bad," John insisted. "Not most of the time. She can't concentrate the way she used to or read a book and she's a bit forgetful. But she can talk quite cogently and plan excursions. Well, not plan exactly. But she enjoys them. And she still plays the piano, you know." He heard how he was sounding and shut up.

"John," Sandy said after a pause. "When we get back, you should let me book her in. For a scan."

"Why?" Will asked. "How can that help?"

"So we can know the worst. See how it's progressing."

"You make it sound like a mold."

Sandy pulled a face and dropped his voice so low that John had to lean forward to catch what he was saying. "Well, when you look at the photographs of the progressive damage it does . . . You don't need to talk about this. Not yet."

"Now who's in denial?" John said. "Can I have another?"

"Sure." Will splashed more Scotch into his tumbler. "Dad, are you OK?"

"It was a shock, that's all," John said. "I think it shocked her too. She was sick. I thought she'd had another stroke." He drank, let the whisky scour him out. "It's very kind of you to have us here, Will," he said. "Not much fun for you."

"Don't be daft. It's kind of you to come and keep me company."

"No. This time next year . . . Well . . . Who knows . . ."

There was another pause filled by the sound of wave on sand. The sculpture thing was silent. By common consent, Sandy had tied it up until they got it home and could station it at the far end of the garden. Even there, John foresaw neighborly complaints. The boys had discovered it and kept untying the contraption and setting it clacking. Possibly Sandy could be persuaded to take it home with him.

"It's so bloody unfair," Sandy said.

"Farmer's coming back," John said suddenly. "Your friend Harriet rang to tell me and I clean forgot. It looks as though they're going to extradite him and he'll be standing trial at long last."

"Good Lord," Will said. "Are you glad?"

"After all these years it's become completely meaningless. I'm retired. It's not my problem."

"So why did Hats ring?"

"To warn me. Sweet of her really. She thought journalists might start ringing up, raking it all over. Who knows? They might ring you."

"I was a kid at the time. Why should they want to talk to me?"

"Oh. No reason really."

"Did I know him?"

"He was quite a pal of yours for a bit. You don't remember a thing, do you?"

Will smiled. "Not a sausage."

"It was a long time ago," John said. "Maybe it was one of the others who was your pal."

How could he have acquired this innocence? And how could she lose great tracts of memory and be termed sick when Will could forget things and remain so blithe? Every parent strove for this. Especially now, John had noticed, when childhood had shrunk back to its eighteenth-century brevity and technology and fear were shrinking the years in which children could be kept in happy ignorance, parents craved the restoration of innocence. But innocence in one's adult child was somehow insulting.

"I should have let her go years ago," John said quietly. "Then I'd never have had to endure this slow absenting of herself. I should have divorced her." Then, seeing naked hurt writ across his son's kind face, he added, without thinking, "Not that she ever gave me cause."

And Will smiled grimly, accepting what he was told.

So, John thought. *That's how it happens.*

"Do the boys have any idea, do you think?" Will asked Sandy.

"No. They just think she's ancient. You know how ageist kids are."

"Oh, sure," Will said. "Oz accused me of being fifty tonight. Have you got stronger sunblock for him, by the way? I couldn't help noticing when he was in the bath, he got quite burned on his back today."

"There's another big tube in the car boot somewhere."

John stood. "I'd better turn in," he said. "Keep her company."

The domestic tone between them, almost like that of a long-married couple, was exacerbating his desolate mood. He pressed Will's shoulder to keep him where he sat, and moved inside as their voices continued softly behind him.

The bathroom, so pristine when they arrived, had taken on the damp, chaotic look of one shared with children. As well as a scattering of sand on the wet floor, there was now a clutter of washbags and discarded clothes around the sink and a plastic spaceship lay marooned on its side in the bath. Both boys were prone to eczema so there was a great tub of the aqueous cream they used instead of soap. One of them had peed on the loo seat and John mopped it clean. He washed his face, brushed his hair, scrubbed at his remaining, jealously protected teeth and put his plate to soak in cleaner solution on a shelf out of the children's mocking reach. Then he changed into the pajamas and dressing gown he left hanging on the door's back. Crossing to their bedroom, he saw himself in the looking-glass. Flannel stripes, tartan dressing gown; a silver-haired, suntanned, nineteen-forties schoolboy.

She was asleep but she woke as he climbed into bed. For a terrible moment, thinking of the horror stories Sylvia had told him, he thought she was about to panic and ask, "Who are you?" but she merely drew him to her and kissed him briefly.

"Toothpaste," she said.

"Yes."

"It was a lovely concert," she said. "Spoiled it royally, didn't I?"

"Don't be silly."

"I'm *not*," she said angrily. "Don't patronize me."

"All right. Yes. You probably spoiled it for some stuck-up old trout behind us. But I was ready to leave and I think Sandy was too. How do you feel? Still sick?"

"I wasn't sick. Who said I was sick? I'm fine."

"What did you see?"

"When?"

"You said . . . Back at the church, you said . . ."

"Oh." She pulled back and settled herself afresh into her pillow. "Those carvings. It's so sad. I wonder how she died, poor girl."

"Should I have let you go?" he dared to ask her.

"Now you're being silly," she muttered, sinking into sleep and sounding complacent, even happy. "Where would I go at this time of night? And I've nothing to wear."

If only it got no worse than this, he thought, he would not mind the gibberish so much. Not if she said it kindly. But he knew there was worse. Sylvia had torn aside his last rags of innocence. Frances's vomit pooling yellow on the wet grass had been an acrid reminder of what was to come. There would be rage and shit and even violence. He knew this and had accepted it as inevitable as nightfall.

He could bear almost anything but the leaching away of whatever made her his wife. He could not nurse a stranger, when the time came. He was too shy.

BEACHCOMBER

Julian loved the early morning. He liked to wake early and lie in his bed thinking and listening to birdsong and the ticks and murmurs of a house still at rest. It was a time when no demands were made of him. He could read or not, as he chose, sleep or not. Recently he preferred not. He preferred thought. He had become aware that thoughts unspoken were unpoliced and that he could set aside or seize time, as now, to luxuriate in whatever thoughts came into his head. He found he could ride them like wild horses into places he could not name, could barely describe. It was like make-believe only without a girl asking questions like "How big is my crown?"

One wild horse in particular had taken him to a place where he had supreme control. It was loosely based on the public baths Ma drove him to once a week only utterly, magically silent. As in a dream, he could be invisible at will, which helped with not feeling bad. Badness, feeling bad, came with speaking, which made a thought visible and made people cross or sad. In this place he had people who did exactly what he told them. All of them men, all of them dressed like the man in the Milk Tray advertisement and looking like him too. As people arrived at the baths the men knew without him actually saying it aloud, what he wanted. And because he did not say anything, it was not his fault. They sent the children one way, the women another and the men another. He knew this was pretty much what happened in the baths anyway but he needed control over it. He needed to be sure that no one would suddenly come into the wrong room or open the wrong door. Then one of the Milk Tray men would secure one of the swimmer men on the ground, like a sort of rocking horse, and Julian would climb on and squeeze him very hard between his legs.

That was all. The last bit was the most important but it was over very quickly because he sensed there was a next but had only vague ideas of what it involved or required. Curiously he found he could not freeze the last bit in his head but always had to begin the story at the beginning again, reestablishing the place, the Milk Tray men, the people, before he could reach the delicious squeeze. It was worth it though because it was a sort of magic, a way of feeling without touching anything, as though mere thoughts could give one the sensation of eating.

He had no idea how he knew that this was not something to be shared with his parents. It was not like wetting the bed or being sick, despite being every bit as dramatic the first time it happened. It was like a magic power in a book, which would vanish as soon as one bragged about it or tried to use it for the wrong reason. But he was inquisitive and longed to know whether he was alone in being able to do it. Or was it something everyone learned to do sooner or later, something they never spoke about but which kept them in bed of a morning as long as they dared? He once heard Ma boast to the chaplain's wife, "Oh, Julian's one of the ones who needs to be *fetched* in the morning. He's *never* woken us up since he was tiny." Perhaps this was her polite way of telling Mrs. Stibson, "Isn't it heavenly! He never wakes us up so we can all lie in bed thinking unspeakable thoughts!"

And if they all did it, did they all think the same thoughts only using different changing rooms? He knew there was more to it. Somewhere between his thoughts and the no more speakable words that Henry had taught him lay the truth. But it was as mysterious as his parents' love.

He knew they loved each other. It was something he seemed to have been born knowing because he could never recall a time without its constant reassurance. All parents should love just as all princesses should be beautiful. It was a given of life, like the difference between sand and water or Lady Percy and a seagull. Nonetheless he had always spied on them, just to be sure. He knew from his reading that only children were like orphans, were more vulnerable. So in a spirit of needing proof, he routinely eavesdropped on their impenetrable conversations, read their letters, tried on their clothes, lay on their still warm bed. It was necessary that he possess them as they possessed him.

These last few days he had been watching Skip too, comparing her situation with his. He could almost taste her envy like a salt breeze. She wanted his father or wanted something of him. His fixedness, perhaps. The way he was like a rock whereas Uncle Bill was more like a girl in that he was all over the place and you never really knew how he was going to be from one day to the next, quiet or noisy, studious or like a big boy. Pa was always the same, like the father in the learning-to-read books. Julian watched Skip on the beach, so he saw how although she sneered at what she called *girly girls* in their mini bikinis or frilly swimsuits (she wore a plain navy Speedo one) she also stared after them with a kind of pain, as though she was swallowing a hard toast crust but didn't want to cry. She dressed like a boy still. The new frock hung on the back of her door. She had worn it once, just once, but everyone had made such a fuss about how pretty she looked, especially Bill, that she had almost torn it off in her angry hurry to get back into jeans, and no amount of cajoling would persuade her to wear it again. But she had chosen the dress when she could have chosen a Tonka lorry instead. And she kept it neat, on a padded hanger, the way some girls kept their dolls tidily on display even though they claimed they were babyish and played with them no longer.

His mother kept her wedding dress in the same way. It was in a big wardrobe in one of the spare rooms. The dress was huge, like a white mountain, but sometimes he took out the headdress that lived in a box on the shelf above. It had little white flowers and pearls and an old lace veil and he put it on and pretended to be a ghost or Miss Havisham. Ma had caught him parading in it on the long landing and looked as though he *was* a ghost. He thought she was making-believe too, because she did sometimes, so he went *whoo whoo* some more and laughed. But actually she was rather cross and said to take it off at once. He had not worn it for months.

Thinking of her, Julian felt a sudden wish he knew to be infantile to get into her bed with her still in it. When he was smaller he used to pretend to have nightmares. He would wake in the night and want his mother with an insistent, unanswerable hunger. He would try to sleep again but could think only of her warmth, her soapy, musky smell, the rustle of her nightdress and how safe she made him feel even in her heavy-breathing sleep. When he began to cry out, it was with frustration at not being able to gratify this hunger. Then someone would come, either Ma or Pa, and he would not need to say what he wanted because they would say, "It was a bad dream. Just a bad dream." And he wouldn't need to do anything but hold on and cry.

Recently however he had started to have real nightmares, in which skeletal figures, whispering, long-fingered, with skin like old purses, clawed at his legs as he fled up the curving staircase at Wandsworth and if they caught him, they held him down and squeezed him between bony legs that cut like scissors. Sometimes they cut him off at the waist before he could escape them by waking up. These dreams had begun at about the same time as he had discovered he could have the unspeakable thoughts, so he dared not describe them aloud when asked, for fear something in them would betray his discovery to his parents. So he made something up, a babyish tale of goblins under a bridge or vampire bats in his cupboard, knowing that only by telling the truth could he make the dreams go away.

He wanted her now, he decided. Wanted to share that early morning sweetness of her bed, like farts and shortbread, and have her stroke his hair and ask how he slept. So he got up and went to find her. But when he opened her door she was still asleep and he found Skip in the bed where he should have been. Skip just stared at him in a fierce, go-away manner, as if she would tell bad things she knew about him if he loitered. So he backed out, pretending he was happy to see her, and saying he was having Frosties for breakfast even though there were none left, because he knew she would want some too.

He wanted to pee but Bill was in the bathroom singing along to a song on the radio so he played with Ma's camera for a bit then went outside and watered the springy grass that grew from the sand, pretending to be a dog and panting. Then he took out Lady Percy and played with her and buried his nose in her fur, which always felt good.

"Hi, Julie." Bill came out, wearing just swimming trunks. His chest was hairy in the pattern of a tree, like the identification silhouettes in the Ladybird handbook. Julian wondered how it might feel to nuzzle it the way he did Lady Percy.

"Hi," he said and turned back to feed her a dandelion she didn't really want. Pa said hi was bad and hello was good, like thanks instead of thank you and pardon instead of what. "How did you sleep?" he asked, because that was what you were meant to say next.

Bill laughed. "Fine," he said. "Like a very proper English log." He crouched on his haunches beside Julian and Julian could smell minty shaving cream and toothpaste and something else. Something good. "What's his name?"

"Her. She's Lady Percy."

Bill laughed again. "Whose idea was *that*? You don't know Shakespeare yet."

"Only in Lamb's *Tales*," Julian admitted. "I tried but it's too hard. I was going to call her Percy but Pa said she was a girl and how about Lady Percy. I know what play she's in though. I found her speeches."

"Good. Do you miss your dad?"

"Yes," Julian said, feeling suddenly deeply sad and wondering if, perhaps, that was why.

"He'll be back soon. I'm gonna swim before breakfast. Wanna come too?"

"Yes."

He put Lady Percy away, went behind a gorse bush and changed quickly into his trunks which were hanging on the line, all damp and clammy. Bill waited on the edge of the beach. He stretched high up then out behind him then pulled up first one knee to his chest then the other. Julian did it too. Bill offered him a piggyback. Julian said all right because he did not want to be rude but he was scared of Skip seeing.

Bill did not give him a piggyback but a shoulder ride. He had Julian climb right up his back and sit on his shoulders then he ran down to the waves and jumped so that Julian flew up in the air and crashed down into a wave. The water was freezing and he screamed and spluttered and got a mouthful, which made him want to spit. Bill laughed and quickly swam hard out to the mouth of the cove as if it was a race. In the moments before the jump and the shocking cold, however, Julian had felt Bill's big head and neck between his thighs and Bill's thick, black hair between his fingers and Bill's hairy chest on the back of his dangling legs and a connection was made.

Treading water as his mother had taught him, peeing some more because the water was so cold it made him go all tight inside, he realized it was possible to have unspeakable thoughts outside his bedroom and to put real people into them as if they were just toys you could move around. He watched Bill swim away from him and in his head made him turn round and swim toward him. He made him put him back on his shoulders. He thought of the story in *Tales of Ancient Greece* where Pandora opened the box and let things out which could never be put back in. He pushed the hair out of his eyes and swam after Bill, determined to do the crawl properly, however hard and slow it was and however much bitter brine it made him drink.

B L U E   H O U S E

Sharing a bedroom with Sandy, sleeping with him literally as well as figuratively, and in the same house as his parents and nephews, was dangerously beguiling. Will had never expected it would feel so natural. Had there been a photograph of his sister to hand, he would have propped it on a table just beside the door so that he could remember the truth of the situation and adjust accordingly whenever he had to face the family again. Instead, Sandy placed a chair across the closed door. This was intended to clatter and so serve as an early warning system should one of the children have a nightmare and come blundering in during the night, to give Sandy time to pull his bed away from Will's. However Will found the small irritant of having repeatedly to move the chair reminder enough that whatever pleasure he was feeling was temporary, built on lies and not to be shown.

For Sandy, as ever, the pleasure was entirely physical. As Will had feared, the risk of exposure made him doubly randy. He was growing bolder each day and was no longer confining fun and games to the bedroom but had taken to pursuing Will when he went swimming so as to grope him under cover of water. For Will, the pleasure was entirely domestic; the waking up together, in contrast to their habitually snatched encounters, the shared preparation of meals, even the illusion wrought by the presence of the children that they were an acknowledged family unit. Sandy's single-minded priapism brutally emphasized this disparity in their feelings. And yet Will knew now that this pleasure he felt in seeming innocence and naturalness was about the situation and not about the man. Could he, as in a boyhood fantasy, have recast the scenario with the mere squeezing shut of eyes, so that its focus was another man, not Poppy's husband, he would have done so the moment Sandy arrived.

Ever since their breaking into the fourth room and his discovery of what it held, he had been itching to see Roly again to find out why he had felt the need to lie. He had been married, of course, for fifteen years, but to the man in the painting and photographs. Whenever he saw signs of life at Roly's trailer, it was when he was surrounded by family. Whenever he was free to get away, he found the place deserted or unapproachably in darkness. His hunger for the truth frustrated, he returned repeatedly to the fourth room, feeling less guilt on each visit, and with tidy rapaciousness combed it for clues. He found a big album of cuttings and photographs, and more photographs, maddeningly jumbled, in a shoebox. There were some tapes of concerts which he could hardly play in the house without arousing suspicion but, such was his fascination, he snatched solitary drives in the car so he could play them in there.

The dead lover was a professional violinist called Seth Peake, several years younger, Will guessed, and they had become involved when Seth was still a music student. There was a small family: a stern-faced mother and a poised sister who looked just like him but rarely figured in the pictures. Possibly she lived in America, for in several photographs she posed with the couple by palm trees, a convertible or a swimming pool. The mother usually appeared with a spaniel, looking slightly pained. They lived in London, in a flat with a balcony over a shop, on to which they occasionally squeezed friends for dinner. Roly sculpted, exhibited to some good reviews, Seth studied and performed, gaining far less press coverage. In the early pictures they glittered.

Then Seth changed. Either aging had stolen his glow or he suffered some disappointment. And then there were different pictures, fewer dinner parties and dressing rooms, more crowded gatherings and demonstrations. And suddenly the flood of pictures petered out. There were just two more. In one, taken on an excursion to the seaside, to Brighton perhaps, somewhere with a pier, Roly was looking away, stony-faced, and Seth, pointing at the photographer, was barely recognizable. Wearing huge dark glasses like an opera diva's and wrapped against the cold despite the evident sunshine, he was laughing but his face and hands were impossibly thin, a death's head on a day trip. The other picture, which lay on the very top of the jumble in the box and so gave away the ending as it were, showed a fresh grave. A heap of flowers and wreaths and fluttering cellophane and cards could not quite conceal the deep brown of freshly turned clay. There were wheel marks visible on the grass, left by a mechanical digger presumably. Roly had written a bald caption on the back: *Highgate* and a date. The rest of the album was empty except for the order of service for the funeral. Seth Felix Peake and his dates. He was thirty-one when he died. There had been readings from Auden and Ben Jonson and string quartet movements by Ravel and Britten. How could one possibly stick in nephews and nieces and birthday celebrations and trips to Ibiza after such an event? Undeterred, Will looked on the shelves and searched through the shoebox again, but found no hint of a sequel. Every family had its archivist and storyteller. In this one Seth, not Roly evidently had been the album-keeper.

Lying in bed listening to seagulls, he heard Dad get up and take his and Mum's tea and biscuits back to bed. Sandy stirred as he lifted the sheet, and threw out an arm to catch his thigh. Eyes still glued shut, he mumbled sexily, a faint smile on his lips. Will gently prized himself free. The two of them had ended up on one bed, impossibly cramped in their movements and he ached all over. Sandy mumbled again as Will pushed the second bed chastely away.

"It's early still," he said. "Save your strength. You promised them a theme park today, remember." He planted a kiss on his stubbled chin. Sandy groaned and rolled away from the light. Will pulled on his trunks and retrieved a dryish towel. Standing near the gap in the shutters, he looked back at the man sprawled so greedily across the bed, at Sandy's heap of clothes neatly folded the night before, at the glass of water he religiously brought to bed to drink when he woke, the book about the SAS he was reading. This was a glimpse, he realized, of the husband rather than the lover. A man for whom he felt tremendous affection but whom he could never love. "Sandy?" he said softly.

"What?"

"This has got to stop, you know. All this."

The noise Sandy made was more like a child deprived of pudding than a man facing the end of a relationship. But that was surely the whole problem; it was no relationship, to his thinking, but something stickily addictive, no less desirable for being contrary to doctor's orders.

"Why?"

"She's my sister, for fuck's sake, and I don't want to hurt her. What more reason do you need?"

"So?" He did not even look at Will to speak, head still half-buried in pillow. "We're *both* mad about her."

"And I want my life back. It's gone on too long. It's not healthy." He bent over Sandy's bed again, pressed a hand to where his ass was clearly outlined through the twisted sheet and kissed his shoulder. "We can talk later on. Tonight sometime. But I wanted to tell you now. So you can think about it."

Sandy made the small boy wants pudding noise again so Will pulled back hastily and left him to sleep. He regretted telling him to think about it and promising a discussion since it sounded as though he required a decision when what he needed was a handshake. They had held versions of this conversation before so Sandy probably interpreted that morning's announcement as nothing more serious than one of Will's periodic fits of conscience. And perhaps it was. Perhaps they would still be sleeping together when he was fifty.

As Will walked down the deserted beach, however, the dazzling sun, cold sand and colder water strengthened his resolve and the exhilaration that went with it. "This is real," they said. After the rain in the night everything looked freshly made and it was easy to imagine it the dawn of a new era in his life, a new, healthier period of truth and accountability and commitment. He was still a lousy swimmer but even that could change. The time he had formerly devoted to seeing Sandy, and waiting for Sandy and mentally recovering from seeing Sandy, he could devote to swimming lessons. He might start singing again, join the Barrowcester Glee Club, which was famously a second-chance marriage market. He trod in a tangle of seaweed and recoiled, having to kick to break free of it. He might, he reflected sadly, merely give up more time to helping his troubled parents.

There was a bark and Fay came racing down the beach and into the sea to cool down. Rather than swim, she ran through the surf parallel to the beach, raising spray like a small horse cantering. Roly came behind her from the cliff path, a brace of large rabbits slung over his shoulder like a scarf. He called Fay to follow him then saw Will, who raised a hand from the water. Without even a glance to see if they were overlooked, Roly slung down the rabbits, stripped off and swam out to join him. "Should have brought my soap," he said.

Will took him in afresh. Despite all the photographs, he had forgotten how he looked and had rebuilt him in his mind, larger and less vulnerable than he was in the flesh. "I've been wanting to see you," he said.

"Should have come over, then." Roly swam in a circle around him.

"I couldn't get away. My family."

"Ah."

"No. I mean it."

"So come today. Run away. I've got to go over to Fowey. You could come too."

"When?"

"Whenever you're ready. Just turn up and we'll go."

"I need to dress and grab some breakfast."

Roly smiled. "Me too. You could help me choose what to wear."

"Will!"

Will turned at the squeaky voice. Oscar, the youngest, was racing across the beach in his pajama bottoms, his red hair like a flash of flame. He backed off as Fay bounced over to inspect him then saw she was

friendly and laughed as she licked his face. Then he was transfixed by
the dead rabbits.

"A nephew," Will said. "Better go. I . . . I'll see you, then."

Roly swam back faster than him and dried himself on his shirt. Oscar
was fascinated.

"He's naked," he pointed out.

"Yes," Will said. "He was in a hurry." He winked over at Roly as they
turned away. "How about breakfast? I bet you haven't even washed
your face yet; you've got sleepy-dirt in your eyes."

As they walked back up to the house, Oscar recounting at length a
marvelously egocentric dream he had just enjoyed, it struck Will there
was now nothing to stop him being entirely open. He had met someone,
the sad young man in fact, and was going on a trip with him. He could
do as he pleased. They were all adults. They would survive without him.

"Are you coming to the theme park with us?" Oscar asked.

"No, Oz. I'm going on a trip with my friend."

"Who?"

"Roly. The naked man back there."

"With the rabbits?"

"Yes."

"Oh. OK. Can I have mashed banana on my toast?"

"Of course." Will ruffled his hair, smiled at the matter-of-fact toler-
ance of early childhood and thought what a pity it was that the crowd
politics of school would soon educate it out of him.

Hugo was already breakfasting while browsing the Internet. "It's all
right," he said, catching Will's anxious glance. "I'm using Dad's mobile,
not yours."

"You'll be giving him an almighty bill, won't you?"

Hugo tapped on his mouse. "He doesn't mind. Mum says it keeps me
quiet." He giggled. "Look what I found."

Oh God, Will thought. *Porn.* But Hugo had found Henry Farmer's
home page.

"This is the robber Grandpa let out of prison," Hugo told Oscar.
"He's so old! He was a rapist too."

"Yes," Will said, leaving Hugo to answer Oscar's inquiry as to what a rapist did exactly. "Eat your breakfasts both of you while I have a look."

There was a beaming photograph, a lengthy diatribe against the injustice of trying to extradite Farmer and an extract from his forthcoming life story. There was also a special offer: one-pound notes, signed by the old rogue himself and purporting to be a share of his original haul. *All major cards accepted* it announced and proceeded to ask for a disturbing number of personal details.

Will stared hard at the sun-lined face, its heavy white eyebrows, a gold tooth, gold dog tags on a neck chain, but felt no glimmer of recognition. There was an e-mail option. Perhaps he could send him an e-mail asking, "Remember me? Because I don't."

"Don't let Grandpa see this," he said, turning back to his toast. "It would only make him cross."

Sandy was in the shower so he could dress quickly and excuse himself.

"I seem to have hooked up with your sad young man," he told Mum, who was discreetly queuing for the bathroom, reading spines on a bookshelf. "I never told you, did I? He's the sculptor."

"No! So that's what all the driftwood's for."

"And it wasn't a wife who died. It was a boyfriend."

"Ah."

"I said I'd help him drop something off. You don't mind, do you?"

"Of course not. We'll see you when we see you."

"Thanks, Mum." He kissed her cheek, guilty that he had just dumped a pile of information on the person in the household least able to process it, and hurried off before Sandy could come out and start asking questions.

Roly was butchering the rabbits as Will arrived. As he peeled the fur away from the pale, fatty flesh beneath, Will remembered childhood bathtimes and the instant of delicious confusion as his father peeled a turtlenecked jersey over his head and crooned, "Skin a rabbit," while Will's face was held tight in woolly darkness. He saw how apposite the phrase was. The carcass did indeed have a look of naked child about it and the limp jacket of fat-lined fur looked indeed like a garment that might as easily be slid on again.

"Sorry about this," Roly said, tossing the parts he did not want to his feet where Fay fell on them, fur, fat and all. "If I don't do them straight away, they start going off."

"How did you learn to do this?" Will asked. It seemed a far cry from dinners on a Notting Hill balcony.

"From a very old American cookery manual. There were also instructions for dealing with bear and ground squirrel."

"Bear?"

"That was a bit wasteful. You only took the paws. For stewing."

Out with it. Out with it, Will thought. *The longer you leave it the harder it'll—*

"I've got a confession," he blurted.

Roly looked up from washing his hands under the rain butt tap. He let Will suffer a few moments before saying, "You broke into the fourth bedroom. It's a bit *Bloody Chamber* isn't it? Impossible to resist once you've taken a first peek."

"How did you know?"

"Persons who look at other persons' photograph albums after dark should close the shutters first, then read by torchlight."

"There's a good explanation."

"I'm sure."

"One of the boys broke Mum's pearls. They rolled under the door and before I could stop him Sandy, that's my brother-in-law, just bashed it open. So I couldn't help seeing. I saw everything."

"Even the everything in the bookcase. Night after night."

"Why did you pretend to be straight?"

"Did I?" Roly opened the back doors of his old van and started nestling sculptures on a heap of blankets in there.

"Well, you let me believe it."

"You assumed it. I only let you think I'd been married."

"And you had."

"In a way, yes."

"But why?" Will pursued. "I feel so stupid."

"I didn't think I'd see you again, so what was the point? I won't see you again. You're only here for another week."

"Who says? I might decide to stay."

"The house is let all month," Roly said, not missing a beat to consider what he had just heard. "What makes this place so attractive suddenly?"

"I've been doing a lot of thinking."

"You make it sound as though that makes a change."

"It does. I mean the kind of thinking I've been doing does. Roly, I think I love you."

Roly merely looked at him then looked away and carried on loading sculptures into the back of his van. "That's very sweet, William. Sweet William. You must get that joke all the time."

"I don't, actually. Everyone calls me Will."

"Oh. Well that's very sweet of you but you have a life elsewhere, with your shop and your café and your family and friends and I have a life. A precarious life. And an even more precarious kind of . . . I was going to say happiness. Christ! What I mean is—"

"It's okay," Will butted in, catching Roly's upper arm to stop his restless pacing to and fro. "I wasn't proposing marriage. I'm not a complete fool. I know these things can't be rushed. I was just . . . I just felt good about how I was feeling and wanted to let you know."

"Oh. Well, good." He looked down at Will's restraining hand, took it in both of his, seemed to read its palm a moment then pressed it to his lips. He raised an eyebrow. "Shall we go to bed straight away or would you really like to see Fowey?"

"Would you be very hurt if . . . I'd love to go out, for once."

"For *once*?"

"I mean," Will hastily covered his tracks, "people are always so keen to leap into bed and it would be really good just to spend time with you, watching what you do. You know?"

"I know."

"And then maybe . . ."

"Hmm?"

"Maybe later."

They kissed against the side of the van. In his excitement, Will had quite forgotten where they were standing. If his mother had taken her usual cool seat at Blue House's rear, she would be enjoying quite an eyeful.

"Tell me about Seth," he said.

Roly broke away. "We should go if we're going." He opened the passenger door and carried on talking as he walked around to the driver's side. "He was a violinist. One of the many prodigies who don't make it. Or not as big as he'd hoped. He taught and he played in a string quartet that now has a new first violin."

"But you were happy together."

"Oh, as happy as two difficult, creative people can ever be. First he was disappointed. Then he was ill. And that became what he did. And gay politics for a bit. Now, do you mind if we don't talk about him any more?"

"Sure."

"I mean, not for a while." He gave one of his snatched, nervous smiles and clicked the ignition key, waiting for the diesel light to go off. "Still a bit raw."

"I shouldn't have asked."

"You're not to be polite. It's one of the things I hate. Which reminds me . . ." He fumbled in the welter of old toffee papers, parking tickets, seashells and nails and found something. "Fay!" he yelled. Fay startled Will by leaping in at his open window, crashing across his lap and taking up, as to the manner born, an alert sitting position between them. She was still chewing some rabbit organ. "Her breath stinks, I warn you," Roly said. "I tried chicken toothpaste but it felt sort of demeaning. For both of us. Here. While I remember."

He reached across and Will thought he was going to run a hand through his hair but instead he only tapped a finger to the middle of Will's forehead as if to admonish wrong thinking. Then he started the engine and, smiling to himself, lurched them off up a track along the valley, skirting the golf course and the old manor that was now its clubhouse.

"That's where my cousins used to live," he muttered. "Smug bastards."

A minute or two had passed before Will caught sight of himself in the wing mirror and spotted the small, yellow star on his brow.

BEACHCOMBER

The sun was so warm Frances felt she was melting, drop by waxy drop, into the sand. Skip was helping Julian build a castle from pebbles. They were being supremely methodical, sorting stones by size and color so they could start with the largest and build up to the small ones while executing patterns in the masonry. The challenge, inspired by the day's lesson in church, which she had demanded, to Bill's amusement, they all attend, was to build a house on sand that could withstand the tide and thereby the ordinances of God.

Julian was as brown as his cousin now, his hair stiff with salt and his legs streaked with mud and sand. He looked good enough to eat, especially the back of his neck and the vulnerable backs of his knees. "Little savage," she murmured when he caught her eye and smiled again at that day's Psalm line, *Neither delighteth he in any man's legs.* Across the beach she could hear the insistent clacking of Bill's typewriter where he worked at the veranda table.

She had been deeply touched to wake from desolate dreams to find Skip in the bed beside her. Sleep rumpled, the girl was warmly childish and confiding, offering her trust in a way that penetrated Frances's guard. Perhaps John had been right and her surliness was simply muffled sorrow. She certainly responded to attention and, once Frances set her talking, fairly bubbled over. It was mainly questions about *girl stuff*, as Bill would term it. The poor thing was fearful about having her first period. Half the reason she favored loose-fitting dungarees was her terror that it would start without warning and show through her clothes. She wanted to discuss the various merits of Tampax and Dr. White's towels, which Frances assured her were more suitable for a young girl. She was also terribly worried about breasts. Would they hurt? How could you tell when they'd stopped growing? How did you measure them? How many bras did you need?

Frances did her best to comfort and advise and was surprised to find that talking like this made her feel her age as giving birth or getting married had never done. Skip let her brush her hair, which was really a very pretty color if only she would let it grow again, then trim and file her nails, which scrabbling on the rocks had battered, and give them a coat of clear nail varnish to protect them. In the hours since, Skip had assumed her defiant, faintly bossy manner and given no sign to betray what had passed between them but now that Frances knew the manner for what it was, it touched rather than offended her. She was startled to realize how much of what she took for her own attitudes had in fact been formed by John. This must have been the case, since now that he was not here to keep tabs on her reactions, she felt less and less obliged to voice a high-minded indignation.

She was about to turn on to her belly to roast the other side while she read some more of the John Updike book she had borrowed off Bill, when she heard motorbikes and twisted her neck to see three of them being ridden along the beach. They were monstrous things of black and chrome and as they drew nearer, causing people to jump indignantly out of the way, snatching back towels, children, dogs, she saw the riders, long-haired, unshaven, leather-jacketed, sunglasses lending their faces impassivity. The children had stopped their building work to stare.

"You have Hell's Angels here?" Skip asked.

"Of course." Julian was defending the honor of the country, apparently. "We have everything."

But his show of nonchalance crumbled as the bikers drew nearer, passed only feet away from where he was watching and headed up the cove toward Beachcomber. There was a girl on the back of one bike, long hair blowing in the wind, bare feet shockingly dirty. When they stopped below the veranda, she jumped off and called out something to Bill who, to Frances's amazement, came out to greet her. He shook hands with the girl and reached into his pocket for some money, which he gave her in exchange for something she unbuttoned from a little pouch around her neck. He sniffed it before handing over the money. They continued to stand there a few moments, apparently just passing the time of day, then hands were raised in laconic greeting, engines revved unnecessarily loud, the girl jumped back on behind the same man, the biggest of the three, with the thickest beard, and the bikes swung away from the bungalow. Rather than take the track, they returned the way they had come, cutting a swath through the sunbathers once more. The bike with the girl on showily struck out into the surf to raise a spray.

"Does your father *know* them?" Julian asked aghast.

"Sure," Skip said, blasé in her turn. "He knows lots of people."

The children returned to their building and Frances rolled on to her front and tried to return to her novel but something like indignation was welling up and stopping her. She ran her eyes over the same paragraph repeatedly but the words acquired no meaning because her mind was too occupied with him reaching for money, the girl's billowing hair and filthy bare feet and the casual way he had accepted her ostentatious arrival.

Behind her his typewriter began to clatter again. More romantic, moneymaking lies about his marriage. Her neck grew stiff from holding her head sufficiently far above the book to focus. She flopped over on to her side instead but could not rest her head on her elbow without crushing her sunglasses against her temple. So she rolled back on to her spine and raised the book on weary arms, shielding her face from the broiling sun even as she tried to read. The book grew impossibly heavy however and sweat mixed with sun lotion kept trickling into her eyes and stinging them.

To the insistent chatter of the typewriter she walked down a corridor. She knew that her baby, her new daughter, was behind one of the doors but found only useless things, dried roses, a mound of sand, a great pool of suntan oil, a circle of prisoners playing Totopoly. The last door took her to a snugly furnished room with a view of a river. A man was lying on a sofa looking at the ceiling but talking to her, talking and talking, all about himself.

"Julian grown up," she said aloud but somebody shushed her so she strained to make out what he was so relentlessly telling her. She could not make out his words however, any more than she could bring his big adult face into focus.

She awoke to music. Bill was standing, shading her from the sun. He had her radio in his hand. It was tuned to a pop channel. "Listen," he said and smirked.

"Ssh," she said. She despised people who played radios in public places, even had they played real music, which they never seemed to. He stared at her and turned the volume up.

"It's your song," he said.

"What is it?" she asked, cross and sleep-soured, sitting up.

"Aretha Franklin. Listen."

"I hate this sort of music."

"Listen."

It was a big, harsh voice. She could tell the singer was black. No white woman dared voice that sort of abandon. There was no melody as such, only rhythm and a sense of a repetitive framework over which the singer could wind herself up. *Oh when me and that man get to lovin'*, she sang. It was mortifying, like someone undressing in the middle of a church. It sounded so real, not faked at all. No one could conjure up this sort of frankness to order. The song must come out differently every time. Watching her, he grinned. He tapped a foot, actually swayed his hips a little as he continued to hold out the radio between them like a kind of offering. He nodded his head, as if at the truth of the singer's words.

"Ssh," she hissed. "Turn it down!"

People were staring. Julian was staring. Bill carried on playing it regardless. At last she could stand it no longer. She jumped up, snatched the radio and turned it off.

"What?" he said.

"That's not music," she told him. "That's just noise."

"Of course it's music!" He laughed.

"I'd find you real music only the powers that be have made the signal too weak to reach us down here."

"You mean spineless stuff. Polite string quartets."

"They're not polite. Not all of them."

"What are you so *scared* of, Frances?"

"I'm not scared." She sat down again, brushed some sand off the radio's blue housing with a clean corner of her towel. It was a good one. It had been a wedding present. "I just don't think everyone else should have to listen to what you want to play. It's inconsiderate."

"No," he said, crouching before her. "That's just an excuse. You're scared."

"You think I'm a prude, don't you?" she said. "You think I'm some kind of dried-up, middle-class, inhibited bitch of a prude who can't let go and so has to hide behind her respectable good behavior to protect herself from the things she daren't surrender to."

"I didn't say that."

"You implied it. You said that trashy *thing* was my song. You think you can understand me and save me from myself."

"No I don't."

"I hate being patronized."

"I just wanted you to hear the song. It's got funny words."

But anger had taken hold of her. She had to show him. She grabbed the radio and turned it back on. The song had finished and a new, rougher sound had replaced it, throbbing electric guitars and some man with a voice like a yowling tomcat. But there was a rhythm there, lax and smoky perhaps yet something to hold on to. She turned the volume as high as it would go so that the voice began to be distorted even further than the singer intended, jumped up and began to dance. She clapped her hands, rocked her hips, stamped her feet. Laughing, Skip jumped up and joined in. Julian was shocked. For a moment he stared at her with his father's eyes so that she laughed at him and beckoned. Then he giggled and jumped up too, shaking his limbs with no sense of rhythm,

the way little boys did playing musical statues. The music was wild,
demonic.

"Who *is* this?" she shouted down at Bill, who was still only watching.
He murmured something. "Who?" she yelled.

He jumped up, took her hands, danced too.

"The Doors," he shouted in her ear so that it half-hurt, half-tickled.

They only danced for a few seconds, barely a minute, feet going
everywhere, treading on each other's toes, kicking sand over the towels,
over the radio. Then a man came up, scarlet in the face from heat and
anger.

"Will you turn this down?" he barked.

Frances let go of Bill's hands, stopped dancing. She was breathless.
The man was ridiculous. He wore a loose white hat and voluminous off-
white shorts and black ankle socks above tennis shoes. She wanted to
tweak his nose or laugh in his face or simply push him hard so that he
fell over. Instead she turned down the music and faced him again.

"I'm sorry," she said. "What did you say?"

"That's not music," he said, slightly taken aback, she fancied, by her
politeness and accent.

"No," she said. "Not really. But I suppose it's sex, isn't it?"

The man actually opened and shut his mouth like a fish. Julian
laughed, the only one dancing now. As the man turned away, Skip
laughed too and both children continued to laugh immoderately, falsely,
forcing the sound out.

Frances picked up the radio and handed it back to Bill. "Don't get
this sandy," she said. "These ones last forever if you treat them well. Tea
anyone? Julian, you've had too much sun. Take a swim to wash the sand
off then come and sit in the shade for a bit to cool off. Just look at that
rampart! You've done brilliantly! When's the tide coming in again?"
She heard herself chattering like a mad thing and broke off to walk back
to the house. She filled the kettle and turned it on for tea then went to
her room and lay on cool sheets, tasting salt on her lips and panic in her
chest.

Desire for him had sprung on her and for a few seconds on the beach
she had failed to recognize its hot, unfamiliar breath at her ear. Had the

ridiculous man not intervened, she would have held Bill close, rested her head on his shoulder, kissed him even. Once recognized as the thing that had lurked behind all her discomfort, her combativeness and mistrust, desire suffused her being like a crimson blush. It was so entirely strange, as unlike the steady love and respect she felt for John as sunstroke after warmth and just as unpleasant. She looked the same—she checked in the looking-glass as soon as her bedroom door was shut—but she continued to feel that the disorder must be painted bright on her face like a high temperature on a child's hectic cheeks.

She ought to ask him to leave, only he had done nothing wrong and she could not ask him to go without telling him why. And she could not bear to have him laugh at her. The alternative was to leave herself, concoct some story, pack Julian into the Volkswagen and go. There was no reason why Bill and Skip should not enjoy the remainder of a holiday already paid for. She went so far as to pull out her suitcase and open it on the bed. Somehow that brought home the ridiculousness of her behavior. She shut the thing away again, sat at the dressing table and brushed the sand from her hair. Hairbrushing was always immensely soothing. Perhaps her mother had brushed her hair when she was fractious as a child. Frances had certainly done it to Julian when he couldn't stop crying and it worked like a dream. Forty tugging strokes one side and forty the other and she felt her equilibrium restored. Or almost. By the time Bill led the children in for tea, she was cutting banana sandwiches as though nothing had happened.

She fancied he looked at her inquiringly but deflected his glances with redoubled brightness. They could both stay. She could act like an adult instead of a frightened child, recognize her desire as the impossible thing it was and enjoy his presence like good weather. She might even flirt a little. There could be no harm in it. Beverly, her friend at the kindergarten, maintained that flirting was a kind of knife-sharpening for marriage. It kept one all the more desirable to and desirous of one's husband. Only Beverly was not married, so what could she know? And Frances, she realized now, had never thought of desire and John in the same context, only of John and babies, which was not the same thing at all.

They took back sandwiches and milk to the beach on a tray to watch the tide reach the children's pebble-built house on the sand. One small section of the wall collapsed but the rest withstood the snaking carpets of foam and she found herself caught up in their jubilation. She remembered she had packed a camera and took a series of silly, laughing pictures of them posing with Bill in the water beside their structure, sandwiches held aloft in a kind of salute.

She ordered hot baths all round then drove them to the cinema in Wadebridge—Skip actually wearing the new dress—to see *Oliver!*, which was very sweet. It made her feel tearful and nostalgic, which was preposterous since it was set long before even her grandparents' era. They ate fish and chips afterward, on the old bridge over the Camel so that the car would not stink of fish. Julian was delighted to find his father's photograph on the newspaper wrapping his chips. They unfurled it in the light of a street-lamp. It was a piece on Farmer's breakout. There was a photograph of John, looking tense and handsome at his desk, and an equally large one of Henry, dating, presumably, from the time of his admission.

"Can we ring Pa?" Julian asked.

"Of course," she said. "I was going to anyway."

They found a call box and rang him and she let Julian and Skip do most of the talking. When she came on she barely had time for a *hello darling no I'm fine* before the pips went.

"I can't call you back," he said. "There's been a development and—" Then he was cut off so her good-bye went unsaid.

She took a wrong turning when they drove over the bridge and they were on the outskirts of Bodmin before she saw her mistake. The children fell asleep in the back, each lying full length on a seat with their feet against a window. Bill found a music channel on the radio and played it softly and she tried to guess whether each singer was black or white. She got it right every time except for someone called Dusty Springfield.

"What's it short for, Dusty?" she asked. "Dorothy?"

"Or Drusilla?"

"Probably Janet. It sounds like a group of Wiltshire villages; Higher

Springfield, Nether Springfield, Springfield Monachorum, Dusty Springfield." She heard herself trying too hard to amuse him and fell silent, letting the song fill the space between them.

The children barely stirred as she bumped them down the drive to Beachcomber. They carried them inside, one apiece. Julian woke up as she was unbuttoning his shirt. "Is Pa famous now?"

"No," she assured him. "Hundreds of people are in the papers and on the radio every day, most of them only once. Every day hundreds more. By the time you start your new school in the autumn, no one will remember him."

"Oh," he said and yawned so she could not tell if he was relieved or disappointed. "Does Henry know I'm here?" he added suddenly.

"Of course not. Not unless you told him. Skin a rabbit."

"I didn't tell him anything," he insisted. "He did all the talking." He was suddenly troubled, his brow creased, almost tearful. Perhaps he was worried about starting at choir school. She brushed his hair, tickling him and laughing at how it was rebelliously standing up at his crown.

"Will you lie down!" she told it, mock-indignant and tapping it with the brush. "Lie down at once!" By the time she had soothed him and had him say his prayers and played the game where he pretended to blow out the light, Bill had long since finished settling Skip. When she emerged, the house was silent and she thought for a thankful moment that he had gone to bed too. Then she heard him cough out on the veranda and saw the glow of his cigarette.

"Come for a walk," he said softly. "There's a moon. Come see."

The tide had filled the bay and was beginning to recede. The moon seemed huge and yellowish as though swathed in muslin. She fetched a cardigan and walked with him up the track away from Polcamel to the clifftops. From up there they could see not only the sprinkling of lights around the bay and the estuary mouth and the lighthouse on the headland beyond but also the occasional boat far out on the water. There was a well-placed bench, nestling against an outcrop of rocks so it was sheltered. She was breathless from the climb so sat there. He stood smoking and looking out to sea awhile, then came back to join her.

"Listen," she said.

"What?"

"You can hear sheep munching. In the field behind us." He listened, laughed and she smelled the odd, nutty smell she had smelled in his room. "Is that cigarette herbal or something?"

"Nope," he said. "Try some?" He held it out to her.

She shook her head. "I don't smoke. I tried it once, at school, and the tobacco made me sick."

"It's not just tobacco. Go on. Try it."

"It's drugs!" she exclaimed, remembering the girl on the motorbike. "You bought drugs!"

"You make it sound like capital letters," he laughed. "How do you people do that? No, it's not *Drugs*. It's pot. I scored some off those bikers. I'd run into the girl at the post office and smelled it on her."

"Fancy."

"So try it." She shook her head. "You'll never know until you've tried."

"I don't want to get addicted."

"One puff will hardly make you an addict. You don't even smoke!"

"No. Thanks. Honestly."

He inhaled again and his voice was momentarily tight, as if the smoke were strangling him. "Becky was so right about you," he said. "Uptight. Completely, certifiably uptight. Even when you danced on the beach you managed to look respectable, like some mum at a kid's groovy party."

"Oh give me that!" She grabbed the cigarette, or roach or whatever one called it, dropped it, swore and stuck it between her lips, feeling with a shock the moisture of his own lips on its paper. She inhaled, fought the impulse to cough, then let the smoke out. The moon caught it so that it momentarily obscured his face. "Nothing," she said. "Tastes of dusty corners. What book was that in?" She held the cigarette out to him but he left her holding it.

"Have some more," he said. "You need to catch up." Humoring him, she inhaled again. "Hold it in this time," he said. "Don't let it out so fast."

She breathed out more slowly, imagining the smoke streaking

through her hair and leaving mossy trails. "Nothing," she said and passed him back what was left of the cigarette.

He dragged on it again, watching her, then grinned and it seemed to her that he had the most perfect teeth she had ever seen. It felt, all at once, as if her skull had opened to the night sky and the stars were shedding chilly light on her glistening brain. The night felt huge and velvety about them, the cliff higher, the bench more exposed. Her nose was suddenly full of the smell of him, which somehow was never going to be enough. "Oh God," she croaked. "Is it always like this?"

"Like what? I'm feeling nothing at all."

"I . . . I can't really say."

"You can let go of the bench. You won't float away." She watched him prize her hand off the bench and warm it in his. "Tell me," he said. "Tell me what you're thinking. Trust me. I'm a novelist."

She pulled away her hand sharply. "Can't," she said but instead of clutching back at the bench for the anchorage it gave her, she flung her arm around the back of his neck. "Oh God," she said, "I think I have to kiss you."

"So, Frances? Kiss me," he laughed softly.

"But I can't possibly."

"Well I can't kiss you."

"Why not?"

"You're a respectable married lady. And my sister-in-law."

"Only very distantly."

His eyes were sparkling. He was laughing at her. His neck was warm and hard beneath her hand. It was the easiest thing in the world to pull him toward her. And then she felt his lips on hers and, oh Lord, his tongue in her mouth and his alien mustache against her cheek and nose. And she knew no kiss would be deep enough. She kissed him furiously, as though his mouth withheld a secret. She fed on his face, rammed her fingers through his absurdly long hair, pulled him down against her. "No," she said. "Stop. We must stop."

"OK." He kissed her once more, chastely, with closed lips, then sat back and looked at her sprawled over the back of the bench against cushions of thrift. But the space between them ached.

"Come back," she said. "I can't bear it."

So he stood now and lifted her up and back so that she was squarely before him and he leaned over her and kissed her anywhere but on the lips. On her cheeks. Her neck. The opening of her blouse. Then he held her more tightly and crushed her against the carpet of plants so that she felt all his weight safely holding her there.

"It hurts," she said.

"Sorry." He began to pull back.

"No. I mean normally. Normally it hurts. I've never told anyone. When we . . . you know . . . it hurts me."

"Have you told him?"

"Of course not. The very idea." She began to laugh. "Where are you? Shouldn't we . . . ? Oh Lord."

He had reached up under her flimsy skirt. She felt herself with his hands and knew she was rough with gooseflesh. She ached for his weight on her again and he was sliding her pants down so presumably he'd soon be on top of her again and she did not care if it hurt she wanted him so. But instead he disappeared from view and began to kiss her in places only the midwife and obstetrician had seen and then, to her amazement, began to lick her in great, long strokes that seemed to run from the base of her spine right around to her belly button, and with a hot tongue that felt as huge and broad as a bullock's.

I'm melting, she thought. *He's melting me in half.*

He cradled her thighs on his arms so that he could drive his face deeper and deeper into her. A part of her thought how comical she must look and what would people say if they came along the coast path and saw her, but she was beyond caring, and the quiet, satirical, respectable voice was silenced by the shock of small explosions he seemed to be detonating deep within her. She heard a seagull crying and thought how peculiar this was because seagulls never cried out at night. And then she realized it was her and began to laugh until tears wet her cheeks. He stopped then and kissed his way up her front, nuzzling through her blouse then lay on top of her, squeezing her thighs together inside his so that her groin seemed to be on fire and pressing her head against the flowers with the flat of his hand on her forehead. Had he not pinned her down like that she might have flown clear off the bench, over the cliff's edge and out to sea. He lay quite still and when he spoke at last it was a shock to hear his voice so close in her ear.

"That hurt much?"

"No," she said. "Not a bit. Oh God."

"Leave God out of it. You mention him way too often."

"Do you think he was watching?"

"I think he has better manners. I think he wreathed us in our own private cloud for as long as it took. Kiss me." She kissed him, realizing only as she did so that she was tasting herself on his lips. Then her straying hand felt him pulsing hard against her thigh. "Nothing that won't keep," he said. There was a pause before he added, "Come away with me?"

"Don't be silly."

"I'm not. You and Julie. We could all live together in Norwich. There's room; they've found me a house."

"That's ridiculous."

"OK. You're right." He kissed her again, then sat on the bench beside her. He kept a hand spread on her belly as though he sensed her light-headed need to remain anchored. "Come away with me," he said again. "I think I love you."

"You think no such thing."

"And you love me."

"I hardly know you. I cordially disliked you when you first got here, in fact."

"And in the sort of books you read that always means love. Love denied. Come away. Let me save you."

"So I can wash your socks. I love John. I'm married to John. This is absurd. It never happened and we must get back to the children." She tried to sit up but his hand felt as heavy as lead and she had no strength to lift it off her. "I was going to run away," she confessed. "This afternoon. After . . . You know. On the beach. I was going to take Julian and leave you both here."

"But you chose to stay. And aren't you glad you did?"

"I'm not so sure."

Now she found the strength to sit up. He helped her off the bench and, once she was on the path again, held her in his arms from behind and rubbed some of his warmth back through her cardiganed arms. "Oh Frances, Frances!"

"Stop it," she said, feeling suddenly wretched. "It doesn't help. Nothing helps."

"Can I come to your room?"

"You'd wake the children."

"I could be quiet as death."

"Yes, but I'm not sure I could. Stay here a bit. I . . . I need to go back on my own and think."

"OK."

She left him smoking a normal cigarette this time, sitting on the back of the bench. She went directly to bed, avoiding all looking-glasses. She did not brush her teeth or bathe and the sheets felt sticky on her salty skin but she needed to feel the events of the day were still about her. She strained to think of John at his desk or reading in his armchair or asleep in bed but all she could conjure was Bill's eyes and the way they pinioned her and the way the smell of him mounted in her head like smoke. So she cried herself to sleep. They were not wild tears of grief. She was not racked with painful sobs. They were rather tears of a kind of homesickness; tears for the loss of a safe place she now knew she had outgrown forever. There was a shade of fear, too, at the complete uncertainty of what lay before her.

She slept before he re-entered the house. She woke with him in the bed beside her and pulled his arms about her and breathed him in as though she had known him years not days. They made love quietly, deliberately. It hurt at first, as it always did, but he saw her wince, because he had refused to let her turn out the light, and he slipped out to the kitchen and came back with a pot of yogurt which he encouraged her to spread over him before he pushed into her again. And it felt better, much better, and he actually cried when it was over for him so that she had to hold him and rock him as though it was something bad and wounding she had done to him, something of his she had stolen. And she saw that it was not only for her that the process was irreversible. He must have held her until she slept for she had no memory of his leaving her and when the sun woke her through curtains left carelessly undrawn, she experienced a short-lived, sleepy innocence of all that had passed.

BLUE HOUSE

Apparently she had been going through a bad patch, but she had no memory of it other than feeling apprehensive. This was a new development. They were still watching her, even the children, prepared for her to do something unexpected.

"I don't know what I was frightened of," she told John as Sandy drove them all to the theme park. "Probably you lot bloody gawping at me."

Hugo and Oscar laughed at this so she laughed back.

The theme park was not at all the feast of sickening aerial rides and finely tuned technological nightmares the children had been expecting. Instead there were lots of men and women in period costume in a re-created nineteenth-century mining community demonstrating traditional activities, like churning butter, splitting slates and spinning wool. Once one got over the shock of the costumes, it was rather charming and Frances enjoyed herself, happily sampling fudge and clotted-cream ice cream and scrumpy when they were offered. The boys were in a deep sulk, however, which only two trips on the mineshaft railway, once with John, once with Sandy, would alleviate.

As they were queuing to visit a pilchard cannery, an old man, apparently on a day out with his daughter, suddenly unzipped his trouser fly, thrust in his hand and started to rub himself with evident relish. The children laughed, naturally, but other people's reactions were astonishing. John looked politely away but, like a lot of the men around them, Sandy became aggressive. "Can't you control him?" he shouted at the daughter, who had given up remonstrating with her father. "There are children here, you know." As if she could have failed to notice. One man pushed the old man quite roughly then another joined in and they tried to bundle him into a corner, like a naughty child, still playing with himself.

"Leave him alone," Frances pleaded. "Can't you see he's ill? He's very ill." And she smiled at the poor daughter to show she sympathized and understood. But the daughter only scowled at her then started shouting at her father too, as if she hated him.

"Put it away, you disgusting old man," she said. "I'm never bringing you out again. That's it! Never again. You hear?" And she pushed between the bullying men to slap her father hard on the top of the head, so that his sun hat fell off.

"If she did that to a child," Frances said to anyone who would listen, "the police would be involved. Stop her, someone. John? Why's everyone so stupidly puritanical?"

But no one wanted to listen. Sandy was hurrying the boys ahead and John took her arm and only steered her out of the way, saying, "I know. Awful woman," but in a way that showed he was thinking of his own discomfort.

They ate a pub lunch, then Sandy placated the boys by stopping off at something called a water park where children, and quite a few adults, flew again and again down slides and convoluted tubes, all of them filled with water, all of them ending in a deep pool where the riders were discharged, sank and re-emerged like creatures reborn only to climb the stairways to ride down again. It was futile and nightmarish, like the worst kind of public baths, with a stench of chlorine and overheated air. Screams and laughter bounced off the tiled walls and huge expanses of smoked plate glass. Heads aching, waving to Sandy and the children when required, Frances and John drank not very nice tea out of polystyrene cups at a sort of café beneath an artificial palm tree. They seemed to be the only people wearing clothes so they felt like visiting dignitaries among a newer, simpler race.

"Nobody's swimming," she said. "Isn't that odd? They're just splashing about. Do people not swim anymore?"

"Of course they do," he said, but he had escaped into a long Russian novel so his thoughts were not with her.

"Where's Will?"

"With a new friend," he said wearily.

"Oh yes," she said, remembering, "the sad young man." Twice that day she had asked where Will was and had been patiently reminded. Why could she not remember? Did she, unconsciously, find the facts unpalatable? "Don't worry. I remember all the facts," she told John as the water tubes thundered about them and calypso music wailed through loudspeakers in the palm trunk. "It's only the irritating details that elude me." He looked at her oddly and offered her another polystyrene tea. "No thanks," she said. "It was bloody awful." And he retreated back inside his novel.

She was tired when they arrived home, too tired to talk, although she was truly curious to hear about Will's day out with their melancholy neighbor. She drank a glass of wine, to be sociable, then excused herself and went to bed. She did not sleep immediately. It was a pleasure simply to be horizontal between cool sheets and to admire the pattern made on the wall by the dipping sun through the slats of the shutters. She heard the boys having their baths, chattering, arguing because they were tired, and sighed, content that they were not her responsibility. She smelled sausages and chops sizzling on the barbecue and imagined how good they would taste with the salad of brown lentils and vivid herbs Will had been dressing as she kissed him good night.

She thought of the blessing and the curse of children and mulled over the words *labor of love*. The novels she liked to read, when she still read novels, tended to end with a couple declaring their love for each other. As though that constituted all that was needful for a happy future. Few romantic novels began at that point, then proceeded, because romance was all about overcoming obstacles not hard work, but the truth of the matter was that love was a burden and from the moment someone said they loved you, they were under an obligation constantly to prove the truth of what they had said, and you were under the possibly greater one of proving worthy of so much ardent demonstration. The love of children was burdensome in a different way, of course, because you had no choice in the matter, especially not nowadays when the ordinary accident of loving one child more than another had been worked up into a kind of crime against nature and the state. Nuns had it very easy, she considered, loving only the world in general and God in particular. Small wonder that their faces in repose wore that look of unstrained complacency.

She awoke with a start, convinced she heard a child weeping. One of the boys must be having a nightmare. She had been so profoundly asleep that it took her a while to reorient herself. It was quite dark. There was no moon. She heard heavy breathing and realized her husband was asleep beside her. She had been caught before, losing her way when getting out of bed in the dark and waking John by making a dreadful crash or falling on top of him. She had learned to use the glowing digits on her alarm clock to piece together her relation to remembered furniture around her before she tried to get up. This room was easier than the one at home because it was so uncluttered. She swung her feet out, found her slippers and dressing gown, took a moment to let any dizziness recede, then stood and, taking steps to avoid stubbing a toe, found her way out. The doorway was easily reached because it glowed slightly, backlit by the boys' little nightlight Sandy had plugged in outside.

That noise again. Or was it not a noise but a feeling? The memory of the feeling she felt when she heard that noise in the night and Will or Poppy needed her? Magic pearls.

She had said that to Oscar the other night. Tucking him into bed—although one did not really tuck now because children had duvets—her temporarily restrung necklace had dangled in his face and he said it smelled of perfume. "Magic pearls," she said and he threw her a look of sobering disdain. Abashed, she had launched into an involved description of the bedtime rituals of his uncle and mother's childhoods and he had merely looked blank and said *oh*. It was hard to believe such worldly, scientific children ever had nightmares. She found the presence of their nightlight reassuring, not for dispelling any fears of the dark—she had always loved the dark—but for suggesting a continuity in some things, at least.

She turned right, to the boys' door, to check on them. One of them might have had a dream because their reading lamp was on but both were now fast asleep. She allowed herself the merest breath of a kiss on each dreaming head. They had lost the tiring odor of cross little boy, all potato crisps and sugary heat, and had drawn about them the temporary innocence of apple shampoo. She turned out the lamp and left them to sleep.

She was wide awake now. If she went back to bed she would only wake John with her restlessness and make him worry. She was also hungry. She went to the kitchen and grazed, standing up at the fridge door, on a lone cold sausage and a small bowl of surviving lentils. Then, needing to kill the garlic and chili now raging on her tongue, heated herself milk for cocoa. Will had packed her some marvelous stuff from an old Italian firm in San Francisco that was full and rich and intensely chocolatey. She crossed the house with her warm mugful carefully held so she would not wake to cocoa stains, and let herself out on to the veranda so she could sit on the teak bench out there and sip and let the repetitive sounds of the sea restore her sleepiness. What a shame, she thought, the family was not present here in its entirety so she could sit here and indulge in the sense of being its guardian.

Then, like a jolt through her spine, she felt that feeling again, of a child in pain, and became sharply aware of raised voices through the dark, open window behind her. "That cannot be true," Will said and she knew at once this was an argument. She knew from the way the air went still, the way it used to when she sat on the landing with her brothers and listened to the awful clarity with which her mother harangued her father. Now as then it made her want to run between them pleading, "Stop, stop, stop!" Then as now, the enormity of eavesdropping, a servant's sin, proved stronger than her need of harmony.

"Of course it is. It's always been true," Sandy said and his voice had a soft, wheedling quality she did not recognize. "I love you."

"Oh, you just say that the way everyone says it. To control me. You've got it so easy. Wife. Kids. Good thing. If I stop this . . . this *arrangement* we have, it ruins the cozy set-up and you have to look outside and you daren't do that because it's far too risky, and it would mean taking that step and becoming a gay man, which you're not."

"Who says?"

"Oh Sandy, Sandy." Will's voice was soft again, even loving.

Frances felt sick. She spilled hot cocoa on her hand and tossed the mug violently from her over the veranda rail. There would be a mark on the sand tomorrow. They would know she had been here, know she had listened. Some instinct told her their silence was being filled with a kiss.

"You're not gay," Will went on at last. "You're not even bisexual. These labels don't figure with men like you. You're just a married bloke, a happily married mensch who happens to have stumbled on an incredibly convenient way of getting his rocks off twice as often without really having to think of himself as an adulterer. And you run no risk of me ever making demands or insisting on having you full-time because you *know* how it would make me look and feel to the family."

"And don't you?"

There was a pause.

"What?" Will asked.

"Don't you want me full-time?"

"Have I ever said I did?"

"No, but that's because you've always been so brilliant about it. You could have made my life hell but you never made any demands. But it must have crossed your mind."

"I never dared let it. Oh Sandy, please! I didn't even want us to have this conversation. Please. Just let me go."

"You've met someone else, haven't you?"

"Since when did you have rights in me? You've got Poppy. You've *always* had someone else!"

"I sensed it the moment we got here."

"Sandy?"

"Oh Jesus! God! You have!"

"I have not."

"You've no idea how I feel. None at all. You think it's just sex, don't you?"

"And isn't it?"

"Only because that's all we ever seem to have time for. I've been dreaming about this holiday. About just spending time with you. As a couple."

"With my parents and your children. Oh yes. Just like a couple. Get real, Sandy."

Then Sandy broke down and wept. It was not loud but even where she sat Frances could feel the force of it, the great hiss of pent-up emotion escaping.

"Stop it," Will said. "Oh. Please, I had no . . . Sandy? Ssh. You'll set me off." He laughed. "Sandy, *please!* Here. Ssh."

Gradually Sandy's sobs were replaced by other sounds, kisses, a muffled groan, and Frances was freed by disgust from feeling pinned to the bench, and not caring now if they heard her, she jumped up and ran in her slippered feet.

The telephone box was where she remembered it, and not even replaced with one of the drafty modern ones. The only change was that it was scrawled over with magic marker like everything now. The ugly look-at-me signatures of the young. It even smelled the same; sugar and sand, melted ice cream and sickly suntan oil.

"Operator services. This is Polly speaking. How can I help you?"

The woman sounded so wide awake, she lent Frances courage as though people did this all the time. "I want to place a reverse charge call, Polly. To Barrowcester." She dictated Poppy's number. They were the only telephone numbers she invariably remembered; her son's and her daughter's. Her own she forgot so routinely, she had it written in the front of her diary along with her address, on the Personal Details page most people scorned to complete.

There was the sound of a familiar, trusted voice, confident even when half-asleep, and then an instant of fear that she might reject the call. But of course Poppy accepted it because she was a mother and a mother's panic about her children functioned on a hair-trigger reflex, summon-able at a moment's notice.

"No, no. It's not the boys," Frances assured her. "They're fine. I just checked on them and they're sound asleep."

"Mum, it's the middle of the night. It's one thirty. Does Dad know where you are? Couldn't this have waited?"

"Darling, it's Sandy."

Fresh panic, of a different kind but no less sharp. "What's happened? Oh Christ, not a car crash! Please not that! Mum? Tell me? What?"

But now that she was on the verge, Frances had no idea what to say. She had seen no further than making the call. "You must come at once. We all need you," she said, picking her way through words as through thistles. "Sandy especially."

"But what's wrong with him?"

"Nothing. Come, darling. Say you'll come."

"But my squash course is . . . You'll be back on Saturday. Oh, Mum. Have you been having a bad day?"

The abrupt change in her voice, from keen-edged fear to patronizing, practiced concern, infuriated Frances. "Just get your fucking ass down here and ask your dirty little brother what he's been up to," she said and slammed the receiver down in its cradle.

As she walked away across the car park, aware now that she was in her night things, she shivered less from cold than from hunter's adrena-line. The phone rang behind her, a piteous, unimportant chirruping which she ignored. She was implacable. She was powerful. She, Frances Pagett, could straighten the twisted path and free the imprisoned.

A cat froze in her path, saw the wildness in her eyes, and fled.

BEACHCOMBER

Like most clinics in or around Harley Street, this one was designed to overcome fear and disgust. Just as lawyers' and accountants' businesses were founded on no nobler motive than profit and therefore strove to muster a compensatory air of respectability so, John imagined, the more intimate the ailment, the less mentionable the organ, the more a clinic called on hunting prints, brass and chintz to evoke a saving gentility.

The word *fertility* appeared nowhere, any more than did *egg* or *sperm*; there was only the doctor's name and flourish of abbreviated qualifications on a brass plate. The waiting room was a drawing room, complete with standard lamps and piano and the thin, middle-aged receptionist who opened the door and showed him to a sofa was dressed not in nursing uniform but like any hostess at a smart but informal lunch. The domestic effect was heightened by its being early evening. Waiting amid soft pools of welcoming light, John half-expected her to return with cocktails and a bowl of nuts.

He had first called in at lunchtime, little expecting to be summoned back so soon. Speedy results as much as discretion and superior knowledge were what one paid for, presumably. He had not met the doctor earlier. The twin-setted receptionist had instead brought him a questionnaire to fill out, an intimate document reassuringly masked by a thick leather folder, like the kind in which the better restaurants delivered one's bill. This completed, she led him upstairs to another chamber, a former bedroom presumably, and left him with the request, murmured with lowered eyes, that he *prepare a sample* and *take as long as he liked*.

Suffering a torment of inhibition he might, ironically, have been spared had she only worn a nurse's uniform after all, he turned to find the room furnished with not only a buttoned leather couch and prints of peachily naked nymphs, but an array of leather-bound continental pornography catering to every conceivable taste. Aghast at the thought of fleeing the room empty-handed, as it were—in fact there was a dumbwaiter in which the sample jar was to be tucked from view—he was startled by the pornography's efficacy.

The afternoon was spent in conference with police and senior officers, piecing together what the investigations had so far established. As soon after his escape as unrest among the men allowed, Farmer's cell had been searched and the men known to be his friends or confederates questioned in the hope of some clue as to where he had gone. Allies or thieves had already cleared his cell however and nothing was left but a few tatty pin-ups and a Gideon Bible. There was also a thick railway timetable. It was unmarked, which was strange given that Farmer had been a keen member of the prison trainspotters' club which recorded train numbers as they passed through a cutting clearly visible from a C-block washroom. As a rule it was depressingly easy to persuade men to betray one another. The offer of perks or even a sentence review was all that was required. Their loyalty this time was such that John could only imagine their discretion had been purchased already with promises of jobs, preferment or cash once they rejoined Farmer on the outside. Friendship was never reason enough. How a robber whose pre-criminal status had never amounted to anything more powerful than post office worker could muster any credible inducements lay beyond John's reckoning. Unless Farmer had some kind of heist planned, but this seemed unlikely in a felon whose only known robbery was executed alone. And so the line of inquiry had gone round in circles and threatened to eat itself.

That morning, however, a link was found that made the situation more humiliating than John had imagined. A newish recruit among the officers who had called in sick ever since the break-out was found to have disappeared. Then an officer overseeing a maintenance work party found bolts missing on a C-wing skylight. The escape now revealed an ingenuity that was surely not Farmer's own, or not his alone. It had in fact been a kind of double break-out only the man over the wall was not an inmate at all but the missing officer.

Malone, who looked far older than he was and had Farmer's build, had taken his clothes and place in the exercise yard while Farmer concealed himself in a lavatory. At a preordained hour, a removal lorry, already parked a few yards down the street, pulled up outside the prison wall and a rope ladder was thrown over, weighted by a crow bar. It was this, not a garden implement, that Malone, posing as Farmer, had seized to strike down the warders on duty before climbing out. The ruckus that followed was not entirely planned, John suspected, but had grown in part from a fight between other prisoners trying to use the ladder while another inside accomplice fought them back so that the ladder could be safely withdrawn to the lorry once Malone was over the wall and away. Aided by the disorder that followed, in which all officers not pursuing Malone and raising the alarm were occupied in driving the men back to their cells, Farmer had succeeded in climbing up the caging that enclosed C-wing's stairwell and out through the skylight to the prison roof. From there he had made his way across the landscape of gully and chimneys to the adjacent roof of the Governor's House and come via a small window into one of the many unused attic rooms. There he had concealed himself until the fuss had died down and the van's driver had successfully led the police on a wild goose chase to Dover before eluding them in a lorry park at the port, where the removal van, stolen of course, was found abandoned.

Malone, like the driver, was still at large, having stepped from the van on some street corner in South London and blended into the crowds, an unsuspected prison officer laid up with toothache. He had phoned in sick daily until that morning, when questions started being asked when his flat was found to be empty. Ferries' passengers and freight were still being checked devoutly. Farmer meanwhile had dined on John's food and left in a taxi wearing his clothes and holding his silver and his painting and his freshly plumped wallet. With insouciance calculated to insult, he had left fingerprints all over the Governor's House.

Uncleaned, soured by the cigarettes of investigating officers, the kitchen stacked with washing-up, the house was beginning to feel as male as the prison it abutted. However, it was Farmer's concealed presence about the place John could not stop imagining. Going about his morning's work, he pictured precisely how Farmer or any other intruder using the same route might have killed him, stifled him in his sleep, drowned him in the bath. Then he thought of Farmer listening in as he made phone calls. He thought of Farmer touching Frances's things with meaty hands.

Far from arousing a low desire for vengeance or even an obsession with wanting to see Farmer caught and humiliated, these thoughts and visions only induced an unprofessional euphoria. Spared, not nearly as badly robbed as he might have been, John found it hard to concentrate on the business in hand and the questions of the police. He was consumed by an intense sense of his own luck and healthiness. The only area in which his life was lacking was his apparent inability to father further children, and in this mood there was no problem he was not prepared to tackle head-on. No sooner was his morning "surgery" over than he tracked down this clinic in the Yellow Pages and, reminding himself he had been cheated of holiday, made a lunchtime appointment. Taking a leaf out of Malone's book, he told his deputy it was for some urgent work on a filling that had worked loose.

The usual suspects had been checked and relatives' houses were being watched, but Malone and Farmer had vanished with an efficiency that spoke of months, if not years of planning. Farmer's hours in the prison library, a fact of which John had only recently bragged to visiting inspectors, had clearly not been wasted in reading poetry but devoted to poring over Ordnance Survey maps. For all he knew the bastard had taught himself to fly from manuals.

Someone had helped him, however, someone with intimate knowledge of the prison's less obvious geography, which ruled out Malone who was too new on the job. Someone had shown Farmer the link with the Governor's House and the ease with which a man could pass from one to the other via the attics. By the time John returned after his lunchtime appointment, spikes and razor wire had been erected to separate one roof from the other and bars had been bolted across both skylight and offending window, but the helper went undetected. Mrs. Coley, the cleaner, was eliminated from the inquiry, though not before her glowing references were found to be bogus. Her duties never took her above the first-floor rooms and her bad knee—authenticated by a police-approved doctor—would surely have prevented her climbing the steep wooden stairs to the area of attic in question. She had been sacked over the reference business amid gaudy imprecations and threats to *take her story to the papers*.

It came as a shock to discover that Dr. Alberti was a woman. The hunting prints and leather, not to mention the ingenious library of pornography, had led him to imagine a clubbable man of the world, the type who would display a photograph of wife and children on his desk by way of male qualifications. Instead Dr. Alberti displayed only a small bowl of roses, whose full-blown pinkness was in contrast to her iron-gray hair and chainsmoker's complexion. She had on the female equivalent of a charcoal lounge suit and as she shook him by the hand and waved him to a chair with a brisk motion of her free arm, he caught a distinct whiff of roast lamb and cigars.

His deputy had a sister in the profession and John recalled Mervyn saying how women doctors were tiring of being corralled toward pediatrics and, like homosexuals, were swallowing their pride to colonize the specialities at the dirty end of the field—gynecology, venereology and sexual dysfunction.

"Well, Mr. Pagett," Dr. Alberti said. "You have nothing to fret over.

Your sperm count is normal. Now, I need to ask you more questions, I'm afraid, of an intensely impudent nature. You'll think me eccentric but I like to borrow a technique from the Viennese and have you face away from me by lying over there." She indicated a leather couch identical to the one in the sample-room. "You'll find it makes it far easier to answer, almost without thinking." A small smile lit up her bullfrog face and John was touched to see that she was as bashful as he. A lack of eye contact would spare them both.

He lay down and began to answer questions. Her technique was to fire them off so fast that one felt obliged to answer just as quickly. How often did he and his wife have sex? Why so rarely? What were these pamphlets he had read? What did they advise? He told her everything, unburdening himself of years of secrets in light-headed minutes. Whereas merely making the appointment had left his cheeks aflame, he found himself talking from the couch dispassionately and as unabashed as if he had been describing his breakfasting habits or the prison menus for the coming week.

"You and your wife are Catholic?"

"No."

"And you're sure—forgive me for asking this—she isn't taking birth control pills in secret?"

"Quite sure."

"It does happen. They come in thin foil packets. Not bottles."

"I'm quite sure."

"And forgive me if I'm underestimating the breadth of your education, but what do you know about a woman's ovulation cycle?"

"Erm . . ." John was so relaxed he actually laughed. "Apart from her monthly headaches bugger all, I'm afraid. They taught us about frogs and mice but I didn't really concentrate."

"You see, you're not firing blanks. Far from it. But it sounds as though you're firing when the target isn't in place. And if you were to persist in following the, forgive me, misguided advice of your pamphlets, you could continue *missing* one another indefinitely. If you want another child, Mr. Pagett, holding back is the last thing you should be doing." So saying, Dr. Alberti walked back into his field of view in order to open the consulting-room door. "Don't hesitate to come back if the problem continues but I think the prognosis is excellent!"

Now it was John's turn to shake her hand warmly. As he signed his check at the hall table, the unlikely receptionist standing by, his signature emerged larger and bolder than usual and he bade her good evening with a kind of hilarity. His euphoria of the morning was as nothing compared to this. Riding the train home, he fantasized recklessly about having a huge family. Why stop at one more baby when they could produce four or five? Governors' houses were large enough to accommodate them all. Frances and he should found a tribe. The house would ring to the noise of a crowded nursery. Mealtimes would be deafening with competing voices, Christmas an orgy of present-giving. He thought of Julian, on his own all his short life, and realized how dreadfully lonely he must have been. No wonder the poor boy was forever reading; books were his brothers.

John hurried through his evening business at the prison. He wished he could ring Frances to tell her the good news and resented more than ever being held a prisoner by his work when he wanted to be with her. He fried himself a celebratory steak and was just pouring a second glass of wine when she rang from a call box in Wadebridge.

He had to hear the children's news first, which married nicely with his earlier fantasies, but when Frances's low, calm voice replaced their chatter, he became tongue-tied. He could not tell her, when she was squeezed into a kiosk with his brother-in-law and two children. He could not tell her, in any case, when the fears just dispelled had never been discussed between them. When the pips cut her off, all too soon, he was left with unspoken happiness caught in his throat, an eye-watering obstruction no amount of wine could rinse away.

The third glass raised his mood, however. Whatever the ingenuity of his escape, Farmer could not be on the run indefinitely. He would make a mistake soon or be betrayed to the police. One or the other usually happened within days of a break-out, most prisoners rarely planning beyond their initial flight over the wall. Then John would seize the remains of his holiday and return to Cornwall. Frances would learn everything.

Dr. Alberti's cunning blend of frankness and discretion had shown him how it could be done, under cover of darkness, perhaps, or while one of them was driving the car. He would tell her of his foolish fears, the pamphlets, the agonies of abstinence, the curiosity of being instructed in the mysteries of human reproduction by a suited woman who smelled of Sunday roast and cigarillos. They would laugh and they would begin again.

The night was oppressively hot and John slept with both windows open and no more than a sheet to cover him. It had taken him hours to lose consciousness and the jangling telephone rang in his confused dreams before it woke him. He answered still in a fog of sleep. A mail train had been halted by a sabotaged electric signal and robbed at gunpoint. The thieves knocked their victims unconscious before making off with six million pounds in cash, bonds and share certificates. Only men with an intimate knowledge both of railway timetables and the arcane nocturnal workings of the post office could have known which train to rob and where on the network to do it.

During a brief struggle, the driver had unmasked his assailant sufficiently to give a description that matched Farmer's. A second felon, with a younger voice, had a near-identical build and wielded a prison officer's truncheon.

Unable to sleep again, unable to read, John shaved, dressed and crossed to his office past startled guards. There were still two hours to go before dawn. There was nothing further he could do and little routine business he could attend to while the prison was still asleep. The robbery had pushed the matter of the escape squarely into the hands of Scotland Yard. However, an overwhelming sense of duty required him to be at his post, albeit uselessly, and seen to be putting obligation before family. Amid the nausea caused by being up before his stomach had woken, he saw the dreams of hurrying back to Cornwall for the irresponsible fantasies they were.

Frances would ring soon. She would hear the news on the radio. She would ring to let him know she understood.

BLUE HOUSE

Wife and daughter were forever accusing him of not noticing such things but John found the holiday household full of strange energies. Frances was herself again, thank God, but had woken edgy, would not sit still and seemed to do most of her talking to and through the children. This did not worry him unduly; she was like a child herself in her ability to tire the mood out of her by keeping them entertained on the beach. Perhaps because she had kept her figure and was still a good swimmer, they were not embarrassed by her in the way little boys would normally be by a woman her age wearing anything less than a knee-length dress. Where her unpredictability made adults nervous, it delighted them. They were especially keen on her new habit of swearing and, despite Sandy's best efforts, were starting to emulate it.

More disturbing were Will and Sandy, who seemed to have stopped talking to each other. Rather, they talked but without their customary liveliness and each kept starving the dialogue with monosyllables. No doubt the strain of two men sharing a room was beginning to tell. Ordinarily John would have escaped the unhappy atmosphere by strapping on his walking boots and binoculars and taking himself off on a hike

sufficiently punitive to deter the others from accompanying him. Today
of all days, however, he had agreed to stay in so that a journalist who had
been pestering Harriet could interview him on Will's mobile. They were
not due to call until noon, a time he had stipulated so as to give himself
a free morning, but now he found himself poleaxed by the past and un-
accountably nervous that his memory might play him false under questioning. Will had thrown himself into preparing a needlessly complex
lunch dish and Sandy was prowling around like a man under a death
threat, clutching some medical journals he kept announcing he was going to *catch up on.*

John had taken refuge on the veranda. There he could keep half an
eye on Frances and the boys, who were building something with pebbles and sand. Both children wore brightly colored wetsuits, which
seemed to him the worst kind of mollycoddling. "The sea's not *that*
cold," he had exclaimed when they first produced the things. "Granny
doesn't wear one! You just have to keep moving." Apparently this was a
faux pas however, since the ulterior purpose of the suits, while pander-
ing to the boys' enslavement to the vagaries of fashion, was to protect
their white, Scottish skin from the effects of the sun.

He had helped himself to one of Sandy's drug company pads and was
noting down the facts of the prison breakout as he remembered them.
Of course they had wanted to talk to his old deputy, Mervyn Mc-
Master, who after all had been acting governor when Malone helped
Farmer escape, but Mervyn was dead long since. He noted dates and
the few facts he could recall about the subsequent inquiry. Then he felt a
kind of despair. The journalist would already have the facts in all their
dryness at her disposal. What she wanted were the personal details that
passed for journalism now. What had Farmer been like? Was it true that
he was a family favorite among Wandsworth's red band work parties?
Had John feared for his life or his family's lives at any stage? How did
John *feel* now that Farmer was immensely rich and about to be returned
to justice? He had no training in how to field such questions. In his day,
governors had never had to face the press.

"I'm retired," he thought. "I can say what I bloody like. That I don't
care if Farmer's now an old man and a regular donor to Brazilian chari-

ties and a pillar of his adopted community. I want him to rot. I want him to die behind bars. Why? Because I blame him for . . ." For what? Blame him, quite unjustly, for personal events that just happened to co-incide with the breakout? Well why not? Those events still caused pain, long after the victims of the robbery had died, in the case of a railway guard brain-damaged by bludgeoning, or recovered, in the case of several wealthy institutions.

"Dad?"

A woman's voice. He looked up and saw a taxi turning back up the hill and Poppy standing there, sunglasses pushed up on her hair, a large bag slung over one arm.

"You're so brown!" she exclaimed. "I hope you've been using total block."

"Where did you spring from?" Finding her before him was like not realizing how thirsty one was until someone offered one a glass of iced water. He stood to kiss her. She allowed herself to be properly hugged these days. It was one of the aspects he appreciated most to her becoming a mother. When she had first left school, she went through a phase of pecking him on the cheek which he had found deeply depressing.

Sandy appeared on the veranda too. "Hey!" He gave Poppy a kiss. "How come?"

"Oh. The squash course was postponed till the autumn," she said. "Not enough takers. So I stuck around for a couple of days just doing things I hadn't done for ages, like going to galleries and seeing old girl-friends. Then I thought, this is silly, I can join them. So here I am. You don't mind, do you, Will? Is there room?"

"Course I don't mind," Will said from the doorway. "And Sandy's broken into the fourth room, so I can sleep in there now."

"You must have left at dawn," John said.

"Pretty much." She looked pale compared to the rest of them. Citi-fied. "This is lovely."

"The boys are on the beach with Frances," Sandy said. "I'll go and get them. They'll be over the moon."

"No," she said suddenly. "Wait." She frowned. "Can I have a drink or something? I'm boiling."

"Of course. Come in, come in," said Will, playing host, and John felt how relieved he was that Poppy was there. "Water, then something stronger?"

"Just water," she said, following him in and glancing around her. "Look. I'd better be quick before she comes in. Is Mum OK?"

John exchanged a glance with Will and realized how guilty they must look. "Well," he began.

"She hasn't been brilliant," Will added. "She got terribly distraught one night at a concert and her mood's been all over the place ever since."

"She seems OK today," John said. "Why?"

Poppy sighed, took the water and sat heavily on the sofa. "The squash wasn't postponed. I was really enjoying it, actually. But I came because I was worried. She rang me last night. In the middle of last night. It was really scary. She ranted about needing me here and . . . and she said Will could explain. In fact she got quite obscene. For her."

"There's been a lot of that," Will said.

"You should have rung me on the mobile if you were worried," said Sandy. "You didn't need to come all this way."

"I tried last night but it was turned off. And several times at the station and on the train but you were permanently engaged."

"Hugo was on the Net first thing," John said.

"I'll bloody murder him," said Sandy.

"Her actual words, if I got this right, were that she was worried about Sandy. Then, when I asked how she was and was she having one of her bad days, she completely lost it and said, *Just get your effing butt down here and ask your filthy little brother what he's been up to.*"

Will shifted uneasily and sat beside her. "God," he said.

"She's worse than I realized," John said. "Darling, I'm so sorry. It must have been vile."

"Don't be silly," Poppy said. "But I had to come. You see that?"

"Oh yes," Will said. "Absolutely. I mean . . . You didn't think she was serious about me . . ."

"No." She laughed. A little tensely, John thought.

"Or you'd have rung me on *my* mobile."

"You promised to leave it at home," she said sharply.

"Yes, but, well. Old habits. I was worried about an emergency at the shop."

"You are hopeless. Has he been pestering poor Kristin every day?" she asked John.

"No," he said. "I've been taking more calls on it than he has."

"Which reminds me," Will said. "I thought that journalist was ringing you half an hour ago. You're not going to let them ruin lunch? Not now we've got a surprise guest."

"What journalist?" she asked.

John was starting to explain about Farmer and the proposed extradition agreement when Sandy, who had fallen quiet, jumped up and interrupted.

"Come and look round," he said. "Come and see our room." She looked puzzled but Sandy was holding out a hand so, bemused, she smiled and took it. "There's something I want to tell you," he added.

"Sandy?" Will said, then jumped up for all the world as if to hold them back. "How about drinks first?" he said. "What about Bloody Marys? I'd love a Bloody Mary. Dad?"

"Oh. Well, yes?" John said uncertainly.

"Sis?"

"Sure. Let's be devils," she laughed.

But when Sandy led her into his room and shut the door, Will made no move toward the kitchen but merely stared for a while before walking out on to the veranda. John thought he would be fetching in Frances but he only stood out there, staring at the people on the beach. Then, when the breeze fluttered his shirt, he reached to unhook the sculpture thing Frances had wasted her money on and nudged into motion the wind vane that drove it. The sculpture began its regular thwacking noise, which Frances had explained was a rook-scarer but which John thought served merely to crank up an unpleasant sense of tension in all who were forced to hear it. Perhaps it was Will's playful way of summoning Frances.

Suddenly there came a gasp from behind the bedroom door followed by the unmistakable whack-whack of a double-handed face slap. Then Poppy emerged even whiter than when she arrived and John jumped up. "What the hell . . . ?" he started.

Fury made her lips tight. "Where are they?" she asked. He had not seen her like this since she was a girl.

"On the beach," he told her. "What's going on? I'm sure they'll be in any second."

But she was flying out through the French windows.

Will stood in her way. "Listen. Whatever you think . . . It was over. Don't listen to him, all right? Whatever he's told you wasn't true. He loves you."

"I'm not speaking to you," she said, her voice dangerously level.

"No," he said. "Of course you're not. I'll get the others. You'll be wanting to pack." He turned toward the garden gate.

Poppy hesitated, torn, robbed of a gesture perhaps, then marched back inside. "Dad? Where were they sleeping? Hugo and Oz, I mean."

"In there." John gestured to the middle bedroom. "Look, would someone please . . . ?"

But she marched on into the room and started hurling the children's clothes and toys into a suitcase. She packed with single-minded fury, even leaving out dry clothes for them to change into. As awed as he was confused, John merely watched. Sandy emerged slowly from his room, heard what was going on and walked to the bathroom, whence he returned with the children's plastic carrier bag of wash things. "You'll be wanting these," he said, standing outside their bedroom door.

"Thanks," she said, and grabbed the bag.

"Please," John said, firmly this time. "What in God's name has happened?"

She looked up, startled, as though she had forgotten he was there. "Sandy can tell you. Can't you, Sandy? He has a little speech all ready."

"Look, can't we just . . . ?" Sandy began but Poppy slammed the door on him and continued thumping around behind it. Sandy looked mournfully at John, shrugged and said, "You were bound to know sooner or later. The thing is, John, I'm gay. Bisexual. Whatever. And the reason I've realized this is because as long as I've been happily married, I've also been having an affair with Will and he tried to split up with me last night, which is what made me see. That I'm . . . not straight."

The room felt very still and very small, as though someone had switched off the beach. While Sandy was making his announcement, Frances and the children arrived on the veranda, Oscar shouting. "Mum!" Hugo only staring solemnly. Poppy emerged with their suitcase and a hand held out.

"Keys," she demanded.

"What?" said Sandy.

"Car keys. Now." Obediently he handed over a bunch and she marched past Frances and the boys—Oscar was starting to cry—saying only, "Come on. Quickly. Get them out of those things, would you, Mum?"

Sandy ran after her. Frances struggled to comfort Oscar as she freed him from his wetsuit. Hugo peeled off his own. John took them out their dry clothes. Frances was crying too. And all the time the bloody sculpture was going *thwack! thwack!* Returning from the car to help, Sandy obviously became maddened by it too. He tried to fasten it again but his hands were shaking and he shoved it instead. There was a sound of splintering wood and the thing tilted over and became disconnected so the wind vane spun on in silence, to no effect.

"Sorry," Sandy said, possibly for breaking the sculpture, possibly for more.

There was a yell from the car. "Will you come *on*!"

"Come on, small fry." Sandy picked Oscar up while Hugo ran on ahead. With a desperate glance round at John and Frances, Sandy ran over to his car, loaded the boys in and went round to the passenger side. But the car flew off before he could open the door.

John turned to find Will standing on the veranda behind them. He had their bags packed too. He must have moved like a demon. A shirtcuff trapped in the lid of one case bore testimony to his speed. He had even slung Frances's precious herbs and spices and the remaining drinks bottles into the cardboard box in which they had traveled down.

"What . . . ?" John began.

"I think you'd better be off too," he said.

"Darling," Frances began and he turned on her.

"Go," he said. "Just go. You stupid, meddling, *ignorant* woman."

"No," she whimpered. "No!"

"It was over. It was all over. I had ended it. No one would have been hurt. But you had to put your . . . your *fucking* oar in and now this happens!"

"Look, Will," John began.

"Go." Will was like a stranger. A tall, gaunt, exhausted stranger. There was real hate in his eyes as he spoke to Frances but when John, thinking to stall matters, asked if they might at least use the bathroom before they set off, the hate melted and Will crumpled against the doorjamb. "Yes, of course," he said. "Do whatever you need."

John checked quickly for their belongings and Frances's drugs and filled a few more bags. Will's mobile telephone rang. John answered, thinking *bloody journalists*, but it was Harriet. "This really isn't a good time," he told her.

"Really? God. Sorry. John, look, it's just to say that Heather Sutton won't be ringing after all. The extradition's off."

"It's off?"

The tone of her quick explanation was one of real concern but it could not have mattered less. Will had disappeared. Frances had sunk on to the teak bench outside. No longer crying, she was vacant, utterly lost. Sandy was standing in the drive, no less helpless.

John assumed control. He led Frances to the bathroom to tidy herself up and change out of her swimming things then, having easily persuaded her to take a couple of sleeping pills, shepherded both her and his son-in-law to his car.

Many fathers in his position would have refused Sandy a lift or, at best, have taken him no further than the nearest station. But they were on the motorway, buying petrol, before this thought dawned on him, by which time any such gesture would have been both limp and inconvenient. Besides, he felt dismay, not anger. Sitting on the back seat, while

Frances snored quietly in the front, Sandy seemed intent on making himself as small and inoffensive a presence as possible. He was, John thought, as much a victim of fortune as the rest of them.

When they finally reached the outskirts of Barrowcester, John dropped him off at the foot of the drive to walk to his wife and house like a lost thing. Frances had woken by now and gave Sandy a farewell kiss that was nonetheless loving for her having temporarily mislaid the unfortunate circumstances.

"Farmer's not coming back after all," John told her as they drove on. "Harriet rang to tell me. Court found in his favor and said it would be an infringement of his civil liberties because in Brazil a crime no longer holds so many years after the event."

"Oh darling," she said, eyes wet again. "Do you really mean that? Clean slates all round? Oh I'm so glad!" and she shyly stroked his forearm as he changed gear, a gesture that took him back to 1968 and another crime entirely.

BEACHCOMBER

It was a Saturday so the beach was crowded with people who were not on holiday but happened to live nearby. The tide was extraordinarily low, which made matters worse. Skip, like Julian, had come to think of the small cove before the bungalow as *their* beach and joined him in despising the invasion. As the tide receded past the last rocky defense against the hordes of Polcamel and the first few people waded round in their flip-flops, the two of them talked in scornful voices and stared as witheringly as they could but no one seemed bothered. Before long the precious private sand was a maze of striped wind-shelters, folding chairs and lunch boxes. There were numerous dogs bounding around lifting their legs and worse on sandcastles and one family who knew no better had actually produced a portable gas burner and was boiling a kettle.

Ma did not seem to mind the crowds for once. Normally she would flatly refuse to step on to a beach she deemed too crowded. Now she was enjoying a prolonged surfing lesson from Bill, reckless, heedless of more sensitive souls in her care. Julian returned from Beachcomber with a plate of peanut butter and banana sandwiches, made the way Skip had taught him. He stood for a moment, scanning the surf for his mother then found her far out behind the main crowd of splashers and jumpers. She and Bill were floating, hunched over their boards like a couple of waterlogged shipwreck survivors as they waited for a wave worth their effort. It seemed they had been out there for hours and he felt a babyish impulse to go after Ma and impose his will. But she had been acting strangely all day. She was doing everything too much, talking, laughing, listening even, with the kind of embarrassing intensity he had learned to associate with the wet afternoons when she had been practicing the piano for hours and was left like a moody stranger in his mother's body.

He straightened his towel, being meticulous about not flicking sand, then sat crosslegged at one end of it with the sandwich plate before him like an offering. Skip was pretending to be a grown-up. She lay flat on her back, her face a mask behind sunglasses, her arms and legs glistening with tanning oil. But she spoiled the effect by wearing a baggy tee shirt over her swimming costume in an effort, he supposed, to look like a boy. She was growing breasts, though. He had seen.

"Mmm," he said, chewing a sandwich and she sat up and took one too.

"Not bad," she said, tasting it. "You're learning." He had learned already, it was ridiculously easy, but it was too hot to argue so he simply offered her a second one. "I guess you think this buys you another surfing lesson," she said, eating.

"No. It's all right," he said and added as casually as he could, "Bill said he'd take me out later."

"You really like my dad, don't you?" she asked.

"Of course," he said. "He's fun."

She gave him one of her assessing stares. He could tell, even though she had sunglasses on, by the way her mouth pinched together like a cat's bum-hole. "You know, he thinks you're girly too. Why else do you think he calls you Julie?"

"I don't care," he said, stung.

She took the last sandwich. "Anyway, I don't want to go out there now. Not with all those *awful* people."

He smiled and she smiled back. She had imitated his way of speaking nastily at first. Now she did it as a sort of game. She was quite good at it, although she would never pass for English. She unwrapped a piece of gum and began to chew, the way she always did, when she had barely swallowed the last mouthful of any meal. He knew his mother hated this but he held the information back from Skip because it was more useful that way. When you were younger and more girly, he was coming to realize, you needed more ammunition.

"Truth or dare?" she asked suddenly.

"What?"

"It's a game, stupid. For when you're bored. Truth or dare?" He must have looked blank. "If you say truth you have to give the true answer to whatever I ask and if you say dare you have to do whatever dare I set you."

This did not sound like a very happy game. "Can't we just play make-believe," he asked. "You can be an evil queen if you like and I'll be your slave."

"I'll go first," she said, ignoring this. "To show you." He was beginning to suspect she had no imagination. "Go on. Say it."

"What?"

"Truth or dare."

"Truth or dare?"

"Dare. Now you dare me."

"Oh." He looked around them. "I dare you to kick that boy's sandcastle over." He indicated the fat six-year-old attached to the family with the kettle. It was an instant castle, made with one of those buckets with built-in crenellations, so had taken no time to build. It didn't have a garden. Not even any shells to decorate it.

"Consider it done." With extraordinary sureness, Skip walked up to, over and past the sandcastle, crushing it underfoot as casually as if she had not seen it lay in her way to somewhere more important. The family was too preoccupied with tea to notice. Only the fat boy saw and he stared after her, plainly uncertain whether to complain or merely cry. Skip returned to her towel by a circular route and flopped back down.

"He'll tell," Julian warned her.

"So? I've been here for hours, asleep. Haven't I? Truth or dare?"

Julian pondered. He sensed the dangers in this game now. "Truth," he said.

Skip lowered her sunglasses to examine his face as she asked him. "OK. One of your parents has to die. It can be quick and painless but they gotta die. Which'll it be?"

"Pa," he answered without even having to think about it. He had never thought about it before but now that he did there was no question. His father would have to die. He gasped at the ease with which he knew this.

"So you love your mother more?"

"No. I . . . Well, Pa isn't around so much so I'm not sure I . . . Oh I don't know. I don't like this. It's silly."

"No it isn't. Your turn."

"When is it over?" But she wasn't answering. "Truth or dare," he sighed.

"Dare."

"Don't you ever choose truth?" he asked.

"Dare, I said."

He had to punish her. "All right," he said. "Show me your thingy."

"*What?*"

"You know. Down there."

She stared at him, unable to believe he would be so impudent.

"Right here," he added.

"I can't," she stammered.

"Does that mean I've won?"

"No!" She was furious. "I'll show you at the house. Come on."

She marched into Beachcomber and as he tailed after her, he wondered how she had turned triumph into punishment. Skip stamped into the bathroom and shut the door.

"Wait," she said firmly. He waited outside. He heard her pull her T-shirt over her head and heard something slap on the floor. "OK." Her voice sounded muffled. "Ten seconds. That's all."

"I really don't have to—" he began.

"Get on with it or they'll come back and catch you."

So he opened the door. Her swimming costume lay flopped around her ankles and she had thrown a bath towel over her head and shoulders so that all he could see were her legs and the portion in question. The towel trembled slightly as he approached.

"Look," she commanded. "You're not looking."

How could she tell? He looked. Very quickly, but he looked. He saw how different she was. How she had begun to grow hair though not as much as his mother yet. It looked small and secret, like a cross between an anemone and a sort of mouse.

"Thank you," he said politely and left the room.

She was dressed in seconds and seemed charged with a kind of hot fury when she re-emerged so that he knew what she had shown him in the bathroom could never be discussed. "Truth or dare?" she asked, inexorable.

"Dare," he said, feeling he must offer some sort of atonement and his humiliation would serve as well as any.

She thought a moment. "Steal one of my dad's cigarettes and smoke it."

"I can't."

"So I've won."

"No! You keep a lookout in case they come."

"No way. If I did it wouldn't be a dare."

He went into their bedroom, looked around him and found a cigarette packet. But it was empty. So he felt in the pockets of Bill's heavy leather jacket. In one there was just his wallet, made of even older leather, and a handful of coins. In the other, though, he found a foil packet, just like Henry's Golden Virginia only without the label, and inside some tobacco and a packet of papers. This was easy. Skip expected him to fumble and be childish but here was a dare in which he could astonish and trounce her, better than sticking his finger in a sea anemone. He would show her. He would prove he was not a girl.

He folded a paper as Henry had taught him, filled it with a generous pinch of the tobacco—which was different from Henry's, stringier and less smelly—licked the paper's edge and rolled it into a neat tube.

She seemed duly impressed when he emerged with the finished article. "Where'd you learn to do that?"

"Prison," he said, enjoying the way this sounded, and holding it in a corner of his mouth the way he had seen Henry do it, he lit it with a kitchen match.

"You can't smoke that!" she hissed as the smoke reached her. "It's wacky baccy!"

"So? It's still a cigarette." Praying he wouldn't be sick or cough, he breathed in a generous lungful and nearly did both.

"Stop breathing," she said. "Hold it in, then you won't cough. For Chrissakes!" She was right. But the moment he made as if to breathe, he started to cough again and he couldn't hold his breath indefinitely. "Give me some," she said and snatched it from his lips. While he felt free to splutter, she took a deep drag and, he was pleased to see, had to stifle a coughing fit too. "One more each," she said, "then we have to hide the evidence."

She held the cigarette out while he took another hesitant puff on it. Then she dragged on it again herself before wetting it thoroughly in the kitchen sink and throwing it hard through the open window. While she waved the veranda door speedily open and shut in an effort to disperse the smoke and the strange, nutty smell, Julian felt a sudden need to sit down. He climbed to the back of one of the armchairs and felt he would never walk again.

"I feel strange," he told her and his voice didn't work properly.

"Of course you do, Girlface," she laughed. "You're stoned."

"Oh."

"You're meant to enjoy it." She too flopped in a chair now and swung sandy legs up on its arms. "Now. My turn."

"What?"

"Truth or dare. My turn."

"Do we have to? Can't you just win?"

"No. My turn."

"Truth or dare?" he asked.

"Truth," she said. "So? Ask me something."

Julian thought but his head seemed to be like a deep, dark pond where his thoughts twitched away from his grasp like crested newts. Then he found a question dangling in the waters like a dead thing. "If you could go back in time and make Bill fall out of the window instead of your mother, would you do it?"

"What kind of a question is that?"

"Truth," he said and giggled and could not stop. She looked at him giggling and started too. It was all the funnier because Ma might come in at any moment and smell the wacky baccy and find them with squidgy legs that had stopped working.

Suddenly Skip stopped laughing and said, "They're having an affair."

"What?" He did not understand.

"They're in love. They're having an affair. My dad and your mum."

He tried to giggle again but it wouldn't work so he shut up and waited.

"You must have noticed," she insisted.

"Don't be silly," he said. "She can't be in love with him. She's married."

"Listen, Julie," she said. "I've been watching. You're only a kid so you don't know what to look for but I'm sharing a room with him and I can tell you he doesn't come to bed until early in the morning."

"He goes for walks. They both do. I've heard them come in."

"Duh. Yes? *And?* They go for walks like they go for swims. To get away from us and spare our feelings. Then he gives it to her and she's loving every minute of it."

"Gives what to her?"

"Sex. She lies down or back or whatever and he puts his thing in her. You know. You must have seen dogs do it."

Julian had indeed seen dogs do it, in a car park on the way to school. His mother had tried to distract him but he saw and she knew he saw and it was disgusting. And that was what she was doing and that was why she had been all strange and talking in high voices and laughing too much.

"Actually," Skip went on, "I think it would be really neat."

Julian just stared so she carried on.

"I mean, your dad's really great too but she's obviously way too young for him, anyone can see that, and she and Dad, my dad, are so good together. It'd be fun. Maybe we could all just live together? Your dad too. Some people do that, you know. My dad knows some people who do that stuff."

"Shut up," he told her. "Shut up shut up shut up!"

"OK. Jeez. I thought you knew. I'm going back to the beach. Look, it's no big deal, Julie. Maybe I'm wrong. Don't say anything. Oh Jeez."

She was like someone who had dropped everything in her bag and did not know what to pick up first. She only went as far as the veranda then she flopped in a lounger and shut her eyes.

"Skip?" he called out. "Skip?" But she seemed to be asleep.

He sat on, staring through the open door to the beach. He wanted to cry but he could not force the tears out. It all made sense but he did not want it to. He had been gathering the signs but ignoring their meaning but now that she had spoken the truth aloud it would not go away. It was like when one walked in dog shit. It never smelled that bad until someone pointed it out—*There, on your shoe, oh God no, don't walk anywhere, just take your shoe off, no, don't put it down, sit down and take your shoe off, carefully*—and then the whole room stank and you wondered why you never noticed it earlier.

He wanted his father not to have left. He wanted Bill and Skip not to have come. He wanted so many impossible things. If Henry had not escaped none of this would have happened, and perhaps if he had not told Henry about . . . But there was another level of wishes, darker wishes, on the level of his unspeakable early-morning thoughts, that was glad Bill had come but furious with his mother. It made him want to fill her bed with sand or her shoes with seaweed. He wanted to tear her dresses and stick her hairbrush somewhere dirty like behind the stove or down the lavatory.

Bill was coming up the beach. On his own. Julian just stared for a minute. It was like early-morning thoughts. He could stare as much as he liked from in here and not be seen. Stare at Bill's hairy chest. At his legs. At everything. He held his hand before his face and slowly brought his finger and thumb together until they framed Bill like the viewfinder on Ma's camera and seemed to be holding him like a toy soldier. Then

Bill waved, so he must have seen and thought Julian was waving and suddenly Julian thought of the wacky baccy. He ran into Bill and Skip's room and stuffed the tobacco and papers back into the jacket pocket and hung the jacket back on the chair, just the way he had found it. Then he felt a little strange so he sat on the end of the bed. Then it seemed nicer to lie down, so he did. And he could tell from the ashtray which side of the bed was Bill's and he rolled on to it and smelled the sheets because it was so good.

"Hi there," Bill said as he came in. "What have you been up to? Junior's dead to the world too."

"Nothing," Julian said. "Playing."

"Oh. *That,*" Bill said. He was toweling himself, though he did not really need to because the sun had dried his skin off on his way up the beach. "It's so crowded out there. Your mum walked into Polcamel to get some food. I said I'd get lunch together. Want some lunch?"

Julian did not know where the courage came from. Maybe the cigarette supplied it. Maybe it came from his being so cross with his mother. But he sprang just as Bill sat on the edge of the bed to pull down his trunks. He pretended to pretend to be a tiger so Bill would think it a game. He made a growling noise like a tiger. But actually it was like the unspeakable thoughts. He held Bill tightly from behind, as he had on the motorbike, then when Bill laughed and stood up as if to give him a piggyback, he slid down and held him tight around the legs, his hands holding so hard on his thigh it must have hurt.

"Hey!" Bill said. "Hey!"

And Julian thought that, since he had got this far and would probably be punished anyway, he might as well go further so, not sure exactly why, he reached up and tried to pull Bill's trunks down. But he had barely got his hand on the waistband than Bill slapped a hand across his and said, "Hey!" more firmly. "Stop that. What are you doing?"

"Pulling down your trunks," Julian said quite truthfully. He was still trying to pretend it was a game but it didn't really work anymore and he felt he had to put on a babyish voice, which he knew even as he did it made things worse.

Bill hauled him off, still grasping his hand. He was so strong he lifted Julian right off his leg and off the floor like a little monkey and dumped him on the bed. Julian giggled and made a monkey noise because perhaps they could make it a game after all but Bill was terrifying.

"That's disgusting," he said. "You understand? That is *disgusting*. You are never to do that to another boy, OK? You're lucky it was me because I can tell you, try that with someone else and he'll break your face open. You understand me?"

Julian nodded. He wanted to cry. He pictured Bill and his mother with no clothes on, bottom to bottom on the sand like a funny crab and it did not seem fair.

"Now get out of here and we'll say no more about it," Bill said more quietly.

Julian left the room slowly. He had his dignity. But as soon as he was in the hall, he ran, ran as fast as he could, out of the house, across the veranda, up the stony track to the top of the hill and the car park and the telephone kiosk. Someone had peed in there. There was a puddle and it stank. He made himself stand right in the middle, in his bare feet, because it was a spell and would help make things all right again. The receiver was so hot it burned his skin but he pressed it hard against his ear because it hurt and that was a useful spell too. And so was the number. One hundred. Like abracadabra.

He had been taught several things as soon as he was old enough to understand. Not to talk to strange men or accept sweets from them. His address. His telephone number and a magic phrase you said when you rang a hundred and a nice lady answered.

"I would like to make a reverse charge call please." He gave Pa's office number and waited. When Pa came on the line and said, "Hello? Julian?" it was as though someone had pulled out a cork in Julian's head and all that would come were tears. He cried and cried. Pa was embarrassed, he could hear that, and a bit cross. Julian tried to talk back but it was so hard.

"What's happened? What's wrong?" Pa asked and he wanted to tell him everything but he realized it was like bad dreams and you had to tell grown-ups what they expected you to say otherwise they'd be frightened too.

So he said, "I miss you. When are you coming back?"

"Soon," Pa said, obviously relieved that they were finally having a conversation. "And I miss you too," he said. "It's horrid here. Listen, Julian. Is your mother all right?"

"Yes. She's fine."

"Oh. Well, you've got to tell her we spoke, all right?"

"All right."

"It's very important. Ask her if she's seen the papers. I can't think why she hasn't rung yet. Will you tell her to buy today's *Times*?"

"Yes."

"Good boy. Now I'd better go. Reverse charge calls are very expensive. They're really only for emergencies, you know."

"I know. Sorry."

"That's all right. Bye."

"Bye."

His mother was home when he got down the hill, and wanted to know where he had been but he just said he had been for a walk and was not hungry. She felt his head and frowned and said he had had too much sun and should stay off the beach that afternoon. Skip winked at him. He just stared back. "All right," he said and left the three of them eating a big lunch with boiled eggs and pork pies and crisps. He was hungry. He could have eaten two pies and a packet of crisps at least but not eating was a spell too. It would help. He did not tell her about *The Times* because he was still cross with her, more cross than ever now because she could not tell at once what was wrong. He heard her laughing with Skip at something Bill had said and he pulled a face to himself.

He went outside and sat with Lady Percy for a while, stroking her rosettes in a special order and feeding her a dandelion leaf. He told her everything in a low whisper only she would understand, until it seemed she was darker and heavier for the secrets he had poured in at her ear. Then he lifted a corner of the fence that was rotten and posted her through.

She seemed unaware of her good fortune at first.

"Go," he said to her. "Quick. Before they catch you again. Go!"

But she just sat on the other side of the fence sniffing and munching. Inside he heard plates being stacked and someone filling the kettle. The liquidizer buzzed for a few minutes. His mother must be making one of her nasty leftover soups. Now Lady Percy ran, frightened by the noise, ran as she normally only ran on a carpet or the hall floor. She headed further and further into the field up the valley and, without so much as a nostalgic backward glance, vanished with his dark secrets down a rabbit hole.

He had meant to create a drama, something that would give him a reason to cry and be pitied and held close by his stupid, ugly mother but all he had done was make an empty hutch and a no less empty field. He saw a buzzard wheel overhead hunting mice and rabbits and remembered a comment his father had made on their first night here, something about foxes having plenty to eat. He was possessed by a marvelously dramatic sense of guilt, like hands steeped in blood. It would show in his face. No one would be able to keep quiet now and say it was too much sun and stay off the beach that afternoon.

"Here. Brought you this." Skip held out a milkshake. "It's banana. Your mum said that was your favorite. I put ice cream in too so it's really thick."

"Thanks." He took it from her and sucked on the straw. It was good. It tasted of sin. "Lady Percy escaped," he said.

"No kidding."

She made no attempt to raise the alarm. She knew better than to make futile rescue suggestions. She just sat with him in silent witness to unswervable change. Julian stole a glance at her as he drank more of the milkshake and realized that it might be possible to be her friend after all. He felt envy too though, not so much of her being a girl as of a kind of flexibility in her which he sensed was part of what it meant to be female. His mother had it too. All women did. He knew that the envy was a low thing, reprehensible, and that he must always be extra nice so as not to let it show.

B L U E   H O U S E

The heavens should have opened. Thunder and lightning were called
for, driving rain and a bone-gnawing wind that would reduce the beach to
a littered waste in apocalyptic minutes. The entire ridiculous, ugly scene
had been played out in balmy sunshine, however, and the chattering, playful holiday parade closed over his departing family like a brightly-colored
soup. Will watched his parents and Sandy drive off, sitting on a rock on
the far side of the beach, children playing in a pool at his feet.

The first thing he did when they left was to hurry back across the
beach to the house. He half-expected to find a note from one of them
but there was nothing. He could not quite believe they had gone. In the
pregnant minutes between hearing the well-earned slaps to Sandy's
cheeks and losing his temper with his mother—for the first time in his
life, it seemed—he had expected discussion, the kind of merciless picking over of the situation at which families were supposed to excel. His
mother's tears, his father's gentlemanly acceptance, his sister's righteous
fury and the revelation of Sandy's complete lack of spine had all passed
so swiftly that he had to replay them in every detail in his mind in
case there was some clue he had overlooked.

In his impulsive impatience to have them gone he had forgotten their bed linen. He stripped it all now, amassing a great pile as he went, then stuffed too much into the washing machine at once so that the load squeaked against the glass as it turned and probably would not clean properly.

The kitchen was full of food, an elegant unserved lunch that would now go to waste. A four-layered fish terrine was not the sort of thing one could eat on one's own. He knew it was delicious, he had made it before, but shock had killed his appetite. He poured himself a glass of wine instead, sat in the rear garden, in his mother's chair, and rang Harriet, prepared to tell her all at last. He rang her direct line as usual but her secretary intervened. Ms. Rowney was in conference until four and could not be disturbed.

He sat on, drinking steadily until his churning emotions arrived at a glassy-eyed stasis. At last the van came bouncing along the valley track to the encampment. Watching Roly climb out and stoop to tether Fay, Will saw not the answer to his problems but only an added complication. Still, he lifted his glass in greeting and Roly raised a hand back. When Will waved him over, Roly merely waved. Will beckoned him again and in response Roly went into a wickedly funny parody of the presenter of a program for deaf children that must have featured in both their childhoods.

"We cannot," Roly signed, "return all your pictures."

When Will beckoned again, Roly teasingly responded with an ever more furious set of gestures: a triangle, a wavy line, a handclap. Will laughed despite his mood.

"You're a cruel tease," he told him when Roly finally came over.

"Must be something you bring out in me." He looked around, taking in the deserted house. "What happened to the sculpture?"

"I didn't heed the warning."

"And where is everyone?"

"Gone."

"*Gone* gone?"

Will nodded.

"But I thought you weren't leaving till Saturday? And how are you leaving without a car?"

Will had not thought of that and felt a spasm of fresh weariness as he thought of an entanglement with local taxi services and over-subscribed end-of-season trains. He sighed.

"Did you have a row?" Roly asked, helping himself to water from the fridge. "All this food! It's like a canceled wedding."

"We had a huge row," Will said. "Terrible things that can never be unsaid." He sighed. "Eat whatever you can. Actually no, I'm lying. There was no row, just a stupid scene and I lost my temper and told my parents to leave too."

"So the row wasn't with the brother or the children?"

"Brother-in-law. No. Do I know you well enough for this?"

"You're leaving soon and you'll never see me again. Why not risk it?"

"I was sleeping with my brother-in-law."

"Shit!"

"I shouldn't have told you."

"Yes you should." Roly leaned against the fridge, eating terrine with a fork. He was looking particularly fetching in old, sun-faded shorts, an even older shirt and work boots. Will would far rather have dragged him to a convenient rug and peeled them off him than make his confession but that would have solved nothing.

"It was all over. I ended it when I met you."

"*Because* or when?"

"No. Yes. I dunno. I ended it but somehow my mother found out and she told his wife—my sister—who just arrived like the wrath of God and swept the children to safety. And I let my mother have it in the neck, which was quite unfair because she's got Alzheimer's and didn't know what she was doing."

"How do you know?"

"They've done tests."

"That she didn't know what she was doing?"

"Oh. I don't know. I don't know anything. And now they won't speak to me and Sandy's going around saying he's gay and in love."

"Is he?"

"No. Not really. Oh fuck, it's all the most hideous, unnecessary mess."

"I think you should use a past tense there. It sounds as though it was a mess and you've just managed to cut yourself free of it."

"But my parents!"

"A mess. You're free of them."

"But I feel so guilty. Not about Sandy, funnily enough. But about Poppy and the children. About what I said to Mum. I've never shouted at her before. We get on so well."

"Then it was probably long overdue. Would a hug help?"

Will nodded.

Roly took him in his arms and held him tight so that he could smell the faint tang of glue and sweat on his shirt. "I was an orphan, which is a bit of a cheat," he said. "But I know what families can do. When I met Seth he was sixteen to my twenty-one, which is nothing if you're a girl but if you're both male . . ." He squeezed Will again, remembering. "His mother had him feeling guilty even when he was *dying*, which is quite an achievement. Sorry. This probably isn't helping. I'm in a good mood because Bron's just sold the lot and the tourist season's nearly over and I'm about to get my house back. And that was insensitive."

"Very."

"Give me another slice of that outstanding fishy thing and I'll take you on a trip. And stop looking so glum. It's lost on me."

It was a pagan site. No signpost marked its whereabouts but there was a well-beaten path through shoulder-high gorse and bracken that buzzed with insect life. Quite suddenly the path opened out into a clearing where, on a plot of land raised above the scrub, twelve ancient stones stood in a perfect circle about a thirteenth. The central one was twice the height, an unashamed skyward phallus. At its base, offerings and spells were heaped. Scraps of bright cloth, rain-sodden messages, bundles of flowers and a limb wrenched from a doll.

"So," Roly said. "We should do this properly. You need some ragwort. There's some. No, you have to pick it or it won't work. And some red campion. That's it. And some honeysuckle and a spring of gorse."

"Ow," Will said, cutting his fingers as he wrenched the gorse off a bush.

"Perfect. Now let a drop of your blood fall on the flowers. That's it. Now . . . a hair off your head." He tweaked out a hair.

"You are in a good mood."

"Ssh. Concentrate. Now. Wrap it all up in one of those dock leaves, like a *dolma*. That's it. Now you put one hand on the center stone."

Will did as he was told. "Now what?"

"Now squeeze the bundle as hard as you can and make your wish."

Will wished with all his might.

"Now you lay the bundle with the others."

"And that's it?"

"That's it. The gods will listen."

"And this works?"

Roly shrugged. "It was fun making it up, though."

Will made to chase him but stopped dead in his tracks. In a clearing beyond the first, on higher ground still, stood a great roundel of stone on its side, a hole through its center. "What is it?" he asked.

"The pagans claim it lines up with the others at the summer solstice and the rising sun shines clean through the circle and makes the inner stone in the ring light up. It's also used to heal things. Children with rickets used to be made to crawl through it and people with arthritis and stiff joints still swear by it."

Will crouched for a closer look. The inside was worn smooth by the constant passage of bodies. He shut his eyes and thrust his head into the middle.

"Got a headache?"

He opened his eyes to look up at Roly. "No," he told him. "I'm just confused."

Back on the coast the weather had finally changed to accord with the events of the morning. Thick banks of fog were rolling in off the sea, blotting out the light and chilling the air.

"Fay, listen," Roly commanded. The dog put her head on one side. Out of the mists came the mournful wail of the foghorn on the lighthouse across the bay. Fay whined. "She hates that noise," Roly said and ruffled her ears.

Will gazed at where the sea had been and breathed salt and bladder-wrack. He saw the darker, introspective appeal the place must acquire off-season.

They went to bed less from lust than because it was a comforting place to be. But for Will the bungalow was permeated with conflict and unpleasant reminders of a family he felt sure must be standing in judg-ment, so they retreated to the trailer and spent the rest of the evening there. Roly made occasional forays back to Blue House for more wine for Will or to raid the fridge.

Will did not dare speak as he was thinking, of dreams and futures. They both observed the correct form for concluding a holiday romance. The mobile phone was kept turned off so that any callers, plaintive or otherwise, would have to make do with the answering service. For a few hours at least, Roly saw to it that the world could not find them. Then he packed Will's suitcase and books and bin-liners of damp laundry into the van and drove him to the station. They sat together until the eleventh hour, talking inconsequentially. Then Will broke the rules.

"I don't want to go," he said.

"Needs must."

"Yes," Will sighed. "Bookshop to open, garden to water, family feud to heal."

"Why should *you* have to deal with it? With the right therapist, you could come to see yourself as the injured party." They chuckled sadly. A bell rang on the platform. "That means your train's coming," Roly said.

"I know," said Will, not moving. "Our timing was so lousy. If only I'd sorted all this out first; come on holiday on my own *then* met you."

"I think our timing was pretty good," Roly said and ruffled Will's hair, making him feel about eight. "Be brave, you."

"Needs must."

"Yes."

They raced madly for the luggage and, chased by Fay, ran over the footbridge just as the train was pulling in. The carriages were already heaving with holidaymakers returning from the far west, so full that there were already people standing in the corridors.

"Oh God," Will said.

"Get on and don't be such a sensitive flower. Read a book. Time'll fly."

"Yes."

He pecked Will's cheek and pushed him toward an open carriage door.

"Can I write to you?" Will asked. "Maybe?"

Roly smiled, properly, without wiping it away again. "Of course," he said. "If you like."

"But I don't have your address."

"You've been staying at it for twelve days."

"Oh yes."

"Go."

"Yes." Will threw in the bags, jumped in after them and shut the door. He flung down the window as the train started to move. "I forgot the sculpture!"

"I'll post it on to you."

"You don't have my address."

"So write to me, then."

"I should have a hat for this."

"That was the ugliest hat in cinema history."

He liked *Brief Encounter*! There was so much they had failed to discuss. Improvising a seat out of his suitcase and the laundry bags, Will took out a novel but failed to read it immediately.

A bored little girl was leaning against the wall opposite him. She stared at him and played with the lock on the lavatory door, opening and shutting it repeatedly. Will listened to the sound, thought of a child's plastic sandal thwacking on a piece of driftwood and carefully wiped the smile off his face.

BEACHCOMBER

Frances would never have believed herself capable of such heedless selfishness. It was not that she specifically did anything—like neglecting the children for hours on end for the pursuit of her own pleasure, or not very often, not unless she was sure they were amusing themselves. It was rather that, while continuing to do everything a mother on holiday should, she allowed herself to become entirely self-absorbed.

She had always feared her piano-playing was a self-indulgence because of the romantic and rebellious notions it fed within her, but now she saw that it was still largely about the entertainment or impressing of other people. *This* was selfishness, this impatience to be alone with her thoughts, this intense awareness of how she looked and felt from hour to somnolent hour, this ridiculous, she knew it, mad hunger to feel his body against hers however fleetingly, above all, this sense of being what the French called *well in one's skin*.

The danger, of course, was that for all that she was treading a tightrope, risking love, marriage, motherhood, those gimcrack medals of social standing and parental approval, because of Bill and what she was doing with him, most of these feelings and changes were not about him at all. The sensation of herself was as novel as the first pangs of child-birth had been. That experience, at once terrifying and fascinating, had felt so far removed from the father of her child, without whom et cetera, that it had been something of a shock to emerge from her etherized labors to find him holding her hand and looking pleased with himself. Similarly she now had to remind herself afresh whenever she felt Bill's touch under cover of lunch table, crowded wave or merciful darkness, to make an effort to focus on this clever, dangerous man whose first laughable declaration of love had begotten this upheaval she was riding so casually.

Part of the trouble was the lack of a courtship. By the time she mar-ried John, by the time he first kissed her even, she had known his life story, the names of all his significant relatives, alive or dead, and even his taste in cake and thoughts on God. Bill, by contrast, was still a stranger in many ways. She would have liked to think the daily small surprises about him were a part of falling in love only her rational self knew they were a symptom of her having met him mere days ago. He, however, knew her too well, read her like a text and could predict her every move. It was a text that inexplicably fascinated him. He wanted to save her and Julian, apparently, from the dead hand of respectability. So far, so patronizing. And goaded by thoughts of Becky, she dealt with *that* by laughing demonstrations of just how capable of unrespectability she was.

More touchingly, he looked to her to save him from what he had thought an inability to love again, a lingering mistrust of women indeed. Even when the children were in earshot, so that he was reduced to en-coded declarations or mere speaking glances, he laid delicious siege to her. He had somehow seen, that day in Trenellion, how restless she was, how ready to be set free and by saying the words aloud and encouraging her, fool that she was, to admit the truth of them, he had made mere thoughts a fact and now built each hour on that crumbly foundation of dissatisfaction so that it was becoming a thing apart from her she could assess and fear.

She wanted to argue, to defend John and their marriage against criti-cism she knew to be unjust, but was only ever in a position to do so when they were alone together. And at such times she found herself a mere groping animal in her desire for his rival.

They lay together now on the sand, hidden by a clouded moon, spent and therefore briefly in a position to hold a sensible conversation but instead she seized his hand and tugged him into the icy water where they washed the sand and lovemaking from each other's bodies and shouted aloud because, after all, they were now only swimming and swimming, even by moonlight, was allowed. They ran back to their heap of ripped-off clothes and she snatched a towel and, rubbing herself, shivering, moved apart from him. As if to assist her, the moon emerged again and they seemed suddenly floodlit, forced into decorum on a sandy stage.

"Julie's a little fruit," he said. "You know that, don't you?"

"He is sweet," she agreed. "He's really blossomed out here. We've brought out the savage in him."

"No. I mean he's a *fruit*. A fag. A queer."

She was shocked, repelled. "Don't be silly," she said. "He's only a baby still. He's only eight. He doesn't even know what it's for yet."

"So? He's still . . . I can tell. He tried to pull my shorts down."

"He showed remarkably good taste."

"He was *looking* at me, Frances."

"Oh, Bill." She was impatient now. This was not what she had wanted to discuss. "The whole world is not fixated with your . . . thing."

"Say it."

"Penis. Penispenispenis." She laughed. "Just me. Come here. I'm cold."

"No." He sat on a rock, threw her clothes across, quite roughly, and began to dress himself. "We need to talk," he said.

"You're right," she agreed, trying to seize control as well as the moment. "We must stop. It's been lovely, amazing, but enough's enough. I'm sure Skip suspects something and I don't want it going any further. I have to go back to John next week and get on with our life and you have a new job to start in Norwich and—"

"No, Frances."

"What?"

"I've asked her already."

"Who?" For an absurd moment she thought he was going to say Becky and, in her shock, she took a second or two to focus on what he was telling her.

"I took her aside after dinner tonight and asked her how she'd feel having you for a new mother."

"But that's . . . You shouldn't have! Not without asking me."

"She was so happy, Frances. She loves you. You can be more mother to her than Becky ever could. To Becky she was just a hindrance, a sort of ironic accessory at best: *My Child.*" He mimicked Becky's icy accent.

She stood, pulled on her jersey because her teeth were chattering with cold as well as adrenaline. "But I'm not free to *become* her mother," she insisted.

"I know. And you're scared and I understand that. But listen. I'll tell him for you. You never need see him again. I've thought it all out. I'll leave Skip here with you and I'll go to the prison and see him and tell him everything. He won't put up a fight. He's way too well brought up to stand in your way."

"But I love him." She walked away, as though she could walk away from the problem, but the house was before her, with Skip inside it, Skip who now knew and was unlikely to keep silent. How could he force her hand like this? How could he say he loved her and be so calculatingly vicious? "I love him, don't you see?" And she heard doubt in her voice, in her need to repeat the declaration and she sank on to another rock, her back to him, watching the house as though for answers. His voice stung her like salt in a cut.

"You're still so fucking respectable. It's making you paranoid."

"It's Skip I'm thinking of," she said. "Not what you call my respectability. Really, Bill," she sought refuge in snobbery, "if you're to survive in your new job, you really must lose this touching American belief that all the English are in thrall to the Royal Family and good manners." But anger made her stammer and she knew he was unconvinced. "It's her I'm thinking of," she reiterated. "You can't just play around with a child's feelings like that. What's she going to think when I *don't* become her mother? Think of the rejection that represents!"

He came up behind her, kissed her neck, kissed her shoulders through her jersey. "Stop fighting it," he begged. "Just let go. Let me worry for us both. Let me make up to you for the lost years. Let me give you the self-willed life you should have been having by now."

His hands were around her now, skating under the cotton and across her belly. She felt hot again, constricted by clothes. How could she feel hot? "I'm not a caged songbird," she said.

"Frances, please." He pressed against her and somehow she found herself sliding backward on to his lap and then they were both where they started, back on the sand, kissing lips already sore with kissing, cheeks already sore with sun.

"Don't make me choose," she pleaded. "Not yet. I can't. Please?"

For all her resolve, the next morning saw no change. The weather was still glorious. She still sat before her looking-glass and was amazed at how full and ripe she was looking, lambent with preposterous desire as much for herself as for him. She cleared the breakfast things in a coffee-scented daze, even singing along to the cheaply repetitive songs on the radio and swaying her hips as she wiped down the table. Then the news came on, the little news that such stations allowed one, committed as they seemed to be to keeping the listener anesthetized and happy, and she heard the bare facts. A six-million-pound train robbery had taken place, one guard was now in a coma from a blow to his head. It was thought to be the work of the man who had recently escaped from Wandsworth jail, possibly working with outsiders. Ports and airports being watched. She grabbed the radio and tried to find other stations but there was only pop music, interference and gobbledegook. Shouting a mere, "Back soon!" to the others, she raced to the car and thundered up the lane.

The Polcamel Stores still had a copy of yesterday's *Times* in a back room. She bought it as well as that day's because it had John's face on the front next to Henry Farmer and another, younger man she did not recognize. She read, astonished, how Farmer had been in the house with John. He could have ended up in a coma like the guard. Or dead. She thought of the hours she had left Julian free to chat to Farmer in the garden. He might have been taken hostage, raped. Anything could have happened. Why had John not told her when they rang? He could have at least sent a telegram. Cursing her slovenliness in not ringing him more often, not wanting to bother him in a "little woman" way, she gunned the engine and raced back up to the car park and the telephone kiosk. She rang the direct line but his deputy answered.

"Mervyn, it's Frances. I've just heard. My God! Is John there?"

"Frances, don't worry. He's on his way down. He said to tell you if you rang."

"What train? I could meet him."

"He didn't say. Actually. I think he half-hoped you wouldn't ring so he could surprise you."

"Surprise us," she thought as she returned down the hill, and flinched at her instinctive assumption that *you* had referred to her and Bill and not to her alone. Should she tell him before Skip did? Or Bill? She could tell him and thus preclude any grand destructive gestures on Bill's part.

I did this. We did this. But I love you and I want to stay. Or *I did this. I love him.*

Did she love him? Did she love either of them? She was racing around the house with these questions in her mind, tidying and dusting as though her guilt had left sandy trails about the place that he would see on arrival. She checked herself. This was preposterous. She would say nothing. Not because there was nothing to say but because she no longer knew what she wanted.

A weariness assailed her. They had not come to bed much before three and even then Bill had pursued her to her room and seemed to have held her all night, pawing her, murmuring in her ear until she pawed back as much in a desperate desire to push him away to let her sleep as from the need to feel any reassurance his warm flesh could offer in return.

She sat on the veranda with a cup of cold coffee from the jug he liked to keep in the fridge. They could decide it for themselves. The men. She knew the decision to be ignoble but she began to feel she no longer cared. They could fight it out and then she would decide, when the bloodshed was done, *then* she would go with one or the other.

He had set up his Olivetti and begun typing but the children or good weather must have proved too great a distraction and the three had gone off somewhere. Idly, she read the paragraph or two he had tapped out. A description of a woman packing in a hurry, including typically male assumptions of the things a woman in such a position would think to take with her: silk stockings and lipstick rather than pearls, a good book and a stash of housekeeping money. She smiled to herself. He would learn. Perhaps it would fall to her to teach him? The rest of the novel in progress, or such of it as he had worked on since arriving, lay in a ring binder under the chair. She marveled at his lack of fear. What if rain came suddenly and soaked the pages, or someone upturned a cup of coffee, just as she so easily might have done before she noticed the binder was there? He used no carbon paper.

She picked up the file, opened it and flicked to the back, wanting to read the page that would give more context to the one still in the machine. He had barely touched these pages, just fed them in and out of the machine, and yet they were, she felt sure, more imbued with his essence than any discarded shirt. She read, frowned, flicked back a further page and read again.

Stop fighting it, the hero, she assumed he was the hero, breathed, his mouth hot against the woman's collar bone. *Just let go. Let me worry for us both. Let me make up to you for the lost years. Let me give you the self-willed life he never let you have.*

She grimly noted the subtle improvement he had made to the rhythm of last night's text then shut the folder and put it back beneath the seat.

She no longer felt wearily passive but energized to the point where angry static might have crackled off her fingertips and hair. She could not resist. She grabbed the folder and read more, amazed she had forborne to do so all this time. John Updike was nothing compared to this.

Having grown up in her father's prison and moved to her husband's she was caught between her ache for freedom and open spaces and her terror of the world outside the perimeter fence.

Furious, she snatched a pencil and underlined the last sentence jaggedly before scribbling in the margin,

"But English prisons have walls not fences. Try 'guarded walls.' Better rhythm?" She flicked on, making other suggestions. When she reached the climactic discussion about leaving the heroine's husband for her love and his motherless daughter, she scribbled, "No. Absolutely not. She loves the daughter and *respects* her far too much to endanger the exclusive relationship the girl has established with him. She only *lets* him think she's coming to him to shut him up and satisfy his ego. In fact she's going off on her own. ALONE!"

She heard Skip's raucous laugh and threw the folder down. They were coming down the cliff path to the right of the cove. She waved. They waved back, all three, so neatly. But he was just a man. A rather ordinary-looking man with a droopy mustache. Not a great love. Certainly not a god of any kind. How could she have risked so much for so little? And unless she worked fast, all was still to risk. She felt like a sleepwalker awaking on a quarry's edge, stones already slipping beneath her dirty, bloodied toes.

"Guess what!" she shouted, jumping up to greet them. "John's coming back. Isn't that great? Crisis over and he'll still be in time for some holiday."

She saw the pain in his eyes, real pain that startled her and brought fear up in her throat. She would keep him at arm's length with brittle, excited chatter. She would use the children as a buffer zone, talking through them if necessary. She would cleave to her little boy's side, even to ridiculous lengths, take him to meet a succession of trains if necessary, until John was safely back to protect her.

There would be no further discussion. Words were dangerous and entirely untrustworthy.

BLUE HOUSE

She had to be very careful. They pretended not to guard her but they did and venturing out alone like this would not be approved of. They were right to worry. She worried too. To venture out alone was to walk across a thawing lake on bobbing floes which shrank even as one paused to recollect the route. As well as her home address, firmly in the front of her diary for showing the taxi driver, she had a bag from his shop, carefully smoothed away in her jersey drawer, which had the shop's address on it. She counted out her money twice and tied the purse on a piece of tapestry wool, fastening the other to a button on her coat so there should be no chance of losing it. She did not even have to read. When the taxi driver asked, "Where to?" all she had to do was hold out the bag and say, "Here, please."

He gave her a funny look but he drove off without fuss. She had made a logical request and spoken no gibberish. She shut the little window between them in case the driver tried to make conversation. She could no longer trust her mouth with strangers. She used what the therapist girl called *inappropriate language* sometimes. Swore, in other words. And she tended to forget who knew what or whom and baffle them with talk of friends and family members they could not possibly know.

She had come in the afternoon because that was the only time she could slip away, stepping out through the window while they thought she was having her afternoon nap. But she also recalled him saying this was his least busy time. The taxi cost so much she was not sure she could afford a tip, so she said an extra special thank you then wrinkled her nose and apologized that she was so poor. The driver used inappropriate language, which made her laugh.

Of course she remembered his shop! She recognized it as soon as she turned on the curb. The vivid orange and yellow awnings. The café tables where pretty, summery people were eating cake and late salad lunches. The window display where new books hung on fishing lines so they seemed to be floating.

She let herself in and breathed that lovely, glossy bookshop smell, so unlike the sad, stale fetor of libraries. Only this was even better because there was coffee too and Casablanca lilies in a big vase. Piano music floated, sad and beseeching, which it took her a moment to place.

"Fauré," she said to a tall girl who had approached wearing a how-can-I-help-you face.

"I'm sorry?" the girl said.

"The fourth nocturne. So lovely, but nobody plays it. He's out of fashion, you see."

"Oh. The music. Yes. Did you want the music section?"

"No. I'm after Julian but he's probably busy."

"There's no Julian here. There's a Jillian. She's helping someone just now but—"

"It's all right," Frances said. "I've seen him. Thanks."

He was walking down the stairs with two men in suits. She gave a little wave, not to demand his immediate attention but simply to let him know she was there. She would be quite content to browse. There were unusual magazines here, she remembered. She might even have a coffee. Wandering at liberty like this had become such a novelty she would not mind waiting for him in the least. He saw her and the shock on his face, quickly masked, reminded her how angry he had been at the seaside, calling her horrible names.

"Julian?"

"Mum? What a lovely surprise. I'm just showing these gentlemen Gaia's café. Can you believe they want to buy this place?"

"Bob Black," said one man, and shook her hand.

"Gary Tucker," said the other.

"Frances Pagett," she said, "proud mother. Pay no attention."

Will glanced nervously at her and continued steering the men toward the café area, where he presented them to the cross woman behind the counter. Then he shook both their hands and left them ordering coffee and came back to find her. "Dad not with you?" he asked lightly.

"I . . . No," she admitted. "But it's all right. I came in a taxi. You're busy, aren't you?"

"Not anymore. Come backstairs and we can have peace, otherwise people'll start asking me things."

He led her up past a series of posters advertising new books and through a door to a warm, chaotic room where two ancient sofas faced one another across a filthy coffee table. "Well. What a surprise," he said again. "Sit."

"Do you want to sell?" she asked, peering into a mug, amazed that there was actually blue fur growing in there.

He sighed heavily and sat himself. "Oh, I don't know. They're from a big American chain that's moving over here." He jumped up again. "I'll just ring Dad. OK? In case he's worried." He darted through another door. She heard him dial. "Dad? Yes, she's here. . . . Don't worry. . . . Just got here . . . Do you want me to run her back later? . . . Oh, yes. Of course. OK. Whenever you like . . . Bye. What? Well, yes. That would be good."

The little room, its mess, the dirty crockery, the jumble of papers and faxes, the heaps of damaged books, the gutted sofas with their greasy arms brought a fit of desolation on her and she started to cry. She heard him apologize to John and break off from arranging a drink. He ran back to her.

"Mum? Mum, don't worry. I'm here."

"Don't leave me," she wailed. "I don't want to be left."

"No one's leaving you." He hugged her then gave her a great roll of paper towel. She tore a square off and blew her nose on it.

"Ruined everything," she muttered.

"What? Look, Mum, I'm sorry about the things I said."

"No," she said firmly and blew her nose again to shut him up. "Let me. I need to tell you."

"What?"

"I need to tell you and it isn't easy nowadays, so please *please* don't fucking interrupt."

"OK." She saw him stifle a smile. She sat. "Sit over there," she told him. "Where I can see you."

"All right." He sat on the other sofa, over the tide of filth.

"I swore I wasn't going to apologize to you ever," she said. "Because that would make it all less important and it couldn't be, shouldn't be, apologized away."

"What shouldn't?"

"But you shouldn't have seen. I had no idea you'd seen us. When two people love each other, or think they love each other . . ."

"Yes?"

"No. That's not right. Deep breath. Julian, listen."

"No one calls me that anymore, Mum. I'm Will."

He looked thinner than she remembered. Much better without the mustache. "Of course," she said, then frowned. "No, you're not. Don't be silly. Listen to me, please."

"I'm listening."

"People make wrong choices. Terrible choices. I could so easily have gone. I wanted what was best for you."

"I know, I know." He came over to hug her again. "And you were shocked and rightly so and you didn't think properly."

She did not want her truth stifled with a hug. She pushed him back. "No! Whatever gave you that idea? I wasn't shocked. But I . . . I was very young. Desperately young. Even forty is still young, believe me, however it feels at the time. I didn't want you trapped."

"And I'm not."

"Of course you were furious, because you wanted him too. Deep down I understood at the time but I couldn't face it and then it was too late."

"Ma, it's OK. Honestly."

"Honestly?" She searched his face for kind lies.

"You've done me a favor. Probably them too. I'm sure Sandy will end up—"

"You're not *listening!*" she shouted.

"I am, I am," he assured her. "Tell me again if you like."

She snorted with impatience. Brother and sister, both alike, always thinking they knew what she was going to say next.

"I didn't realize Poppy would move in with you," he said. "I thought maybe she'd kick him out."

Lucidity dawned on her mind, only it was much quicker than dawn, more like a light switched on. "She's with us to look after me," she said.

"You don't need looking after."

"Thanks," she said wryly. "I think it's an excuse. She needs time."

"Does she hate me?"

Frances shrugged. "You're her brother. She has to deal with you. Give her time."

"He's been trying to speak to me," he said. "I won't see him. He's too confused. It wouldn't be fair. Or right."

"Good. Do you mind if we change the subject?"

"Not at all."

He started to speak about the business, the people who wanted to buy it, the opinions of employees whose names and faces were a blur to her and she felt weary and began to long for her bed. Why had she come here? All the way into town for what? She had a dim memory of a tremendous, urgent sense of mission but now found herself bored and tired on an ugly sofa with no sense of having accomplished anything.

"Oh," he said suddenly. "I forgot. Roly sent your sculpture back."

"Roly?"

"You know. Your sad young man." She must have looked blank. "Hang on," he said and banged through the door and up the stairs to his flat.

A girl, a complete stranger, shuffled in without saying hello, dumped a bag on the floor, repaired her makeup in the cracked looking glass over the sink and went out again. The encounter made Frances feel invisible but she was used to this; she had become invisible to young people, male and female, twenty years ago. Now they only noticed her to offer her seats, drinks, open doors, in a brisk effort to neutralize her disconcerting presence with good form.

Will came back in with some pieces of old wood with a plastic sandal attached and a wind vane. "Look," he said. "All in one piece still despite Sandy's best efforts to demolish it."

"It's rubbish," she said. "A child could do better. Can I leave it behind?"

"Oh. Of course. Er, listen, Mum. Dad's here. He can't come in because he's on a double yellow. I'll walk you down."

"I'm not a cripple."

"I know. But you're my mother and I've missed you."

"Shut up."

She walked downstairs with him at her elbow like some kind of flunkey. This was not what she had hoped for. Her anger could sweep these stupid books off the walls, could wilt lilies, scratch girls' insincere faces and send scalding coffee into laps. She stopped abruptly at the foot of the stairs, needing breath. She saw John in the doorway to the street. He waved, smiled, pointed along the pavement and walked out of sight.

"Mum?"

"I hated you, you know," she began. "I blamed you. I think I still do. It was all your fault. Which made me guilty, so I hated you more. Then you came home on Sundays and I loved you again. So it was all right really. Wasn't it? Were you terribly unhappy?"

"When?"

"In thingy. Prison."

He grinned. "Happiest years of my life," he said, understanding apparently, and kissed her cheek. He brushed off the makeup girl, who wanted to know something, and steered Frances out of the shop and into the waiting car.

He spoke to John briefly. Perhaps *that* was the point of this excursion? To make son and father speak again. Not that they were speaking any more than they ever did or any more deeply. As ever, they were like fellow pupils in boarding school, or submariners obliged to take shares in a hammock with the minimum of social intercourse. If anything, the great filthiness each was strenuously overlooking made them even more polite. She yawned loudly. John apologized and drove off, winding up the window.

"Did you worry?" she asked after a while of their driving in silence.

"I was glued to the cricket," he said, "And Poppy was deep in *Dead Souls*. Neither of us had any idea you were gone."

"Oh. Good," she said and she saw amusement crinkle the edge of his eye.

BEACHCOMBER

Bodmin Road station was strangely placed, deep in a thickly wooded valley at least a mile outside the town. Possibly local landowners had funded this stretch of the Great Western line and had insisted on a convenient stop where houseguests could be met—John had noticed the discreet drive that curled away from the car park among rhododendrons. Only a few years ago, locals could have changed to a branch line train not only into town but all the way along the Camel and its estuary to Padstow. Now, thanks to Beeching's swingeing economies, they were reliant on sporadic buses and the occasional mercies of a taxi service. John saw other passengers, luggage-laden, being met at the ticket barrier and half-expected Frances to be there peering effortlessly over the heads in the crowd as she searched for his face. He was glad that she was not. She would surely have brought the children and Bill and the barrage of questions and anecdote would have frayed his nerves. This way, climbing out of the valley in a taxi and winding through the fields to the sea, he could readjust gradually back into a holiday frame of mind. With no luggage and wearing his work suit, he felt he must look like a commuter or bringer of bad news, queer among the silly hats and sun-pinked legs.

In fact his news was good. The papers did not know it yet but Malone had been recognized and caught boarding a plane to Chicago under an assumed identity and a bad wig. In exchange for a lighter sentence he had already begun to spill beans. Farmer had left the country and, unless he had deliberately misinformed Malone as insurance, would be in Cuba by now where he would lie low before heading on to Brazil. There was no extradition treaty with either country but preliminary inquiries were being made. Most of Malone's share of the haul had already been traced to his sister's house in Plaistow where it was hidden, with laughable innocence, in a trunk on top of her wardrobe. The sister, like the two other accomplices, had vanished, tipped off about Malone's arrest. Either she had no idea of the worth of the certificates she had hidden for him or had not dared return to a house under observation. Inevitably he would have salted the rest away somewhere else, passed it to a contact for laundering. Whatever, it was not John's affair. Farmer's share, the lion's share, had yet to be traced. Malone suspected it was traveling to Brazil or Switzerland under separate cover by some hired hand or other. It was as good as spent. Lloyd's underwriters could foot the bill. Already detectives were trawling through records of previously unsolved heists on the basis that they had underestimated both their man and his past record. Podgy, underachieving Farmer was well on his way, John wryly saw, to being reinvented as an ice-cool master criminal.

What Malone had been unable to tell them was how Farmer knew to hide in the Governor's House. Farmer had refused to tell him every detail of the escape plan, arranging only how they could make contact a few days later. John felt reprieved, exonerated from all blame. Only the niggling suspicion that someone on his own staff besides Malone had betrayed him, had put his and possibly his young family's lives at risk, checked his satisfaction.

Frances heard the taxi and met it at the foot of the drive. Her face was clouded with concern and for a foolish moment he thought she was going to tell him bad news—an adder bite, a drowning, that wretched motorbike—but then Julian ran out to join her and they were both smiling so he knew all was well.

A large family, he thought. *Five children? Six?*

"You're not meant to be here. Julian and I met two earlier trains just in case," she said. "Then they said not to bother until eight."

"Well it's half past that now."

"Is it? Oh blast!" She slapped her watch, then rewound it. "I'm having a useless day."

"She's been forgetting *everything*," Julian said and shyly took his father's hand. John had to drop the hand to hug Frances and when he looked down again, the moment had passed and Julian's hands were in the pockets of his shorts.

The little party had made a touching effort at a feast of welcome. Frances had tracked down a bottle of his favorite claret, Bill had improvised a barbecue on the sand dune and was cooking chicken legs and sausages and Julian and Skip had written WELCOME BACK in shells and seaweed on the ground before the veranda. John shook hands all round, said, "Well this is nice," several times, was persuaded by Frances to change out of his suit then, changed and washed, sat on the veranda with a glass of the wine. And it was good. The heavens were laying on a spectacular sunset, swallows were swooping across the fields behind the house and his nearest and dearest had missed him. He was back in the charmingly extended family he felt he had only just left. What could be sweeter?

And yet something was wrong. The children were overexcited and on the verge of turning fractious, tired perhaps after a long day of sun, play and anticipation. Frances was almost manic in her insistence that he relax, put his feet up, have another drink and in her exhortations to the children and Bill to confirm just how good it was to have him back again, to ask him about the escape and robbery now that he could talk freely. Bill was unmistakably muted, almost sullen. Definitely not the brash, oddly likable man John had left behind.

"What's going on between you two?" he asked Frances, snatching a moment alone with her as she finished decorating a trifle in the kitchen.

"What do you mean?" Her voice was tight. "Damn!" She had spilled a great blob of hundreds and thousands on to the cream and crossly stirred them in with a finger.

"Have you had a row?"

"No." She laughed, turned, licked her finger. "Don't be daft. Why?"

"Well, you're not talking to him and his feelings seem to be hurt. Be a little nicer. It's only for a few days."

"Did he say something?" she asked. "About them leaving?"

"Not exactly." Skip came into the room, stole a handful of crisps for her and Julian then hurried out again laughing wildly. "He just said what a wonderful time he'd had and something regretful in his tone made me think—"

"Oh. I see. So he didn't say when they were leaving?"

"No."

"Oh." She smiled brightly. "Don't look so worried. You're on holiday again." She topped up his wine. "Gosh, that meat smells good. Don't know about you but we're all famished. Did you bring any post?"

"Not much. I left the bills. There's a letter from your mother."

"Oh God."

"Oh, and a parcel for Julian. It's not his birthday?"

"You know it isn't. Where's it from?"

"Well I don't know. London postmark."

"Julian?" she called out. "Pa's got a parcel for you."

Julian came running, closely followed by Skip. John was glad to see that at least these two had bonded. He had worried the age difference would be just too wide.

"I'll get it," he said and opened his briefcase. "Letters for you," he said, handing Frances a small handful, "and a small and mystifying package for you, my boy."

Grinning, Julian took it. "Can I open it now?" he asked.

"Of course," Frances said. "We all want to know what's in it." She gave Skip a hug to show she included her, worried perhaps that she would be jealous.

Julian tore at the packaging.

Bill appeared in the doorway. "Meat's almost ready," he said. "What's all this?"

"Mystery parcel," Frances told him. "Isn't it exciting!"

She was making the poor child self-conscious and he was struggling with the thick brown string that held the package closed.

"Here. Let me," John said and gave the string a slash with his penknife to get it started.

There was a small box, from a jeweler's in Hatton Garden, and inside, a gold watch, a real gold watch, far too expensive and heavy for a child. Skip gasped. Julian picked it out uncertainly.

"Is this for me?" he asked. "Who's it from?"

Frances had found a note in the outer packing. "Well it's come direct from the jeweler's and it's definitely addressed to you, not me or Pa."

"Maybe there's an inscription," Bill said.

Julian turned it over in his hands. "It's really heavy," he said. He had no idea of the value of the thing. It was just a watch and he had a Timex already. John could see he was trying not to look disappointed. "It says *A token of esteem for my young friend . . .*" he began.

John started to understand. He took the watch. *"A token of esteem for my young friend for services rendered. HF,"* he read then looked hard at his son.

"I don't understand," said Frances.

"I do," John said. "It's from Farmer. It's from bloody Farmer. The nerve of the man!" Anger made his hand shake and he pretended he needed a sip of wine to give it something to do. "It's from your friend Henry," he told Julian. "Isn't it?"

"How should I know?" Julian asked. He made a silly face, a sort of grin which looked even stupider with his black eye and for a second John despised him.

"What services, Julian? What did you do for him?"

"Darling, I really don't think that—" Frances started but John cut her off.

"Tell me!" he said and grabbed Julian's wrists. "What services?"

"Ow!" Julian said.

"You told him. Trailing after him in the bloody garden, you *told* him."

"You swore!"

"He could have killed me," John said and slapped him.

The blow was hard enough to make the boy stumble back against a chair.

"Beef curtains," Julian said, beginning to cry. Frances reached out for him but he smacked away her hand, hard enough to whiten the skin through her tan. "Fucking chutney ferret," he said. "Buggery fuck arsehole."

John slapped him again. He did not want to hurt him, just to silence him, silence this filth that was like Farmer jeering out at him like a devil in the child's body. Julian fell over. Frances screamed. Skip giggled nervously.

"Hey, steady!" Bill shouted.

The second slap made things worse. Julian did not cry out but as he got back to his feet he continued to mumble a litany of obscenities, words he could not possibly understand, words he could only have learned from the prisoners. The rest of them just stood and watched and listened as though, John thought, he were not a child at all but the mouthpiece of some brutal oracle. Then he started to make sentences.

"They've been like dogs in a car park," he said. "At it like dogs in a car park. Round and round. Bum to bum. And we're not meant to look but we do and it's filthy. Filthy. He squeezes her between his legs on the floor and gives it to her and she loves it. He sticks his thing in her beef curtains."

Now Frances slapped him. As soon as she did it she cried out, a terrible, wounded, "Oh I'm so sorry!" that could have been meant for any of them but Julian just spat back, "That's right. Break my cunting face open." Then he ran.

For a second, as the boy's slapping steps ran over the veranda, the house felt impossibly small and hot. John looked at his wife and saw a stricken, white-faced stranger, then he pushed past the others and raced across the darkening beach.

Julian was up ahead, already churning out through the waves. John followed and, startled by the mineral chill of the water, realized that he might be about to have to swim and would need to discard his shoes. By the time he had pulled them off and hurled them to the shore, Julian was executing a furious crawl.

"Julian!" he called after him. "Wait. For God's sake. Bloody hell." And he threw himself after him.

Water was not his natural element—faced with a beach holiday he would walk while Frances swam—but he had been efficiently taught in the freezing, river-fed pool at his school. He had no practice at swimming in sodden clothes, however, and Julian had anger on his side as well as a head start. It was getting dark so fast he was guided more by sound than sight, following the splashing of reliably inefficient technique. Julian never swam for long unless forced to. He would tire soon and give up. But the tide was pulling out and they were in quite the worst part of the bay for being seized by a rip current and pulled farther out than their feeble strokes alone would carry them.

"Julian, stop!" He tried to yell over the waves. "The tide's too strong. Julian!" But the child was like a clockwork thing, churning on regardless, his arm strokes regular for all their wildness. It was so cold John had lost all feeling in his lower body so God alone knew what a mere boy in shorts and tee shirt was suffering.

When, after what seemed an eternity, John realized he was in grabbing distance and managed to seize his shirt and then his chest, there was little fight in him. Julian kicked once or twice, from rage or automatic desire to keep swimming John could not say, then went quite limp. It was impossible to fight the tide back into their little cove. Instead, lungs burning from the effort, John swam parallel to the shore past the rocky headland and into the wider, more welcoming space of the main beach. It was only when they flopped on to the sand, thrown by one wave and smacked on the backs by a second, that it occurred to him to check whether Julian was still alive.

The boy was breathing still, but clearly near-catatonic with cold and exhaustion. John held him tight against his chest, thinking to share what little warmth was left him, and lurched up the beach to the steps to the car park. His mind was empty of everything but the need to run a hot bath and get the child in it, closely followed by the desirability of a shot of whiskey. The sound of the motorbike engine therefore came like clamor from a room he had thought empty. Its headlamp swung on to the drive and he had to jump aside as the machine roared up the track. He felt the wind it made on his chilled limbs as it passed.

In the cruelty of the hour, he had quite forgotten Skip. He merely assumed, too weary even to do more than register the fact, that Frances and Bill had left together. *She's gone,* he thought, staring after the motorbike's receding lights. *She's left me.* But he said aloud, "Nearly there, boy. Nearly there. Hot bath and cocoa and bed. Nearly there."

Julian had been keeping up a regular if exhausted lament since they left the sea, a faintly feral keening, turned to an involuntary sobbing by the pressure on his lungs as John jolted him up and down as he hurried homeward. So it was a moment before he made out a second voice, also sobbing. Skip was standing at the base of the track. In the light from the house he could see the tears that washed her cheeks. "Skip? Skip, we're OK. He's OK. What is it?" he asked, stupidly, thinking of nothing else to say.

She had lost all her swagger and was a child again, a little girl, weak and frightened. "He left me behind," she said. "He's never coming back."

"Come," was all he could say. He wanted to hug her but Julian was already a dead, shivering weight in his arms.

"He took his typewriter," she wailed. "He took his typewriter instead of me."

BLUE HOUSE

John had been trained by first his sister then his wife always to find at least one thing on which to compliment a woman. "If all else fails," Frances used to say, "tell her how well she's looking. Her nerves may be in shreds and hearing that could be her first step to recovery."

"My God," he told Sylvia. "What happened to you?"

It was hard to believe that a few weeks could have wrought such alteration. She wore no jewelry. In place of her usual tailored jacket and skirt she had on a navy-blue shift affair which, because he had never seen her in anything so loose, struck him, for one absurd moment, as a nightdress. Her hair, normally so shaped and finished, had somehow become limp, as though wilted in damp heat. Perhaps most disturbing of all were the dark glasses failing to conceal a bruised cheek, and a sticking plaster over one ear lobe, through which blood had seeped and dried.

"Get me another of these first?" she asked.

"Of course." He fetched her a gin and tonic. That at least had not changed; her quaintly feminine short beside his overbearing pint.

"How was your holiday?" she asked as he sat down.

"Good," he said. "Then bad."

"And Frances?"

"Not so good. Sylvia, tell me!"

"I've put him into care," she said swiftly and immediately glanced across at another table of drinkers, facing down fancied disapproval. She gulped at her drink, which visibly relaxed her. "I've stopped recycling," she said, seeing him notice. "Glass, that is. I'm too ashamed. Isn't that stupid? I stick the bottles in the dustbin."

"Your face . . . Did you fall?"

"I'm not drinking *that* much," she snorted.

"Sorry," he said. "I didn't mean . . ."

"He hit me. He'd been doing it for a bit. Usually in the bathroom, because it's worst in there. But you wouldn't know about that yet."

"Frances wet the bed the other night."

"Oh Christ. Me and my big—"

"That's all right. We managed to see the funny side. She'd been dreaming about the sea. But . . ." He stopped short of mentioning the ear, not wanting to make her feel awkward about the state of her sticking plaster.

"He'd slap me when I was wiping him clean. That sort of thing. A bit like a toddler only it hurt because he was bigger. At first I used to make a joke of it, even smack him back. But then he started to scare me. I mean, he was always quite a strong man. He used to lift weights. And he'd start doing this thing where he'd grip my wrists suddenly and not let go. Just grip until he started bruising me. 'What is it?' I'd ask him. 'What do you want? Please stop that, you're hurting me.' And sometimes he'd stop and even say sorry and sometimes he'd cry. But then these last times it got worse. He punched me, really punched me, so I fell over. And then he . . ." She touched a hand to the sticking plaster. "My fault for wearing the things," she said, shortly. "Anyway, I had to see the GP for this, to get it stitched and it all came out. I wouldn't have gone along with it only I . . . I was starting to hate him and I was scared of what I might do. He wet himself just after I'd cleaned him up. Just stood there and peed and I was so fucking angry I let him just stay like that for a whole hour. That's not good. That's not right. So . . ."

"Where is he?"

She sighed and began scratching the label off her tonic bottle. "The nursing home I had him down for wouldn't take him," she said. "Maybe earlier but not now, not with a record of violence. And after I'd saved all this bloody money to pay fees. He's in the psychiatric ward."

"God."

She shook her head. "Of course he's quiet as a lamb now because he's rattling with pills. He can hardly walk he's so stoned."

"Does he know where he is?"

"Probably. He cried when I went this afternoon. Said 'Don't leave me don't leave me!' I felt I was leaving him in boarding school. But there was nothing for it. I have to get my life back. For both our sakes. And now that I'm not mopping him up all the time, carting him in and out of the bath, it's easier. I can just visit him and be nice, you know? He's become a patient. A sick friend."

"What's the ward like?"

"Don't ask," she laughed. "Funny really. You spend all this time worrying about them ending up in an old folks' home before their time, sitting in some sun lounge with a load of dribblers and bleaters twenty years older, and instead he ends up with a bunch of psychos and depressives. But he's not mad. He's just . . . not *there*. Telly on full blast. All the time. In that respect it's *just* like a home. No one watching it but the cleaners. They showed me the scan, you know?"

"My son-in-law's booked Frances in for one."

"Yeah, well, prepare yourself. I had no idea. I mean . . . there were holes. Actual holes. Sorry. I'm going on. I've been holding back with Teresa so I don't drive her mad and now I'm dumping. Go on. Dump back. Why was the holiday bad?"

"Oh, it wasn't bad really. More sad. But she enjoyed herself."

He had never intended to tell her of the drama of Sandy and Will, still feeling that the fewer people knew about it the sooner its ripples would subside. But he found he could not tell her about Frances either. Not only did it not seem fair, but her story of Steve and his sudden deterioration had frightened him and he felt the need for comforting half-truths.

For the first time, she let him drive her home. Intending to drink, she had come in a taxi. As they drove, talking of neutral subjects, things they saw outside the car, new restaurants, posters, children up to no good, she made a brave attempt to reassemble her old self. Repairing her lipstick, she caught sight of the bloodstained plaster and quickly replaced it with a clean one, tutting that he had not remarked on it. She even applied a fresh squirt of scent from the tiny silver spray she carried in her bag. Who was this for, he wondered, as she pecked his cheek and he smelled the gin fumes beneath the jasmine. Surely not for him?

They had arrived at a house whose exterior, standard rose bushes and newly washed car, betrayed nothing of the recent turmoil within. She asked him in for another drink. He knew this was no more than politeness on her part, or loneliness, or a fear of entering alone a house crowded with accusations, and gently declined. He said they must meet again soon but, as he waited, like a good taxi driver, to watch her unlock her door and let herself safely in, he reflected sadly that now that she lived alone, their meetings would assume a new ambiguous tenor and would have to cease.

Frances was playing the piano when he came home. Apparently specialist skills, like specialist vocabulary, could be among the last areas of conscious thought to be damaged by the disease. Rocket scientists rendered incapable of holding a toothbrush or using a telephone could converse with their research students better than with their relatives. There was some hope, too, that so long as the impulse to continue was there, regular piano practice and the intense stimulus and evident pleasure it involved, might hold the disease at bay longer than if her only hobby had been thimble collecting or painting by numbers.

Apparently she had missed her piano in Cornwall for she had taken to practicing with a vengeance since their return. Now, more than ever in their life together, he felt the music spoke of things she could not divulge. Depending on her mood, she filled the house with its anger, charm or sensuality. One Debussy prelude, apparently depicting footsteps in the snow, had become a recurring motif in the past few days. He found its blank soundscape, too chilly even for despair, unbearable and would retreat to the garden or his study on hearing the opening bars.

Poppy was sitting in a pool of light where one normally sat to watch television. The television was off and she was reading, reflected in its dead screen. He kissed the top of her head. She mumbled in reply and turned a page.

She only set foot in her house to retrieve clothes or to drop off the children, whom she collected from school every day, brought to their grandparents for high tea, and dropped off when Sandy returned from surgery. She had not left him, not officially, hence the lopsided arrangement whereby Sandy had the children most of the time. At first she had been too angry to deal with him, then she had needed *space to think in* and now she was here to help John care for Frances.

Had the offense been more ordinary, involving, say, someone both female and not a relative, the obvious course of action and reaction might have been clearer. The ambivalence, the sheer bloody awkwardness of it all, however, which everyone seemed too uncomfortable to discuss, had left her marooned. Poppy had always been quick to take action and quick to speak her mind. Her anger, so dramatically and swiftly demonstrated in Cornwall, had dissipated, leaving her in a curious, regressive limbo. Quite unexpectedly in so disarmingly literal a child, fiction had become her refuge and, for all John could tell, principal resource for advice and comfort. The first day she had woken in the spare room, still sentimentally furnished with things from her and Will's childhoods, she had begun to read her way through bookshelves she had so long overlooked. She began rereading novels from her girlhood, *Little Women, What Katy Did,* in a self-conscious effort to find solace in their familiar, premarital sphere. But now she had read her way through the spare room and begun asking John what she should devour next. This morning, a little mischievously, he had passed her his much-thumbed Penguin of *Anna Karenina*. Glancing down to her lap, he saw she was more than halfway through already.

"Making sterling progress," he said.

"It's good," she said, not looking up. "She's just given up Seriosha. Mum's fine. How was your drive?"

"Fine. Wet."

"And the pub?"

He hesitated.

"I've got a nose, Dad."

"It was fine. Coffee?"

"No. There's a parcel for you."

"Really?"

"Next-door's nanny took it in by mistake. It's in the hall."

He made himself a coffee and went to investigate. It was a largish, rectangular parcel, thickly padded. The stamps were foreign but without his glasses he could not see where from. He tucked it under his arm and pushed into the drawing room. Frances stopped playing.

"Don't stop," he said. "It's lovely."

She turned back a page or two and began the piece again. He recognized an old staple of hers, Schumann's *Prophet Bird*. It was a strange piece; a pretty enough evocation of fluttering flight, it became neurotic and unsettling if one listened too closely, full as it was of perverse accents and unexpected turns.

He sat and pulled out his glasses, leaning into the light thrown by a standard lamp. A mountain and a lake; Switzerland. He disliked customs declarations forms because they lessened any element of surprise. *Reproduction,* someone had written carefully. *Sans valeur commerciale. Cadeau.* Mystified, he tore it open. Paper gave way to bubblewrap, so tightly wound round and sealed that he had to use both hands to wrench it open. This, of course, was how letter bombs worked, he reflected seconds too late; they were not letters at all but parcels, playing on the recipient's residual childish greed for presents.

It was not a reproduction at all but a painting. It took him a moment or two to recognize it because the surface had been cleaned so thoroughly and what had once seemed a farmyard scene at sunset or dusk, a sow and her piglets enjoying the last of the day's warmth, now lay in dazzling, almost too colorful daylight. So many details had emerged from beneath two centuries of cigar smoke, fireplace fumes and household dirt that a whole new picture was revealed. A blossoming rose grew up one side of the sty, wild flowers glowed in tufts across the farmyard and, most unexpectedly, where the murk had been deepest, a small girl, dressed in artless country style, leaned on the sty wall to admire the basking family of swine. Always assured by his father that it was a Morland, or as near as damn it, the painting was now revealed as something altogether less distinguished and more sentimental; an image of the sunnily innocent kind one might pick as a greetings card for an unmarried female relative. The cruelest transformation had been to the fine, eighteenth-century frame. Once plainly of greater value than the painting, it had been coated with yellow gilt paint so shiny that an ignorant customs officer might have read the declaration, glanced at the contents and assumed the whole to be fresh from Woolworth's.

There was no letter. Nothing betrayed the sender. On his way over to interrupt Frances to show her, John glanced at the back. Following reframing, the rear had been taped and papered up, for all the world like a painting finished yesterday. On the paper was scrawled, *From one old boar to another. Ta for the loan of this. Having my lad send it back while he stops off to do some banking for us. Sorry I won't be seeing you soon. No hard feelings! Your old guest, H. Farmer.*

Even were it still a Morland, in today's skewed marketplace, he supposed, the message and signature would probably have swollen the painting's value as an authenticated but minor artist's imprimatur could never have done.

Frances had stopped playing and was looking up expectantly.

"Look," he told her. "Remember this?"

"Pretty," she said, remembering nothing. "The boys'll like that. They like pigs."

BEACHCOMBER

When the first Friday came, he waited in the playground with the day boys, assuming Ma would be there to collect him. Boy after boy was collected and still she never came until at last a master found him, Mr. Thomas, and said why was he not in tea with the other boarders and was he lost. And there was an embarrassing scene in which he explained and Mr. Thomas took him to Matron in front of all the other boys in the dining room and asked her. She turned to him quite kindly, although she was still in her starchy uniform so he knew it did not count.

"Oh no, Pagett," she said. "You're not a weekly boarder. Whatever gave you that idea? You're a *full* boarder like everyone else. We don't have any weekly boarders. Now sit by me and have your tea. Look. Doughnuts for when you've had your bread and butter and sandwiches! You can see Mummy and Daddy in three weeks, when they take you for a Sunday out."

He had not cried then but he had cried at night, when several other new boys were crying and some boys were kind and said everyone cried at first but that it got easier. And some boys were harsh and told him to be quiet. Only it did not get easier and it seemed to him that the smell and taste of tears was in his nose and on his tongue ready to surprise him and at a moment's notice he would start to cry again.

It was a choir school attached to Tatham's, the college where the much bigger boys went, and it was very old and very beautiful. He had almost forgotten he would have to sing. Twenty-four boys in the school were choristers, which meant that their parents paid no fees, or hardly any, but they had to sing hours and hours every day, in the chantry or the chapel, after breakfast, before lunch, after tea and on Sunday mornings. Music was a mystery to him. He had learned to read it at his other school. That and some perceived beauty in his singing voice had won him a place, apparently, although the voice trials had taken place so long ago he scarcely remembered them. Faced with new music to learn every day, however, most of it in Latin, which he would not start learning until next year, he found the notes melted under his hot scrutiny and meant nothing. And if that and the feeling apparently called homesickness were not reason enough to weep openly in choir practice, the beauty of the music was. There was one particular anthem all about the lame man leaping as a hart and the tongues of the dumb shall sing which they rehearsed all week and which he had to mime to for fear that his voice would crack with emotion.

It was a punishment, of course. He realized that by the middle of the second week when the initial shock of being abandoned, hastily and without proper good-byes, had begun to wear off sufficiently for him to look around him and take in the strangeness of his surroundings.

There was absolutely no contact with the outside world. There was no privacy. They slept in big dormitories, twenty or thirty to a room, brushed their teeth in communal washrooms with more washbasins than he could count and even bathed in communal bathrooms where there were six baths plumbed in around the walls instead of just one. Only in the lavatory was there freedom and even there the walls stopped short enough from the ceiling for boys to peer over and high enough off the floor for messages, and worse, to be passed. The lavatory paper was hard, scratchy and unabsorbent which was almost as much of a shock as only being allowed to bathe twice a week and there being no armchairs or carpets or curtains in the entire place.

Then one of the boys ran away, or tried to. He got no further than the railway station because he was still in uniform and someone recognized him and handed him in. It was then that the truth dawned on Julian; Barrowcester Choir School was a prison. Not like a reform school or a Borstal, because nobody smoked and the boys spoke nicely and were not obviously criminal or far too polite to talk about it if they were. But a prison for boys whose parents needed to have them out of the way for some reason. This did not upset Julian as it might have done a few months ago, when the idea of being sent away first entered his consciousness. In fact it reassured him and was the start of the infinitely slow process by which he did what Matron called *settling in*.

Boarding school was a place of menace. But prison, so dire to others, was a thing he understood. He knew its smells and rules, its beehive divisions of labor and control. He knew how to behave and had a fair idea how best to survive it.

In the first weeks he had several discreetly arranged meetings with a man who pretended to be a friend but who was plainly both a stranger and some kind of doctor. He asked Julian lots of questions, about home and the prison and how much he loved his parents and missed them. He also asked about Henry, which was difficult because Julian found he remembered very little about him, and about his uncle, which was frankly embarrassing because the man wanted to know if his uncle had touched him and, because he didn't explain properly first of all, got very interested when Julian, quite truthfully, answered yes, meaning piggybacks and so forth.

In particular the man wanted to know why he wanted to be called Bill. The truth was he had no idea. He was mainly called by his surname and number in any case, so it didn't often come up. But the nice choirmaster called him Julian when he cried during choir practice on his first full day and something had made him say, "No, sir. It's not Julian. It's Bill."

Word passed round and Miss Fermity, his form mistress, and beautiful Mrs. Smith, who was to teach him piano, and several of the boys all began to call him Bill. He told the doctor man it was because he liked the name and, to his surprise, the name was allowed to stay. It also helped him to settle in. He could think of Julian as a rather weak little boy, a girlface who made sand castles and cried, while Bill was braver and stronger and sang and slept in a big dormitory and only occasionally had bad dreams, which he had more sense than to share. As in any prison, nicknames were essential. Even the seniors with flawless singing voices and frighteningly correct posture had friendly nicknames which even juniors could use, like Spud or Baby or Goliath. The story of his assumption that he was to go home every Friday for a whole weekend soon spread, probably via Matron who was given to gossip as she dispensed plasters and cough sweets, so he was christened Weekly or Weeks, which evolved to Weekly Bill and so to Will. Which was not a nickname at all but just another name, but he did not greatly mind as it was better than teasing.

Some boys were teased so relentlessly they screamed and threw sort of angry fits, which everyone gathered to watch as it was as good as television which, unlike adult prisoners, they were not allowed. Well trained by Skip's example, Will began to suspect he would make a good teaser when his turn came.

His mother wrote every day for the first few days then Matron had a word with her about how it was not helping him settle in and they changed to weekly letters like everyone else's. She did not say much. She just chatted on paper, about the garden and what his father was doing and the possibility of their moving from Wandsworth soon to take on HM Prison Barrowcester and be closer to the school. She sent things too, almost, he felt, as a substitute for saying anything. Not cakes with files in, of course, since she put him here and hardly wanted him to escape, but books and easy piano music for him to learn and photographs in case he forgot what everyone looked like. She sent the new Parker pen set they had bought him to replace Henry's watch. There was money left over from the sale, she told him, which had been used to buy him Premium Bonds.

Boys were expected to write back but only on Sunday mornings, between breakfast and choir practice. They had to write two sides, very neatly with no blotches or crossings-out. When they finished they had to show the duty master before it went in the envelope, which they also had to show him. Officially this was to check for spelling mistakes and messy writing but Will knew it was actually to make sure they weren't writing *help me please take me away I'm so unhappy people are horrid to me take me away please.*

Dear Mum and Dad, he wrote. Only girlfaced Julian called them Ma and Pa. *Matron says I am settling in at last so it must be true! My bed has a nice view of the cathedral and a big old cedar tree. Some of the corridors, and especially the ones in Tatham's, where we sing mainly, are meant to be haunted so I go along them quickly. But I'm not scared really. I have made some new friends. Hodges 3 who comes all the way from Africa (but isn't black!!), Schoenveldt, who plays the oboe and Honey, who is Cornish and has the other bit of my bunk. The upper bit. Next term I get an upper bit too. New boys go on the bottom. Matron says in case they fall out! I hope you are both well, I am well but a bit horse from all the singing. We are singing Vittoria,* Missa O Quam Gloriosum Est, *this morning which Honey says is dreary but I really like it. Aren't I queer? This comes with lots of love, Will. (a.k.a. Bill)*

P.S. Julian sends his love too!!

He knew better than to write the truth. He knew how untrustworthy adults could be and how sad. Sometimes you had to help them. Children were stronger, perhaps, because they had lived less long so had suffered less and not started to wear out like old cars did. Funnily enough, although the letter was happier than he felt, by the time it had been inspected by Dr. Feltram and he had converted *horse* to *hoarse* and was sealing it in an envelope, the happiness felt real.

Perhaps, like Latin and unspeakable thoughts (which worked even better in a dormitory for some reason), happiness was something one could learn.

BLUE HOUSE

A Saturday lunch at Harriet's was a rare pleasure. They were a regular feature but Will had always found it too hard to turn his back on the shop to attend one. The holiday had proved, however, how much Kristin, his assistant manager, had been hankering after a taste of autonomy and what good use she had made of it. He had resolved therefore always to take Saturdays off as well as his usual Wednesdays. He had also rewarded his third-in-command by creating the post of events manager for her, which would preclude the need for him to fret any more over the meet-the-author lunches.

Like many commuters, Harriet was obsessed with wringing every hour of pleasure and profit from her weekends. She had friends to stay, she threw long Saturday lunch parties, she slaved in her garden and, now that Vera was old enough to appreciate such things, took the child on excursions.

"Look at you, so brown and beautiful still!" she said, opening the door and kissing him stealthily. He pressed a bottle of wine on her. "You shouldn't."

There was laughter from the kitchen. He felt a pang of regret. It would be Harriet's idea of self-indulgence; two of her similarly driven women friends talking him into a drunken haze. His day off shrank before him, wasted on people he did not care about who would require him to perform when he would rather just be talking to their host. "Who else is here?" he asked brightly.

"No one. I wanted you to myself. Anya's taking Vera to some cartoon."

"Oh."

"Don't look so relieved. When I die—"

"She's all mine. Don't remind me."

Vera thumped up the stairs to meet him.

"And you have to take Anya too," Harriet said. "They come as a package."

Vera grabbed his wrists and stamped hard on each of his feet in turn. Even through thick brogues, she made a lasting impression. "Hello fatty," she said.

"Princess pig." He gently tugged her pigtails. "How do?"

"Come, Vera. Coat on." Vera went obediently to Anya who wrapped her up and led her away. Anya's patience was unshakable. Harriet claimed her life as a refugee had been so grim that she would have submitted to the torments of three Veras if it meant she could continue to live in comfort and relative safety. To be on the safe side, she was paying for Anya's evening classes in English and computer skills so that she could retain her as a nanny but find her day work once Vera started school full-time. Such obliging treasures were harder to find in a provincial city than the proverbial good man.

They ignored Harriet's elegant sitting room, where she would have steered him were they not alone, and went immediately downstairs to her kitchen, with its cozy fug, dog-eared sofa and view of her sloping garden. The autumn sun shone sharply through dripping beech trees. Smoke drifted across the lawn from a neighbor's bonfire. They kicked off their shoes and lolled on the sofa with a bottle of Pinot Grigio and a dish of fierily spiced olives. The fridge so thickly pasted with Vera's artwork would, he knew, be full of good things from Hart's, the high-street

delicatessen. One of Harriet's principles was never to cook when someone else could do it better. The Aga was purely for toast, comfort and
for heating things through.

"So, tell Mother," she said. "You're in love."

"Looks like it," he told her.

"With someone you've spent, what, ten hours with?"

"Longer than that." He dug her in the ribs with a toe. "And we've
been writing. Proper love letters. Well, I write him love letters. He
writes me letter letters. We write about all sorts of things. Probably stuff
we wouldn't talk about face to face. Not easily."

"And he's encouraging you?" Expertly she fired an olive pit into her
palm.

"He's got more sense." Will sighed. "He has no television or
telephone and what you'd call no social life at all, so I think I'm his
amusement."

"But what about Sandy?" Harriet had heard all about Master Mystery's rude unveiling and had recovered both from her pique at not being confided in earlier and her horror at so incestuous a coupling.
"Having wrecked his home, shouldn't you do the decent thing and offer
him a new one? You'd be a brilliant stepdad, the children already love
you, Sandy loves you . . . She can have half his pension *and* his house.
Your family—"

"I don't *want* to be a stepdad. I don't want Sandy. This is stupid. I
split up with him, remember? Anyway, I wrecked nothing."

"He hardly did it on his own. Those poor boys," she sighed wickedly.

"Shut it."

"And poor Poppy."

"Well, that you *don't* mean. If it hadn't been me, it would have been
someone else."

"I'm sure that comforts her no end."

"She'll go back to him. She just hasn't found a way of doing it yet that
won't damage her pride."

"You don't take straight couples very seriously, do you?"

"Well, do you?"

She shrugged. Point taken. "Are you hungry?"

"Not yet," he said and grasped a cushion. "Oh, Hats. I don't know what to do. I'm single again. Properly single for the first time in years. And I ought to be out there enjoying myself."

"It's cold out there," she said with feeling.

"I wouldn't know," he said. "I don't go out. Give me a free evening and all I'll do with it is sit at the kitchen table writing Roly another sermon-length letter. I've never felt like this about anyone."

"So you said."

"All the books say not to put things into writing. But I don't care how much of a fool I seem or how deeply I commit myself. It's probably just the fact that it's so romantic and he's so inaccessible."

"Nowhere's inaccessible anymore. Not if you've a phone line and a computer."

"And what about the shop? And Mum, for God's sake."

"You cannot let her be an issue. Let someone else take a turn. Leave her to Poppy. If you sold your place here the money you made would pay for weekly train trips home, if you felt that strongly. Why do you think Frances ratted on you both, anyway? Does she envy what she never had?"

"I think she . . . she tried to tell me the other day, only her wires were so crossed I couldn't make much sense of it. I think it was drastic measures."

"She was setting Sandy free? But he's the father of her grandchildren."

"Not Sandy. Me."

She took this in, interrupted with an olive in her cheek. "In that case it's easy," she said at last. "Take the Americans' offer on the shop."

"But it's my life!"

"Take the offer. They can only retain you as a manager so long. If you don't sell to them, they'll only open yet another rival store and drive you under. It's a miracle you held out against one chain. Two would sink you."

"So I sell. What then?"

"Move to Cornwall. Start again."

"I don't want to move to Cornwall. I . . . I want Cornwall to move here."

"That's not an excuse. It's a whine."

"And there aren't any bookshops there," he pursued.

"Perfect."

"Because there aren't any people. Not enough. Not book-buyers. I've asked the reps. Even before everything went online, most didn't bother going west of Exeter because it wasn't cost-effective."

"So dare to be modern. Sell books over the Net."

"Mail order?" Will pulled a face. "Where's the poetry in that? And I'd need premises. A warehouse."

Harriet stood, irritated, walked to the fridge and began grabbing packages. "You're raising obstacles that aren't there," she said, in the tone that warned she was spoiling for a fight. "You could change direction. Run a café. Sell wetsuits. What does it matter, if you love him so much?" She turned on him, eyes narrowed. "You're scared."

"Am not."

"You're a typical mistress, that's your trouble. A fence-sitter. Using someone else's husband for years rather than committing to a man of your own. It's so selfish!"

"Coming from the woman who conceived with a turkey-baster."

"He wasn't a turkey-baster. He was—" She snapped her mouth shut too late. This was the first admission that Vera had a flesh and blood father.

"Aha!" Will crowed.

"Not now," she said, slamming plates on to the table and slapping down packages of cheese and pâté and deli delicacies as though leaving the food in its wrapping and treating it roughly could somehow lessen the meal's extravagance. "Hang on a moment."

She grabbed the telephone and her diary, checked a number and dialed. "There's something I have to do . . . Dr. Chadwick? . . . It's Harriet. Harriet Rowney. Have you got a moment? . . . Good. I wanted to book some sessions for a friend . . . That's right. I know it's a bit unorthodox but . . . Would it? Oh good. And you'd send the bill to me? . . . Fine. I think he'll need at least six." She caught Will's eye and something mischievous in her expression made him understand which friend she was talking about.

"No," he mouthed, shaking his head. He tried to wrestle the telephone from her but she skipped out of his reach.

"Yes. His name's William Pagett. I'll get him to call you to make the appointments. Thanks so much. Bye." She hung up. "She's very good," she said. "The first six sessions are on me. It's an extremely generous birthday present."

"But—"

"You said you preferred things you could use up."

"I meant a case of port."

"This," she said, cutting a slab of foie gras, immensely pleased with herself, "will have much better aftereffects. Now. Sit at the table like a Christian, eat the lovely food the nice lady brought you and stop looking like that. You can write me your thank you letter when the couch has done its work."

BEACHCOMBER

It was a wretched, pointless occasion; a funeral for an atheist who had never lived in the parish. And with no coffin and no certainty that he was dead.

"We have to do it," John insisted. "For her sake. Certainty, however grim, is easier than this not being sure. She needs to grieve. We all do."

So kind of him, that *we*, when he could have said *you*.

There were several old women a few pews behind them. One of them coughed as the vicar finished the Sentences and announced the twenty-third psalm.

"No singing," Frances had told him. "It's too hard." So they all stood now and recited it. There were so few of them that singing might almost have sounded less self-conscious; at least then they would have had an organ to back them up. Thank God for old women. Frances stole a glance at them. They were not regulars or she would have recognized them. They could not be friends of Bill's. He had no friends here—their exhaustive searches and newspaper announcements had made that brutally clear. The new colleagues he had never got to know in Norwich had sent a wreath, as had his publisher in Boston and his old faculty in

Berkeley. These were funeral *aficionadas* then, cemetery crones. To connoisseurs of last rites this event must be a novelty. Word must have spread. Perhaps such people had a newsletter produced on someone's smelly Roneostat and discreetly circulated. *Odd one in Trinity Road today. No coffin. One twelve-year-old daughter now orphaned. Possibility of suicide following exposed adultery. Family small so support doubtless appreciated in their time of need.*

They sat again and as the vicar began his useless address, groping after significance in a hopeless muddle, Frances reached for Skip's hand and squeezed it. The poor child had been quite wild at first, to the point where they had to get a doctor to sedate her, the same one who had seen to Julian's black eye. For two or three days she had been impossible, either weeping or angry and full of a terrible aggression toward Frances, dropping dark hints about what she knew and what had been promised her and what she expected.

It was Frances who dealt with the police. The afternoon after Bill left, any fantasies about completing their holiday shattered, she told John to drive the children back to Wandsworth. Polcamel was no place for them now and she was unfit company. Julian had to be made ready for starting at choir school and Skip enrolled in the junior year of Putney High School to give her some stability while her future was still uncertain.

"Good idea," John had said, seizing the chance of activity, and packed their things.

She had never felt so alone as when watching them leave. John was civilized, of course, that was to be expected, but the children were utterly cold. Skip hurried to shut herself in the dormobile without saying goodbye or even glancing round. Julian, dwarfed in one of John's jerseys as well as his own, because he was still chilled from his ordeal in the sea, stared at her curiously then kissed her, but it was a kiss of obedience with no hug to warm it.

She sat on the veranda for an hour after she had watched them drive away, then the sounds of happiness from the crowds on the beach became oppressive and she retreated indoors. Indoors was worse. His things were everywhere: ash in an ashtray, dirty clothes in a heap beside his bed, swimming trunks still on the line. She took refuge in blind housework. The model tenant, she cleaned, aired and dusted the house then squeezed his things and hers into a single case, hid the key of the bungalow as instructed and hauled her case up to the car park where she rang for a taxi to Wadebridge police station.

She edited the facts for the police, confining her report to what was necessary for them to make out a missing persons registration. Her brother-in-law had driven off after a family argument, she said, which was true after a fashion. She had reason to fear he would *do something foolish*, she said, because he had not taken his daughter or belongings with him, nor even his passport. When she said he was a novelist, she saw how the word was taken almost as a synonym for psychological instability. The policeman she dealt with was wonderful; avuncular yet unintrusive. He took details of Bill, of the motorbike, of anyone he might be likely to contact—the new university, for instance—and even recommended a small hotel for her to check into while she waited for news.

She rang the prison at once and gave Mervyn the hotel's number then she lay on her bed hugging herself and waited. Had one of John's thick jerseys or Bill's old leather jacket been to hand she would have pulled it on for comfort; either would have done since it was the comfort she required, not the man. Instead, she lay on the bed, pulled up the quilt and hugged herself, taking in the pictures of fishing boats, the pastel-dyed dried flower arrangement, the skimpy nylon curtains, the powerful scent of flykiller. The hotel was as oppressive as the bungalow in its way; very much a family establishment and not a place designed for romantic afternoon liaisons nor, for that matter, distraught adulteresses. The excitement when she arrived by police car was palpable.

John rang her that evening to say they had got home safely and to see how she was. She snapped at him, "How do you think I am?" and he rang off soon afterward.

She slipped out to an off-license and bought a large bar of chocolate and a bottle of wine which she smuggled back to her room. She wolfed the chocolate then drank herself to sleep. The police rang in the early evening to say there was no news then called again, halfway through the next morning, to say they were sending a car for her.

His motorbike was not found at once because he had hidden it. He had driven half an hour's distance up the coast to Trebarwith where a long beach bounded by high granite cliffs and a grim quarry faced the open sea. It was chosen, the police imagined, because it was the first beach to the north from Polcamel Strand that was accessible by road and was well away from the complex currents of the Camel estuary mouth. The motorbike lay at the very back of the largest of several caves that plunged up into the cliff face. Had he wished to retrieve it later, he had fatally misjudged the hiding place. At low tide, when he would have arrived there had he come directly from Polcamel, by police reckoning, a broad expanse of golden sand would have been presented in the moonlight. At high tide, however, a few hours later, the entire beach vanished and the caves were scoured out by booming surf. Its engine sluiced with salt water and sand-clogged, its bodywork brutally dented by the repeated battering it had taken against the rocks, the motorbike had finally become wedged on its side behind a boulder and left half-buried in sand by the receding tide. Children had found it and played on it for hours before an adult had come across them and alerted the police.

The registration number would be checked for confirmation in a day or two. Meanwhile Frances made her identification in a corner of the station car park where the motorbike lay on a trailer. There was dried seaweed caked on the handlebars and twined about the cables. No other trace of Bill had been found, the policeman told her, or of his typewriter. The poetic explanation was made that he had picked a beach facing the open Atlantic to reduce the risk of being washed up then used the type-writer to weight his body before swimming out and drowning himself.

Returning to Wandsworth with the news rather than merely passing it on by telephone, Frances found that John and poor Skip chose to inter-pret the evidence as charitably as the police had done. Skip had to, of course, since the alternative, that he had abandoned her, was more than a child could comprehend. Frances could not, however, would not let the matter rest. She spent a great chunk of her savings placing an-nouncements in Cornwall, in Norwich, in Berkeley, and nationally, in *The Times* and *Telegraph*. She asked for news and reported sightings and received only a steady stream of crank notes and shocked letters from friends and colleagues of his. She fantasized about placing a final notice addressed to him in person, saying *call me* and giving her number. Common sense held her back, but also anger. Just as it was disgust and anger that prevented her shedding a single tear.

It was John who visited school outfitters and packed Julian's trunk. It was John who took Julian away to Barrowcester to start at his new school. Frances watched it all as in a dream, unable to participate as she knew she should. Since her return the children had played without her, avoided her even. The house was so big it was quite possible to meet only at mealtimes. She tried to rouse herself to see Julian off at least—he was excited in the way she knew masked terror—but she was checked halfway down the stairs by something she overheard.

"Why isn't she coming too?" Julian had asked.

"Your mother isn't very well," John said.

As for Skip, since the news of the motorbike a change had come over her and she became a model of good behavior that was almost more aggressive than the wildness that preceded it. She was quiet and studious, eager to begin at her new school and, as she put it, *get on with life.* Her anger now only surfaced when, seeking a companion in confusion, Frances tried to make her talk about her feelings or hopes. After a few attempts, Frances gave up trying.

The school uniform, a really rather pretty dress in a mauve and white stripe, was donned without fuss as was the name her mother gave her; not Petra Louise, as John had misremembered, but Poppy Louise. She returned from her first day at Putney High announcing that she wanted to grow her hair and, with astonishing ease, she began to drop her accent. This morning she had said *fortnight.* She was becoming English. She was also coming to seem less and less like Bill and more and more like Becky.

"This will be my punishment," Frances thought. "To acquire a daughter after such longing only to find her grow into the sister-in-law who despised me." For she felt she must be punished. Even if Bill had not committed suicide but merely elected to abandon his daughter and *lose* himself somehow. Even if he had simply hit his head and lost his memory. She blamed herself and the stupid inhibitions she was so keen to deny she possessed. John, after all, would not have killed himself had she left him but would by now have been well supported by cohorts of adoring women from the officers' wives' club. In time he would have married another as easily as he married her, because men like him had to be married.

And Bill and she? They would have managed. Passion would probably have been checked by the grim process of the Law and the replacement of holiday fling with domestic regularity but perhaps something good might have grown in its place, something difficult but interesting and vital, like a marriage in a book. Perhaps she would have left Bill too and ended up an impoverished piano teacher with an aura of fading disgrace about her under-furnished apartments. Even that would have been better than this.

The service was over now. John stood and she thought he was offering his arm to her but of course it was to Poppy Louise, who looked so sweet and shattered in her new black coat and school uniform. Frances walked behind them, smiled dutifully at the old ladies, waited in the porch for the inevitable word or two with the vicar and his wife and lamented again the lack of a coffin so that they could follow due process and proceed to a graveyard or crematorium and so to a funeral tea and a neatly prescribed period of mourning. Instead they were cut adrift, left to walk alone to the ridiculous, brightly colored Volkswagen, which spoke, as always, of escape and giddy irresponsibility.

"Home for tea?" she said. "The Stibsons aren't joining us although I offered. I baked a seed cake." Poppy Louise and John's silence felt like disapproval so she shut up, unlocked the car and elected to drive while John sat in the back with Poppy Louise, who at last could relax sufficiently to cry and was holding on to him so tight that Frances envied her and felt disloyal.

Words had got her into trouble so she used them less and less but she still dreamed of a phrase that might work like a charm and make everything all right. But John had been distant ever since her return from Cornwall, presenting a united front to help Julian cope with leaving home but otherwise talking to Poppy Louise rather than to her and using the demands of work, wherever possible, to avoid her. He came in to eat and to sleep, otherwise the prison absorbed him utterly, which left her feeling imprisoned too. Occasionally, as now, when she pulled up in the drive and waited for everyone to get out before she parked in the garage, she caught him watching her and the mute reproachfulness in his gaze enraged her. In a book they would have argued but he wanted to know nothing. There had been no cross-questioning, no grand scene. Only mute bloody reproachfulness.

She watched him cross the drive and climb the steps to the great, smoke-blackened porch, a protective hand steering Poppy Louise by the small of her back. She started the engine again and drove into the garage.

"What if I just sat here in the darkness?" she wondered. "What if I didn't go in? How long would it be before one of them came out to find me?"

If only John had come back to Beachcomber ten minutes earlier than he had, shoeless, soaked to the skin and carrying what had first struck her as her son's dripping corpse. He would have seen her and Skip and Bill frozen in a tableau as on a stage, heard Bill saying *Come* and her saying *I love John too much*. Always so reliable, he had missed his cue however and had entered only to tears and hysteria.

Frances took a barley sugar from the tin she kept to hand in there, sucked it for a minute then crunched it carelessly, violently, imagining she was crunching up her own teeth and not sugar.

She let herself out and prepared to enter the louring house. She became aware of a party of red bands piling lawn mowings into the compost heap. They were watching her dither on the gravel. She stared back at them, briefly defiant, then made herself go in.

BLUE HOUSE

Poppy was restless and Frances knew why. It was Sandy's birthday and she was wanting to be with him but feeling she had to stifle that thought along with any curiosity about where he had taken the boys for the weekend. The tension was exhausting to behold. She had read for a while then abandoned the attempt. She had taken Frances on a riverside walk so brisk that it left Frances breathless and sweaty. She had cleaned the kitchen so thoroughly that even the jam pots and sauce bottles had been washed and the cupboard shelves left spotless. Frances had tried playing the piano but that only made Poppy worse, as though each successive key change of scale or study were winding up her internal spring. The sound of John's rake as it scraped dead leaves along the lawn could not have helped matters either. Frances had always hated that noise, which seemed the very sound effect for mortality. She preferred even the drone of the lawnmower or the strimmer's bluebottle whine.

"The state of this cupboard!"

There was a very useful cupboard, a walk-in one, constructed across what had been a deep alcove beside the sitting room chimney breast. It contained shelves of old board games, matches and firelighters, wrapping paper old and new, newspapers awaiting recycling, unfinished tapestries, the sewing machine and great bales of assorted fabric from when Frances had been inspired by some Canadian novel to begin stitching Poppy a patchwork quilt as a feminist heirloom. Though to the untrained eye the cupboard's state appeared chaotic, Frances had a rough idea of what was in there and on which shelf to find it. Privately she thought of it as her *memory hole*; if she could not remember where she had put something, the chance was it would turn up in there. It had taken a while for her to discover that the reason for this was that the cleaning lady had long since seized on the cupboard as a convenient door behind which to toss anything that impeded her dusting.

"Oh fuck," she said but she was too slow for Poppy was already bringing out armfuls of dust-furred junk and stacking things on the carpet. Dust soon filled the air and made them both sneeze, but Poppy proceeded with a relish bordering on mania.

"The first thing," she declared, "is to get everything out in the open."

"Everything?"

"Absolutely everything, and give the cupboard a damned good clean. I bet Joyce never cleans in there, does she?"

"Why should she? It's a cupboard."

"Then we can decide what to throw out."

Frances came over from the piano and Poppy immediately handed her a large box silver with dust.

"They'll all need wiping down just so we can see what they are."

Frances ran a finger through the grime. "Totopoly," she read aloud. The mysterious name recalled a long evening and the scents of wine and seaweed.

"You may as well throw all the games out," Poppy said. "Hugo and Oscar won't play anything unless it has batteries."

"I think Oscar prefers books to games. Like Will," Frances said quietly.

"I hope not," said Poppy. "Games teach them how to behave. Where does Joyce keep your dusters?"

"She brings her own. She finds mine too venomous."

Poppy sighed. "Venerable. I'll try the cupboard under the stairs," she said and marched off.

Frances looked around her at the contents of her memory hole spilled across the carpet. A toasting fork. A pot of hand salve someone had given her, called Farmer's Friend. The Christmas tree lights which had to be mended afresh every year although they saw less use than any other bulbs in the house. A set of placemats with parrots on them. When Poppy returned, with the Hoover and dusters, she found Frances exactly where she had left her. She plugged in the Hoover and scoured out the cupboard, leaving Frances to begin dusting off the boxes. Frances sneezed again and had to use a duster as a handkerchief. She stuffed it up her sleeve so Poppy would not try to use it and smear something and be cross. Then Poppy came to dust too, or rather took over the dusting while Frances watched. She began to make a heap of things to take to an Alzheimer's Society jumble sale.

"The Chinese believe that clutter makes you ill," she said. "Now where did I read that? They think it causes problems in all sorts of areas of your life. You don't want this anymore, surely? You always hated it. Apparently you draw a floor plan of your house then draw an outline of a person on top of it, with their head at the door and the rest sort of laid out as it comes and then you walk around and mark all the parts of the house where clutter builds up and that tells you the areas of your life and health that will give you trouble until you tidy things up. I wonder where this glory hole would be."

Frances thought a moment. She imagined herself Wonderland large, her head squeezing up against the front door and her limbs snaking through the rooms, forcing nervous occupants to flatten themselves against walls and windows to avoid them. "Bowels," she said decisively. But Poppy was already, reluctantly, stacking things back on the emptied shelves.

"What's that?" she asked, pointing.

Frances looked down at the box in her hands. *Basildon Bond* it told her. *Wedgwood Blue.* "Photographs," she said.

"Do you want them still?"

"Of course."

"So why aren't they in an album like the others?"

"It's my horror box; they're the silly ones. They're the ones that didn't come out right or weren't flattering. Things like that. I should have thrown them away only it didn't seem right. They're you and John and Julian. They're people." She broke off, hearing herself plead. "You're right. Let's chuck them out."

"No. Let me see." Poppy made a grab for the box.

"They're only silly. We've got so much to do." Frances resisted her. "There's the roof space next."

"But I want to see. It'd be fun. Come on."

"No!"

Trying to tug the box back from Poppy's grasp, Frances succeeded only in bursting its fragile seams. Photographs and old negatives littered the hearthrug. They were mainly black and white but a few were color, with that intensity photographs seemed to lose once color became the norm and not an extravagance reserved for weddings and guaranteed sunshine. "Sorry," she said but Poppy was already on her hands and knees, picking the pictures over with gleeful nostalgia.

"Your hair! I remember that day. And look at this! My God, you and Dad look so young!"

"We were."

"The holiday house. Look. And . . . Oh . . . I've never seen this."

"Show me."

"It's great."

The picture an early color one, showed Julian and Skip grinning from inside a rampart of pebbles on a beach. They clutched sandwiches above the water as a wave broke around them. Behind them, mugging, dangling a stalk of seaweed over Julian's head like a wig, stood Bill.

"He looks so young too." Poppy was staring hard at the image, as if willing it to give up more information than it showed. "This must be the last picture taken of him," she murmured. "Why haven't I seen this ever?"

Frances remembered finding the camera, film still in it, months after the memorial service. It was nearly a year later. There had been no reason for pictures before, no celebrations. But they were about to set out on their next summer holiday, their first one as a family of four. They were going to Wales, to a cottage near Llangollen, and she had sent the film in for developing before they left and hidden the pictures away like a dirty secret amid the flurry of their return home. The memory returned to her in such immediate detail that the panic and guilt of then were briefly more real than the dust and daughter of now.

Carpet, she thought. *Curtains. Clutter.* And the past became like music from another room again.

"I didn't want to upset you," she said. "By the time I had it developed you'd become so happy and settled."

"Well you were wrong. I'd have liked it. I'd like it now. Can I take it?"

"Of course you can."

Poppy raked through the pile. "Are there any others?"

"I don't remember."

"How about you? Pictures of him and you?"

Frances forced a smile and shook her head. "You were too young to use the camera."

Poppy was sagging over her knees. It took Frances a while to realize she was crying. "Stop it," she told her. "Please don't cry. Darling, it was so long ago. So much has changed."

"Nothing *changed*!" Poppy gasped. "You just moved on. Dusted yourself down and moved on."

"I took you with me, though."

"You didn't *take* me anywhere. You just stuffed me in that school to make me English so I could fit in and be tidy."

Frances felt faint. She sat on the sofa. She reached out an arm to stroke Poppy's shoulder but she had sat too far away and her fingers fell short.

"I feel such a blithering idiot," Poppy said. "I had no idea about Sandy and . . ." She made a face as though she had found her brother's name too bitter on her tongue to pronounce. "It was you I wanted to . . . I couldn't believe it when I saw that place advertised. I even checked when I rang up, to make sure it was the same. I knew he'd ask you two. Especially if we all urged him not to. Ever the dutiful little boy. I wanted you to remember. I wanted to bring it all back. How you killed him."

"I didn't kill anyone."

"You know what I mean." Poppy was shouting now. Curiously, it was only when she was angry that she sounded American again.

"We were never sure he died. He could still be alive somewhere. He might have . . . what I have."

"Oh don't give me all that old crap again."

"Frances? What's going on?" Hearing raised voices, John had run in from the garden. There was a golden leaf caught in his hair. Frances looked at it, then back at Poppy.

"He became a non-subject with you two, didn't he?" Poppy was saying. "That was how you coped. His death was never remembered. It never occurred to you how that must have made me feel. You never observed an anniversary for it, never talked about him."

"You only had to ask," Frances managed. "You never asked so I thought—"

"Huh!" Poppy shouted and started stuffing photographs into a carrier bag, heedless of damaging them, then actually scrunching them up in her hands. "Putney High made me too fucking polite. Of *course* I never asked!" She stood and added quietly, "I'll take this lot out to the bin."

She left with the bag of photographs and a bin liner full of old wrapping paper and other rubbish. Frances sat on the sofa. She could hear John's voice in the hall calming Poppy as it had always done, talking soothing sense.

She looked at the photograph which she had managed to snatch in the confusion of their tumbling, her old hand as swift and undetectable as a lizard's darting tongue. It showed a young, hairy-chested man with a mustache. A young woman was lying on her stomach, trying to read and he was rubbing oil on her back. Interrupted, sensing the photographer perhaps, he had glanced up and was looking straight into the lens. His expression was somehow naked, too surprised to have mustered a suitable smile. The picture must have been taken by a child. It was low down and hopelessly lopsided and there was a veranda post in the way.

Staring at it horrified, on the pavement outside the photography shop, she had assumed it was taken by Poppy, who she had already discovered to be capable of slyness. It was, she had always assumed, Poppy's way of saying *Don't pretend. This is something I saw and I know.*

Now she imagined Julian instead who even as a child, had been uncomfortable and clumsy with mechanical things. She saw him in the afternoon shadows on the veranda, in his blue shorts and snake belt and bottle-green Aertex shirt, feet bare and muddy like a little savage's. She saw him frown as he unbuttoned the leather case and struggled not to drop the camera, saw him peer through the viewfinder and twiddle the focus the way he had seen grown-ups do, saw him click the shutter then stare at Bill with the cold eye of childhood.

BEACHCOMBER

She hesitated a second or two, darted back to her bureau and grabbed two pairs of new stockings from a drawer and a favorite lipstick from the cute china bowl his mother had given her. They lent her courage somehow and, as she took one last look about the house she had failed to make a home, a half-smile was born on her lips. She was afraid, yes, but excited, precisely because each step toward the front door was a step nearer an irreversible decision. She forgot her keys until they jingled against the lipstick in her bag. She kept only the one to her car and the smaller one to the safe-deposit box. The rest she stuffed into the mailbox. "There," they seemed to say. "Done." But what of the

The manuscript stopped there and, despite himself, despite his impatience with the breathless, trashy style not to mention the crudely autobiographical subject matter, John found himself tantalized, wanting to read on. But what of the what? The qualms? The second thoughts? The ice in her pumping heart? The dagger in her glove compartment?

The furnace fired up suddenly, startling him and bringing him back to his senses and his reason for being down in this hellish room. He slapped the folder shut, stood up from where he had been sitting on the old table where he had seen the trusties playing cards and drinking tea and strode over to open the thick steel door so he could throw the manuscript on to the flames beyond. Then something stayed his hand until the handle grew too hot and he backed off.

He questioned his motives. He had told himself it was an unfinished, therefore unpublishable novel by an author of little distinction and that burning it was a kindness to his niece as well as to Bill's memory. Was there an element of cheap revenge in the gesture? And embarrassment too, given that such text as there was gave what appeared to be graphically accurate descriptions of an adulterous affair enjoyed with his own wife? But what if there were? Why should he not be embarrassed and avenged? He had behaved with every restraint so far. Every bloody restraint.

Footsteps sounded on the stairs. It was too late for it to be one of the officers. "Poppy?" he called. "In here."

But it was Frances. He had thought her in bed long ago. Soon after they returned from the memorial service, she had excused herself from the dinner she had prepared, saying she felt a little ill, and had spent an eternity in the bathroom. All was quiet when he came down here and started reading so he had assumed her in bed. She might have been for she had on her night things. Finding him, she stopped short, pulling her dressing gown about her although the room was unpleasantly hot. The orange light from the window in the boiler door showed a tanned ankle above the slippers.

"No," she said. "It's me."

"Frances." He slid the folder on to a chair and sat on it. Burning it would be burning a piece of her, however that piece pained him, and he could not let her see what he was about.

"Sorry. What are you doing down here? It's so late."

"I . . . The furnace was making an odd noise," he said. "Thought I should check."

"Oh." She absorbed that then began in a rush. "John I . . . I'm so sorry. I hate this and I wanted you to know I never . . ." She looked up and briefly met his eye.

He was as tongue-tied as she was. He longed to say the right thing but she had been so tight-lipped, so forbidding, these past weeks that he was afraid of saying anything to make matters worse.

"Really?" This was signally inadequate since he only hoped, but was not entirely sure, how her sentence had been going to end. He said it anyway.

"Yes," she said with a ghost of a smile. "Really." She came further into the room. "God, this bulb's bright. Do you mind if I . . . ?"

"Not at all."

"Thanks." She turned off the overhead light so they were lit only by the dancing glow from the furnace and the thin light off the stairs beyond. "I'd begun to think I was pregnant again," she said. "But I wasn't. If I had been . . . it would have been yours, you know."

"You really needn't . . ." he began, appalled by the details she might be about to share, which would horrify him and make him hate her.

She persisted, however, telling him nothing about Bill at all but instead an incoherent description of some dream she had experienced the night before John was called back to London by the breakout. "It sounds childish," she said, "but I knew it was yours and I think it would have been a girl. I'm . . . John, I'm sorry. But listen—No. Let me say this. It's not easy and I've . . . Just listen."

"I'm listening."

"Now that . . . there's nothing to make you stay by me, you can divorce me. If you want. I'll quite understand."

He could not believe they were having this conversation. How had they come from silence to such extremity in a few sentences? "Is that what you want?" he asked, finding he could not look at her, so little did he want to see her tentative nod. "I don't want to keep you against your will. And now that this particular chapter seems closed . . ." He despised the pomposity in his voice, the well-schooled phrase, the Latinate syntax. *Caesar, however, having subjugated the troops of the heretofore triumphant Vercingetorix and his slaves and his wives . . .* He needed to talk as freely, as sloppily as his rival had written. His feelings were bound round with grammar that he longed to shrug off. He wanted to tell her about Dr. Alberti's prognosis, about his dreams of a huge family, how they would try again.

But then, quite as if she were not listening, she began to say that they could file to adopt Poppy Louise formally. "She's so happy in that school. Well, I think she'll be happy. She seems calm there. And it's the least we owe him and . . ." She began to cry. She slumped into the other chair and wept, grinding her knuckles against the tattered Fablon-topped table as if that could check her grief. "Skip can fill the space," she howled, then could make no more words.

He could not reach her from his chair so he had to push it back and come around the table and stand behind her. At first he only dared put a hand on her shoulder but when she snatched at it and held it that gave him the impetus to crouch down and hug her properly. He was too low now, of course, so that he was almost pulling her forward off her chair. He held her up. The strain was agony on his calves and he couldn't keep it up indefinitely. It was probably the least comforting hug man had ever offered wife.

He opened his mouth to speak but could only talk to her as he had talked to Poppy in the car earlier, shushing her grief rather than finding words to console her. He wondered if he would ever be able to tell her how much he loved her or whether, as now, it would always have to be done as clumsy demonstration. Perhaps, eventually, if she would grant him the time, he could accumulate enough small, loving gestures to make something big enough for her to notice.

BLUE HOUSE

Beneath the standardized posters and racks of leaflets nudging one toward debt, it was a bank of the old school, with yards of mahogany paneling, brass chandeliers, a high, paneled wall between cashiers and public that still had brass spikes along its top. There were broad mahogany desks around the parquet floor with deep leather armchairs beside them, as though clients might need rest from the emotional strain of writing checks.

While they waited to be dealt with, John went to withdraw some cash and Poppy sank into one of the armchairs. He admired her discreetly, the thick chestnut hair, the long legs, the lap left capacious from childbirth. He could not be sure, because she was always well turned out, but he had a suspicion she had succumbed to some marvelously old-fashioned instinct and dressed up for the occasion. She wore her gold earrings, instead of her more usual colored glass ones, and some heels that made her even more imposing. There was an ancient studio photograph of his mother looking severe with one elbow on a black marble pedestal. He had never known if the picture was a good likeness, having little physical memory of her, but repeatedly now Poppy's stances, reading or merely waiting, brought it to mind and so gave him an idea of the kind of woman his mother might have been.

"Mr. Pagett?" A female clerk in a gray suit was at his elbow.

"Yes?"

"If you and your daughter would like to come this way."

He raised his eyebrows to Poppy who joined them as they crossed to a heavy door in the paneling.

"I must ask if either of you wears a pacemaker," the clerk continued. "Because of the security equipment we have to pass through."

She led them through the door and across the cashiers' office, then along a corridor and downstairs to the vault, where she politely asked them to look aside while she punched in a code. He suspected this did not happen often these days, when so many people had safes at home, and that she was enjoying herself, in her quiet, gray way. She left them in a room that was stark compared to the lush public chamber upstairs, a brightly lit cell with only a table and two plastic chairs. It put him in mind of a police interrogation room.

How suitable, he thought.

The clerk returned with his deposit box and left them with instructions to pick up the intercom when they were ready to hand the box back in.

It was a very good necklace, he knew. The rubies had been his grandmother's and had legally passed to Becky, who scorned them and never bothered to collect them from the bank's custody.

"Your mama, your real mother, never wore them," he said, opening the battered leather case and pushing it across the table for Poppy's inspection. "I think she thought they were too old-fashioned or vulgar or something. I suppose the setting is a little heavy."

"But they're incredible!" Poppy smiled, lifted them out so that the light set off the fires within them. "Very Anna Karenina."

"They're yours. I should have given them to you before, on your wedding or something, but . . . well . . . something stopped me. Caution of some kind. I didn't want you feeling you had to sell them for school fees or sofas. But now that . . . Well, I thought . . . you could sell just a few. Have the others made into a bracelet maybe."

"I wouldn't dream of it." She did not try them on, merely held them up so that he glimpsed how well they went with her hair, then laid them

carefully back on the still bright green velvet in their box. She kept a finger resting on them.

"No," he said. "Maybe not. I just thought you'd like to know, you
know, that they're yours to do with as you like. Not Sandy's. Not the
boys'. You know?"

"A running-away fund," she said calmly.

"An independence," he suggested.

"Thanks," she said. "I don't know what to say. I'm touched." She
glanced at her watch. "Dad, we should get on. The boys finish school in
twenty minutes."

"Hang on," he said. "That wasn't really why I got you in here. I had
to come up with something that I could say in front of Frances and she
knows about the necklace. She wore it herself, once or twice. But she
thinks I burned this long ago."

He reached into the back of the deposit box and drew out the manuscript. It was a little dog-eared, stained with a streak of coal dust on the
front, held together with two ancient rubber bands tied on in a cross.

"What is it?" she asked as he passed it over.

"Your dad's novel. It's the one he was working on. When he
went. It's not publishable. It's not finished and, frankly, it's not very
good. I think he was writing out ghosts. It tells you a bit about Becky,
though. But more importantly, it'll tell you a bit about his affair with
Frances."

She looked up as though he had slapped her. Had she forgotten, perhaps, that he knew? That he had, eventually, been there? For all her rage
earlier in the week that it was a *non-subject*, she could hardly expect him
to have spoken of it lightly and often. She sat staring at it. He helped
her, pulling off the rubber bands, one of which was so fatigued that it
broke, thwacking his hand.

"Look," he said. "You should read the whole thing obviously, when
you've got more time, but if you turn to the last pages he worked on . . .
Look." He turned the pages for her. Some were stained into orange
translucence by suntan oil. "Here," he said. "This is the passage where
she's wondering whether to leave her husband for the hero, her lover.
And in his first version she was going to. See? She packs her bags and

goes to join him and his daughter at the airport. The daughter's you, of course. But she had second thoughts. Look at these notes he scribbled." He turned a page and read the notes out to her. "You see? Something she did or said was forcing him to change the story to match the truth, the emotional truth she was showing him. She had too much respect for you to come between you. She was going to leave both of us, him and me, rather than try to be your stepmother, which she knew you wouldn't have wanted. But he left before she could, and I kept her and got you too."

"But how could you know that and forgive her?"

"I love her." He shrugged. Looking back, it seemed so simple. "I never stopped loving her. How could I not forgive? I was just overjoyed that she chose to stay. For days after he disappeared I kept thinking he'd be found or reappear and she'd go off with him and take you and maybe even Juli—sorry, Will. And having you to care about was a sort of blessing, do you see? Because we could love each other through you and gradually feel our way back into . . ." He faltered.

"Trust?"

"Lack of fear. I was so afraid. I was like a condemned man, even after the police gave up and we had the memorial service and set about adopting you officially. Everyone thought I was tense about Henry Farmer, waiting for someone to turn him in, but it was your father I feared."

"I can't forgive him," she said. "Sandy, I mean. How *can* I? It's all a mockery."

"He was a good husband. You were happy."

"Yes, yes. And he loved me and we even had a good sex life." She saw him blanch. "Sorry. But we did and that's important. But now all that seems like a sham, if he was . . . doing what he was doing."

"Your happiness is still real. And his love."

"But he hurt me."

"Yes. Of course he did. Like Frances hurt me."

"That was only a holiday fling, Dad."

He thought about this a second. "No," he said. "It took place on a holiday, that was all. You don't plan to leave your husband after a fling.

She was in love. It was a . . . a real thing. What hurts isn't the length of the affair, it's the moment you find out about it and *how* you find out. You might fool Sandy and your Mum but you don't fool me. I've seen you on the phone to him. I *know*."

"Yes but—"

"And he still loves you. He's not in love with Will."

"But he's gay."

"I . . ." He stopped, seeking the right words. "I don't find these things easy to talk about. Sorry. But I just think he's a bit lost. Like Frances was lost. And if you don't get back in there, somebody else will, man, or woman; it probably doesn't matter."

"We must go." she said. "Shit!" She jumped up, grabbed the intercom and apparently ended the discussion. She left the rubies where they were but took the manuscript, borrowing a plastic bag from the clerk to hide it in. They collected the boys from school and he drove them, at her request, to Sandy's house, her and Sandy's house. She made an excuse about clothes and needing to check on the boys' sports gear, but when Hugo and Oscar had raced ahead up the drive, she turned back to John's open window.

"I'll call you later," she said. "I might just hang on a bit. Have a talk with him or something. You know?"

"I know," he said. "Don't be too easy on him."

She prepared a retort then saw he was joking and scowled good-naturedly. They were neither of them much given to hugs or tearfulness so she merely turned after the boys and he drove home feeling light-headed. He and Frances loved her dearly but she was a powerful, thundery presence, always had been, and it would be a relief to have the house to themselves once again.

BLUE HOUSE

The drive, which had seemed so merciful in the summer, had taken hours longer than Will had expected. Traffic had not been especially heavy but it had begun to rain soon after he reached the motorway south of Barrowcester. Sheets of water lay across the tarmac so that every lorry sent up waves of blinding, muddy soup. Having once seen such an accident happen at high speed, Will went in dread of aquaplaning across the lanes, and cut his speed drastically, thinking to crawl in relative safety and listen to a talking book until the rain blew over. He could not turn off the wipers until Okehampton, however, hours later. Where the dual carriageway crossed Bodmin Moor, loose curtains of fog, that seemed to twitch away then envelop the car again with no warning, delayed him still further. By the time he was pulling through Polcamel, one talking book, two quartet recitals and an orchestral concert later, his eyes were sore from squinting and his mouth raw from the succession of searingly salty and cloyingly sweet snacks whose wrappers now littered the passenger footwell as their crumbs littered his lap.

The place was almost deserted. Most of the houses lay dark, as did the little complex of shops and bars beside the beach that had been so lively every night in late summer. He imagined the landlords of the rambling B & Bs confining their quiet winter lives to a few, cheaply heatable rooms at the backs of their establishments, turning their gaze from the churning sea that brought them their livelihood in high season but now brought only mists and brine-laden winds. He could not possibly run a profitable bookshop in such a place. Not even a café. Confining her life to the unseasonal wealth of Barrowcester and central London, Harriet had no idea of the economic realities of truly provincial life.

And neither did Lindsay, as Dr. Chadwick had asked to be known. She, of course, had offered no advice at all, but merely repeated his comments back at him in a mildly interrogatory fashion, for him to confirm or qualify until, like an intimate conjuror, she had been able to stand back with a quiet flourish, as if to say *"You see? This is how you truly feel and this is what you fear and this is what you want to happen.*

"If you come to me anymore," she said, "this will stop being therapy and become full-blown analysis."

"Which you know I think is self-indulgent."

"So?" she asked.

"I know, I know," he said. "Be happy. Don't be happy. It's my choice."

She only smiled. "You have my number," she said at last. "You can call it whenever you like. If it's not convenient, I'll tell you."

Naïvely he had expected a more rousing finish, perhaps even a little human warmth now that the boil on his psyche had been lanced. A hug, a good motherly urging to get out there and chase his personal rainbow. Even a smile that showed her teeth for once. But no. A handshake and her habitually cool air of what he had first read as secret amusement, but which was more probably a stifled yawn, were all she offered by way of parting blessing. The bill came later. He had overrun the six sessions paid for by Harriet, surprising no one but himself.

He wound down a window to clear the hours of fug he felt were clinging about him like a dank second skin. The smell of the sea not only roused him but awoke his sense that, for all that he had a small suitcase on the back seat and the biggest deposit he had ever seen nestling in his private account, and for all that he had just driven five hours without a proper break, he was effectively here to go on a date.

Washing, shaving, changing, changing again was out of the question but still he felt it was impossible to plunge directly down the drive to the house without some preparation. He parked in the utterly empty car park, turned off the headlamps and radio and breathed sea air for a minute or two. There was an apple on the passenger seat, bought in a service station, in the trust implanted in boyhood that apples, so fresh and green, cleaned one's teeth, or at least imparted a cleaned-teeth sort of freshness. He ate it, although nerves, now that he was finally here again, had replaced hunger with a certain queasiness.

Eating, he unzipped the side of his case and took out the last letter. It had arrived only this morning. He had read it, called the shop and jumped in the car. He could not ring ahead; there was no telephone and he cringed at the thought of acting on Roly's suggestion of ringing Bronwen's gallery in Saint Jacobs to leave a detailed message.

What can I say after such a letter that will not seem banal or, worse, polite? Now that the enigmatic Dr. Chadwick can spare you and now that you've succumbed to the overtures of Texans bearing gifts, I think you should come down here. Obviously I haven't done a nearly good enough job of putting you off me and, strange as it may seem all these pages of yours—yes, they're in a rather handsome, marbled-paper file now and yes, I've been rereading them—they make quite a novella—where was this sentence going anyway? (The beach-bum reads but he never claimed he wrote.) Strange as it may seem, these letters of yours haven't managed to put me off you. Quite the contrary, I fear. So come back and remind me how twitchily, prissily urban you can be. I also need to show you just how depressing and vile it is here mid-winter. And let you hear me snore. Et cetera.

Fay is mightly pissed off. She tore her shoulder on some barbed wire and is confined to walks on a lead until the stitches come out. We'll have to walk her extra far, I warn you, to give her the mileage she's accustomed to clocking up on her speedy own.

Yours with something worryingly close to ardent, R.

Will locked the car and pulling his coat and scarf about him, walked between the single row of houses to the path above Polcamel Strand. It was low tide, far lower than he remembered it ever getting in summer.

There was no street-lamp, only the dim glow from a few upstairs windows and the regular, swinging beam from the lighthouse at the estuary mouth, and yet the beach was not quite dark. The waves had a kind of brightness in them and moonlight spilled through a note in the clouds further out to sea.

He made his way down the brown granite steps he remembered being bright with holiday litter, and walked out across the sand. He came as close to the thundering surf as foolish suede shoes allowed then walked to the right, away from the Strand and black-eyed bungalows and past the headland at the point cut off at high tide. When he could walk no further, he stopped and looked up to the dark mouth of the little cove.

Blue House was ablaze with light, even its forbidden fourth bedroom. The shutters were snugly shut against the cold and damp, but light spilled through their cracks and picked out a rim of green paint about each window. In the darkness it was not blue, of course, so he could see Beachcomber before him as well. So many memories, shocking memories, had been stirred up in his sessions with Dr. Chadwick that for a minute or two he was obliged to do no more than stand and stare while past and present intermeshed.

He drew nearer and smelled woodsmoke. There was no music. Somehow he would have expected music, but perhaps that was crass. It was a subject that had never arisen in their letters, he realized. He remembered no music in the fourth bedroom beyond the handful of homemade concert recordings. Perhaps since Seth's death Roly had preferred to live in silence? Will wondered if he could cope with this, he for whom turning on the radio was the first thing he did on returning home, after flicking on lights. Could this house become home?

He let himself in at the garden gate and peered through the French windows.

A fire was burning in the stove, the little door at the front left open to create the sense, more comforting perhaps, of a normal hearth and grate. Roly was sprawled on the sofa, his back to the door, the dog asleep between his legs, her head lolling over one of his thighs. There was a deep, white plastic collar about her neck to prevent her chewing the stitches in her shoulder. It lent her a quaintly Elizabethan air.

What right had he to disturb them? The scene was one of total, independent peace.

Will raised a hand and knocked twice.

She walked across the sand not caring if her shoes became wet, drawn forward as much by the great blue moon up ahead as by the sound of the breaking waves. The moon had a ring around it which promised or threatened something, she forgot what exactly.

The chill of the foam shocked her skin. She stood still and felt the delicious tug beneath her as the water sucked away sand. The water was as cold as death.

If I stood here long enough, she thought, *just stood, the sea would draw out more and more sand from under me and bring more and more back in. Little by little I'd sink, ankles already, knees soon, then waist, then belly.*

She imagined standing up to her tingling breasts in sucking, salty sand. When the first, disarmingly little wave struck her in the face, would she panic? Would she, instead, laugh, as they said, *inappropriately?*

She dared herself not to move.

The moon was nearly full. She could see the headland on the far side of the estuary mouth and its stumpy, striped lighthouse. She could see the foam flung and drawn, flung and drawn about her. He was striding across the little beach behind her; she could tell without turning. Would his hands touch her first or would she merely feel the rough tweed jacket he draped about her? Would he call out from yards away or would she hear his voice soft and sudden when his lips were only inches from her neck?

I love you. She felt the words well up. *I love you more than words can say.*

"Darling?" he said. "Shall I help you back up? You're getting mud all over yourself. Here. Take my hand."

She let him take her weight as she lunged back on to the landing stage. The river mud sucked one of her shoes off but it did not matter greatly. She stopped, turned and kicked the second one after it then let him lead her, barefoot, across the garden to the house.

He was rather old for a nurse, much older than her, in fact. But he was tall. Tall was good. She liked that in a man, being so tall herself, and she liked the way he did not seem to mind her walking smelly river mud across his kitchen. She smiled at him as he lowered first a towel then a basin of warm soapy water to the floor before her, because it was all rather funny.

Then she asked him his name.

Author's Note

In the mid-sixties, when Ronnie Biggs the train robber made his successful escape from Wandsworth Prison only months into his thirty-year sentence, my father was that prison's governor. My mother had spent much of her life to date on the periphery of prisons since her father was also a prison governor. As children we interacted with some of the prisoners, and my sister and brothers risked life and limb playing in the house's rambling attics and on its roof. There begins and ends any resemblance between my own family and the wretched one just depicted.

Henry Farmer is entirely ficitious.

Ronnie Biggs is still at large having, like Farmer, avoided extradition on the grounds that under Brazilian law, his crime was committed too long ago to be prosecutable.

I am indebted to my father for providing salient details of 1960s prison routine, to Podge and Meg Brodhurst for that first, life-changing invitation to pass a school holiday at Wavecrest, and to the Civitella Ranieri Foundation for their extraordinarily generous hospitality which allowed me to finish this novel in such inspiring, peaceful surroundings.

The Alzheimer Association's helpline number is 800-272-3900.